MOON FLOWER

BOOKS
by
JAMES P. HOGAN

MOON FLOWER

BY
JAMES P. HOGAN

Moon Flower

A Baen Books Original

Baen Publishing Enterprises
P.O. Box 1403
Riverdale, NY 10471
www.baen.com

ISBN 10: 1-4165-5534-X
ISBN 13: 978-1-4165-5534-6

Cover art by Alan Pollack

First printing, April 2008

Distributed by Simon & Schuster
1230 Avenue of the Americas
New York, NY 10020

Library of Congress Cataloging-in-Publication Data
Hogan, James P.
Moon flower / by James P. Hogan.
    p. cm.
ISBN 1-4165-5534-X (hc)
I. Title. PR6058.O348M66 2008
823'.914--dc22

                                    2008002987

Printed in the United States of America

10 9 8 7 6 5 4 3 2 1

❧❦❧❦

To my Nieces and Nephews:
Phillip & Roger
Janet & Lynda, Barrie & David
Carol & Susan
Tony & Bobby
Tony & Alan

❧❦❧❦

PROLOGUE

Some of the equipment deployed by the larger defense and security contractors thriving off the ongoing strife as the world reached the middle of the twenty-first century would have been worthy of many national governments in times gone by. *Marduk* was the newest addition to the arsenal of Milicorp Transnational, based in San Jose, at the southern end of Occidena, one of the regions that had seceded from the former United States. An orbiting bombardment platform carrying beam weapons, missiles, and guided bombs, *Marduk* was capable of shifting its orbit to target any place on the Earth's surface within three hours.

The Indonesian breakaway state of Tiwa Jaku had been established following takeover of the island by a military junta bankrolled and equipped by foreign commercial interests keen to secure access to the considerable tropical hardwoods reserves and recently confirmed deposits of rich nickel and tin ores. When the actions of a growing popular reactionary movement threatened to destabilize the regime, President Suwarko, who had liaised with Milicorp as a general under the former government and taken out his own contract with the corporation upon coming to power, called in their services to suppress the rebellion. For the directors and technical staff of Milicorp, the event provided a welcome opportunity to test *Marduk*'s capabilities.

Flanked by staff officers in gray Milicorp tunics bearing the gold-lightning-flash-on-red shoulder insignia designating Tactical Orbital Command, Myles Callen stood in the center of the Opcon

1

Room on *Marduk*'s Control Deck, staring down into the display "tank" presenting a composite 3-D image, reconstructed from direct observation and data from lower-altitude surveillance drones, of a magnified portion of the terrain below. Callen's executive status as corporate "Facilitator" in charge of the operation placed him above the hierarchy of uniformed ranks. He wore a plain dark suit with traditional narrow tie and was addressed as "Mister."

The view being held in the tank showed an area of broken, rocky hills rising above scattered forest and plantations to the west of the capital on the island that was now called Tiwa Jaku. Colored icons and data superimposed on the image indicated the dispositions and strengths of the rebel units that had pulled back to take up a defensive stand there. The plan devised with Milicorp's cooperation had been simple enough. A feinted retreat by the government forces and false reports spread by infiltrators of a general uprising had drawn the rebels out onto the plain, believing that they had an open road through to the city. When they had converged into columns, they were annihilated by remote-piloted ground-attack drones unloaded secretly by Milicorp personnel and deployed in the previous few days. Falling back to the hills, the survivors found themselves penned in by government troops who had moved in surreptitiously from the rear through the surrounding forests. The classical move would then be for government reserves to advance from the city and seal the trap, followed by a bloody and protracted operation of assault, reduction of the defenses, and mopping up. But *Marduk* offered a swifter and more economical option.

The Ordnance Director spoke from his console to one side of the tank. His voice sounded also in earpieces of the active optic spectacles that Callen was wearing. "Pilot laser registered on Hill 327. Main beam armed and primed to fifty percent."

"Frame synched and locked. Opportunity window one minute, twenty-seven seconds," another voice announced over the circuit. That was the time they had before *Marduk*'s progression along its orbit would take it out of effective range.

Callen murmured a command that was picked up by a sensor that doubled as a tie pin. A zoom field opened up in the spectacles to show a close-up of the part of the display that his gaze was directed at. Hill 327 was a natural amphitheater of rocky scarps and shrub, formed in what could have been the remains of an ancient volcano, that the rebels were turning into a strong point overlooking their defensive positions. He could make out groups of figures digging slit trenches and filling sandbags for gun emplacements, and below them lines of others hauling packs and equipment up the slopes. The ravine at the reverse foot of the prominence—in the direction that *Marduk*'s firing window was moving—had been identified on the previous pass as a staging area for materials and munitions. Beyond that, in the forested valley slightly to the north, were the camouflaged hideouts housing the families, support base, and supply caches.

Callen called up a countdown check and nodded to the Ordnance Director. "Fire sequence pattern. Take out the full list."

For an instant, a thin finger of radiance illuminated the ground zero point shown on the target designator screens as a reddened circle, ionizing a conducting path from the orbiting platform and perceptible on the ground as a faint column of violet coming down through the thin veil of cloud. Then a bolt of high-energy electrons flashed to the surface to hit the target area with the force of a mini-nuclear bomb, vaporizing everything inside a radius of a thousand feet. Callen had a brief impression of the blast wave sweeping outward from the fireball in a turmoil of rocks, debris, shattered trees, and bodies before the frame stepped to the next indexed target zone. Even after observing the test firings in Nevada, he was still impressed.

In all, six bursts of devastation were delivered before *Marduk* stood down from active operations on that pass of its orbit.

But by then, the battle was already over.

The following day, Callen put a call through to Colonel Guadalez, commander of the Milicorp ground force. Shots had been coming through all morning of government soldiers bringing in trucks full of bewildered survivors, many still in shock or suffering from flash burns, to wire detention cages erected outside the city. "What are the latest numbers?" he inquired.

"It's looking like around twenty-eight hundred to three thousand. Could be up to three-quarters rear echelon." Guadalez's swarthy face with its thick mustache broke into a grin showing strong white teeth against the background of the trailer that he was using as a local command post. "That means we really hit their fighting edge hard. They shouldn't be much of a problem for a long time now. You guys up there got it right on."

Callen acknowledged with a noncommittal nod. "I just do my job."

"Do we have word on what to do with them yet?"

"San Jose have been talking to Suwarko. He's decided that he needs to teach a lesson to discourage other would-be troublemakers. Our contractual commitment is fulfilled. Stand down your mission and turn them over to Suwarko's people. They'll deal with it. We'll be airlifting you out the day after tomorrow."

Guadalez returned a matter-of-fact nod. It was to be expected as part of the business. Being seen to be involved in the liquidating of prisoners was not good for corporate public relations. "That gives us two nights here to celebrate," he said. "Much appreciated. I've heard wild things about this city. I guess you guys don't get to party much up there, eh?"

"I wouldn't have the time anyway," Callen told him.

"Still working?"

"Always working."

"It, ah . . . doesn't exactly sound like what I'd call a life," Guadalez commented, picking at a tooth with a thumbnail.

"I just do my job," Callen told him.

Callen took a lander down to the surface on *Marduk*'s next pass over the West Coast. The summons from Milicorp headquarters had said simply that he was required back urgently to be briefed on his next assignment. Rath Borland, the Operations Vice President in San Jose, had not gone into detail when Callen called to inquire further, on the grounds that the matter was sensitive. He had confided, however, that the job would be of a long-range nature, far from Earth.

CHAPTER ONE

Einstein's theory of gravitation, better know as General Relativity, revolutionized physics by interpreting gravity as an effect arising from geometry. Basically, the presence of mass induces a curvature into the structure of space and time that determines the paths that moving objects, light, and other forms of mass-energy follow.

A common analogy to illustrate the idea imagines a cannonball resting on a stretched rubber sheet, creating a dish-shaped depression. A marble introduced to roll frictionlessly around at some equilibrium level does so not because the cannonball send out an invisible "force" to attract it, but because the geometry of the space that it is moving in constrains it to.

In the 1950s, a German physicist by the name of Burkhard Heim, who had been badly crippled by a laboratory accident in the course of his work during World War II, investigated the problem of reconciling General Relativity with quantum theory, which while immensely successful in predicting experimental results, seemed incompatible in terms of many of its basic concepts and requirements. Heim's approach involved a geometrical interpretation of the electromagnetic force similar to the way in which General Relativity had treated gravity. It turned out as it required two extra dimensions in addition to the earlier theory's four. In them, it became possible to interconvert gravitational and electromagnetic energy, one to another. Extensions of Heim's work carried out in the first decade of the twenty-first century introduced a further two dimensions, bringing the total to eight, and involved two new types of force previously unknown to physics. An implication that Heim had not really pursued was that a suitably equipped vessel could exploit these new realms of existence to travel between points without physically traversing the dimensions of ordinary space in between—analogous in a superficial way to air travel enabling journeys from one point to another at speeds much higher than anything attainable on the ground. When detailed studies produced the startling revelation that the transit times implied worked out at somewhere in the order of a few hours from Earth to Mars, and perhaps a couple of months for distances measured in tens of light-years, experimental work began in earnest, and practical demonstrations took place within a decade. The long-speculated interstellar "hyperdrive" had arrived.

Exploration of other star systems and discoveries of new worlds followed with astonishing rapidity. Those who for many years had thought and written about humanity one day expanding across the solar system and beyond had envisioned it as beginning an epoch of unparalleled scientific advancement and adventure. However, such was the nature of the powers who controlled these enterprises that the prime motivation behind the missions sent to open up the new frontier was the insatiable demand of the predatory beast that the global economic system had become for more resources to exploit and new outlets to "develop" for the further generation of profit.

A major player in the race to acquire assets and create fresh markets—either in the form of suitably advanced and susceptible native populations, where such opportunities presented themselves, or by promoting Terran emigration and colonization—was Interworld Restructuring Consolidated, with headquarters functions distributed across offices in China, Japan, Europe, the Central Arabic Federation, and North America. Alien native cultures, however, were not always immediately appreciative of the benefits that would flow from such interference in their affairs, and one of the attractions for Terrans who chose to emigrate tended to be the prospect of being left alone and enjoying greater independence. It was therefore regrettable but unavoidable that to recoup a reasonable return on the expenditure and effort that had been put into a venture, the corporations that had been entrusted with protecting their investors' interests sometimes found it necessary to apply forcible measures when irrational opposition was encountered, or threats to order and security put the maintaining of sound policy at risk. Hence it followed that Interworld Restructuring was also a major contractor for the services of Milicorp.

Rath Borland was a small, sinewy man with a shock of black hair and gnarled features that gave the impression of having accumulated over greater than his actual number of years, which were somewhere in the late forties. A woman on the marketing executive staff had once confided to Callen that he put her in mind of a "simian walnut," which seemed to fit well. Like many small men, Borland overcompensated by being generally more contentious than circumstances required, and displaying an insistence on being assertive, even when it didn't matter. This was especially true when dealing with men like Callen, who were bigger physically and capable of projecting a certain social charisma when it suited their ends.

As far as Callen was concerned, this didn't affect their working relationship one way or another. Despite his four years of deputizing for Borland, the feelings between them had never acquired a measure that went beyond the purely professional. Earlier phases of Callen's career had involved work in intelligence and industrial espionage that had left him with few delusions about the world of corporate realities that lay behind the public imagery. As a professional, he acknowledged Borland's capacity for objective analysis and ability to exercise intellectual detachment in the pursuit of the efficiency that the stockholders expected. Both of them had passed on the order for the execution of the prisoners taken at Tiwa Jaku with the same impartiality. Should the corporation's objectives ever so require it, Callen could have arranged for Borland's assassination, with equal dispassion.

They met in Borland's office suite on the penthouse level of the Milicorp headquarters skyscraper dominating the eastern fringes of the sprawl extending from San Jose. Borland stood by the picture window that formed one wall of the office area, looking out over sparsely built hillsides toward the Alum Rock launch complex a few miles away—although Heim drives were not generally used for surface-to-orbit shuttling, more efficient, sustained-thrust nuclear engines and ground-based power lasers had made obsolete the blast

zones and remote siting associated with the earlier chemically pro-
pelled behemoths. Callen listened from a chair turned away from the
conference table on the far side of the room from Borland's desk, his
elbows spread easily, one foot crossed over the opposite knee. The
decor was angularly geometric, with the furnishings all of black
leather and chrome. Visitors sometimes commented that the atmosphere it imparted seemed cold and harsh. Borland said it symbolized
Milicorp's commitment to detachment and efficiency.

"When probes sent back the first surveys and profile reports, the
people at Interworld thought they had an ideal situation."

Borland was referring to a recently discovered planet that had
been named Cyrene, orbiting a Sun-like star called Ra Alpha, which
with a smaller, redder companion known as Ra Beta constituted a
binary system in the constellation of Canis Minor. Its abundant life
included a humanoid race—surprising to some but, as it turned out,
not uncommon—that in what appeared to be the most progressive
region had produced a culture roughly comparable to that of Europe
in the eighteenth century. This made it ripe for an introduction to
the benefits of more advanced methods, along with innovative ways
of extracting from the populace the wherewithal to pay for them.

Borland went on, "So they organized a follow-up mission that
included an ambassador and a diplomatic staff in addition to all the
usual scientists, mapmakers, et cetera. That was about eight months
ago now. The trip out took close to two months. As far as anyone can
tell, they seem to have arrived in good shape. But before they'd been
there for another two, the whole operation was coming apart."

Callen's brow creased. "Coming apart?" he repeated. "How do
you mean?"

Borland turned from the window and made a throwing-away
gesture. "Disintegrating. The reports back started getting fewer and
fewer, and what did come through wasn't making any sense. People
started saying that the mission objectives were all wrong or didn't
matter, and talking about needing time to 'rethink values'—whatever
that's supposed to be about. I'm talking about experienced
Interworld task-group directors and project managers, not a few
academics with some cuckoo-land theory of sociology who went along
for the ride. Then they started disappearing—first the scientists;
pretty soon it was everybody. Before long it didn't seem there were

enough left in the base to run the communications properly. As I said, it was all coming apart."

Callen frowned while Borland waited for a reaction. There had been a few cases of disaffected groups taking off to fend for themselves in uninhabited wilderness worlds, and one instance that he knew of where a religious sect who helped set up a colony among a population of primitive tribes had decided to go native and departed from the Terran settlement to spread their word. So long as the numbers were small and not sufficient to affect the main enterprise to any significant degree, the normal policy was to let them go. With scant resources at their disposal, the Terran authorities took the attitude that if there was discontent wanting to express itself and potentially disruptive energy that needed dissipating, everyone would be better off if they did so elsewhere. In any case, anything that helped spread Terrans and their ways farther abroad could only be good for business in the long run. But he had never heard of anything on this kind of scale, affecting virtually the entire mission.

"What kind of values were these people talking about?" Callen asked at length.

"You tell me." Borland made an exaggerated display of showing both hands.

"What did we get from the SFC?" Callen asked. Since Interworld was a client, the mission would have carried an armed Milicorp contingent for security and defense. The Milicorp Security Force Commander would be able to communicate directly with headquarters at San Jose, independently of Interworld's regular channels.

"He was a general officer, second star," Borland said. "Name of Paurus."

Callen shook his head. "Can't say I know him."

"It doesn't matter much. He vanished somewhere across Cyrene, along with just about all of his unit. It's lucky for the rest of the mission that the natives don't seem to have much inclination toward hostilities. The coop's wide open, and the guard dog has gone AWOL."

"The whole unit?" Callen looked disbelieving. "You mean it even got to our people too? Along with their officers?" This *was* serious. That the subject was not general knowledge within Milicorp, and even Callen had not been brought into it before now despite his executive status, was no great cause for surprise. Extraterrestrial development demanded high stakes with a prospect of high returns, at high risk. Information that could deter or unnerve investors was treated as highly sensitive and dispensed strictly on need-to-know basis.

"It gets worse." Borland moved from the window to his desk, and turned to support himself in a half-sitting position against the edge, arms folded. "A second follow-up mission was thrown together at short notice and arrived at Cyrene on a ship called the *Boise* a little over a month ago. The Milicorp SFC was Carl Janorski."

This time Callen nodded. "I know him. He was in charge of the air strikes we ran in the Zaire coup a couple of years ago." Callen had been there to handle Milicorp's ground liaison. On that occasion the rebels had been supported by funding from South American drug sources and been able to outbid the government, which had resulted in a regime change.

Borland nodded. "That's the one. This time we kept careful tabs, and again everything indicated that they arrived in good shape. . . . And now the same thing is happening again."

"Even with someone like Carl there? I don't believe it!"

"He's still at Revo base, sure enough. But the person they sent as Director—a guy called Emner, who was supposed to find the previous ambassador—is saying he can't follow the policy directives because whoever dreamed it up at Interworld doesn't understand the situation. Meanwhile, the scientists have started taking off. It's the same story."

"And no one knows why?"

"No one knows why—and Interworld are in panic mode. And since we provided the security on both missions, we're not only involved contractually but our professional image is at stake." Borland paused. A big part of Callen's job was being called in as the Mr. Fixit when regular measures failed. He had already recognized the pattern. There was no need for him to say anything. He nodded resignedly and waited for Borland to spell it out. "A ship called the *Tacoma* is being made ready for a relief mission to Cyrene to see what can be salvaged. We're putting together a team to investigate what the hell's been going on there, and I want you to head it up, Myles. Take a day's break to unwind after this Tiwa Jaku business. Then we want you back here to start briefing on what's being put together.

Liftout from Earth orbit is scheduled six days from now. What kind of situation you're likely to find when you get there, I've no idea."

Callen made a face. "If it's a two-month trip, then if things can deteriorate as fast as you've indicated, nobody could have." He made a so-so shrug and curled his lip cynically. "Okay, apart from the unknowns it sounds pretty straightforward."

Borland let things hang just long enough to give the impression that it might be that simple. Then, "There's one other thing," he said.

There always was. "Of course," Callen replied.

"Interworld has a considerable investment in the work of a research scientist called Evan Wade, who was one of the scientists who went missing from the first mission."

"What kind of work does he do?" Callen asked.

"Some kind of physics. He did private work on contract before enrolling for Cyrene, but in years gone by he was with the State University at Berkeley. He got himself a reputation there as something of a subversive with left-leaning ideas. Ran off-campus student meetings, organized demonstrations; that kind of thing. Interworld are concerned that he could be working some kind of deal with the Cyreneans to give away know-how for free that would enable them to develop the resources there themselves, which could undermine investment opportunities here. We need to keep relations with Interworld sweet. I want you to find this guy Wade and bring him back—by persuasion if possible, but forcibly if necessary."

"It doesn't sound as if he's likely to be very persuasively inclined," Callen commented. "What kind of leverage do I have to use? Anything?"

"Interworld claims that he still has unfulfilled contractual obligations with them," Borland replied. "The terms don't say anything about being nullified by jumping ship. You might be able to make something out of that. If not, as I said, do whatever you have to."

Callen got the impression that Borland held little stock in the first option and had mentioned it merely for form. Giving a direct order for abduction by force was not the approved management style. There was just one small but very pertinent point that hadn't been touched on. "That's fine," Callen said. "But do you have any suggestions on how to go about persuading him, one way or the other, if he's vanished?"

Borland had evidently been expecting it. "As a matter of fact, I do," he answered. Callen inclined his head in mild but genuine surprise. "Shortly after the *Boise* mission arrived—just before Wade disappeared—he filed a request for an assistant to be sent out to work with him at Cyrene. Details of the job spec found their way around the usual circuit, and one of the names that has applied is somebody called Marc Shearer, who as it so happens was Wade's colleague when Wade worked Berkeley. In fact, Shearer took over his work there after he left."

"Did they stay in touch?"

"Almost certainly. As a former faculty member, Wade worked out a deal that still gave him access to their lab facilities when he needed them."

Callen nodded slowly. "It sounds as if Wade and Shearer could have had it set up."

"Possibly. But that's beside the point. The point is that he's familiar with Wade's work, and they obviously get along. So it makes Shearer a natural to work with Wade on Cyrene. The disappearances on Cyrene haven't been widely reported, and so there's no reason for anyone to see anything amiss. A few words from the right people at Interworld will make sure that Shearer's application is approved, and that he's on his way a lot sooner that he expected."

"You mean with the *Tacoma*? In six days?"

"Sure. The wheels are already moving." Borland unfolded one arm to make a casual gesture in the air that said it was all that simple. "And when you get to Cyrene, Shearer will lead you to Wade," he completed.

CHAPTER TWO

Fifty years before, it had been purely the stuff of fringe fiction and far-out-fantasy movies. Now every month seemed to bring news from robot probes reaching a new world, or human follow-up arriving at a previously located one to send down exploration teams and establish a surface presence. There were some that didn't orbit a parent but maintained a fixed position intermediate between mutually gyrating binary stars. Several examples of prolate forms had poles extending beyond their atmospheres. Some had barely cooled from incandescence, while others were wastes of frozen methane and ice. Those that supported life included low-gravity environments in which gigantic life-forms flourished, comparable to the great reptiles and other fauna that had once lived on Earth but could never exist under its present conditions. At the other extreme were a high-density microplanet with a species of intelligent insects that farmed fungi plantations and built adobelike dwelling with tools, and a world surfaced entirely by water, where life had moved up onto floating islands formed from coagulated detritus by photosynthetic microorganisms.

And there were some that had types of life very similar to those found on Earth. A few cases included humanoids in various stages of development. Quite how this could be was still a matter of heated controversy within the scientific community as well as between science and such other departments of learning as philosophy and theology, because according to generally accepted theory accumulations of random change should diverge, not progress toward similar endpoints. So evidently, more was going on than generally accepted theory recognized, which was about as far as any agreement went, and proponents of principles that were contradictory all managed to claim vindication. Whatever the explanation, it seemed that evolution in comparable environments was somehow preprogrammed to unfold along comparable developmental paths.

Along with everyone else, Marc Shearer was assured that social evolution everywhere was likewise destined to shape itself toward a world of Hobbesean nastiness and Darwinian callousness in ways that, sooner or later, the laws of nature made unavoidable. He didn't accept it. It seemed ironic that laws once held to be self-evident fact underpinning the whole of biology should now be admitted as questionable in that field, while remaining immutable with regard to the field of human affairs to which they had been unceremoniously coopted. He didn't accept the inevitability of a society in which unchecked avarice set the norms, exploitation and injustice were regarded as natural and equated with realism, what used to be called lying formed the basis of well-rewarded professions, and ruthlessness was admired.

As a talented young physicist who could focus on achieving results when he put his mind to it, he could doubtless have secured himself a good job with one of the corporations if he chose. But the lifestyle and conformities that such a move would have entailed ruled it out as an option. He often wondered what nascent alternative patterns might be emerging among those other worlds out there, that the news bulletins reported and scientific commentators babbled on about enthusiastically for hours. In his mellower moments, he would sometimes share with friends visions from his readings of social philosophers of years gone by, and debate the possibility of an order founded on compassion and cooperation, with the longer good taking precedence over short-term gain, and knowledge being sought for its own sake. For the most part they were skeptical and called him a hopeless idealist. Be that as it may, people like Shearer weren't going to change.

He caught Rogelio's eye meaningfully for a moment as he picked up the large bag of unshelled hazelnuts from the counter and carried it over to where the other four were sitting around a plastic-topped table in the center of the kitchen. The kitchen was a shabby affair of cheap cabinets, faded wallpaper, and aging appliances, shared between the five rooms which along with one full and one half bathroom made up the basement and ground-level floors of the tenement house. The street and its surrounding blocks were typical of a working-class residential part of south Oakland.

Larry drew his hands back from the wooden fruit bowl that Marc had told him to position in the center. "Uh-huh! Now we get to see the big mystery," he boomed to everyone. "Okay, Professor, what's this all about?" Larry was a stocky two-hundred-sixty-pounder with a tuft of beard and a gung-ho politics, who worked as a security guard for a company in Hayward. He and his wife Nancy also managed the rooms, in return for which they enjoyed their own kitchen area in a two-room unit on the top floor.

On the opposite side of the table, Brad smiled faintly in a way that said they would find out soon enough. He was one of the house residents, an Army Reserve veteran whose disability benefit had failed to materialize despite his suffering a dragging leg and a knee that would only half bend. That had been in the Secessionist Rebellion, when the southern parts of California, Arizona, and New Mexico had broken away from the original Western Federacy under immigrant pressures to join the Greater Mexican Union. The remainder, comprising central and northern California, Nevada, northern Arizona and Utah, parts of New Mexico and Colorado, and territory west of the Rockies up to Alaska, had renamed itself Occidena.

"Nuts," Ursula said. "Hey, I hope this isn't your way of telling us this is all we get to eat tonight." She was a social worker—blond, intense, inclined to be defensive.

"What a thing to say to a friend." Larry looked around imploringly.

The fourth, called Duke, was black and in his early twenties. He was one of those who hadn't migrated to Martina, which extended from Louisiana to the Carolinas but excluded the lower end of Florida, now affiliated with Cuba. He also lived in one of the rooms above and had a musical talent that he was having trouble getting recognized. Shearer had been trying to introduce him to the right people at the university. "We're going to play the nuts game," Duke told everybody. Rogelio moved around to the far side of the table, watching Shearer, who had taken off his wristwatch.

"Yes, that's right, Duke," Shearer said. "And the nuts game is this. I'm going to pour a quantity of nuts into the bowl. When I say 'Go,' the idea is for each of you to end up with as many as you can." They looked at each other as if searching for hints of things to expect.

After a few seconds, Larry said, "That's it? We just go for broke?" Ursula frowned, glancing up at Shearer suspiciously as if to say, *It can't be that simple.*

"There's just one other thing before we start," Shearer told them. "Every ten seconds, I'll stop you to check the bowl, and I'll double whatever the number is of nuts remaining there, by replenishing from the bag. Everybody got that?"

"The aim is just to get as many as we can," Ursula repeated.

"Exactly right," Shearer confirmed.

"And whoever ends up with the most wins," Larry checked. Brad shrugged in his easygoing way and said nothing.

Shearer didn't answer, but held his watch up in readiness. They waited, tensing almost palpably. Duke bit his lip, thought for a moment, then looked at the other two, seemingly about to say something.

"*Go.*"

Larry dove in with both hands. Ursula, anticipating him, moved the bowl away before plunging in herself, in the process of which they tilted it, causing nuts to spill out onto the table. Brad helped himself to a share obligingly but didn't seem able to muster the same zeal. Duke hesitated, shaking his head; then, seeing the contents of the bowl diminishing rapidly, he succumbed to the pressure and grabbed into it, at the same time scooping up strays on the tabletop with his other hand. The combined violence of all their hands upended the bowl and turned it over, spilling nuts out onto the floor. Duke consolidated his take, while Larry went down with a whoop to sweep the ones on the floor together into his other hand. Ursula followed him with an indignant shriek and managed to salvage the few that he had missed. Brad was unable to reach the floor due to the stiffness of his leg but found several nuts that had remained underneath the dish. When Shearer called "*Time!*" they had all completed scavenging and were guarding their collections protectively.

"I win!" Larry announced triumphantly. He had both hands

cupped around his pile. There was no need to count. Ursula and Brad were next, with about the same amount each—Ursula had been more energetic but Brad had bigger hands.

Shearer leaned over and righted the bowl. "Let's see now, there doesn't seem to be anything left in there, so I guess that's it. Game over."

"You've gotta be fast, guys," Larry said as Shearer slipped the watch back onto his wrist.

Ursula was looking perplexed. "Well," she said, shaking her head, "I guess that was supposed to prove something. Don't ask me what, though."

Duke seemed to want to say something again, then dismissed it with a sigh. He stared down at the nuts in front of him. His initial moment of hesitation had put him clearly behind the others. "Like I said, you should have gone for it," Larry told him. He cracked one of the nuts with his teeth and looked up at Shearer while he separated the shell. "Okay, Prof. Look, I won. Do I get a prize? So now tell us. What was it all about?"

"I never said anyone had to win," Shearer replied. "I just said the objective was for all of you to end up with as many as you could." He glanced again at Rogelio, who was staring at him fixedly, and winked. "Now, I'm going to keep you all in suspense and not say anything more about it right now. What I want you to do is think about it, and then we'll talk some more when we next get together. Okay?"

"No, not fair!" Ursula protested. Brad accepted it with a shrug.

Larry flipped the kernel of the nut into the air with a thumb and caught it deftly in his mouth. "Oh, this *is* the mystery man!" he exclaimed. "Hey, these are good. What say I open a few beers to go with the rest of them?"

"I thought you'd never ask," Ursula said.

"Great idea," Duke agreed.

"I'm not starting any partying tonight," Rogelio warned. "I have to meet someone back across the Bay at eight." He looked over at the clock readout on the microwave. "In fact, I'm gonna have to be leaving pretty soon."

"Oh, really? That's too bad," Ursula said.

Larry got up and heaved himself over to the refrigerator. It was an old, bulky model and served as the rooming house's message board, with magnets on the door holding an assortment of notes, reminders, clippings, and postcards from various places. Postcards had become something of a rarity compared to the old days. Ordinary people didn't travel as much as they used to. The restrictions were a deterrent, and most of even those who had jobs were living on the edge. As he got there, he took his phone from the pocket of his shirt and thumbed a preset number. "Hey, Nancy. We're opening a coupla beers in the kitchen. You wanna come down?"

"What else have you got to eat in there, Larry?" Brad asked, looking interested.

Shearer decided that he could use an early evening too. The lab was scheduled to begin some more tests in the morning. "You catching the BARF?" he asked Rogelio, using the popular version of the acronym for the Bay Area Rapid Transit subway.

"Uh-huh." Rogelio nodded.

"I'll walk with you."

"Sure."

That was the custom. Walking alone in the streets on the wrong side of the gated community walls and business park security fences could have its risks. Shearer picked up the jacket that he had draped over the back of a chair and pulled it on, zipping it up halfway. "Say, that's too bad," Larry said, turning his head from the opened refrigerator.

"I have to be in first thing tomorrow."

"Take care," Rogelio told the others as he and Shearer turned for the door.

"You too."

"See you around."

"You two take it easy, eh?"

"Don't get stuck in a time warp tomorrow, Marc."

Shearer and Rogelio came out into the cool evening air and started walking in the downtown direction, toward the subway terminal. Shearer's apartment was a block farther along. The streets were shabby and littered, the houses run-down, with fences disintegrating around overgrown yards, paint flaking from tired clapboards, and dingy windows, many barred, showing bare blinds or old, sagging drapes. Shopwindows were shuttered or protected by heavy mesh. A red-brick building, originally a hotel, now converted to low-income rentals, was decaying behind a parking lot covered in trash and stripped automobiles. Fading relics from an age that had died.

Rogelio had a sturdy, deep-chested build, with dark features crowned by a heavy mane of hair, and strode with an air that bespoke confidence and purposefulness. Originally from south of what had been the border, he had kept going when most others halted somewhere in the jumble of shantytowns, strips malls, businesses, and smallholdings that had sprung up in a belt from San Diego to Los Angeles. He worked as a lab technician for a pharmaceuticals company in south San Francisco and still had faith that the system would reward ability, hard work, and diligence. Shearer had predicted what the outcome of the nuts game would be.

"You'd think, Rog, that people would figure out that if they all just waited, and didn't take anything out for a while, the amount of nuts in the bowl would soon get very big—automatically doubling every ten seconds. . . . Or maybe if they just took half between them and let the bowl refill every time. Then they could carry on dividing up a pot that paid everyone well. That was all I told them to aim at. But they never do. Most times, it doesn't make it to the first ten seconds—like just now. I never said anything about competing, or somebody having to win. But people always assume it. It's ingrained from the culture."

Even though the game had gone the way Shearer said it would, he had no illusions that Rogelio would be convinced that easily. The objection would be either that it didn't mirror the real world, or yes, that was the way things were, but human nature wasn't going to change any time soon, and to imagine otherwise was unrealistic. Sure enough, "Okay, it went like you said. But it's still just a game. Contrived." Rogelio swung his head briefly as they walked, hand thrust in the slit pockets of his windbreaker. "You're not telling me that's how the free market works."

"Oh, I know how it works in theory," Shearer agreed. "But what we saw was how people act in practice. They don't trust each other. And that's why they can't figure out that everyone being rational about it would result in more for everybody. Because if somebody tries to do the sensible thing and hold back, he just gets creamed by the others."

"I think that Duke was maybe thinking something like that—right up front."

"Oh, you saw that, did you?"

Rogelio nodded emphatically. "Yes. And look what happened to him. You see. It makes my point."

"That most people won't react rationally," Shearer said. "But since your free-market theory is premised on everyone rationally pursuing their best interests—that's even supposing they know in the first place what their best interests are—I'd argue that no, it makes *my* point. In the world of people that we've got, a free market isn't going to exist. Or at best, it'll be too unstable to last."

"How do you figure that?" Rogelio asked.

Shearer waved a hand briefly. "Okay, suppose that somehow a system comes into existence that works just the way your theory says. It all interacts, and as things work themselves out, you're going to see differences. For whatever reason, whether it's because of ability, hard work, being born in the right place, or plain luck, some people are going to do better than others."

"Okay."

"And this is where your human nature comes in, Rog. Wealth buys power. The ones who are raking in a bigger share will use it to influence the political process in ways that benefit themselves and penalize their competitors. The pitch gets tilted," Shearer snapped his fingers, "and as soon as that happens, a free market ceases to exist. And what you just saw is what you get."

They walked in silence through the gathering dusk while Rogelio chewed it over. Even if it took until the next time they met, Shearer knew he would find an angle to come back from; but that was what made friends interesting. A panhandler approached them from a doorway. He looked despondent, weary, his face a mask of hopelessness. Not a scam artist. Rogelio fished some change from his pocket and dropped it in the scrawny hand. Other eyes followed them from groups lounging on corners or squatting on front steps as they passed. A police surveillance drone came lower to direct a spotlight beam at something in the next street. On a vacant lot where some offices had been demolished, a group of derelicts were warming themselves around a fire built from the debris. Did all roads converge on the same inevitable end in those other worlds out there too? Shearer wondered again as they came within sight of the razor-wire-topped fence and gate through to the subway terminal. Or had some of them found a different way? Perhaps the answer depended on having a nature that wasn't "human."

He saw Rogelio on his way, and then stepped up his pace to walk the remaining block and a half to the house. A strange car was parked in front, with a third seat that folded down to provide extended luggage space in the rear. It was loaded with the bags, boxes, and oddments of somebody moving home. The light from the lamp opposite and the strip above the door revealed glimpses of coats and wall pictures that Shearer recognized as Fay's. He stopped, checked again, and then changed direction to walk up to the driver's door. A man in an overcoat and cloth cap was sitting inside, smoking a cigarette. "Hey, what gives?" Shearer demanded, gesturing, as the window rolled down.

"Don't ask me. I'm just a mover for hire, okay? She's inside."

Frowning, Shearer felt for his keys and turned back toward the door of the house.

CHAPTER THREE

The door into the bedroom was open. Fay was inside, packing the last of her suitcases. A couple of plastic bags filled with last-minute oddments, and several of her pricier dresses draped on hangers lay across the foot of the bed. She looked up with a start when Shearer appeared and leaned with a shoulder against the jamb, his arms folded loosely. Fay had long made it clear that she looked down on his choice of friends, and she seldom accompanied him on social visits. He usually came home later.

"So . . . moving on to the Big Time, eh?" he said. His mouth formed a parody of a smile. Such a turn of events was not totally unexpected, but he hadn't been prepared for things to come to a head this suddenly. The strain in their relationship had been building up for a while. A queasy feeling rose in his stomach with the realization that this was finally happening after two years. Fay was trying to suppress a shaking in her hand. If it was a nervous reaction from fear of a fight or a yelling match, she needn't have worried. They were past things like that.

"Big Time? Is that what you call it?" She shook her head shortly, still looking down at what she was doing, causing her hair to fly out in agitated flares of blond. She was wearing a hip-length coat of imitation white leather and fur trim over tight jeans and spike-heeled boots, with lots of rings. Her wrist jewelry jangled as she laid a sweater on top of the contents that she had already packed, and began stuffing the final few smaller items into the spaces around the sides. "Just wanting a decent house, and to be somewhere where it's

22

safe to walk the streets? Someone got stabbed outside the subway today. . . . Cops all over the street. Did you even know?" She made a quick half-gesture that could have indicated the room, the house beyond, or the rest of the world outside. "I can't live like this. I mean, what are we—day-jobbers who've never seen a week's work in one stretch, or some kind of sharks that need to be where the action is? You're a *physicist*, Marc, for Christ's sake! With degrees. I always thought that meant somebody with brains and some common sense. Well, isn't that what it's supposed to mean? Instead, you have these weird ideas about . . . oh, I'm not sure what they're about anymore. All I know is I can't live with it." They had been through all this before. But it seemed that Fay had a script set in her head that she had to get out, as if to leave no doubts that could invite accusations afterward.

"It means trying to understand reality the way it is, and not being deflected by how you'd want it to be or how you think it should be," Shearer said tiredly. "To do that, you have to be free to accept what the evidence is telling you."

"Free? You call this free? Free is being able to do what you want, right? Well, I *want* to mix with company that's got some class and style, okay? And I *want* to be able to look around me and see things I don't see here."

"And eat in places where they dress for dinner, and pay someone to come in and clean the house."

"Is there supposed to be something wrong with that?"

"Only the idea that it's what being free is all about."

Fay glared at him as she slammed the lid of the suitcase. "Do you know how much physicists make at places like Stellar Dynamics, or Milicorp Transnational just across the Bay? Or there's a whole bunch of them up the coast around Portland."

"Space engineering. Mercenary warfare contractors. . . ."

"Sure. What of it?"

Shearer sighed, straightened up, and moved into the room. Fay stiffened, but he turned to sit back against the vanity, one foot on the floor. "That's not being a physicist; it's being a whore. To fit in means you conform. You see only what you're supposed to see, even when you know there's something wrong. Reality becomes whatever the guy who's paying wants." He shook his head. "No, that isn't what I call being free."

"It's being *paid* something *decent* for what you *know!*" Fay closed the catches with a couple of fierce swipes. "Don't you *have* any self-respect, any pride?"

"Maybe a little too much. So I could help them make better molecular disruptor beams. Can you imagine what it's like to be fried slowly from the inside? That's what human beings in other places are paying so that people can live the way *you want*. Does knowing that still make it worth it to you?"

Fay lifted the suitcase onto its side and collected the other items together, grasping the bags with one hand and draping the garments over her forearm. She looked at him scornfully, her other hand resting on the handle of the case. "All I know is that I can't deal with all of the world's problems. It's the way life has always been. That's the *real* reality that you've never been willing to face, Marc. Or couldn't. To win, you've got to be a player. But you just won't, will you? You don't even get in the game." She lifted the case off the bed and paused to check around for anything she might have missed. "And don't start giving me the line about cooperating instead of competing, and the world not having to be this way, because I've had it up to the ears. It's never going to change, and you won't. So . . ." She let it trail away and shrugged "So that's it. It's over. Have a nice life."

Even as she moved toward the door, her manner seemed to be saying that if he'd only show her she was wrong by asserting himself enough to stop her, maybe it could be different. But he couldn't. It would never be any different, and he would have been acting a lie. All the same, he couldn't hold back a stab of bitterness.

"So where are you going? Found yourself some starter husband material with a cool pad and the right wheels?"

Fay sighed wearily in a way that asked if this was necessary. Inwardly, Shearer was already regretting his words. "No, I'm moving in with a girlfriend until I get myself straightened out. Okay? But at least it's inside some walls and has guards with guns on the gates." She crossed the living room to the outer door, which Shearer had left open. As she disappeared through it she tossed back over her shoulder, "And no, don't ask me where. That isn't your concern anymore."

Shearer listened to her bumping her way down the stairs, then moved over to the window and watched her emerge into view below.

The driver in the cloth cap came around, opened the near-side rear door, and helped her load the things in with the rest. Fay climbed into the second-row seat, and the driver returned to the front. Shearer heard the car's engine start. The lights came on, and moments later it pulled out and moved away along the street. He went through the living room to close the door, then came back to the kitchenette and filled the kettle to heat some water for coffee. The place looked bare without Fay's pictures on the walls and a lot of familiar ornaments and knick knacks gone from the shelves and worktops. An odd numbness seemed to have come over him, making him unable to decide quite how he felt. . . . For the time being, any-way. All that would come later. But already he knew deep down that it was best this way.

He turned to the refrigerator and opened it to see what there was that would make a sandwich.

CHAPTER FOUR

Although the quantum physics developed in the course of the twentieth century had led to such stunning practical applications as the Heim drive with its opening up of interstellar space, an understanding of exactly what constituted the physical reality underlying the mathematics remained as elusive as ever. Various interpretations had been put forward over the years to account for such mysteries as how an entity could be both a wave and a particle at the same time, or how a choice of which experiment to perform in one place could apparently affect instantaneously what was observed somewhere else. But no conclusive way had been found for deciding between them, and the debates between schools of philosophical bent continued to rage, while more practically inclined scientists got on with such workaday business as devising more efficient ways of sending some people to the stars and others to eternity.

A curiosity that went back to the earliest years of quantum theorizing was that the wave equations describing both massive and massless particles yielded two forms of solution, known as "retarded" and "advanced." The retarded solutions described entities possessing positive mass-energy, and were the ones employed in formulating the quantum descriptions of the world that had proved so successful in modeling physical phenomena and predicting experimental results. The advanced solutions, on the other hand, not only invoked the peculiar property of negative mass-energy, but also traveled backward in time. Hence, through most of the history of quantum theory, they had been dismissed as a mathematical artifact having no physical meaning.

26

However, a view of quantum mechanics that emerged toward the end of the twentieth century and known as the Transactional Interpretation took the position that they were real. And when, to the consternation of many, it proved able to account for many aspects of quantum weirdness that were still causing all the rival interpretations difficulties after the best part of a century, it began attracting a dedicated following to add to the already noisy debate.

Evan Wade had reasoned that if "A-waves" were real, it should be possible to demonstrate their existence experimentally, and doing so became his consuming ambition. His interest had its roots in earlier work he had been involved in that had come to be known as biophotonics—the emission of low-intensity photons by organic cells and their role in intercellular communication and coordination. For many years this had been a controversial subject, with the reality of the phenomenon being hotly disputed. When the matter was finally settled in the affirmative and legitimized with an officially recognized label, Wade's mind turned to the possibility that here could be Nature's key to establishing the existence of A-waves.

Unlike the macroscopic processes that classical physics describes—ones involving the motions and interactions of matter in bulk—biological systems are able to manipulate individual quantum entities. Examples are the passing of single electrons along atoms of the ATP chain by the energy metabolism, or the handling of ions in the nervous system. Such behavior is governed not by classical physics in the way that biologists had attempted for a long time, with limited success, to apply, but by quantum physics. Biophotonics research confirmed that certain molecular structures were fine-tuned to couple with specific frequencies and modes of electromagnetic radiation; hence they constituted highly efficient antennas. Wade became convinced that the key to creating an A-wave detector would be found in the architecture of natural molecular radiators and absorbers. That had been the thrust of the work he had pioneered at Berkeley, and he had continued to oversee the project from his private practice through a deal that he'd worked with the administrators. Shearer, who had come on board initially as Wade's assistant, took over when Wade left with the mission sent to follow up discovery of the planet Cyrene.

For Shearer this was pure physics at its most exciting and

intriguing—the chance of being the first to gain a new insight to how a part of the universe worked. By comparison, he was unable to muster much enthusiasm for the thought of being a development physicist concerned with devising practical applications in some field where the basic discoveries had already been made. It didn't matter how well it might pay, or where it ranked on the totem pole of what was conventionally recognized as "success." The regular rewards followed precisely *because* the most fascinating and challenging part was already accomplished. Shearer had tried explaining it to Fay, but there were some things that some people would never understand. That was why it had been better to let things take their course.

The apparatus occupying the small basement room in the Physics faculty of the State University at Berkeley looked like a regular piece of laboratory optronics that could have been anything from a holophotometer for analyzing the geometry of proteins to a test rig for a neurally controlled music synthesizer. It comprised a couple of racks of circuitry and crystalogic arrays in a floor-standing frame, some bench-mounted optics and holoware, and an adjacent desk doubling as a control console, sporting a main display and several smaller ancillary screens.

Shearer sat at the desk, entering settings for the next test, while Rob Vowley, a postgrad who had also been there since the time of Evan Wade, read parameters off the schedule sheet from a lab stool pulled up on one side. Merritt Queale, their young, petite, dark-haired technician of several months now, tidied the bench of tools that she had been using to fix a minor coolant leak.

"We'll use the same offsets. I'm taking the range up to two seconds," Shearer said.

"Check," Rob acknowledged, and made a note in a column on his sheet.

"And keep the correlation filter at five-point-six."

"Gotcha."

Shearer hadn't told them about Fay yet. There was a time for bringing up personal matters, and a morning with a busy work schedule wasn't it. They worked well enough, sharing either through temperament or as a result of circumstances, a resignation to life on the fringes of the physics world.

Rob had idolized an older brother who bought a military recruiter's line at age eighteen and had been butchered in one of the central African interventions. Grief and anger had driven him to activism against overseas aggression, as a result of which he was officially listed as "subversive," which effectively debarred him from any regular employment above janitor. Most of what he made went to keeping his disabled mother, whose compensation payments from the military had foundered on a technicality that the state authorities showed no inclination to investigate. Yet underneath it all, Rob had the same kind of dedication as Shearer to wanting to know what was true. If it hadn't been diverted into campaigning for political truths, he could have made a first-rate scientist.

Merritt was a very private person and divulged little about herself beyond domestic details and day-to-day trivia. She lived to high personal standards and distrusted large, powerful institutions of any kind, governmental or corporate. Shearer's assessment was that while she could no doubt have made the grade for many more highly paid and prestigious callings, she preferred a low-profile existence that didn't involve endless interrogations and background checks, which she looked on as being treated like a criminal suspect. But she was precise and competent in her own unassuming way, and had proved totally dependable. Shearer had little time for loud people who were always telling the world how good they were. The ones who really were good, he had found, were those who, when the facts spoke for themselves, didn't interrupt.

For his own part, Shearer, at thirty-three, was on the young side of average to be heading such a project. But Wade's departure had left no other likely successor with knowledge of the work that came anywhere close to Shearer's, and none at all who shared Wade's confidence in the outcome. For Shearer, that in itself was reward enough.

Rob glanced across at Merritt. "How's that joint looking?"

"It's back up to full pressure. Seems okay."

"Let's roll it, then," Shearer said. "We'll make this the last one before lunch."

"Fine by me," Rob agreed. Merritt moved around to stand behind Shearer's chair, where she could watch.

A set of coordinate axes marked by scale graduations appeared down the left side and across the lower part of the main screen, with the graphing area showing as a lighter-toned panel. What made this different from other laboratory setups was the tiny configuration of molecular-scale fibers embedded in a cryogenically stabilized crystal matrix housed within the cookie-jar-size aluminum cylinder in the lower section of the floor-standing frame. The device was a modified form of one of Evan Wade's attempts to design a detector of A-waves—waves of "something" that traveled backward in time. He had dubbed such a device an *adtenna*, from "advanced wave detector-antenna."

Shearer checked the status indicators showing on one of the smaller displays. The procedure they had developed was somewhat more elaborate than Wade's original trials, but still conceptually straightforward. A set of random number generators, which could be varied with regard to how many generators were employed and the range of numbers that each could produce, sent their outputs via a delay circuit to a device that produced a complex wave function from the collapse of a superposition of quantum states. The particular combination of quantum states to create the superposition would be determined by whatever numbers happened to be generated. Hence, until the delay had elapsed—in the present case Shearer was making it two seconds—there was no way of knowing what form the result-ant complex function would take: It didn't yet exist, and the numbers that would define it hadn't been produced.

However, according to the theory, the function, when it did come into existence, would send an A-wave back in time, which the adtenna would pick up. The output from the adtenna was then merged in a holographic-like process with a reference signal derived from the original random numbers to produce an interference pattern that could be decoded as a frequency spectrum and dis-played. The spectrum would result from combining two inputs: the set of random numbers, and the A-wave coming back from quantum function that the numbers would cause to be generated two seconds in the future. As such, it would contain information pertaining to a situation that had not yet come into existence. At least, that was the idea.

Shearer touched a key to initiate the run. Rob turned on his stool to watch the screen. A countdown window opened and ticked off the seconds from five down to zero. A pale violet fuzz, like the bristles of a wide brush but irregular in height and shimmering and shifting, appeared above the horizontal bar, extending from left to right across the screen. A ghost. But not the ghost of anything gone; a ghost presaging something that was yet to be. . . . Then, suddenly, a solid, blue trace consisting of irregular peaks and troughs added itself. The image froze. And that was it.

"Logged," Rob murmured matter-of-factly. Merritt straightened up and moved away to sit down on another chair near the desk, while Shearer went through the routine of verifying that the record had been annotated and filed.

Theoretically, the initial violet trace showed the wave function that existed in the future—not a prediction computed from a model or a probability forecast, but a *physical manifestation* generated from the backward-propagating A-wave. That state of affairs had persisted for two seconds. Then the delayed numbers had been delivered to the quantum superposition device, causing the function to happen, and the blue trace was the result. But if a precursor of the blue waveform did indeed exist within the violet fuzz, it was so buried in noise and uncertainties as to be far from readily apparent. The only indication would come from complex statistical analysis of the signals. Shearer and the others had seen this many times now, and at best the results were marginal. Technically, the correlations they were getting were significant. But convincing the rest of the world was another matter.

Other scientists had read the papers describing the project; some had even come to see the experiments for themselves. But it quickly became apparent that their motivation was to debunk and discredit, not to evaluate, and the reports they subsequently wrote had not been favorable. Shearer often wondered if that might have been the real reason behind Wade's sudden departure—as if Wade had kept up a brave face outwardly, reassuring them through his infectious enthusiasm that it would all work out in the end, but all the time harboring a growing disillusionment inside, until one day he decided that he just wanted out.

And so the project had limped along on shoestring funds that the administrators had managed to wring out of an office of the state defense intelligence apparatus on the strength of deliberately exaggerated accounts that Shearer, following the precedent set by Wade, had written into the renewal applications, intimating the imminence of a method for "seeing into the future," with juicy implications for military intelligence and political decision making. But that kind of deception was standard practice that researchers were forced to follow if they hoped to attract any attention at all. The funding authorities knew it too, and so a senseless kind of game ensued in which neither side believed the claims that were written, each knew that the other didn't believe them, but both were required to act out the farce with straight faces and due solemnity. When the tune being called for was one that the piper couldn't deliver, if he wanted to eat, he had little choice but to promise that it would be learned by tomorrow.

And so they had carried on, and the experiments continued to deliver their marginal results. With Wade gone, Shearer had found himself gradually losing heart in the whole business too, and asking himself more frequently if they were reading more into what they were seeing than was there, and if the reality was as inconclusive as the skeptics said. One of the biggest pitfalls in science was the ease with which wishful thinking could distort the vision of true believers.

Then, about a month previously, he had received a terse message from Wade saying that he wanted Shearer to come out and join him. However, this would have to be framed as a request for an assistant, and university regulations relating to equal opportunity didn't permit someone of Shearer's grade to be stipulated by name. Hence, Wade would have to go through the regular channels of putting through a request for a slot to be approved and applications invited; but he would make the description such that only someone with Shearer's background would fit. Details of an opening on Cyrene had duly appeared in the professional situations-available lists, and Shearer had put in his bid. Although he hadn't fully admitted it consciously to himself, he knew deep down that it signified his acceptance that the project at Berkeley was as good as over. He was open to the thought of starting again with something new elsewhere. He knew too that his mood had communicated itself to Rob and Merritt. None of them had come out and said so, but he could sense that they all had the feeling of living on borrowed time.

"Got any thoughts about lunch?" Rob asked, turning around on the stool to address Shearer.

"Not really. . . . Sammy's?" It was a deli along the block from the campus, one of the regular haunts.

"Could do, I guess."

Shearer looked over at Merritt. "Coming with us?"

"I brought something in today. No reflection on the company, but it means I get to read for an hour on my own in peace and quiet too."

"What are you reading?" Rob asked her curiously as she got up and went over to unhook her duffel bag from the rack behind the door.

"An old Victorian novel. English." Merritt came back and sat down again, taking out a plastic lunch box secured with a rubber band, and a flask. She rummaged some more and handed Rob a battered-looking volume with faded red covers and worn edges. "Besides, I don't like the security hassle of getting back in again. So I only go out if I have to."

"Original?" Rob inquired, thumbing through the pages

"No, a nineteen-twenties reprint."

"That's practically the same to me. So what's it got? Swooning heroines, cads, and decent chaps with character and breeding that tells?"

"At least they were written by authors who knew their own language," Merritt replied. "And, you can be facetious if you want, but you're not that far off the mark. Sure—characters with style and taste. Where else are you going to find it these days?"

"Do you know, there used to be a time when there wasn't any security to go through to get into a place like this?" Shearer said. "Or most places, in fact." He inclined his head up at one of the cameras covering the lab area from opposite ends. "Or any of that. The staff would never have put up with it. Universities were public places, funded with public money. They took a pride in being open to anyone who wanted to walk in off the street. No tracker chips in everything you own. No bio-ID profiles."

"Times sure change, don't they." Rob snorted and rose to his feet, passing the book back to Merritt.

"It sounds like another world," Merritt said dreamily.

"That's just what it was," Shearer told them. He got up too and retrieved his jacket from the hook next to Merritt's bag. "Airports as well."

"You're kidding."

"Really. Everywhere. My grandfather told me he could remember just walking through to the gates where they boarded the old flat-takeoff jets. Sometimes there wouldn't be any agent or anyone there. The door of the plane was open. You just got on, found your seat, and waited for the crew to show up."

Rob was staring fixedly when Shearer turned back toward the door. "You know, Marc, every time I listen to you, I end up thinking about something in ways that never occurred to me before," he accused.

"That's because you're not supposed to think about it," Shearer said, and then threw back, "See you later, Merritt."

"Take your time."

As Shearer followed Rob out, his phone emitted its squeaky rendition of *Toccata and Fugue* in his jacket pocket. "Go on ahead. I'll catch up," he said, taking the unit out. Rob nodded and moved away along the corridor. Shearer thumbed the accept key and dropped his pace to a slow walk. The tone selection that it had sounded indicated an audio-only call. "Marc Shearer here."

"Mr. Shearer." The voice was that of Ellis, the department head. "I have some news for you that I am informed is most urgent. I confess that I also find it highly surprising."

"Oh?"

"It concerns your application for an off-planet posting."

"Yes?" Something jumped in Shearer's chest. Although he had complied with Wade's request, there had seemed little reason for it to be considered worth allocating a valuable slot on a mission. Hence, he had not thought too much about it, devoting his time instead to the contemplation of what other future prospects might present themselves.

"It appears that you, or conceivably Professor Wade, must have more influence in the right places than I would have thought credible. Your application has been accepted, and I am instructed to expedite matters by no less a person than the faculty dean himself. It appears that a further expedition to Cyrene is being organized, and is due to depart six days from now."

Six days! God Almighty! . . .

"You are required to be at Interworld Restructuring's offices across the Bay for preliminary briefing and familiarization, commencing tomorrow morning. You'll need to spend the rest of today tidying things up here. Can you come up to my office first thing after lunch to go over the details?"

Shearer's mind was still racing to catch up. "Er, well, yes. . . . Of course" was all he could manage.

"Shall we say two o' clock, then?"

"That would be fine."

"I'll see you then, Mr. Shearer." The line went dead.

Still in a daze, Shearer fumbled the phone back into his pocket and quickened his pace automatically. Slowly, like light growing and brightening the landscape as the sun comes out from behind cloud, the meaning became clear in his mind. "*Yeaaahh!*" he yelled jubilantly, turned a full circle, and punched a fist toward the ceiling. . . .

Just as two girls in lab smocks came out of the doorway beside him.

"Did you just win something?" one of them asked warily.

"Even better than that. I'm going to the stars!"

"Oh, really? That's great. When?"

"Six days from now."

The girls glanced at each other. "Oh boy," the second one murmured.

CHAPTER FIVE

Orange County and other parts of the Los Angeles area that had once provided homes and playgrounds for the rich and famous and the rich and notorious alike had for the most part been taken over by more common representatives of the species. When the influx from the south that had swelled to huge proportions in the early part of the century eventually led to civil violence and then armed conflict, the affluent and mobile transplanted themselves to new enclaves of exclusivity farther north. The area now bordered the Greater Mexican Union, and as the immigrant population consolidated in numbers, wealth, and confidence, strong signs were emerging that it might secede and change over to the other side.

The other factor that played a large part in the secession of the Western Federacy, later reduced to Occidena, was the seismic shift in financial holdings and political power that followed the sudden breakthrough into Heim physics and its rapid development in things like starship drives. Enormous fortunes were made through timely stock transfers and takeovers, lofting names overnight into the *Forbes 400* that longtime subscribers to the *Robb Report* had never heard of. The most consequential of these activities revolved around the corporate empires and research institutions associated with the space and military industries on the West Coast, which was where the bulk of the scientific expertise and infrastructure best suited to exploiting the new physics was concentrated. This also happened at a time when new heights of intrusiveness and excess on the part of the former federal government were increasing general unrest and adding to the internal forces already straining the nation toward fission. When the West-centered interests preempted impending confiscatory legislation from Washington by declaring themselves independent and made clear their readiness to defend their new sovereignty by force—of which it commanded an overwhelming superiority—the Eastern establishment found itself holding a pair of twos against four aces and had no choice but to back down. The resulting shock waves opened up fault lines that had been creaking and deepening for decades. In a rapid series of convulsions the Midwest, Plains, and Great Lakes regions followed suit to end years of growing resentments by breaking ties with Capitol Hill and pledging a return to original constitutional principles, which they symbolized by adopting the name New America; the Southern states yielded to a decisive black majority swollen by migrants escaping the turmoils of other parts, to become Martina; while the eastern rump, in a way that was not without its touch of irony, emerged as a parody of what was almost a reversion to the original thirteen colonies, proclaiming its adherence to the grander vision nevertheless with the amended title of Federated American States. Completing the picture, Texas preserved a balancing act between east, west, north-center, and south by reinvoking its status as a onetime republic; Hawaii went along with the Western Federacy and Alaska elevated its governor to president and declared nationhood, but maintained a close affiliation.

So the children of the new privileged West Coast dynasties were no longer graced by attending such hallowed academies as Harvard, Princeton, and Yale. Stanford still kept its prestige, of course, and by the reckoning of many headed the list of western higher learning institutions by virtue of its tradition. Gates University, in a glorious setting amid the Cascades, was a close runner, noted for the munificence of its donors, as by a slightly wider margin were Corbel, not too far north at Bellingham, and Farrell at Santa Cruz. The last two were formerly existing campuses that had been acquired, expanded, and aggrandized to immortalize names that had swept to super-wealth and fame in the extraterrestrial development boom. A titanium Heim heat shield surmounting polished marble on the entrance lawn had replaced ivied walls as the symbol of tribal roots and social cohesion for the highborn.

One of the founders of Interworld Restructuring was a former Air Force pilot turned business speculator by the name of Conrad Metterlin. Having adjusted to the life of palatial residences in Carmel, St. Moritz, and Brisbane, custom-built Lamborghini, and a personalized Gulfstream that he used as a flying conference room or party suite depending on the occasion, he turned his attention to the business of raising his position on the social hierarchy by outdoing rivals in ostentatious display—a compulsion also coded in the genes that color the tail feathers of peacocks and the hindquarters of mandrills. Among prominent humans, this frequently expresses itself as the making of spectacular donations to worthy and highly visible causes. In Metterlin's case, it took the form of a half-billion-(revalued)-dollar grant to include a Metterlin School of Aviation in Occidena's new National College of Space Sciences and Engineering at Sunnyvale. This in turn was a lavish affair intended as a monument to symbolize the groundings of the new nation's wealth and political prestige, and took the form of grandiose exhibition of surreal space-age architecture and experimental facilities dedicated to the new physics, close to the airport and aviation complex located further north along the peninsula, the military space center on the former NASA site at Ames, and the launch installations east of San Jose at Alum Rock.

The Aviation School's Grand Opening Day was blessed by a flawless sky of sunshine and clear blue. Chefs from San Francisco's noted houses of haute cuisine dispensed salmon tartare with marinated cucumber, and paté de foie gras accompanied by oceans of champagne in a marquee set up to serve the lawn party beneath the name METTERLIN carved in granite above the main entrance, while couples in Adrian Jules suits and Gregg Ruth diamonds gyrated on a polished hardwood floor to amplified swing from a blue-blazered dance band. The orchids setting the tone of the floral backdrop had been flown in from Venezuela, and the winsome, yellow-furred primates somewhat suggestive of lemurs, known as *kerries*—the zoologist who discovered them had been Irish—being led around on gold chains by attendants and frolicking to the delight of the guests, were from a planet of a neighbor to Barnard's Star. At the far end of the lawn, facing the Aviation School building, a pair of

Beech twin-prop trainers stood garlanded in flowers and bunting—
Metterlin's surprise bonus gift, named *Julian* and *Esther* after his two
children.

Jerri Perlok was not there as a result of owning a line of per-
fumery with a Paris label that had become famous, or landing a
husband from Jimmy'z club in Monaco. In fact, she didn't have a
husband, spending too much of her life in wild corners of the world
that few beyond regular readers of *National Geographic* would be
likely to know much about; in any case, even at twenty-nine she had
still to experience a relationship that she could have felt enough
confidence in it to want to make permanent. Despite being accused
by many of being irreverent and rebellious, at heart she was still one
of those old-fashioned few for whom "lifelong commitment" meant
what it said.

She sat on her own at one of the sunshaded tables on the lawn,
sipping a glass of Meursault Chardonnay over an unfinished plate of
smorgasbord salad, and noting the subtle and sometimes not-so-subtle
signaling through body language and preening displays taking
place on the dance boards and around and about of who ranked
where in the status stakes, who was bidding, and who was available.
As an anthropologist and evolutionary psychologist with a secondary interest in mythology, Jerri was more accustomed to observing
the mating rituals of South American birds and Namibian
antelopes, and more familiar with the rewards and punishments
meted out by ancient Greek and Hindu deities than the emerging
subspecies of *Homo sapiens plutocratus*—but it was all very educa-
tional and interesting.

Her invitation had been procured by a friend called Ivor, whom
she had met a little over a year previously on the Hawaiian island of
Maui. She had been staying in a trailer on the lower slopes of a volcano, which she and a colleague had rented as a base for studying
migratory bird habits. Ivor was in a $2,000-per-night suite at the
Four Seasons hotel, functioning in his role as household manager for
the Metterlins and their company of select guests enjoying a week of
mid-Pacific getaway. It was a truism among household managers, or
"personal assistants," employed by the superlatively rich that they
slept with the phone left on and a notepad and pen by the bed to be
always prepared for sudden demands from their charges, so Jerri and

Ivor had not actually seen much of each other in the event. Even principals who were not third-generation hereditary beneficiaries but who had made it to where they were through their own drive and initiative seemed to acquire a sudden learned incompetence in even the simplest of mundane tasks. It was as if having others perform them were a badge that denoted status—much like the women of Imperial China whose crippling by foot-binding advertised that they could afford servants to carry them. But Ivor's anecdotes of life in the top tenth of a percentile had been too intriguing for an anthropologist not to be interested in. She found him personable in himself in any case. His permanently unpredictable schedule suited her own tendency to get stuck into things that interested her for days at a time, and to disappear suddenly from her apartment in the Sierra foothills across the Central Valley for spells in unusual places, and in their own unconventional way they had continued an erratic form of friendship ever since. And so here she was.

The other reason Jerri had wanted to attend the event was that her life had recently taken on a change of direction that she'd known was a possibility but not really taken seriously. Some months before, more by way of a whimsical dare to herself than from a belief that it would lead to anything, she had applied to Interworld Restructuring for a position as an exo-anthropologist (purists in the profession were still debating whether the term was meaningful, since according to some, "anthropo-" meant strictly Terran-human) in response to the ads they had been running for scientific professionals to staff their stellar exploration missions. Maybe hearing a lot about the consortium from Ivor had had something to do with it. For a long time little had happened other than her receiving a routine acknowledgment. Then, suddenly, she was notified that an expedition was being organized at short notice to a planet called Cyrene, and if she could wrap up her Earthly affairs in time, or at least put them on hold, there was a slot for her if she wanted it, and a place reserved on a familiarization course to be conducted in San Francisco.

Jerri had noticed that elderly people seldom argued. If others disagreed with their views, or were too rushed and hurried to listen to them in the first place, they tended to let things be. But when someone did take the trouble to listen, they could learn much that was of value. And one thing that she had noticed over and over again

was that older people never regretted anything they had done. Even
the marriage that hadn't worked, the gold mine that ran dry, the
business that went belly-up—all seemed to evoke the reaction "Well,
I gave it a try." What they regretted were the things they *hadn't* done
when the chance was there: the year or two to see the world that they
had put off and put off because there was always something more
urgent, and one day it was too late; the buy-in option that they
turned down. Even the recollection of a come-on eye and a provoca-
tively revealed leg from fifty years ago could produce a wistful "It was
right there in front of me, but I was too green to see it." Thus fore-
warned, Jerri had consigned herself to whatever fate might have in
store, accepted the offer, and joined the class a week previously.
However, she was playing hookey today after Ivor made good on his
promise to get her an invitation to the Metterlin Aviation School
opening day, which gave her a chance to see close-up something of
the people behind the business that she would be working for. Also,
it would enable her to break the news to Ivor personally of her imminent departure. Things had moved so quickly that she hadn't found
an opportune moment to mention it.

A rising fanfare from the band made her turn her head from
studying the curving geometric surfaces of metal and glass that
formed the roof and upper parts of the building. Two stewards wearing the maroon jackets and tan pants of Metterlin's personal staff
were tactfully but efficiently moving the dancers away from the center
of the wooden floor and clearing an avenue to the side, where a paved
path led from the entrance forecourt. Approaching along it, surrounded by an entourage of officials from the college, local political
figures, more maroon jackets, and a half-dozen two-fifty-pounders
in tuxedos bulging at the chest and the shoulders, was Conrad
Metterlin himself, with his wife, Vera, on his arm.

He was clearly relishing every moment. As the people on the
dance floor fell back into an admiring circle and others converged or
fluttered mothlike from around the lawn and the marquee, he strode
grandly in a sky-blue suit that shone with a silky luster, trimmed at
the lapels and pockets with what looked like sheared mink, beaming
and acknowledging favorites with waves from side to side. Vera
maintained a regal poise, moving proudly in an iridescent gown that
reflected in gold and green, and seemed more drapery than dress, the

effect enhanced by jewelry flashing in the sunlight from her fingers, arms, neck, and hair. Without missing a step, the couple swept to the center of the floor as the band changed tune, where they proceeded to move smoothly into a stylish routine that brought approving murmurs and applause. The steps and twirls looked very technical and precise, but Jerri didn't know enough about that kind of thing to be able to fully appreciate or name them. She took another bite from her plate and continued to watch, fascinated, while the King displayed himself before his court.

"They've been rehearsing it for a week," a voice murmured from behind her. She looked up as Ivor slid down into one of the vacant chairs. He had exchanged his white jacket—the household manager didn't share the maroon of the rank-and-file attendants—for one of lightweight red satin that blended in. Even so, he was taking a risk; staff were not expected to be visible when off-duty, let alone talking with guests. But all attention was elsewhere, which was doubtless why he had chosen this moment to make an appearance. "Had a special dance coach coming in daily for the last month. You don't wanna know what the hourly rate was."

Ivor was medium in height, trim and athletically built, with black hair cropped very close to his head, and deep brown eyes that Jerri had long suspected concealed a greater shrewdness than he tended to let on. He missed nothing and made decisions instantly that almost invariably turned out to be right. Also, he was a perfectionist—as anybody would practically have to be to qualify for the job. Yet despite the diligence he displayed in catering to every whim and need, from seeing that a dish of Esther's preferred brand of ice cream was always available from the kitchen to making sure that a plane from the Metterliln's small private air force was fueled up at all times with a pilot on call, Jerri discerned an attitude beneath it that was not in accord with the image that he was obliged to maintain. She wasn't sure if it stemmed from envy hiding somewhere deep down, suppressed resentment, or simply a reaction to incessantly having to advertise one's subservience. But she sometimes detected hints of rebellion stirring, which was maybe what had evoked a response in herself. His revealing of just how planned and calculated an affair the spectacle taking place on the dance floor had been was an example.

She smiled in the easygoing way that came naturally, whatever the setting. "They give you a break? I don't believe it. The next thing, you'll be telling me they're turning human."

"Hey, why don't *you* try giving me a break? I've been on the go since five A.M. I spotted you here a while back—but I can only manage a few minutes. So hi again. Glad you could make it. What do you think of life in the stratosphere?"

"Some theories have it that elaborate dancing evolved as a selection ritual. Proficiency and coordination are genetic markers for reproductive eligibility. It's still there if you look. But most people have conditioned themselves not to see it."

"Don't you ever stop working?"

Jerri dropped her flippant tone. "I'm enjoying it. Thanks for taking the trouble, Ivor. I appreciate it."

"No problem." Ivor selected a cocktail stick with a black olive, cheese, and anchovy from a dish on the table and sampled it. "Did you come down from Pinecrest this morning?"

"Actually, I was down here in the Bay Area already. That was something I wanted to tell you. I took a day off school."

"School?"

"Off-planet Preparatory Basics. At Interworld's place in Redwood City. Do you remember that crazy application I told you I put in—for an anthropology slot? . . ."

Ivor stared at her for what must have been a couple of seconds at most. She could almost sense the bit-patterns streaming through neural registers. "You got it?"

She nodded. He seemed genuinely pleased for her, even though it obviously meant she would be leaving.

"How soon?" he inquired.

"Four days."

"*Four days*? Jeez! When you make your mind up to do something, you don't hang around."

"It's all happened so quickly. That was why I didn't mention it before—my feet haven't touched the ground. The runaround to get Nim approved was unbelievable."

"Nim's going too?"

"Well, of *course!*" Nimrod was Jerri's dog. She flashed Ivor a reproachful look that said he ought to know better. "So I'm *really* glad that this came up when it did, because it gives me a chance to tell you face-to-face. The ship's up there in Earth orbit already. It's called the *Tacoma*. We'll be shuttling up from Alum Rock. . . ."

CHAPTER SIX

Dr. Ellis, the department head at Berkeley, confided to Shearer that it was probably as well Shearer would be departing. Since the adtenna project had failed to yield worthwhile results, funding was unlikely to be renewed when the present contract expired. He already had a termination agreement and various release documents ready to be signed. Probably, Shearer reflected cynically as he scrawled his name on the dotted lines, a convenient way of getting rid of a surplus body and cutting the departmental payroll without incurring severance obligations.

Shearer had expected that if anything came of the Cyrene application, he would have had a lot more time to prepare for it than this. When he asked about Rob and Merritt, Ellis replied that arrangements would be made to absorb them elsewhere in the university. That was something to be grateful for anyway, Shearer reflected. Consequently, he was able to feel comfortable in himself and to look to the future with curious but guarded optimism when he showed up the next morning to begin the briefing sessions that had been scheduled across the Bay in Redwood City.

Interworld Restructuring's company literature referred to its holdings on the Bay waterfront unassumingly as "offices." The reality was a massive square-built structure the size of a city block, with angled walls and a flat airpad-roof, rendered in glass and various hues of plastic and ceramics. With just about all of the peninsula north from San Jose being urbanized, the complex stood on reclaimed land that had been worth a billion before anything was built on it, and extended out over the water above a system of piers inside a floating security fence of linked buoys patrolled by armed guards in speedboats. The north-facing wall of the massif was windowless and carried a plot of the nearer regions of the galaxy, illuminated at night, showing the locations of the stars where an Interworlds presence had been established. A morphing banner above cycled through the words PEACE-PROSPERITY-PROGRESS.

Shearer's first morning was spent going through bureaucratic procedures that involved various insurances, waivers, and releases, tying up the contractual conditions between himself, Interworlds, and various other interests that had connections with the forthcoming mission, and setting out the limits of liabilities involving the Occidenan government. The afternoon saw a grilling security interview with an unnerving character called Callen, apparently destined to be going with the mission too, who asked some pointed questions about Evan Wade. After that there was a group overview of the Interworlds organization and its operations. The next day began with classroom sessions on general off-planet mission familiarization and essential emergency procedures. After that things grew more interesting. They got down to specifics and began learning something about Cyrene itself.

Ever since the possibility of joining Wade had first raised itself, Shearer had consulted the scientific journals and Interworld's own published reports to discover more about the planet, but apart from general data, the information he'd managed to find was surprisingly sparse. Compared with the publicity and fanfares to attract new investors that accompanied news from other worlds, it seemed odd. It was also odd that despite the much-publicized "miracle break-through" of Heim-physics-based communications that enabled round-trip message exchanges with the new colonies to be measured in hours rather than years, he had not managed to contact Wade for almost a month now, even though the regular net was supposed to access the interstellar system.

After Wade's arrival there six months previously with the manned mission sent following Cyrene's discovery, he had found some moments in what was clearly a busy life to send back a few initial impressions of the new world. In fact, in response to requests from Wade, Shearer had even arranged for some items of equipment that Wade said he needed to be sent with a later robot supply freighter. To Shearer's mild surprise these had included a prototype A-wave adtenna, along with ancillary circuitry and spare parts, which seemed to indicate that Wade intended carrying on with his research pursuits there. However, Shearer's subsequent messages expressing curiosity had produced no reply. When he used the opportunity of being inside Interworld to inquire further about this, he encountered what felt like evasiveness. But with all the new course material to absorb, he was too busy to ponder upon the matter unduly or pursue it further. He would be there soon enough, he told himself.

Cyrene was one of three widely spaced planets orbiting the star Ra Alpha, which formed a loose binary system with a smaller, redder, companion star called Ra Beta. A peculiarity about Cyrene was its orbit. Accompanied by its single moon, Calypso, it moved in a highly elliptical path about Ra Alpha, in the same plane as Ra Alpha and Ra Beta orbited each other—or more precisely, the center of mass between them, which because of Ra Beta's lesser mass lay slightly displaced from the mid-point in the direction of Ra Alpha. Cyrene turned on its axis in a little under 28 terrestrial hours, and took 680 of these days to complete one orbit about its primary. The path it traced was such as to carry it almost three times as far from Ra Alpha at apogee—the farthest extremity of the ellipse—than its closest approach at perigee. The result, compounded by ten-degree tilt of its axis, was an extreme of variation between summer and winter conditions that life on Cyrene had adapted to in some remarkable ways.

One of the consequences of an inverse square law of gravity is that bodies in an elliptical orbit travel faster as they plunge inward to approach perigee, and slow down again as they move back out to apogee. This meant that Cyrene did not cover equal distances along its orbital path in equal times. Just 54 days, or 8 percent of the 680-day total orbital period, occurred within the quarter of the ellipse closest to perigee; 150 days, or 22 percent were inside that half of the ellipse; and the remaining 530 days were spent in the half remote from the parent star, the greater proportion of them far out around

James P. Hogan

the apogee point. Winters on Cyrene, therefore, were long—drawn—out affairs, and the summers short, fiery, and with the daily conditions changing rapidly.

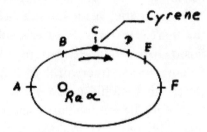

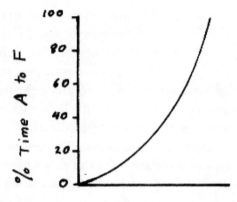

Point on Semi-Orbit	%Distance A to F	%time A to F	Days From A
A	0	0	0
B	25	8	28
C	50	22	75
D	75	50	170
E	87.5	69	235
F	100	100	340

Figure1. Orbit of Cyrene about Ra Alpha.
Total period=680 days. 1day=28 Earth hours.

It didn't stop there. Ra Alpha also orbited Ra Beta (or at least, could be thought of in that way) with a period of 6,118 days, close to nine of Cyrene's lopsided years. Since the ellipse that Cyrene traced around Ra Alpha preserved an effectively fixed direction in space (theory required a slow precession measured in thousands of years, but enough time had not accumulated yet for observational confirmation), the relative movement of Ra Beta superposed a longer 9-year cycle upon the basic 680-day summer-winter pattern, the intensity of which varied depending on where Cyrene was in its orbit about Ra Alpha when the three bodies came into alignment.

According to terms borrowed from Yocalan, the Cyrenean language that had been studied the most, the "Interior Point" occurred when Cyrene was directly between the two stars, and the "Exterior Point" when it again lay on the line connecting them, but on the far side of Ra Alpha. Because of the difference in periods, the place along Cyrene's ellipse where these Points occurred progressed from one orbit to the next as Ra Alpha advanced in its slower path around Ra Beta.

Although perigee was recognized as unique and marked the beginning of a new year for most Cyrenean cultures, the Interior Point, although shifting from year to year, was universally celebrated as more socially and celestially significant. In Yocala it was known as "Longday." This was the day in the year when Ra Alpha began to rise on one horizon just as Ra Beta set on the opposite one, giving two full days with no darkness at all at some point in the transitions between summer and winter, and back again.

When Longday occurred at or near perigee, summers were at their fiercest, with Cyrene close to Ra Alpha and long periods of daylight resulting from two suns on opposite sides of the sky. As Cyrene moved away from perigee, the two suns would gradually be seen to move closer together from day to day, the darkness growing longer, until Ra Beta disappeared in the glare of Ra Alpha, to re-emerge after winter, when Cyrene would again be accelerating inward and warming again. There was thus no correspondingly spectacular point to mark the antipode of Longday, when Ra Beta was in line with Ra Alpha but on the far side. However, generations of Cyrenean astronomers had fixed it from the apparent movement of Ra Alpha with respect to the background stars. It was known as "Henkyl's

Day." Henkyl and Goruno were the Yocalan names for Ra Alpha and Ra Beta, after two rival mythical figures from ancient legends, who battle each other endlessly for control of the heavens. Henkyl's Day occurred when Goruno was eclipsed completely and Henkyl ruled alone for a day.

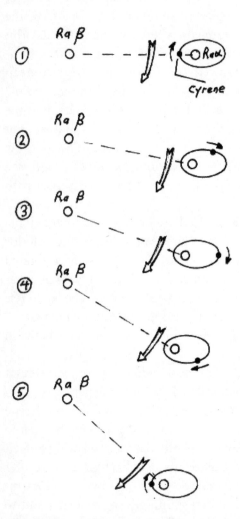

(1) Cyrene at perigree. Day of no darkness. Ra Alpha rises as Ra Beta sets. Time of maximum warmth.

(2) Cyrene at quarter orbital period. Cooling. Day by day, Ra Alpha and Ra Beta are seen to move closer together from opposite sides of the sky.

(3) Cyrene at apogee, halfway into orbital period.

(4) Cyrene at three quarters of orbital period. Ra Beta has closed visually to Ra Alpha sufficiently to be invisible in its glare.

(5) Cyrene completes one orbit. Ra Alpha has advanced 1/9 of its orbit relative to Ra Beta. The next darkness-free day will occur when Cyrene is some distance into its second orbit.

Figure 2. Motion of Ra Alpha relative to Ra Beta for one orbit of Cyrene. Cyrenes's orbit selected arbitrarily to commence from the point where perigree falls on the line connecting the two stars.

When Ra Alpha had made its four-and-a-half year semi orbit around Ra Beta, Longdays would have shifted to occur in the period centered on apogee. The cold resulting from Cyrene's greater distance from Ra Alpha would then be partly offset by the presence of Ra Beta in the winter skies, giving times of both milder winters and less extreme summers, due to their experiencing longer nights. Thus an additional climatic influence existed above Cyrene's 680-day year, which produced periods of blazing summers and harsh winters, alternating with milder versions of each over a nine-year cycle. It was known as the "novennial," and its resulting seasons as carbayis and doroyis, which translated roughly as "hard years" and "soft years."

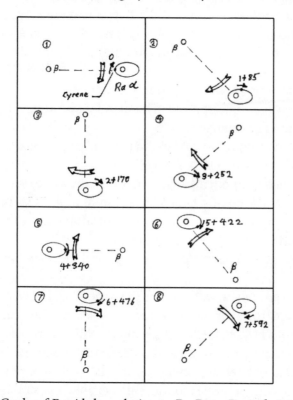

Figure 3. Cycle of Ra Alpha relative to Ra Beta. Period=9.1 orbits of Cyrene about Ra Alpha, i.e. 6118 Cyrenean days. Figures give the number of 680-day orbits of Cyrene, plus additional days of the following part-orbit. Thus, Frame 2 shows Ra Alpha 1/8 of the way into its cycle about Ra Beta, which is reached after 1 orbit of Cyrene around Ra Alpha plus a further 85 days.

এ(৬৯)৩

Shearer collected the plastic pack of insipid-looking cafeteria food from the dispenser, added cutlery and a cup of synthetic coffee substitute to his tray—the real thing had been withdrawn following a health scare and legal battle—and moved on to the payment machine. As he slowed to select a chipped card from his billfold, the man behind lunged past, waved a hand at the reader, and marched through the gate haughtily when the green light flashed. Implants seemed to give people an air of existing on some higher plane above the lowly herd. Shearer cleared the transaction and emerged into the eating area, with its ceiling-to-floor wall of glass on the far side looking out across the lower end of the Bay. The booths by the window were all taken. He slowed again, looking for a table, causing the bearded man bounding through after him to swerve, almost spilling his tray. "Makeupyamindwhichwayyergoin'can'tcha?" the man snarled, catching his bottle of soda as it tipped.

"Pardon me," Shearer said. The man looked at him as if he had spoken a foreign language and walked away.

"That's the wrong way, Marc," a more friendly voice said. "Don't you know you have to be assertive?"

He turned to find Jeff Lang, who was in the same class, holding a tray with some kind of salad and a carton of milk. "Oh, is that what it is? I thought it was just that some people don't know there's a difference between manliness and rudeness."

Jeff grinned. "You just don't read the right how-to books."

"I guess not."

They were fellow oddballs in the group, which was what had drawn them together. Jeff was about Shearer's own age, sandy-haired, with a boyish, freckled face and an obliging, easygoing nature that guaranteed social scorn and professional obscurity. He worked as some kind of freelance researcher and had been commissioned by an encyclopedia publisher to put together the bones of an entry on Cyrenean history. He looked around and inclined his head in the direction of the wall nearby. "There's an empty table that way."

"Sure."

They moved over and sat down. Jeff peeled the lid off his salad, poured a measure of milk into a cup, and opened the pack containing cutlery and napkin. "So, how long does it take Cyrene and the two Ras to come back into the same relative positions?" he asked. "Figured it out yet?"

Shearer groaned. "Jeff, gimme a break. It's lunchtime. My head's still aching from it all."

"Cramming it in all right, aren't they?" Jeff agreed.

"All right. So carbayis and doroyis." Shearer challenged. "Which is which?

"Carbayis is the hard years," Jeff replied. "Blazing summers. Ice-age winters."

"You sure?" Shearer realized that he wasn't himself.

"Make up a memory aid," Jeff suggested. "Carb is hard. Carborundum. Get it?"

"Good one. So what about dor, doroy? . . ."

Jeff shrugged. "I don't have one. It just has to be the other. But thankfully we won't be showing up in the middle of either." Cyrene was currently some months out from perigee, and by the time the *Tacoma* arrived would be comfortably into the intermediate part of its year, with the two stars positioned such as to produce moderate extremes. He looked down at his salad as he prepared to eat. "No egg. I always used to like a hard-boiled egg with salad. How long has it been since everyone stopped doing them?"

"I'm not sure. Not that long. I can remember having them at the university with breakfast. You can still get the powder mix they make into scrambled."

Jeff pulled a face. "Ugh! Wallpaper paste. Health departments. How long before I'm not allowed to cook myself an egg at home in my own kitchen?" He rolled some lettuce leaf around the end of his fork and speared a piece of tomato. "Yes, see, you smile, Marc. But can your remember the things we smiled at twenty years ago that have happened and nobody thinks twice about now? And there's a whole generation of kids out there who've never known any different and think it's the way things have always been. I mean, where does it all end?"

Shearer chewed in silence for a few seconds, then decided that Jeff was someone he could risk a joke with. "Well, you're the historian, Jeff. Line 'em all up against a wall and shoot 'em, and start all over again. Isn't that how people who've had enough have always fixed it in the end? It lasts for a while, anyway."

Jeff snorted in an offhand kind of way. "That might have worked when both sides had muskets and barricades, and you were in with some kind of a chance. But nowadays the firepower's too unequal. How can ordinary guys stand up against tactical nukes and databases that know everything you do? A couple of days ago a whole family in Carson City got blown away for not stopping at a checkpoint. A checkpoint! . . ." He stopped and gave Shearer a sidelong look. "Hell, what am I saying? I don't know you. I could end up in a camp for just talking like this."

"True," Shearer agreed. "So go on, you tell me. Why are you talking like this?"

Jeff shook his head with a long sigh. "I don't know. Sometimes you just have to let it out. I suppose . . . you seemed like an okay kind of person." He checked himself with a mock frown. "You are, aren't you?"

"Yes, you don't have to worry," Shearer said. He eyed Jeff curiously for a second or two. "You're not from here, are you?"

"You mean Occidena?"

Shearer shrugged.

"No, you're right. Minneapolis," Jeff said.

New America, where they said they were trying to get back to the constitution. That could explain a lot. However, Shearer had learned that talking politics with strangers was generally not a good idea, and so he didn't pursue the subject. Instead, he just smiled distantly and looked away. The cafeteria had filled for the midday break. He recognized some faces from their class, and one or two others that he had met while going through the administrative chores on the first day.

"Looking for someone?" Jeff inquired after a short silence.

"Oh, not really. . . . There are some of our people over there. Thomas, and Forrest is with him. What happened to Jerri today?"

"Jerri?"

"Isn't that her name? Tall, slim. Dark hair, sort of reddish, and a kind of pointy face and pouty mouth—not exactly what you'd call glamorous; but sexy."

"Oh, you noticed her too, eh?" Jeff grinned knowingly. "That's right. She wasn't in this morning. I think she's from across the other side of the Bay—up in the mountains somewhere. I'm not sure what she does."

"You don't know? What happened to the memory aids?"

Jeff made a conciliatory gesture with his fork. "You've got me."

Shearer looked back toward the window forming the far wall. A dredger flanked by a couple of barges had moved into view, heading up the Bay. "I thought I caught hints of an irreverent streak yesterday, when that guy was talking about our sacred mission to export the benefits of our way of life across the galaxy," he said. "If you asked me, Jeff, I'd say she's another one of us."

CHAPTER SEVEN

The tone announcing a call sounded from the concealed speakers in the study of Myles Callen's residence west of Los Gatos, in the hills midway between San Jose and the coast. He touched a stud on the wristband of his watch to activate the house system and shifted his attention from the list of items to be attended to before his departure for Cyrene. "Accept to current screen," he instructed. On the desk display that he was using, a window opened to frame the peak-capped face and blue-shirted shoulders of a guard at one of the gates into the community. "Yes?" No doubt it was to advise that Krieg had arrived. The time was about right.

"Good evening Mr. Callen. I have a Mr. Jerome Krieg at the gate, asking for you. His ID checks okay." While the guard was speaking, the view in the frame changed to a shot of Krieg's craggy, close-cropped head scowling from the driver's window of an automobile.

"Yes, that's all right. He's expected," Callen said.

"Thank you. Goodnight, Mr. Callen." The frame on the screen vanished.

Callen tidied up the loose ends of what he had been doing, saved the encrypted updates, then cleared the screen and got up from the desk. He picked up a sealed envelope that he had prepared, left the study with its functional lines and decor of chrome and black leather echoing the theme of his office at Milicorp, and went through to the central living area. Its mood was equally a hymn to masculine opulence, with upholstery of brushed gray suede, shag rugs, and a preponderance of metal in the ornaments and fittings, making no concessions to softness or warmth. The centerpiece above the mantel was by a renowned military artist and showed an aircraft approaching for a night landing on an early-twenty-first-century nuclear carrier. Female visitors told Callen that the place mirrored his soul. The comparison pleased him. He had tried marriage once, primarily as a social maneuver when it seemed required to complete the executive image, but found it to be incompatible with a first loyalty toward the corporation. And besides, monogamy was never a realistic expectation, and he had been surprised to find that was taken seriously. His psyche needed the gratification of repeated conquest as much as Milicorp's business health needed a world of perpetual conflict.

The simview window set in the outside wall was showing a live morning cityscape looking out over the center of Tokyo. Callen voiced the house system again to change it to a subdued artificial composition of moonlight over mountains, and cleared away some sensitive papers that he had been working with earlier. The door tone sounded from the room system just as he was finishing. A reflex glance at the monitor that flashed to life in a corner confirmed that it was Krieg. "Admit," Callen directed. It would have been too condescending of rank to go out into the hallway to greet Krieg; but he remained standing.

Krieg appeared moments later, square-built and solid, clad in a brown leather hip coat and black, crew-neck sweater. He was from Milicorp's dirty work department—on the payroll but not listed officially in the organizational chart. He was, and accepted being, a "deniable," who dealt only through Callen. Thus, the exalted levels that included Rath Borland could legitimately claim no knowledge of his existence or his activities. Precisely how, or in conjunction with whom, he carried out his assignments, even Callen preferred not to know. They had both been in the business long enough to understand what needed to be done without leaving trails of records.

Krieg rubbed his palms together as if he had come in from the cold, even though it was warm outside, and looked pointedly in the direction of the cabinet opposite the fireplace. It was an unconscious way that Callen had observed before of signaling that he had news that was worth something. Callen walked over to the cabinet, opened it, revealing a selection of bottles and glasses, and gestured for Krieg to help himself. Declining anything on his own part, he sat down in one of the armchairs, laid the envelope that he had brought from the study casually on a side table, and waited. Krieg mixed a concoction, added a couple of cubes of ice, and spread himself in the chair opposite. He took a sip and swilled it around in his mouth approvingly.

"Amaranth," Callen guessed.

Krieg nodded. It was the name of a planet that Interworld had "acquired" for development somewhere around two years before, and from which Krieg had only recently returned. This would be a short stopover for him; he would be coming on the Cyrene mission too. "It's all in place. Zannibe's gotten to the head of the roost and told him his knotheads don't have a clue. It's all over the city that Zannibe says he's seen hard times coming and they haven't, and when it happens he'll be the one who'll know what to do. The whole country's ready to buy his line as soon as water starts turning red and there are bodies falling over."

"Sounds like an upstream injection," Callen said.

"Uh-huh."

"What are we using?"

"PF13-C followed up by an aerosol herbicide. If that doesn't work, a denatured local gastric virus. Latency five days. Peaks after two weeks. Mortality ten percent."

"Redesignated operational?" Callen checked.

"Yup," Krieg confirmed. "Code word Bistro."

Callen nodded and made a mental note of it. Then, changing his mind, he got up and went over to the cabinet to pour a measure of brandy while he went over the details again in his head.

Amaranth possessed an anthropoid-pongid race that had spread to most of the planet's habitable areas, and in its most advanced manifestations reached a stage of erecting large stone structures and warring with metal weapons and animal-drawn chariots that looked surprisingly like their earlier Terran predecessors. And, also in keeping with many Terran precedents, the rulers were often jealously protective of their image, and not disposed to subordinate themselves to the authority of intrusive aliens, whatever technological advances or other gimmicks they might have to offer.

The usual Terran ploy was to find an envious rival or ambitious enemy who could be lured by the prospect of commanding unmatchable firepower, after which it was simply a case of playing one against the other until a winner emerged, who would from then on be a dependent, and therefore dependable, puppet to keep the population in line and ensure that the dues for all the ensuing benefits were collected. But it sometimes happened that no suitable candidates presented themselves, and the reigning native powers were relatively settled and content, with differences limited to occasional squabbles and small-scale skirmishes. Such was the situation in Amaranth.

However, such societies could be breached by appeal to religious superstition. Zannibe belonged to an enterprising clan of nomadic astrologer-diviners who made a living out of scaring wealthy and powerful, but gullible, patrons—which usually lasted until they were either lynched or deemed it prudent to move on. On getting some glimpses of the powers and real magic wielded by the alien god-figures who had appeared from the sky, Zannibe had become an instant ally and readily placed himself and the small group of kin currently following him at their disposal to be coached in a scheme to subvert the ruler of a distant nation called Jorst, whose name was Xeo and who was proving recalcitrant.

In essence, the plan was straightforward. By Krieg's account, Zannibe had already been insinuated to speak at the court of Xeo, where he would have delivered a prophecy of a plague about to befall the land, that would be signaled by the river turning red. Xeo's own priests, of course, would know nothing about this, since they didn't have the benefit of a contact man to the Milicorp commando group that Krieg had quietly set up, equipped with the chemicals to make it happen. Synchronized with the arrival of the discolored waters at Xeo's capital city on the region's major river, drones deployed upwind would release a quantity of airborne toxins sufficient to destroy crops and induce sickness among inhabitants and livestock on a scale that no one would have difficulty in recognizing as a "plague." The preferred outcome would then be to see the incumbent priesthood discredited and dismissed and Zannibe installed with honors as the new official seer and advisor to the throne, whereupon the pestilence would magically cease, and in due course a more cooperative policy could be expected to unfold—not the least reason being that Zannibe would find himself in need of comparably magical protection from the vengeful priests.

But if that failed, more drastic measures would be employed. By "denatured," Krieg meant that the viral DNA would degenerate with each replication cycle, eventually becoming nonviable and ending any further spread after a set period.

Callen had no further questions or points to raise. He came back to his chair with his glass and sat down. "Fine" was all he said. It was the kind of operation that fell under the blanket understanding of what constituted "security" interests, without any express directive from Interworld. In the same way, Borland's instructions to Callen had not been in a form that would be found in any company records. It was a subject about which the less said, the better.

Krieg waited a few moments more before changing the subject. "How are things going at Cyrene?" he asked. "I've been out of touch. I hear they've got some kind of trouble there."

"Two follow-up missions have been sent. They both disintegrated."

"Disintegrated?" The furrows in Krieg's naturally plowed forehead deepened.

"People started disappearing. I don't mean just the usual few Lewis and Clarks, or Hayseeds who decide they want to go native. I'm talking about wholesale—Interworld people, our own people, all the kinds who are on contract. We can't even make sense out of what we get from the ones who are still left at the base there. They start talking about seeing the world differently, not being able to communicate. Nothing you say seems to mean the same anymore." Callen shook his head. He could have given more detail, but he was tired. They had two months of voyage ahead of them for going into things like that.

"Sounds like something in the air," Krieg said, kneading the back of his neck with a hand.

"They've tried all the tests anyone can think of. Nothing shows up. But one of the names that's gone AWOL is of special interest. We've got a brief to track him down and bring him back. That was something I wanted to talk about. A scientist. Name of Evan Wade, from the Bay Area, used to be at Berkeley." Callen picked up the envelope from where he had set it down and passed it across. "Apparently he has unfinished business with Interworld that they want delivered. The also see him as a threat to their operation— subverting the natives. "

"Hm. Sounds like something big," Krieg commented. "What kind of scientist?"

"He's into some new type of wave that has to do with quantum physics. That's about all I can tell you. There's more in there." Callen gestured at the envelope in Krieg's hand.

"So all we have to do is find a guy who obviously doesn't want to be found, somewhere on an unknown planet that freaks out everyone who lands there. Anything else?" Krieg made it sound like something he polished off every day before lunch.

"It's not all bad," Callen told him. "Before he disappeared, Wade put in a rec for some help. A guy at Berkeley called Shearer, who used to work with him, applied for the slot, and friends of Interworld made sure it went through."

"So he'll be shipping out on the *Tacoma* too?" Krieg completed.

"Right,."

"And he leads the way. We follow."

"Exactly. You know our motto: Keep it simple."

Of course, Wade would hardly be coming back to the base on Cyrene to meet Shearer, but the two of them would be in touch somehow. So it wasn't going to be quite that simple. "We'll need tabs on Shearer," Krieg said after taking another drink and studying his glass for several seconds.

"We're putting a plant close to him," Callen replied. "To be referred to as Dolphin. In fact, it's already moving along. He's in the same training class as Shearer at Interworld. They had lunch together in the cafeteria there yesterday."

CHAPTER EIGHT

Early on the morning set for departure, Shearer and the rest of his group from the familiarization sessions appeared back at the Interworld center in Redwood City from the hotels where they had been lodged. From there they would be bused out to the launch complex at Alum Rock, where they would be joining other groups who had been processed in other locations. They all knew each other pretty well by this time, and the groupings and friendships that would doubtless take shape during the voyage ahead could practically be foretold. They had learned what basics were known of Cyrene's geography, physical characteristics, and strange climatic cycles, and something about the culture and customs of the inhabitants, as well as more about mission procedures and regulations. And of particular interest to Shearer as a physicist, even though from professional curiosity he was by no means a stranger to the subject, some time had been devoted to elaborating a little on the principles behind the new method of propulsion that would take them there.

A modification to preexisting beliefs that physicists had been forced to accept as a result of the demonstrated success of Heim's theory was that the speed of light that mattered was not with respect to the observer, as Einstein had maintained, but with respect to the dominant energy field in the region through which the light propagated. In the parts of the cosmos where conditions were cool and tranquil enough for neutral matter to form, in which the powerful electrical forces canceled each other, this meant the local gravity field. For over a century, all the experiments relating to this postulate had been performed in laboratories solidly nailed to the ground and stationary in the Earth's field, and hence the crucial difference had escaped detection.

The difference was crucial not only on account of the theoretical implications, but also in a more practical way, in that the operation of Heim ships depended critically on the gravitational field energy of the object being accelerated—i.e. the ship—compared to that induced by other gravitating bodies close enough to be significant. All of which was a long way of saying that they used conventional nuclear drives to get away from Earth's immediate vicinity before kicking in the part that really got things moving.

Another good reason for keeping the flips in and out of Heim space well removed from planets, moons, and busy regions of human space activity was that navigating across Heim space over interstellar distances was not yet a perfected art, and the point at which an arriving craft would materialize couldn't be fixed with precision.

The launch facility at Alum Rock was not, therefore, something akin to a railroad terminal, where, as some enthusiasts had prophesied in the early days, vessels would dematerialize from an underground terminal and reappear in similar environs at the destination, but a more traditional style of base from which travelers and freight were beamed up via ground-laser-powered shuttles to join the mother craft in orbit.

Although, like most people, Shearer had seen such launch centers many times in pictures and news documentaries, and found the image of what they symbolized stirring, the reality as they approached was in some ways sobering. The perimeter of fences, concrete, guard posts, and even watch towers mounting weapons, gave more the impression of a military fortification than what was billed as a gateway to the stars. Even the sight of the shuttle noses rising above their service gantries and the surrounding clutter, and the massive, turretlike mountings of the two pusher lasers on the squared, blockhouselike peak above the sprawling power complex four miles away failed to relieve the feeling. The world ran on plunder protected by violence. Was this the great vision that they were now destined to export out into the galaxy?

Jeff interrupted his brooding from the seat across the aisle. "Why so solemn, Marc? You've been talking for days about going to the stars. This is the big day, man."

Shearer smiled halfheartedly. "Oh, just making the best of the first morning in days when I can tune out, I guess. It's been a hectic week." Jeff was around most of the time. He seemed to have latched on to Shearer as a pal. Shearer didn't really mind. Jeff seemed okay. He could come up with some interesting tidbits of Cyrenean history—no doubt from getting some homework in before leaving on his assignment.

In a seat somewhere behind, Roy was foghorning to somebody about the racial clashes that were threatening to break up the fragile Texas Republic, and how they ought to nuke Mexico City before Occidena lost another piece. He was some kind of market surveyor and forecaster, big and fleshy, boorish in manner, and Shearer did his best to avoid him. The night before, in the hotel bar, he had been calling for bets on who would get the first lay with a Cyrenean.

In front of Shearer, Arnold and Karen were engrossed in what looked like an intense debate about something. Arnold was an appraiser and planner of commercial real estate, Karen a financial analyst. It seemed that behind the scenes, schemes were already advanced for meshing Cyrene's anticipated productivity with the Terran economy and establishing a basis for value exchange. Shearer had found them nominally social and agreeable as was true of most young, upwardly aiming professionals, but in the remote kind of way that stemmed from conforming to expected norms rather than anything real in the way of feelings. They typified the dedicated servants of the system that Shearer abhorred, upon whom its existence depended. What baffled him was not so much that they never questioned, but the apparent inability to conceive that anything *could* be questioned.

The general company was drawn from the younger, relatively more junior elements of those who had attended the various courses and classroom sessions that week. They had also glimpsed and occasionally crossed paths with members of a higher-status contingent who would evidently be traveling to Cyrene too, but none of them were on the bus or the other two buses following behind. They were being flown over from the pad on the Interworld Center roof. Jerri Perlok had mentioned that among them was someone from the

Corbel family, who had bankrolled Conrad Metterlin and owned over half of Interworld. She hadn't said how she knew.

She was sitting a couple of rows ahead on the far side. Through the drive out from San Jose and for most of the way up into the hills she had immersed herself in reading, but set it aside when they came within sight of the launch complex. Now she was upright and alert, her waves of dark, reddish hair prominent above the seat back, moving in short starts as she took in every detail. By nature, Shearer had found, she was the opposite of Arnold and Karen—questioning everything, willing to give unconventional views an equal hearing, and probably incapable of conforming. But he had also noticed that she had the sense not to argue when outnumbered by people who weren't listening. One of the few truly interesting people that life washed up out of its vast ocean from time to time, he had decided. She had a dog called Nim that she was taking with her to Cyrene. The hotel had found a place for him, and Jerri had brought him out once or twice in the evenings to meet the group. A few of them had seemed mildly disapproving, but Shearer liked dogs. They were intelligent, honest, affectionate, and totally loyal . . . traits, it often seemed, that had yet to evolve in much of humanity. Or had they existed at one time, and since atrophied?

He hadn't realized he was staring so obviously until Jeff's voice teased, "You wish."

Shearer raised his eyebrows and didn't try to deny it. "A guy could do worse, Jeff," he agreed.

Just then, the Interworld agent who was acting as courier for the group cut in over the speaker system. "When we get to the gate, there will be an individual security check. Everybody has to get off the bus. You'll all need your regular ID, tax clearance certificate, and counter-signed embarkation papers."

Nobody left the country owing money to the government. It wasn't that the downsized regional governments wielded much real power these days. They functioned as collection agencies for the corporate empires and as caretakers to deal with social unrest and placate—or at least make token gestures toward—the dispossessed victims of the utopian order that everyone was assured now existed.

Jeff snorted and opened a pocket of the briefcase resting on his knee. "Do you think they've got this on Cyrene too already," he grumbled.

"Give 'em time, Jeff," Shearer answered with a sigh.

Once inside the complex, the inevitable flurry of minor last-minute changes to plan, and the final chores to be attended to allowed few moments for reflection. In what seemed in some ways like detached kind of dream, Shearer found himself being routed through seating areas, corridors, and concrete galleries with windows set high in the walls to a staging hall; then, after a short wait, he was staring with the others out at huge steel gantries rising above a forest of service towers and masts as a shuttle bus took them out to the pad area itself. Disembarking from the bus was followed by more weaving through doors, passages, gates, and stairways, and then they were walking though the connecting ramp into the center section of the shuttle, standing with half its body length below ground level in the launch silo.

They had been issued with numbers directing them to assigned seats on the various decks, which were built cross-hull like the floors of a lighthouse. Once in freefall in wouldn't matter which way the floors were, and the seats would be useful only for preventing everyone from floating into a tangle. There were ways of controlling one's attitude and movements in zero-g using the gyroscopic effects of rapid rotary arm movements, but the old hands assured them that the only way to learn them was the hard way. And the same would apply for the first two days or so aboard the *Tacoma*. After that, life for the remainder of the voyage to a point two days out on approach to Cyrene would get easier. A bonus of Heim gravito-electromagnetic interconversion was that once past the "H-point," where the main drive was engaged, a portion of the output could be bled off and transformed to synthesize normal gravity inside the ship.

Shearer was still too absorbed in the newness of it all to take much notice of who was around him as he settled down into his seat and secured the restraining harness. No sooner had he done so, when of course there came the announcement of a short delay while a laser boost station somewhere downrange in Russia reran a calibration. He sat back resignedly, staring at the screen facing the deck from one side like a miniature theater, currently showing an outside view of umbilicals disconnecting and blast doors being closed in the silo walls below the ship. It was the first chance he'd had to be alone with his thoughts since leaving the hotel that morning.

Everything around him—the masterpiece of engineering that he was sitting in; the concentration of technical ingenuity outside that was about to lift it free from Earth itself; and the awesome machine waiting above, along with all it represented—was a triumph of the human intellect, symbolizing surely as strongly as anything could that there were no limits to what intelligent life could achieve. The Golden Age that mythology created in the past could have been the reality of the future that centuries of visionaries had dreamed would one day be. But somewhere along the way, something had gone wrong. In his earlier years of youthful idealism bolstered by faith that human nature was at heart just, and the better side would ultimately prevail, he had crossed the continent, eager to find and devote himself to the further building of the better life that the recruiting ads and promotional agencies had promised for qualified and talented people. For surely, he had told himself, the part of the world that he had seen until then was the exception, an aberration. . . . But no, it was the same everywhere; just in different ways.

Shearer was originally from the west side of central Florida, toward the coast, an improbable product of a trailer-park home and dysfunctional family consisting of a violent and alcoholic father, a mother who survived by means of tranquilizers and other recreational chemicals, and a Bible-quoting sister two years older than he, whom he had last heard of fund-raising for a fundamentalist electronic church based in Virginia. He discovered his own escape in the realms of mathematical physics, revealing him to be something of a prodigy even in middle school, and confirming the suspicions of family and neighbors of his distinct inclination toward the "strange." The fare from the public and even the school's library had been inadequate for his insatiable appetite, but word of his abilities reached a professor at Gainesville who still believed that education meant being encouraged and shown how to think, not behavioral conditioning measured in grade points. Recognizing Shearer's talent, he coached him privately at no charge and gave him unrestricted access to his files and bookshelves. Shearer had seemed set for early enrollment into a degree course on a state grant, which would open the way to better things. The rapid breakthroughs into the revolutionary physics being reported from researchers in both the north and south Americas as well as Europe and Asia portended exciting and unlimited prospects. A creatively fulfilling and rewarding personal future seemed assured, despite the black clouds that had been piling up and rumbling in the political sky. And then the Great Breakup happened.

Central Florida became a primary battle zone as Hispanics and Cubans, who by that time formed a majority in the south, extended themselves northward to defend their turf against the black expansion coming the other way from what would become Martina. Amid the exodus of whites who weren't caught in the crossfire or among those being targeted by both sides, Shearer got away, thanks to arrangements that the professor made for them, on a crowded boat that was ferrying batches of people out of Tampa and across to Texas. The professor himself didn't make it.

Shortly thereafter, Texas assumed independence and was engulfed by turmoil of its own, which had still not abated. But Shearer was already being drawn by the lure of the western coalition of former states whose secession had precipitated the whole collapse. That was where the new science was consolidating, and where the beginnings of amazing capabilities that would spring from it were already becoming visible. It took him another couple of months, but existing from one day to the next and moving on when an opportunity presented itself, he was finally able to present himself before job interview panels of corporations unheard of ten years previously, whose names were already synonymous with visions of the dazzling future that was to come. At least, that was how the Public Relations imagery portrayed it. The effect on Shearer of meeting the actuality face-to-face was devastating.

Yes, they were eager to employ his kind and quality of talent, and were prepared to pay handsomely—if one was looking for nothing beyond material recompense, conventionally accepted notions of prestige and status, and a ticket into an alienating and ruthless competition among peers to secure more of the same. It seemed that the only measure of human worth was the ability to contribute to the efficacy of creating profits or ever more fearsome weaponry to protect them. It was evident even before the sessions were over that he wouldn't have accepted an offer on their terms even if they persevered to the point of seeing fit to make him one, after which the disinterest quickly became mutual. As a last resort before ending up a street derelict, he followed up on a lead to Evan Wade, whose name he knew from the scientific literature, and the professor in Florida had commented on favorably. The result had been a place with Wade's obscure group at Berkeley. True, the work involved a relatively unexplored fringe quantum effect without much promise in the way of immediate tangible return—which was precisely the reason it was unexplored—not the center of mainstream Heim physics that Shearer had dreamed of; but in the way that mattered to him he was free—as free as it seemed possible to get in the kind of society that had come to be, anyway— and still work in advanced physics with any kind of support at all. And that, he supposed resignedly, was about as much as could be hoped for in a world that he was told was shaped by harsh, immutable laws—the work of nature, not humans—that permitted it to be no other way.

"Attention." An announcement from the cabin speakers broke his reverie. "We've received clearance from downrange and are initiating a five-minute countdown. Make sure seat harnesses are secure and any loose objects stowed."

And now he was moving on once again, this time to another world completely, for how long he didn't know. Was there some goal at the end of it all that fate had in store for him, he wondered, like fulfillment at the end of the wanderings of one of those heroes of ancient sagas? Or was it simply nature's way of saying that the world just didn't have a place for him? If so, it seemed that a lot of people these days were getting the same message.

CHAPTER NINE

The interconversion between electromagnetic and gravitational energy that formed the basis of the Heim drive derived from an immensely strong magnetic field rotating at high speed. However, this didn't entail any cumbersome mechanical rotation of anything material. As in conventional electric motors, it was the motion of the field that mattered, and this could be accomplished by a suitably phased combination of currents circulating in stationary conductors—which was just as well since the *Tacoma* was comparable in mass to, and in size somewhat larger than, an old-time naval cruiser. But because of the nature of its primary propulsion system, its basic geometry was circular, thus rendering the notions of advanced space machines in the form of "flying saucers" that had permeated the popular literature for a century fortuitously not far from the mark in terms of what was eventually realized. Indeed, there were still some diehard devotees who took this as proof that the claims had been right all along and the "real thing" was still somewhere out there. By far the prevalent view, however, and one of the few consensuses that Shearer was inclined to share in unreservedly, was the opposite, since if Earth's explosion out from the solar system in recent decades wasn't enough to make any lurking aliens show themselves openly, the overwhelming likelihood was that there weren't any. And for what it was worth, experiences so far in the nearby reaches of the galaxy were consistent with that conclusion. None of the sapient races encountered by Terran explorers had proved as advanced as Earth's technologically, or anywhere close. As a popular aphorism held,

"Someone has to be first." Or as someone in Shearer's group had put it earlier in the week: "UFOs are real, and they are us."

"It's usually called the nuts game, but it'll work just as well with these." Shearer came back to the table with a box lid containing the plastic counters, disks, tiles, and tokens that he had collected from the games scattered about the C Deck messroom, which also served as a recreation center. "Forget what they look like. Everything counts the same."

The four people seated at the long table by the wall waited curiously. A metal bowl emptied of its normal content of fruits and snack items stood in the middle between them. Jerri was one. Roy, the Mouth, of course, had to be there. The other two were Arnold, the real-estate planner, and Zoe, an administrator who would be joining the logistics staff at the Cyrene base. Jeff was watching with interest from a nearby chair, while other figures who happened to be around at the time looked on. The ship was two days past the H-point, now under Heim drive and simulating normal gravity inside. It was also cut off from the familiar universe as far as anything electromagnetic was concerned. The external imagers showed uniform blackness on the screens. The only information reaching the vessel was communications and navigation data received by special instruments.

Shearer went on, continuing as he spoke, "I put some of these objects in the bowl like so. . . . Jeff has the watch. When he says 'Go,' your aim is to end up with as many as you can. Then, every ten seconds, I want Jeff to tell you to stop so I can count whatever's left in there. I'll double the number by replenishing from this box. Everybody okay?"

"Just end up with as many as we can," Zoe said.

"Right," Shearer confirmed. "Play whatever strategy you think will best achieve that."

Roy was flexing his arms and shoulders as if loosening up for a football game. Arnold remained impassive. Jerri's eyes flickered over them in a curious kind of way as if trying to read something or get their attention, but they failed to notice.

Shearer nodded to Jeff. Jeff consulted his watch, waited few seconds, then ordered, "*Go.*"

Roy lifted up the bowl, clearly with the intention of simply emptying the entire content in front of him. It was a good try, but Zoe reacted quickly enough to intercept the bowl in midcourse and dig a hand inside, in the process of which they turned it over to scatter disks and tokens all over the table. As shouts of encouragement and jeers erupted around the room, Arnold dove in smoothly to sweep a heap together with both arms as they fell, leaving Roy and Zoe to scrabble frantically for the remainder. Jerri sat watching them, motionless, making no attempt to join in. The expression on her face was a mixture of exasperation and despair.

"*Stop*," Jeff announced.

The outcome was foreseeable from the beginning. Shearer made a show of righting the upturned bowl and inspecting it. "Game over," he said.

"Some game," a mystified voice said in the background. "That's it?"

"Arnold wins," another declared. "Look at all that! Nice move, Arnold."

"Only because I stopped Roy for him," Zoe said, sitting back to release her assortment of disks and tokens.

"It takes a planner." Arnold grinned as he returned his own pile of spoils to Shearer to separate out.

"Damn, and I had it figured out," Roy muttered peevishly. He braced his arms along the edge of the table and rose. "You just got in lucky," he told Zoe, then rose and turned away. Amazingly he was irked at losing in even something as trivial as this; but Shearer had seen it before.

"So that's it, Marc?" the person who had spoken before called again. "What's it supposed to prove?"

"Tell you tomorrow," Shearer answered. "Let's just say, something to think about."

"What was the matter with you, Jerri?" someone else asked.

Arnold got up and moved around from the bench seat by the wall, looking distinctly underwhelmed. "I'll wait to hear about it then," he said to Shearer. "Right now, I think I might go and check what they've got in the canteen. I haven't had anything since lunch. Want to come along?"

"Thanks, I ate earlier. It was meat loaf, chicken, or fried fish."

"Hey, can I come along?" Zoe asked Arnold. "I could use something too."

"Sure."

She got up to join him. "See you people later." They left.

Jerri stayed to help Shearer sort out the items according to the various games they had been borrowed from. Jeff began picking out the boxes and passing them over, while all around, the chatter picked up again as people returned to what they had been doing.

"No, the pyramids and cubes go with those," Shearer said, motioning with a hand.

"Oh, okay," Jerri acknowledged.

"Why did you just sit there?" Jeff asked her, puzzled. He shook his head at Shearer. "She didn't even try."

"I won't be forced into being stupid," Jerri said. Jeff seemed baffled and looked at Shearer again.

Shearer had never seen anyone respond that way before. He stared at her for several seconds, not quite sure what to make of it. She met his eye unwaveringly, a faint, impish smile on her face and an expression that seemed to say, *You know what I'm talking about. I don't have to spell it out.* "Most people don't see it," he said finally. "And the few who do usually get pressured into going along anyway."

"Just like life," she said.

"That's the whole point."

"And what makes it stupid. As I just said, I won't do it."

It was one of the rare occasions in life where Shearer felt he was communicating with someone, instead of returning expected litanies and leaving half of his person switched off. Jerri regarded him with a measured wariness, as if searching for clues that he was genuine; but the half-smile remained playing on her mouth. There was something precious and pleasingly intimate in the feeling that they were the only two in the room who understood the meaning of what had happened a few minutes ago. Jeff cemented it by doing a double take from one to the other. "Hey, is there something going on here that I'm not seeing? . . . Oh, okay, I get it."

Shearer was starting to find Jeff's eternal presence a little wearisome. At every turn it seemed that Jeff was there, like a shadow. He was personable enough in his way, but at times he could be inquisitive about Shearer's personal business to a degree that went beyond the familiarity of a new friendship. He wanted to know about

Shearer's background, his politics; the kind of work he did, who this person Wade was that he was going to join; did he know where Wade was on Cyrene? It wasn't as if Jeff had ever met Wade, even, or if Wade's work held any particular significance. But Jeff sometimes talked as if he were inquiring after a lost personal acquaintance.

Jerri seemed to sense it, and Shearer found that it didn't surprise him. "It's about time I went to check on Nim," she said. "Want to come and say hello?" Nim was short for Nimrod. Nim and Shearer knew each other by now, from the hotel in San Jose and a couple of times since the beginning of the voyage, when Jerri had brought him out for a walk around the decks. Shearer made a point of keeping a few of Nim's favorite treats in his pocket.

"Good idea," Shearer agreed. He finished putting the last of the games back together, and closed the box. Jerri was already on her feet, waiting. Jeff sent him a broad wink as they turned to go. Shearer was glad that Jerri didn't notice. Or if she did, she pretended not to.

The core section of the *Tacoma*'s generally circular form extended out to about a quarter of the radius and was divided into upper and lower parts. The upper part contained the command and control centers, and officer's quarters. The lower part was designated the E Section and formed an enclave reserved for a more exclusive set of passengers. The remainder, consisting of ordinary professionals, artisans, intended settlers, and military-security personnel, were housed in the midships decks between the core and the power, propulsion, and machinery compartments located around the periphery. Accommodation in E-Section was in the form of individual cabins fitted with full-size beds as opposed to bunks, bathrooms with whirlpool tubs, minibar, office-fitted desk, and an appropriate complement of comforts not found in the regular quarters. It contained its own dining room, pool, exercise center, and entertainment theater, and access from other parts of the ship was through security points that were manned at all times. The two worlds into which society back home had polarized were represented faithfully.

Within E Section, the rigid social hierarchy of Earth's wealth-based elite was reflected in the ordering of the accommodation levels from upper, near the ship's center line immediately below the command

and control decks, to lower, at the bottom of the core. The upper ones boasted progressively more square footage, richer decor, and bigger beds, turning into two-room suites at the top. The cabin assigned to Myles Callen was below those occupied by the independently rich and influential, CEOs, and company presidents, but above upper managers, senior government officials, and top professionals.

He sat in a bathrobe and slippers at the desk and electronic office unit fitted into one corner of the room, watching a transmission from Emner, the Director of the Terran base near the city of Revo, on Cyrene. It had come in some hours previously, in response to Callen's latest questions, sent earlier. Emner's words were as perplexing as ever, and the message not reassuring.

"You don't understand. I've tried to tell you people, but you still don't understand. Cyrene does things to your mind. The things you think are normal from living on Earth don't apply here. How can I explain it? . . ." Emner's hand flashed briefly as a blur in the foreground on the screen. He looked haggard beneath his head of straight, gray hair, as if he had been carrying a burden of worry for weeks. "It's as if you've lived your whole life in a fog, and emerged into daylight for the first time. You see things clearly that you never even knew existed before—yet they were there all along. You look back, and you can see the shapes of people still blundering around in the fog. But you can't communicate with them. There is no common language. They don't have the words."

Callen smacked the edge of the desk with his hand in frustration. He wanted to shout, *What things*? The messages always rambled round and around the point. They were never specific.

Emner leaned back. There was a distant, half-focused look about his eyes. Callen couldn't decide if it signified a fanatic losing touch with reality, or the effects of something local in the environment, as Krieg had said. Emner looked away for a moment, as if consulting something.

"Why do we stay?" That had been another of Callen's questions. If whatever the influence was had caused a majority from two missions to disappear from the base at Revo, what was different about Emner and the others who still remained? "To stop you and what you represent. This world has to be protected. You'll destroy it, just as you have begun the destruction of every other world you've touched. You can't see it and you don't understand, because you're still inside the fog. Maybe Cyrene will make you understand. But if not, somebody has to."

Callen paused the recording there, and sat frowning for several minutes. Then he got up and paced slowly over to the bar, where he poured a shot from the decanter of whiskey. He added one cube of ice from the dispenser, swirled it around with a stirrer while he stood thinking, then tasted it and moved back to the desk. "Cabin manager," he said aloud.

"Answering," a synthetic voice replied from the speakers.

"Connect me to Krieg, audio only."

Krieg came on the line ten seconds or so later.

"Can you get along here when you have a moment?" Callen said. "There could be a problem of running into some resistance at Cyrene. We might be talking about having to mount a forced takeover there, possibly armed. I'd like to hear your thoughts."

"I'm on my way," Krieg replied neutrally.

Callen cut off the screen. If he ended up effectively having to run the base, it would cut too much into the other duties that he was supposed to be taking care of. The other thing he should do, he reflected, would be to have a relief commander and staff sent out from Earth on a fast military clipper as quickly as could be organized. He would get a preliminary message off to Borland as soon as he had finished talking with Krieg.

"So how did you get out of Texas?" Jerri asked. "Wasn't there a lot of trouble around then, with everybody trying to get into Occidena because that was where the money and the military were, and the top-paying work?" She was sitting on a plastic-wrapped pack marked "Coveralls, Medium—Qty. 4," set atop a solvent cannister to make a seat in the storage bay on the lower deck of the Outer Ring, just inboard from the power and engines. Nim's box had been left open to the aisles between the stacks of crates and shelved bays lining the walls to let him move around. The crew joked that it made them feel the place was properly guarded. Nim lay gnawing at a bone between his paws that Shearer had acquired from one of the cooks.

"That's right, there was," Shearer agreed, ruffling Nim's ears.

"But with the new space industries mushrooming overnight, you just walked right in if you had the kind of talent they needed. Physics was high on the list. And I was lucky, too, in knowing someone who'd pointed me to the right names there."

"The professor who never showed up on the boat out of Tampa?"

"Uh-huh." Shearer nodded heavily.

Jerri produced a beef-flavored munchy and showed it to Nim. The dog watched her alertly, ears pricked. She flipped it with a thumb; Nim caught it and devoured it in a couple of gulps. "But you weren't with any of the space corporations there," she said. "You told us you work in this little lab at the back of Berkeley somewhere."

Shearer sighed. "I guess I'll never be a millionaire, will I? I don't know. . . . It just seems to me that there's more to life than buying and selling. Everything you do from one end of the week to the other shouldn't have to be justified by a profit-and-loss account." He cocked an inquiring eye at her. "So does that make me a hopelessly incorrect write-off? You know, all the dreaded words: noncompetitive; underachiever. . . ." He shook his head. "But no. From the little I've seen of you, I'd say it wouldn't matter."

Jerri was looking at him in an odd, thoughtful kind of way. He sensed a guard that she normally maintained being gradually relaxed. She was warming to him. It was an elating feeling. "You see, there's something about you that I like already," she said. "You watch people, and you see what they are. Ninety percent of the people in that class were too busy wanting everyone else to watch *them* all the time." Nim was making pointing motions toward her pocket with his snout. Jerri took out the other beef munchy that he'd known was in there and flipped it. "So what kind of work do you do at Berkeley that isn't going to make you millions? It has to be something interesting."

"An obscure part of quantum physics that has no redeeming social, commercial, ethical, or moral features whatsoever."

"I love it already."

"In fact, until recently it was dismissed as a mathematical fiction with no physical meaning. But there are waves that travel backward in time."

Jerri's brow narrowed. Clearly, she saw the implication at once. "You are serious?" she checked.

"Oh, yes. We think we might have confirmed them experimentally—it's right on the edge of being able to tell for sure. Although most of the others who've seen it don't buy it. They say it has to be a result of sloppy experimental design, wishful thinking, or something like that. A few have come out and said it's a deliberate fraud."

"But you think it's genuine."

"I did at one time. . . . Now I sometimes wonder."

"But it was a big thing with you."

"Oh yes."

"So why leave it?" Jerri asked.

"The guy that I worked with, who pioneered the whole thing, went to Cyrene withthe first mission. We kind of planned that I'd follow him out there."

"So is he doing the same kind of thing out at Cyrene?"

Shearer made a who-knows face. "I haven't heard a lot back from him lately. It's early days yet. I did arrange for some of the equipment that we used to be shipped."

"Why would he want to go there? Wouldn't work like that be easier to do back home?"

"Well, I guess making life easy isn't everything. . . . Evan's about as crazy over a lot of what goes on as I am." There had been some convoluted politics in the circumstances attending Wade's departure, which Shearer didn't go into because he didn't fully understand them himself. Jerri seemed to sense his reservation and didn't pursue the subject. She traced a circle in the air around Nim's nose with her hand, and grasped his jaw playfully when he opened his mouth trying to follow.

"Do you think those waves you mentioned could have something to do with the way animals sometimes know when things are going to happen?" she asked lightly. "You know the kind of thing: when their owner is on the way home, or someone's about to have an accident. I read that people who've done experiments say the only explanation that makes sense has to be something like that."

Shearer forced down an impulse to be skeptical but couldn't contain a smile. "Well, I think I'd like to know a lot more about the experiments before I could comment," he replied.

"Now who's being the stuffy one?" Jerri chided. Shearer got the feeling she had expected it. He hoped they weren't about to get into a debate over it. Repeatable experimental physics was one thing; this was something else. But Jerri carried on playing in silence for a while, making feints as if to take Nim's bone, while Nim parried to protect it. Then she said distantly, "Nim can pick up on things like that. I leave him with friends up at Pinecrest when I go on visits sometimes. They say he always knows when I'm coming back. . . . I don't mean turning in to the driveway, or a few hundred yards upwind along the road. I mean hours before—when I'm getting into the car, not even out of the airport." She looked up at him defiantly—whether challenging him to explain it or daring him to question it, he couldn't be sure. He grunted noncommittally. There probably wasn't a pet owner anywhere who hadn't been convinced of the same thing at some time, but this sounded like politics that Shearer felt it would be as wise to stay out of.

"How much do you know about Jeff?" Jerri asked curiously.

The question caught Shearer by surprise. "Jeff? . . . Well, about as much as anyone. Why?"

"There's something about him."

"What makes you say that?"

"Nim doesn't take to him. I don't know what it is. But something's not right. I've seen the signs before."

This time Shearer was unable to prevent a hint of irritation showing. Respecting the beliefs and feelings of others was one thing, but letting somebody's dog superstitions affect a personal friendship was too much. "Oh . . . I know he can be a bit inquisitive and crowd personal space a bit at times. But Jeff's okay. Anyway, I can handle it." Shearer heard a sharper edge to his voice than he had intended.

But again, Jerri seemed to have expected it and showed no offense. Instead, she turned Nim's head from side to side, and then let go of his jaw and gripped his paw as he raised it. "Are you being silly, Nim?" she asked. "Is it just because Jeff doesn't bring you treats the way Marc does? Or is there something else you're trying to tell us? We'll just have to wait and see, won't we?"

CHAPTER TEN

At breakfast the next morning, Shearer found himself sharing a table in the cafeteria across from Arnold and Karen, with Roy and one of the cronies who had latched onto him farther along, and another couple at far the end. Since Arnold and Karen were into a conversation that sounded private, and Roy was giving forth on the importance of "winning" while he demolished an immense plate of food, Shearer turned his attention to browsing the schedule for the day ahead while he ate. Roy's attitude toward him lately tended to vary between cool and hostile. Roy had never figured out the rationale behind the nuts game, and when somebody explained it, he apparently concluded that Shearer's aim had been expressly to make him look foolish. Jerri's private comment had been that Roy was capable of managing that well enough on his own without need of any help.

The morning session would be about Cyrenean social divisions and languages. After lunch they would be introduced to "sambots" and see some demonstrations. The term derived from Self-Assembling Modular Robot. They were used widely in planetary environments that didn't possess the familiar Terran infrastructure, and since people in most ordinary walks of life were unlikely to have come across them, some familiarization was being provided in advance. It sounded interesting, and Shearer turned to the notes accompanying the schedule.

Early realizations of robots, such as in automated manufacturing plants or space construction and underwater applications, had taken the form of various weird and elaborate contraptions, each specialized for its particular task. A more recent approach that had superseded specialized machines in many areas used the principle of "modular robots." The idea was to create specialized functions on demand from simpler modules. A basic modular unit on its own could accomplish very little; but a sufficient number of them—which could be quite large—when combined together in the right manner, formed a system able to carry out a complex task. By rearranging themselves the same modules could assume other configurations suitable for performing other tasks. In a way, the concept mimicked biology, in which variants of the same basic cellular theme grouped together in different ways to form all the tissues, organs, and organisms making up the living world.

Modules were generally based on some simple geometric form such as a cube, tetrahedron, triangle, hexagon, or some other fractal that preserved its characteristic shape at increasing scales of magnitude. With enough microelectronic intelligence built in, they could be self-assembling according to the needs of a situation and a set of blueprint programs carried internally. Illustrations contained in the notes showed a formation of peculiar stick-and-ball-like modules attached together to form a moving lattice with spiderlike legs crossing a precipitous terrain of rocks and craters, and then reconfigured into a communications antenna after reaching its destination. Sambot work crews were usually landed by the initial survey probes to prepare bases for habitation at newly discovered worlds where manned follow-ups were decided on. Besides preparing the way and making life more comfortable, they proved highly effective, also, at instilling an appropriate level of awe and wonder among native inhabitants before the humans showed up.

"Anyone sitting here?" Greg appeared, bearing a tray, and indicated the empty chair next to Shearer.

"Go ahead."

Greg was a land and civil engineering surveyor, bound for Cyrene to help assess some construction projects that were being contemplated. With a shaggy head of black hair starting to show gray, short, matching beard, horn-rimmed spectacles magnifying naturally intense eyes, and a strong set of teeth that bared ferally when he smiled, he looked more the stereotypical leftist ideologue and anarchist than Shearer, whom Roy had accused of such. He had a robust, forthright manner that he managed to keep congenial, and Shearer rated him among his preferred company.

"No Jerri?" Greg inquired as he set down his tray.

"It's dog-walking time," Shearer said.

"I thought Zoe had taken that over."

"They split it. It's Jerri's turn." Zoe and Nim had taken to each other. A couple of times a day, either she or Jerri, or sometimes both of them, took Nim to the "long gallery," a general utility communications thoroughfare that ran all the way around the ship at the Outer Ring.

Greg pulled out the chair and sat down. "These eggs look great. How are yours?"

"Good."

"That's one thing about spaceships. You get to eat real food." Greg began arranging his cutlery and dishes. "You know, I never really understood what all the fuss was about them. Why couldn't they just post whatever the information was and let people choose for themselves what they want to do?"

Shearer shrugged. "'Choose' isn't a word that's in the bureaucrat vocabulary."

"Did you check the news on the beam before you came down?" Greg asked as he settled down to eating. He meant the Heim-wave link from Earth.

"I don't bother with it much, to be honest," Shearer said. "I agree with Mark Twain. The only thing you can believe in it is the advertising."

"Who's Mark Twain?"

"Oh, a writer from way back. Why? What's happened?"

"That OBP that's been up for a while now." Greg shifted his eyes sideways. Shearer looked uncertain. "Orbital Bombardment Platform," Greg supplied. "It's run by Milicorp."

"Oh, okay."

"It's seen action. That place where the trouble's been out across the Pacific somewhere. What's it called? . . ."

"Tiwa Jaku," Roy said from the far end.

"Yeah, that's it. The whole terrorist stronghold got taken out from orbit—one pass with a saturated e-beam. Apparently it's all over there. Pretty neat stuff, huh?" He seemed excited.

"Haven't there been protests too?" Karen said. "Something about all the prisoners and families being shot?"

"Supposedly," Arnold put in.

"That's a load of bullshit!" Roy fumed. "Some people will believe anything if it runs us down." He motioned with his knife. "And even if it was true, it's the only way to deal with terrorists. Once you've got 'em, the worst thing you can do is leave 'em in one piece and with a grudge to come back at you. See, giving people like that breaks doesn't work. They'll just see it as a sign of weakness." The others exchanged ominous glances. Roy's tone was at its most belligerent, and no one, it seemed, wanted to start their day by getting into this.

"Well, at least they don't have an OBP up over Cyrene," Greg said to change the subject.

"Yet," Arnold commented.

"You're cheerful today," Shearer told him.

"It's the way things happen. You can't change it."

"Although, I did hear a rumor . . ." Karen looked around. "Did anyone else hear it? About some kind of trouble on Cyrene." Everyone stopped eating and waited. The couple at the end turned their heads.

"What kind of trouble?" Shearer asked.

"They've lost a lot of people from the base there. That's why this mission was rushed together. There's a group aboard that's being sent there to find out what's going on. They've got their own military team and everything."

The others looked at each other. Clearly this was news to all of them.

"Who told you this?" Arnold asked her.

"I talked to a Milicorp officer in the gym yesterday. His name's Earl. He was trying to impress me." She smiled, evidently enjoying the attention she was getting. "I think I was getting hit on."

"What do you mean, they've lost a lot of people?" Greg asked in an alarmed voice. "Killed? There's fighting going on there?"

"That doesn't sound like the Cyrene I've been reading about," Shearer said.

Karen shook her head hastily. "No, no. What I meant was, they're disappearing—taking off. Nobody seems to know why. Know what else he said? He said that when we get to Cyrene, he'd be able to get me a place on one of the recon flights out over the planet. Wouldn't that be great?"

Shearer looked quizzically at Greg. He wasn't interested in the last part, but people disappearing at a sufficient rate for another mission to be hastily organized was surely something pretty serious. Why hadn't they been told? The same question was written across Greg's face too.

After breakfast, Shearer left the others talking among themselves and made his way through the various compartments and corridors to the long gallery. A number of strollers and joggers were out, but he didn't see any sign of Jerri, which was as well because he wanted time to be alone and think. He would catch up with her later.

The question troubling him wasn't so much that of why a mission of the kind the *Tacoma* was carrying—a typical complement of professionals, artisans, administrators, even a number of prospective settlers—would be sent in such circumstances. Organizing an interstellar voyage was a complex and expensive undertaking, and from what Karen had said there didn't seem to be any physical threat. If a ship was going to Cyrene, the opportunity would be exploited to serve as wide a spectrum of needs as possible. Nor was he particularly surprised or indignant that they hadn't been told. As with just about everything that went on in the world, profitability would be the first priority, which meant that anything likely to cause alarm and interrupt the flow of funds from investors would be played down until the last moment.

What he had to ask himself was if Wade could be among those who had vanished, which would explain why Shearer hadn't heard from him for a while. He wasn't especially concerned about finding Wade when he got there himself. Wade would be aware of his predicament, and Shearer was confident that he would be contacted in due course somehow. More to the point, the powers that be would obviously know about Wade's disappearance too—hence, no doubt, the evasiveness that Shearer had encountered back in Redwood City when he tried to get information. And that led to the question, Why had they not only accepted Shearer's application to go out and join Wade, but apparently pulled out all the stops to rush it through before the *Tacoma*'s departure?

After considering all the angles that he could think of, Shearer was left with only one answer that made any sense: because they wanted to find Wade too, and they thought Shearer would lead them to him. And that, perhaps, accounted for the undue interest that Callen from Milicorp had shown in Wade when he interviewed Shearer as part of the screening process. It implied that there had been more to the circumstances of Wade's departure than he had talked about. Just when Shearer had thought he was about to begin a new life light-years away from Earth and finally be free from the world of predatory greed and militarized corporate politics that he abhorred, it seemed as if he was about to be engulfed by it again, from the moment they arrived.

He was still preoccupied a half hour later, when he reappeared back in the midships section and headed for the Study Center, which extended through parts of C and D Decks. Course schedules had been provided by the Interworld mission planners as a way of putting the time of the voyage to good use. That morning had Shearer listed for Yocalan Language Basics—the tongue spoken in the region where the Terran base on Cyrene was situated. Jerri would be in the class too. On his way to the classrooms, he spotted Jeff in one of the study cubicles, pondering among screens and papers, and veered across to say hi.

"Some rudiments of Cyrenean history," Jeff said, sitting back in the chair and gesturing. He seemed to welcome the excuse to take a break. Luckily, the Cyreneans seem to be helpfully inclined by nature and pretty free with whatever information anyone asks for. They're a few centuries behind where we are—just about breaking into steam. But they got there faster. The guy who wrote this estimates that from about where the Greeks were in the equivalent of something like two hundred years. And yet the squabbles that they've had from time to time never seem to have gotten out of hand and turned into all-out wars. So pressure to advance military technology doesn't seem to have played much of a part. Interesting, eh?"

Shearer ran his eye absently over the assortment of maps and charts. "Maybe the climatic extremes had something to do with it," he offered.

"Yes, that's been suggested already. Some people even think the two could be connected—that there might be more incentive for working together and burying differences, instead of for greater competition the way you'd think." Jeff shrugged. "Anything's possible, I guess."

In fact, Shearer didn't think that greater competition was the inevitable result of every stress. The received wisdom of the times simply assumed it. But he didn't say anything.

Jeff touched a key to save the notes he had been making. "So what's new with you, Marc?"

"Out of curiosity, have you heard anything about there being some kind of trouble at Revo?" Shearer asked.

The grin that had started to form on Jeff's faced changed abruptly. "What kind of trouble?"

"People disappearing from the base. Our people."

"Where did you hear that?"

"Just some talking around the table at breakfast this morning."

"Who was it that said it?"

"Karen got it from one of the Milicorp people in the gym."

"Do you know his name?" Jeff was always poking for more detail, even when it seemed unimportant. But Shearer was used to it by now. He shook his head.

"She didn't say."

Jeff thought for a few seconds. "Do you figure this scientist that you're supposed to be meeting up with out there . . . what was his name? Wade?"

"Right. Evan Wade."

"Do you figure he might have gone missing too? If it turns out he has, how are you gonna find him?"

"Oh, I guess he'd still be around the base somewhere. In any case, it's no big deal. I'm sure I'd hear from him somehow."

Jeff watched Shearer's face for a moment longer, then dismissed the matter with a shrug. "Well, I'll be talking to some of the admin people this afternoon," he said. "I'll ask around. If anything comes up I'll let you know."

"Thanks. I'd appreciate it," Shearer said.

CHAPTER ELEVEN

Around about 1960, dazzled by the ease with which the new computers were able to convert between the artificial, precisely structured programming languages devised specifically to communicate with them, experts had predicted that fluent automatic translation of natural languages—the messy, ambiguity-ridden stews of metaphors, homophones, homonyms, double meanings, irregularities, and exceptions in which humans speak—would become a reality within five years.

But formal artificial languages and natural human languages work in totally opposite ways. In formal languages, nothing is assumed. Everything that is to be conveyed has to be stated explicitly. The meaning is carried fully in the message. Humans, on the other hand, tend to communicate only that which they consider it likely the listener does not already know. They assume a huge amount of pre-existing world-knowledge in order to be understood. The message constitutes merely an agreed convention of codes for triggering concepts that life, experience, and learning have already created in the head of the listener.

The result was that after many fruitless years and much costly effort expended on ever more elaborate attempts to extract meaning from where it didn't exist, the general agreement had emerged that a different approach was called for.

A possible solution that had been receiving a lot of attention was known as neural cognitive and associative access. The idea behind it was that, irrespective of the particular streams of syllables that different speakers might employ as an intermediary, the meanings they were trying to communicate all started out as—and would hopefully end up as—the same kind of concept existing some-where inside the same kind of mind. The last half-century had seen major advances in various brain imaging techniques, along with sophisticated methods of recovering coherent patterns of meaning from scattered data in particle physics and other fields. So instead of grappling with all the capricious usages, figures of speech, colloquial shorthand, and other devices that plagued every language, seemingly contrived specifically to facilitate literal constructions expressing anything other than what was actually meant, would it be possible to get at the underlying concepts directly?

Early attempts had sought to use the outputs from such a process to drive discrete language synthesizers that would create a rendition in French, Spanish, German, or whatever, depending on the synthesizer selected. But the complexities involved in composing a construction that accurately captured the original turned out to be as irreducible to formal code as deciphering it in the first place, and the results obtained were indifferent at best. Ironically, the best performances were achieved with experiments at translating into Chinese and other Asian languages, where the phonetics were based on symbols more directly related to the concepts involved rather than alphabetical syllabic constructions, and thus eliminated a whole level of abstraction.

The next step, then, was to ask, Why bother going from neural concept to impossible human lingual mishmash, and then back again, at all? If the aim at the end of it all was to recreate a similar—ideally identical—pattern of neural stimulations in the brain of the recipient, mightn't it be simpler to go directly from one to the other?

One implementation of this principle was the Neural Imaging Decoder and Activator, or NIDA, known otherwise as the Babel Box. A still largely unknown factor was how applicable the decoding pro-cedures worked out on Earth would be to interpreting the neural activity of aliens. That was a question that some of the linguists and cryptanalysts aboard the *Tacoma* hoped to be shedding a little more light on. But if it could be made to work, it promised the tremendous benefit of not having to understand and encode all the intricacies for every one of what was already a bewilderingly high number of some-times very strange, alien languages.

Earlier versions of NIDA had required a bulky headpiece with an elaborate array of sensors and a rear neck surround like an ancient Roman helmet, which was fine for experimental purposes but didn't permit the mobility necessary for practical use. The newer pickup was in the form of an elastic mesh cap that was pulled over the head, with lobes projecting downward in front of the ears. It was light enough to carry comfortably, and its settings could be adjusted via a regular phone or from the general-purpose compad that most people carried, often as a wrist unit.

The system had not been used on Cyrene before. It was being taken there as part of a wider program of field trials to gather alien experience and performance data. Those who had decided to study Cyrenean languages seriously still had to work at it the old-fashioned way, using what information the earlier missions had been able to send back on the subject. Fortunately, Cyreneans were naturally curious and valued learning highly. Mastering Terran was already a challenge being taken up by many, and a source of social approval among them.

Jerri sat at one of the tables in the classroom, each seating four people, tapping the studs on her phone intermittently while she concentrated on the "echo" voice that she was hearing in her head. She was trying to adjust her NIDA unit to see if she could lose some-thing of the macho-belligerent quality of the original, which she found overpowering. The original was the voice of Don Olsen, the class instructor, who was wearing a similar device. He was large and burly, with a tanned balding head and a booming voice that years of former military background had left in permanent command mode.

"The mark saw that the boot was on the other foot," Olsen recited slowly and deliberately.

Jerri heard him, but in a subdued kind of way as if in the back-ground. What seemed to be a stronger voice said with a delay short enough to be imperceptible, *The victim realized he now had the advantage.* It was like being at one of those conferences with people from many countries in the audience, where multichannel head-phones were issued carrying a selection of live translators.

The NIDA was picking up the patterns of neural activity that occurred in certain parts of Olsen's brain as he spoke, and trying to induce the same patterns in the brains of the students. The neat thing about the way it worked was that the concepts evoked in response were coupled to the speech and auditory centers, producing the effect of a ghost voice that used the listener's own vocabulary and preferred terms and phrases. So the system would convert somebody else's style of English into one's own English.

Olsen turned off his unit and waited until they had all done the same and written their versions down. "Okay, let's see what we got." He stabbed a finger to single out someone at the back. "West." That was Zoe, the logistics administrator. Olsen never used first names.

"The dupe thought he could turn the tables," she read from her pad.

"Simmons."

"Er . . . There was a way the victim could get his own back."

"Demaro."

"The one who was calling the shots now was the intended target."

Olsen looked around. "That's good. We're getting those settings to converge. What we've been doing is a useful preliminary step before trying it between different languages. When you hear the original in a form you can understand, it provides a lot of clues that help the decoding routines. Now before we break, I'm going to hit you with something else. Ready again. . . ." He turned his NIDA back on and waited while the class followed. "Die Kinder sind in der Schule." The ghost in Jerri's head echoed, with markedly less parade-ground volume, *The children are in school*. She smiled to herself and wrote it down. After a short pause there followed, "Könnten Sie es mir aufschreiben?" accompanied by *Write it down*. And finally, "Wie war das noch 'mal, bitte?" with *Repeat please*. Olsen disconnected again. "Okay, I'll leave those for you to compare among yourselves. We'll get into it more when we pick up again. Fifteen minutes." He peeled off his NIDA cap and set it down, then headed for the door. A couple of people got up and pursued him into the corridor, evidently with questions.

Jerri leaned across to see what Marc, who was sitting next to her, had written. His first sentence was the same as hers. For the second he had *Can you write it down for me?* and for the third, *Can you say that again, please?*

"The second two were questions," he said, inspecting her pad in turn. He turned his head to Al Forrest, who was sitting on the other side of him. "Did two and three come out as questions for you?"

"Yes, right. They did."

Marc looked back at Jerri. "You've made them orders."

"Maybe his manner affects me more and overrode that part," she said.

"You think it could work that way? . . . I guess it might. That's interesting. But you did put 'please' on the last one."

"Yes, well, everyone knows that bitte means please."

"Hey, that's cheating," Marc accused. "You're not supposed to use things like that. You won't be able to when it comes to Cyrenean." He sat back, took off the NIDA headpiece, and looked around the room as he picked up his water glass.

Jerri watched his face, with its clear, olive skin, tanned permanently by a Florida upbringing, lean-lined, vaguely Gallic profile, dark, curly hair, and brown, intensely deep eyes. It was the eyes that had first led her to the person who dwelt inside. By now, she had let down the guard that she had long learned wise to maintain against newcomers into her life. She felt comfortable with Marc because in the ways that mattered most to her she found that both of them felt alike. He enabled her to be herself. And in a world where she had grown accustomed to being an exception who was looked upon by most that she met as eccentric at best, that was no small consideration.

The issue that set her apart the most radically was her attitude toward a social order whose only measure of human worth was wealth and possessions, and the disdain she felt for the kind of behavior that it fostered. As an anthropologist, she found preoccupation with absurdly expensive cars, trendy homes, "in" designer lines, and other such symbols of rank to be indicative not of superior genes but of extended juvenileness. Not that there was anything wrong with making life comfortable; but when taking it to such extremes to assert an imagined superiority became life's single purpose, she began to suspect that it might have more to do with compensating for underlying feelings of inadequacy at not having anything of real worth to offer.

Oh, true, Conrad Metterlin, for example, had played a significant role in founding and building a corporate empire that had swept to success on the wave of the new technologies. But the rest of the clan that she had watched at Sunnyvale, reveling in their newfound celebrity, had been there solely by virtue of their fortuitous circumstances. And even with Metterlin himself, Interworld represented merely a means that his particular background had equipped him to employ toward the desired end, not an end in itself as might constitute a lifetime's vision. If it hadn't been interstellar development, it could equally well have been commodity banking, real estate speculation, minerals exploitation, or ocean mining. The point was that the object of the exercise was foremost a ticket into the club; precisely what one did to get there was secondary.

With Marc, it was the other way around. Like Jerri, he wasn't impressed by the trappings of exclusivity and didn't respond with the reverence and envy that were customary. He knew himself and was content to be who and what he was. He lived for what he might achieve and to one day give to the world, not to take from it. His fascination for the strange branch of physics that he had described, and the passion to learn more—even if it entailed moving to another star system if that was the most promising opportunity that presented itself—were driven by the innate sense of curiosity and wonder that Jerri thought came naturally to any human being who hadn't been blinded by artificial distractions. She was glad to have found a kindred soul as companion on her journey into such a vast unknown. As to her own motive for leaving? . . . Regardless of the things she had told Ivor, she realized that she wasn't sure. Maybe at the bottom of it there lay nothing more than the simple reasoning that if things at home couldn't get worse, then elsewhere they had at least an even chance of being better.

"So what's your take on the NIDA so far?" Marc asked, looking back at her.

"Impressed," she replied. "What else can anyone say? I'm curious to see how it copes with minds that are totally alien."

"Have you tried playing with the tuning yet? I've got mine to sound Southern." The auditory effect could be tweaked to alter the tone and quality of the voice translation that was experienced.

"I was more interested in trying to get Olsen out if it," Jerri said. "He makes me feel as if I'm at Boot Camp somewhere. . . . I guess I'm not exactly the biggest fan of the military mystique. They were supposed to defend people. But it all got subverted, like everything else. Now they're the instrument for keeping people in line. We're brainwashed about terrorists, but the only terrorists I'm scared of are the ones I have to pay for. It's insane." Marc looked at her questioningly but said nothing, as if he knew there was more to it. Jerri realized she had touched on this before. She sighed. "Oh, there was a guy once that I was pretty close to—in Sacramento, after I moved south from Oregon." She was originally from a small mountain community not far from Cave Junction. "He was a media and web commentator with not-exactly-approved views, and pretty outspoken about them. Well, he said some wrong things about some wrong people, had a three A.M. house call and got sent to a camp. He was never the same after they let him out. They messed his head up inside—with drugs or something. . . ." She shook her head, deciding that she didn't want to talk any more about it.

Marc gave it a few seconds and read her correctly, as he always did. "Was that when you moved up out of the Valley to the foothills?"

She nodded. "It was an illusion of getting away, anyhow. And by that time I was traveling a lot. . . . That was when I discovered the stars, too. In the Sierra. I suppose they must have been there in Oregon too, but I'd never noticed. Not to the same degree, anyway. There were suddenly so many, and so bright. . . ." The stars they would see from Cyrene when they emerged out of H-space would be different. She wondered how long it would be before she'd see the familiar constellations of Earth again. "They weren't always the same, you know," she said distantly.

"What? The stars?" Marc looked puzzled.

"The entire skies. Don't believe what the textbooks tell you."

"Seriously?" Marc was looking surprised but intrigued. It was so refreshing to talk to someone who didn't start spouting objections reflexively. "How long ago are we talking about?"

"Within human history. It all changed several times."

"What makes you think that?"

"They left records of what they saw. It's written into their religions and arts and legends from all over the world. That's how I got interested in mythology."

"Give me an example," Marc invited.

Jerri thought for a moment. "You know how to find the pole star, right?"

"Follow the two pointers from the Big Dipper."

"Right. Otherwise known as Ursa Major, the Big Bear. Or you can point from the handle of the Little Dipper, Ursa Minor, which is close to the pole. That's what's called the celestial pole—the point the sky seems to revolve around, that the Earth's axis would extend to."

"Okay."

Jerri loosened her NIDA cap to let more air through her hair. "Well, you can find what are called 'Bear's Son' stories from every culture, that talk about an offspring of parents representing Earth and Sky, who displaces the father—which meant taking over his position at the center. The European *Beowulf* saga is one of them. The *Odyssey* is another. What they were trying to record is that the Big Dipper used to be at the pole."

"So when would this have been?" Marc asked.

"What Hesiod called the Age of Heroes—around seven hundred B.C."

"Then the axis must have tilted."

"Exactly."

"What would have caused that?"

"Good question. People who have looked into it come up with different theories. But the point is, the solar system wasn't always as stable as it's been for the last few centuries. But orthodox astronomy isn't going to come up with any answers if it won't even consider the possibility."

Marc still seemed wary, but genuinely curious. "So what about before then?" he asked. "Are there other stories that talk about something else before the Big Bear?"

Jerri nodded. "Yes. Hercules was there for a short time as a result of an axis shift that's represented by the death of his grandfather, Perseus, who was there before he was. The Hercules myth says that he briefly took over the job supporting the sky from Atlas and moved it. Hence the notion of superhuman strength. The labor of obtaining the golden girdle of the Amazon queen, Hippolyte, refers to the new celestial equator that the shift resulted in. It's been thought for a long time that the Labors of Hercules represent a journey around the heavens, but nobody has ever really been able to make them agree with the zodiac that exists today. But if you plot the equator as it would have been with Hercules at the pole, suddenly it all fits."

Jerri would have left it there, feeling she had said enough, but Marc waved a hand for her to carry on. "Fits, how?" he asked.

"The labors in the story don't seem to relate to any of the constellations that lie on the celestial equator today, but they do fit ones that would have then," she replied. "For instance there's Corvus, the crow, which could have been the Stymphalian birds that Hercules had to drive out of the marsh. Then there's Hydra, the snake, which could have been the Lernean Hydra. Another would be Crater, the cup—the golden goblet shaped like a water lily that Helius lent him to sail to Eritheia in. . . . And the dog, Canis Minor. That would be Cerberus, the Hound of Hell, that Hercules had to bring back from the underworld. You see—an equator that contains those signs matches the story. The one that exists now doesn't."

"And you're saying you find the same thing all over the world?"

"Well, of course the forms of the myths aren't identical. But they can all be interpreted similarly: Middle Eastern, early American, European, east Asian. . . ."

Marc stared at her for several seconds. "Interesting," he pronounced finally.

"I think so," Jerri agreed. "Better than having to keep up with whoever the latest art fad is that you've got to have on your walls." Ivor had told her that an Austrian painter who had recently made it to the rariefied heights produced plain canvases of a single color applied with a roller, and got two thousand dollars apiece for them.

"Can you point me to more stuff I can read up on?" Marc asked.

"Sure. How long have you got?"

"You know, every time I listen to you, you get more intriguing," he said. "How come you managed to hide yourself so well all these years?"

He was telling her something very personal. It produced a warm, gratifying feeling. "I guess you were just looking in the wrong places," she answered. Amid the babbling that was going on around, their eyes met in a way that was just for the two of them.

Olsen's voice boomed from the back of the room suddenly as he appeared in the doorway and strode toward the front. "Okay, people, time out. Everybody straighten up. Let's see how we did. . . ."

CHAPTER TWELVE

Conrad Metterlin's spectacular ascent from onetime pilot to multi-billionaire was a result of two principal factors. One was certainly his own astuteness in recognizing the potential of the new technologies, and his good judgment in backing celestial colonization as one of the major spinoffs. The other was adequate bankrolling at the right time, which he had obtained from the Corbel family, noted for their size-able estates in Delaware and Maryland. Whereas the Metterlin clan were going through the exuberant phase of celebrating and display-ing their newfound wealth, the Corbels had accommodated to the poise and self-assurance of fourth-generation rich, after rising on the tide of energy market manipulations that went back to the mid-twentieth century. When shifting global politics and abatement of nuclear phobia brought an end to American dominance of the scene, it was time to relocate to sunnier climes both figuratively and literally. The Corbels liquidated their Eastern holdings just in time to avoid the crash that came with downsizing to the Federated American States, and moved the operation to where new horizons were opening up, and in which they already had a significant stake.

Acquiring the state college at Bellingham and turning it into Corbel University had been one of the first moves in establishing visibility and status. But the competition to achieve eminence among the new rising social class was fierce, and the present paterfamilias, Joseph Corbel, decided that something more original and attention-getting was called for. The obvious person to entrust with such a charge was his favorite niece, Gloria, who had already earned herself a reputation as a tearaway romantic among the ranks of the staid and stately by whitewater rafting in the rapids of Paraguay, running the Cresta, and being heli-lifted to join a trans-Antarctic survey expedition for two weeks, in the course of which she learned to handle a dog team. And Gloria, after verifying that whatever was going on there didn't involve any physical violence, persuaded Joseph that the ideal way to promote the family name and recast it in an image commensurate with the new, exciting things out in space that they were, after all, helping to make a reality, would be for one of its members to go with the third mission departing for Cyrene—by which she meant herself, of course. Although she hesitated to admit it, she did *so* need a break away from Henry, her marriage to whom had been arranged primarily to broaden the family's economic base into communications electronics, but who really did get so *terribly* dull when endured for too long at a stretch. Whereas she, on the other hand, while mindful of her duty toward the family and its interests, was so young and untamed, capricious and wild . . .

. . . and spoiled, avaricious, brattish, and vain, Myles Callen thought to himself as he finished shaving in the upper E Deck suite's pseudo-baroque bathroom, with its gilded fittings and ornate arches over the whirlpool tub and shower, and rinsed off his face. Her voice came through the open doorway from the bedroom while he inspected himself in the mirror.

"You can't imagine how boring. . . . I mean, he talks to me about profit-and-loss statements, for chrissakes! I'm sure he thinks it makes him seem predatory and exciting. Can you believe that, Myles? The guy who parks my car is more exciting."

His tan was still good, and he had kept his muscle tone solid and firm—a habit acquired from his more active field days. There were bite marks on his chest but no blemishes that would show. His need to dominate asserted itself through rough play during sex, which evidently excited and stimulated a reciprocal side of Gloria. He smoothed on some lotion and picked up a brush to take care of his hair.

"But you're more . . . There's kind of a meanness there, even ruthlessness. I don't care what people say, women are wired to respond to that. It's all about protection, survival, know what I mean? Genetic. So kids will make it okay, and they'll be survivors too—which is how lines get to last. But with a guy like Henry, sometimes I really find myself wondering. . . ."

Callen slipped on the robe provided as part of the cabin service, knotted the belt, and came out from the bathroom. Gloria was lying propped against the pillows in a silk bed jacket, nursing the empty glass from the bourbon that he had poured her before going into shower. The screen facing the bed was showing a recorded news documentary from Earth with the sound turned down. Mush music at subdued volume was playing from speakers somewhere.

"Darwin before breakfast?" he grunted. Gloria held out her glass. He took it and crossed over to the cocktail cabinet and bar. There was still ice in the bucket. He refilled Gloria's glass and mixed a Manhattan for himself.

"There was a thing on a few minutes ago about some kind of epidemic or something breaking out at another colony world, Amanthea? . . . Amanth? . . ."

"Amaranth?" Callen brought her glass over, then moved to stand staring at the vista of jungle waterfall and mountains in the simview window while he tasted his own.

"That's it. The river's turned red, and it's wiping out a whole area. There were pictures of aliens falling down in the streets and stacks of bodies, all blotchy and bloated. There won't be any chance of something like that happening at Cyrene, will there?"

"No one can ever rule out anything a hundred percent," Callen said. "But you don't have to worry. The medical scans and profiles for Cyrene are pretty complete. You'll be properly protected."

"No, I know *we* wouldn't catch it. But who'd want to walk around with that kind of thing all around? And the smell would be *ghastly*."

"Cyrene seems to have a healthier climate than Amaranth allround," Callen said. "Some of the biologists think it has something to do with the cycling between extremes. But they haven't figured out quite how yet."

"Oh, Myles, you're not going to start getting technical on me, are you? I don't have a head for it. That's the kind of thing you hire people to know."

And they hired people like him to protect them, Callen thought to himself. And without people like him, what would their importance and influence be? Nothing. Without guns and people with the mettle to use them, they wouldn't hang on to their wealth and their properties for a week. The utter dependency behind their arrogance and airs of superiority made him contemptuous. And that made screwing their wives and roughing them around all the more gratifying. Just how easy it could be never ceased to amaze him. Spoiled children looking for entertainment. He sensed that she was watching him.

"What are you standing there, looking so serious about?" her voice asked. He turned from the simview and looked at her. She shook her head, causing long blond tresses to fall loose over the orange silk, and stared at him pointedly over her glass as she drank.

"Just things I have to do today," he said.

"Why now? There's still weeks before we get to Cyrene."

Callen moved back to stand beside the bed and looked down at her. His eyes were mocking. "So show me what you do have a head for," he said.

Her mouth pouted, then curled into a wicked smile. "You really can be a bastard." She drained her glass and set it down, then reached for the belt of his robe. "But I like bastards."

CHAPTER THIRTEEN

The *Tacoma* transferred back into normal space inside the planetary system of Ra Alpha a little under two million miles from the point computed by dead reckoning, which was considered not bad by the standards currently being attained. The remainder of voyage to Cyrene, under conventional nuclear propulsion, took two days.

During that time, the occupants who had crossed interstellar space for the first time gradually became accustomed to the wonder of viewing a sky unlike any that had ever been seen from Earth, and watched with fascination and a steadily increasing restless anticipation as Cyrene grew larger and resolved more unfolding detail on the ship's screens. The images themselves were not unfamiliar, of course, having been reproduced in countless shots sent back from the original probes and the two manned missions that had followed since. But this time the images were not retrievals from an archive of data sent back from afar. They were live, of a world that was really out there beyond the walls of the ship. For many of those aboard, it brought home for the first time the immensity of the distance that now separated them from Earth.

Interstellar mission ships like the *Tacoma* were expensive and in high demand, with highly specialized crews, so the previous two had long since departed. The only evidence of Terran presence above the surface were a robot freighter that had arrived a couple of weeks earlier to deliver supplies, currently being loaded with marketable cargo for Earth and biological, botanical, mineral, and other samples of scientific interest, and a network of satellites put up for communications and surface navigation. Under normal circumstances, bases and settlements on newly discovered worlds were left to their own devices between ship calls, maintaining contact with Earth via H-links. But no time had been announced for the length of the *Tacoma*'s intended stay at Cyrene, which fitted with the notion of the rumor that Karen had started, of disappearances among the earlier arrivals. Not that Shearer and his companions saw the situation as necessarily something to be apprehensive about. After all, they reasoned, if something was attracting previous arrivals away, it couldn't be all that bad. The question that concerned him more was what those in command of the Terran presence on Cyrene proposed doing about it.

The planet itself was larger than Earth but with a lower core density, resulting in a surface gravity that was marginally less than Earth's—one of the Terrans there described it in a report that Shearer had watched as "invigorating." On average, about two-thirds of the surface was ocean, but since both polar regions contained large areas of seas that were relatively shallow, the amount of open water varied widely with Cyrene's position along its peculiar orbit. At lower latitudes the oceans were smaller with landmasses more evenly distributed than on Earth, between eight and a dozen of them sprawled over the surface amid variously shaped bodies of water to a sufficient extent to earn a classification of "continent" from one or another of the geographical authorities that had pondered the subject, but as yet no official pronouncement had been agreed. The candidate continents, and the assortments of lesser mainlands, islands, and archipelagos clustered around and scattered between them, extended through regions of jungle, desert, mountain, forest, and plain, each experiencing greater extremes of conditions than any of their counterpart zones on Earth. In fact, the nature of many of these regions was not fixed, but transformed from one kind into another as the climate progressed through its complex cycle. Comments had come back consistently from the few areas so far explored in any detail on the richness and diversity of every form of life.

The city of Revo occupied a neck of land connecting two parts of the deeply indented western coastline of one of the larger landmasses in the mid-northern latitudes, with a long lake extending away into forested mountain country on its inland side, and an arm of sea widening to open ocean on the other. The Terran base was situated ten miles east of the city on a line of low hills sloping down to the south shore of the lake. A stretch of river spanned by several bridges connected the lake to the sea, its mouth forming a harbor always filled with vessels sporting riots of colorful sails and looking almost like bird plumage. The buildings of the town were mostly of red, brown, orange, and gray brick and stone, solid and tall, with accentuated perpendicularity and steep roofs, packed densely along narrow streets and alleyways in the center and by the water-front, but giving way to more open layouts with courtyards and gardens farther out. Domes and towers were evidently popular, gracing the skyline in all shapes and sizes.

The main means of land transport was by animal power. One of the principal types employed—in that area of the planet, anyway—took the form of a four-legged creature used both for riding and drawing in the manner of a horse, which did bear a strong resemblance to a horse, and which earlier Terran arrivals had christened, not too surprisingly, a "horse." There were also a variety of sturdier, more bovine-like and other ungulate-like types, more suited to slower, heavier work, and some without recognizable similarities to any Terran forms at all.

Shearer was with a group that shuttled down from the *Tacoma* four hours after it took up a parking orbit fifteen hundred miles above Cyrene. Jeff and most of the others that he tended to mix with were there too, but Jerri had gone on the previous shuttle. After all the talk and preparation through the two-month voyage, and then the buildup of suspense that had affected everybody in the final few days, finally they had arrived. Yet the descent found them all strangely quiet as they sat staring at the succession of progressively enlarging views on the cabin wall screen, each for the most part absorbed in their own private thoughts.

Three sambot-constructed personnel carriers took them from the pad area to the base compound. They were the first examples that Shearer had seen of working sambots in operation; the classroom examples shown during the voyage had been small-scale affairs to demonstrate the principle. The system out of which the carriers were assembled had been developed to build shell structures, and consisted of two basic types of platelike module: one square, the other triangular, each measuring three to four feet along a side. Actuators and latches located on the edges enabled a newly added module to "flip" its way end over end across the surface of the growing structure to lock into its target location. Special-purpose modules included mobility units, containing wheels that pivoted out on supporting struts and inflated, each with an independent motor, and a variety of service units and operating tools.

Bases established on new worlds were considered to be shop-windows of the Terran culture, hinting at all the wonders and riches to come if the native rulers agreed to be sensible and went along with Earth's policies. The documentaries and news clips showed them as bustling centers of activity, with new constructions constantly being added, machines in motion, vehicles coming and going, and glittering light shows and floodlight displays at night. But as they approached the perimeter, it became evident that Revo base hadn't made it to that league. Unopened containers brought down from orbit lay in lines outside the fence, while construction inside hadn't proceeded much beyond the basic layout of administration building, workshop and storage units, and accommodation blocks that would be expected in the early phases. A clutter of vehicles was parked around the Admin Building, no doubt in connection with the arrivals from the *Tacoma* that had shuttled down earlier, but otherwise the activity going on around seemed scattered and indifferent. The others in the bus were exchanging worried looks. If this was an indication of the defection rate the place had been experiencing, it would mean there was a real problem.

"I'm thinking maybe you were right all along after all," Greg told Karen. She just shrugged and shook her head in a way that said she would rather not have been.

"We'll find out soon enough now, anyway," somebody else said.

Shearer looked out again at the quiet walkways between the huts, and the skeletal upper stories still awaiting completion. He registered in a distant, almost unconscious kind of way that Jeff was the only one who wasn't showing surprise.

They had been told to check with the General Office in the main Administration Building. Personal baggage from the ship would be delivered to the base later. The lobby area was crowded and noisy when Shearer and the others entered, with people jostling around a service desk on one side, and others clustered about several offices opening from corridors leading away left and right. He stopped inside the door and looked around, trying to get some bearings, while others detached from the group to go in search of directions. Then Jerri emerged from the throng ahead and came over, with Nim beside her on a short leash. "Hey, you made it," she greeted. "It's bedlam city if you're not a VIP."

Shearer stooped to ruffle Nim's ears and was rewarded with a head being rubbed solidly against his palm. "Have you got the system figured yet?" he asked Jerri.

"The first thing is to get your accommodation assignment."

"I take it there's plenty available."

"Oh, you noticed."

"It's not exactly Times Square out there. So what do I do?"

"I've already done it." Jerri handed him a plastic wallet that she had been holding. "You're in Block B—Room B6. I'm in D. As far as I've been able to find out, it looks as if you were right about Wade. He doesn't seem to be around. I'm not sure who would be the best person to talk to. There's a guy called Innes, who's listed as the Assistant Scientific Administration Director. His office is along that way, but he seems to be a bit snowed under. Maybe you should try him tomorrow, when things have settled down."

Shearer looked at the people milling around in the corridor that she had indicated. "What about the Director?"

"I'm not sure there is one."

Jeff appeared from somewhere. "You need to find your accommodation slot," he told Shearer. "Hi, Jerri. Hi, dog." Nim flattened his ears and looked wooden.

"Already done. Jerri took care of it." Shearer showed the wallet.

"Some people get all the breaks. Oh-oh, Zoe's waving about something over there. Catch you later." Jeff disappeared again.

"So how about you?" Shearer asked Jerri. "Have you managed to track down this Lemwitz person yet?" Martha Lemwitz was Interworld's Social Sciences Coordinator on Cyrene. The slot for an anthropologist that Jerri had been sent to fill reported to her.

Jerri shook her head. "Not listed on the current contact list, just like Wade. I think I might have become an orphan already."

Shearer released an exasperated sigh. "What a way to run a planet. Do you think the Cyreneans are taking notes?"

"Come on, let's get you fixed up across the way, anyhow," Jerri said. "Be ready for the hit when you walk outside, though. After two months in the ship, it goes to your head like a shot of moonshine."

They left the building and followed a short roadway to the rows of chalet blocks that formed the residential sector of the base. The first minutes of outside air were fresh and mildly scenty, and indeed with a distinctly intoxicating rush; but whether caused by something in the air or simply a reaction after their long confinement, the effect quickly passed. The day was warm and bright, with Ra Alpha high in the sky, and Ra Beta visible as a lesser, secondary sun lower down toward the horizon. As they had learned aboard ship, Cyrene was in the mid portion of its ellipse, moving away from perigee, with the two stars in an intermediate position between those associated with climatic extremes in their nine-year cycle. For the moment conditions at the latitude of Revo were in a subtropical-temperate phase close to ideal, and ship's fatigue clothing was comfortable.

Regular accommodation was assigned as two persons to a room. They came to B Block, and on the way to his room, Shearer saw that the names of the occupants were posted by the doors. He found he was sharing B6 with Jeff. It could have been worse, he supposed—Roy, for example. After depositing the bag and brief-case that he had carried with him, he left again to accompany Jerri in taking Nim for his first outside walk for a long time. At the same time, it would be a chance to explore more of the base and see something of its surroundings.

A building they had passed on the way from Administration turned out to be the Recreation and Social Center, which contained the main cafeteria, a gym, and a pool, although the extension at the rear where the pool was located was still overshadowed by a construction crane and lacked a roof. Behind it were workshops and laboratory spaces in prefabricated temporary huts, which should have been replaced by something more permanent by now. Bordering the fence were the service buildings, housing a small fission plant providing power, a water treatment plant fed from a creek running down to the lake, and sundry other installations. The fission plant was a modular system developed for bases and other facilities on the new worlds being opened up, and consisted of sealed units roughly the size of garbage cans that presented just output connections for delivering power. They ran for years, and when spent could be either opened up for recovery and reprocessing of the by-products, or left to be their own disposal container, inside which the radioactive content would gradually decay away.

Jerri let Nim off the leash to embark on a romp of sniffing, poking, and exploring this new and strange domain. Sometimes he would stand suddenly motionless for maybe ten or more seconds at a time, his head cocked at an odd angle. Evidently Cyrene was a world of new sound experiences too.

They reached the fence and began following it—a double line of chain-link topped by razor wire, running between alloy posts studded with sensors and surveillance cameras. In many places, plants had started twining their way up the mesh. From what he had heard and read of Cyrene, Shearer was unable to fathom why the base needed such formidable protection. Simply because the minds whose business it was to decide these things were incapable of conceiving otherwise, he supposed. They moved out to the perimeter path running just inside the fence and stopped to stare out at their first real view of the world they had come to.

They were on the north side of the base, looking down toward the lake, maybe a half-mile to a mile away, that extended inland from Revo city, which lay hidden behind wooded hills away to the west on their left. The base stood above a ridge of low, rounded slopes descending to become a rocky promontory jutting out from the shore immediately below. To the right, the ground broke up into folds of bluffs and stream beds on either side of a deeper rivulet feeding the lake. The far side of the lake seemed to be similarly hilly, but the details were lost in a low haze. Above, the day was fair. The visible patches of sky seemed to be about the same shade of blue as midday summer on Earth, but somehow with a more iridescent tone—an effect, possibly, of the presence of two suns at this time in the day. The clouds varied from white into mixtures of yellow and orange rather than presenting just a uniform gray scale, the montage of reflected colors giving the lake a quality of intensity and vividness seldom captured in bodies of water on Earth.

The impression of richer color contrast was reinforced by the vegetation covering the slopes below and growing among the mounds and gullies to the sides. The landscape was mostly green, with grasses of various lengths and textures giving at least a superficial reassurance of familiarity, but in places taking on shades that ranged from an eerie blue-violet to red russet brown. There were clumps of mixed bush and scrub, some of fairly normal appearance, others distinctly odd, and clustered around some hollows forming what looked like a tributary valley head to the right, a stand of peculiar trees with massively wide, multiple trunks, reminiscent of swamp cypress, but with broad leathery leaves more like palms. Everywhere, there were flowers. . . . And peculiar birds that perched and jumped in the peculiar trees, or sailed in long, lazy tours that took them far out over the lake. One descended to settle on the top of a fence post, from where it inspected the newcomers more closely and chattered down at them. Nim ran to the base but could only stand panting and looking up, powerless, tail beating a frenzy. Then he gave up and came loping back to where Shearer and Jerri were standing. They resumed walking slowly.

Around a corner formed by an angle in the fence, they came to a gate with a guard post on one side. A dirt track led away on the far side, disappearing around a hump of grass and scrub. The gate was closed, but a smaller pedestrian passage in front of the window was open to the outside. They looked at each other, each reading the same question. "Only one way to find out," Shearer said. Behind the window, a trooper in a Milicorp uniform straightened as they came over. "Any reason why we can't go out?" Shearer asked him. "We've just arrived here."

"ID." The guard went though the ritual of scanning their badges and thumbprints, and consulting unseen oracles on a screen inside the box. He acted as if being agreeable was something to be looked on as weakness, and seemed disgruntled at not finding anything to object to.

"So is it okay?" Shearer asked as the guard passed the badges back wordlessly.

"If it wasn't, I would have said so."

"Gee, thanks. Enjoy your day."

They came out onto a track of yellow gravelly soil bordered by knee-deep grass and speckles of variously colored flowers. The vista below and across the lake seemed suddenly more immediate and accessible without the fence intervening. Nim darted forward at something beneath a shrub, which shot away into the grass before they could see what it was. From behind them, the bird came down off the post and alighted on a protruding rock to eye them curiously.

After a short silence Jerri said, "All ripe for development. I can't wait to see it."

"If I didn't know you better, I'd almost think you were being sarcastic," Shearer answered.

"Do you think the Cyreneans have any idea?"

"If the past examples are anything to go by, I don't think it matters much."

Jerri sighed disconsolately. "It's all so . . . wrong. It was never supposed to be like this. Before star travel became real, people had dreams of it bringing exploration and discovery, learning and enrichment. How did it come to this?"

"The usual reason. The wrong people always end up running everything, I guess."

"I know. But why is it like that?"

Shearer had asked the same question himself many times, but still he found he had to search for an answer. "Because people are dumb enough to believe them," he replied.

They were heading more-or-less west, intending to circle around to the main access gate from the pad area, which lay south of the base. Another angle in the fence brought them around so that the lake was now behind them. The ground on this side was flatter and more open, extending away from the ridge on which the base stood. A roadway, little more than a cart track, wound up from below and disappeared amid grassy folds and hillocks studded with fronded plants that looked like overgrown ferns. From the general direction, Shearer guessed that the track from the gate they had come out through joined the roadway not far below.

Nim stopped dead, ears pricked, one forepaw raised, snout leveled like a pointer's. Shearer and Jerri came to a halt, staring in surprise. Ahead of them, standing fifty yards away or less, was a carriage with a party of Cyreneans.

CHAPTER FOURTEEN

The carriage was cheerfully painted in elaborate colored designs, of lightweight construction, sprung, with high wheels, and open in the style of a chaise. It was drawn by a pair of Cyrenean animals square-built and sturdy in the manner of oxen, but longer in the legs and less squat, both with a black woolly covering and faces that were longer and narrower, more deerlike than bovine. Woolly moose minus the antlers, perhaps. In it were two Cyrenean women in sunbonnets, with two children and a man who looked to be elderly, wearing a gray hat with a cocked brim and high crown like a busby. Two other men were mounted on Cyrenean "horses," one alongside the carriage, the other a few yards away. The first horse was white, the other gray with black markings. In size and general contours they did indeed resemble horses, but their faces were shorter and more rounded than Terran horses', and their tails were furry. Shearer's first impression was of a family group who had brought the children on an outing to see the camp of the aliens.

"Stay," Jerri commanded in a low voice. Nim, who had been tensing like a spring being slowly wound, relaxed back on his haunches but without letting his eyes flicker.

The mounted Cyrenean who was by the carriage turned in his saddle to stare curiously, as did the occupants. One of the children started to say something and was hushed by the younger-looking of the two women. The other Cyrenean, who had been sitting contemplating the base, wheeled his horse around and guided it at a slow walk toward where Shearer and Jerri were standing. Nim came up of his haunches, body straining and quivering. "Stay," Jerri murmured again. Shearer eased his phone surreptitiously from his pocket and held it in his hand at readiness.

The Cyrenaen was olive-skinned with high cheeks and narrow eyes like an Asiatic, but a nose that was longer and thinner than the typical snub and rounded Oriental shape. He had a short, pointed beard, lending a Cavalier effect, which was enhanced by dark hair curling to the shoulders and a purple hat with a broad, floppy brim turned up at the sides and a flap at the back, covering the neck. A dark red flower attached jauntily at the front like a cockade added an element of dash. He wore a black cloak that draped over his mount behind, and under it a green coat with trim of yellow cord, and wide button-down lapels turned back to reveal a knotted, embroidered kerchief at the open neck. A curved sword in a scabbard was slung from the saddle behind him. With the eighteenth-century-looking carriage behind him, and the metal spires of the Terran surface shuttles standing above the pad area in the far distance, the sight was incongruous.

Shearer and Jerri watched, keeping still and saying nothing, while the Cyrenean drew to a halt and sat regarding them curiously for several seconds and casting an uncertain eye over Nim. Then he swung himself down in an easy, effortless movement, turned to face them, holding the reins in one hand, and bowed graciously, doffing his hat. When he straightened up, his eyes were glittering in a way that seemed good-humored. He was tall, at least six feet, with a lean, long-limbed frame that stood loosely. A broad belt carrying a pouch sat beneath the coat, supporting baggy brown pants that ballooned Cossack-style before being gathered into short boots.

"Peoples from Earth. Let it be a good day to you." Evidently— and thankfully—he was one of the Cyreneans they'd been told about who had taken up the challenge of learning English. His voice was deep and resonant, articulating the words carefully, perhaps attuned to a slightly lower pitch,. "My name is Korsofal. I live in this . . ." he made a vague gesture at the surroundings, "near country."

"Yocala?" Shearer guessed. That was what the Cyreneans called the surrounding region.

"Yes, Yocala. Very good."

Shearer indicated himself. "Marc. . . ." followed by "Jerri," and then as an afterthought, pointing, "Nimrod."

Korsofal grinned, showing strong white teeth inside his beard, and extended an arm to indicate the carriage. The other rider had moved a few paces toward them. "My family peoples. And he is the good friend. You come, and I tell the names."

Shearer and Jerri exchanged glances. "This is working out faster than anything I ever expected," Shearer murmured. And then, in a louder voice, turning to Korsofal, "Sure."

Korsofal replaced his hat and began walking with them, leading his horse by its reins. "I have began, as you hear, speaking English. But much is still to learn. I must ask patience."

"It's a lot better than our Yocalan," Shearer said. Jerri tried repeating it using some of the Yocalan words they had learned on the ship. Korsofal understood her and seemed delighted.

"The most useful thing I find to know how to say is 'What is the English for?'" Korsofal informed them. He indicated Nim with a wave. "For the example, Nim . . . rod is the name, yes? Just this one. The special."

"Right," Shearer confirmed.

"So what is the English for . . . the animal that Nimrod is one of? In the way that, I already know, this one here that I have is the horse."

"Dog," Shearer said.

"So Nimrod is the dog?"

"Nimrod is a dog."

"Still, I have trouble with the 'the' and the 'a.' But this is not the time. Or should it be 'a' time? You see—a joke." They both smiled. This was going to be okay. They were drawing near the carriage. The other rider dismounted to await them. He looked some years older than Korsofal, fuller in build, clean-shaven, with a cap like a peaked beret, a long, coarse, brown riding cloak, and a loose two-piece tunic of some dark gray quilted material. The group in the carriage were peering out expectantly. Like Korsofal, they were all of brown to olive complexion.

Korsofal was looking curiously at Shearer as they walked. "My feeling was that maybe I was brought here to meet a Terran," he said. "I think that it must be you."

Shearer shook his head. "Sorry. I'm not meeting anyone. We only just arrived . . . . here," he pointed at the ground, "from Earth." He pointed upward.

Korsofal seemed to understand. He reached inside a pocket of his coat and pulled out a regular Terran, machine-made, business-size envelope. "Your name, you said, is Marc, yes?" He handed the envelope over. Written on it in a hand that Shearer recognized with a start as Evan Wade's were the words, *Marc Shearer*. Bemused, he opened it and unfolded the sheet of paper that it contained. A dried, pressed, pink flower was sandwiched inside. Shearer was no botanist, but as far as he could tell, it was indistinguishable from a regular Terran rose. Unable to make anything of it, he turned his attention to the accompanying note. It read:

Marc,

If you're reading this, you made it. Welcome to Cyrene. There are more incredible things going on here than you ever imagined. You can trust the bearer of this completely, but be careful of the usual spooks. He'll tell you whom you need to talk to. Give the enclosed to the person that he names. That person will understand.

See you soon.

E.

Korsofal was watching him intently. "When I meet you, I am to tell you a Terran name," he said. "The name is Doctor Uberg. He is inside." Korsofal indicated the base. "I do not know why is the flower."

This was one of the strangest conversations that Shearer had ever held. "But I already said, I wasn't here to meet anyone," he protested, trying to clarify with gestures. "We came outside to walk the dog."

Korsofal seemed to have been expecting it. "As I say, I was brought here, but not sure why. For days I have the message paper now that says Marc. When you tell me you are Marc, then I know it was to meet."

"We decided just now. Minutes. You couldn't know that I would be here. *I* didn't know."

Korsofal eyed him dubiously and knowingly. "The only words I have are that the good feelings guided me here to this place today. When I am here is when I find what I should do. But you do not understand, yes?"

Shearer shook his head vigorously. It wasn't making sense. "No, I don't."

"Is so, yes I know. Peoples from Earth do not know these things, do they?"

The Cyrenean nation of Yocala, of which Revo was the largest city, was ruled by a sovereign appointed to office by a voting body composed of members put forward by means that seemed to vary from place to place according to local preferences. Although he was not a monarch in the strict, hereditary sense, the Terrans referred to him as the "king." His name was Vattorix, and his residence was in an estate on the far side of the lake, several miles out from Revo city on the northern shore.

As if Callen didn't already have problems enough, a message had come through from Rath Borland at Milicorp in the last week of the voyage, communicating the latest brainwave from Joseph Corbel, which had come down via Interworld. It would be a great boost for the family and corporate image, and an astute Public Relations move, Joseph thought, if his niece, Gloria, were to be portrayed in the light of an interstellar ambassadress. To this end, he wanted a formal visit arranged for her to meet Vattorix in such a capacity. Since the Corbel dynasty controlled the purse strings, that pretty much decided the matter as Interworld's policy. And since Interworld had entrusted the investigation of what was going on at Cyrene to Milicorp, and Callen was Milicorp's man on the spot, empowered to assume authority as soon as the *Tacoma*'s captain had delivered the mission safely to the planetary surface, it meant that implementing Joseph's zany idea was his baby. So Callen had sent a message ahead to what still passed as administration at the base, asking them to make arrangements for Vattorix to meet the new representative who would be arriving from Earth.

In the meantime, his immediate priority was to make a start at getting some kind of an understanding of what had been happening. On arriving from the shuttle pad area, he and Krieg were met by Carl Janorski, Milicorp's Security Force Commander with the second follow-up mission, successor to General Paurus, who had vanished from the first. Janorski conducted them to the office suite that had been reserved in the Administration Building. Since wasting time was neither part of Callen's nature nor something that present circumstances allowed him the luxury of being able to afford, he decided this would be as good a time as any to broach the subject. Accordingly, after inspecting the room that he would be using and depositing his briefcase on the desk, he gave Krieg a nod and asked him to wait in the office outside. But no sooner had Callen closed the door and started to open his mouth than Janorski preempted him by requesting that he be moved up to the ship, and announcing that he was resigning his command and his commission.

Callen had already discerned that this was not the Carl Janorski that he had known in Africa. The brusque, pragmatic dispassion that had once made an effective military professional had given way to something less combative, more mellow. And yet he sensed that wasn't the result of any softening of character or some kind of breakdown. Janorski's eyes were clear and steady, his manner composed but determined, and anything but defeatist. Clearly, there was nothing to be discussed.

"Why, Carl?" Callen asked tiredly. "What in hell's going on in this goddam place?"

"This whole way of going about things—what we're doing, what the mission is a part of. . . ." Janorski shook his head, as if the words were inadequate, "It can only get worse. The Cyreneans don't need any of it. They'd be better off left to their own ways."

"What are you talking about?" Callen asked, getting impatient. "What's gotten in to you and everyone else here? I demand an explanation."

"It's not something I can tell you," Janorski answered. "How do you describe music to the deaf, or a painting to someone who hasn't learned to see? We just get to know. As you will."

It was the same nonsense Callen had been hearing for months. "Tell me one thing, then," he said. "You were in charge of security here. People have been disappearing in droves. Nothing has been done to prevent them. Why not?"

"I follow the policy as given by the Director," Janorski replied. "He never issued any order to that effect. So you'll have to ask him."

Callen stood with his back to the window in Emner's office on
the top floor, his expression a mixture of irritation and contempt,
while Krieg had assumed a position just inside the door, impassive
and wooden-faced. Emner looked even more disoriented than he
had on the screen in Callen's suite aboard the *Tacoma* several weeks
before. He was wearing casual fatigue dress despite this being the day
of receiving a mission from Earth, when an appropriate observance
of protocol would be expected; the reception arrangements had been
lackadaisical; work around the base was way behind schedule, yet the
base Director had done nothing to alleviate it. Callen was already
wondering inwardly if he was going to have to declare an emergency
as authorized by the Interworld charter and assume overall command himself.

Milicorp's Colonel Yannis, a former space pilot officer who had
been adjutant officer to General Paurus, and since the arrival of the
Boise and the second mission had been reporting to Janorski, sat in a
chair by the wall near an end of Emner's desk. Like Emner, he
seemed distantly focused. Callen had already as good as decided that
he would have to appoint somebody from the *Tacoma*'s Milicorp
force to take charge of security at the base. It would only be as a
temporary arrangement. The relief base commander that he had
requested while the *Tacoma* was still en route had been dispatched
from Earth along with a staff corps via fast military clipper and was
due to arrive in the next couple of weeks.

"The place has been hemorrhaging people for months." Callen
threw up his hands and shook his head to show his incomprehension. "And you did nothing about it? It's fenced and gated. The gates
are guarded as per regulations. Yet you never thought to change the
orders?" He stabbed a finger to point at the panel of monitor displays
beside Emner's desk, where a screen was still showing a frozen image
from one of the perimeter cameras of Shearer and the anthropologist
that he had been getting friendly with, leaving via Gate 3 on the west
side to meet the group of Cyreneans who had obviously been waiting
for them. "We saw it right there. Anyone can just walk out—even
now! For the love of Christ, man, what kind of a circus are you running here?" He turned his gaze on Yannis. "Is there something about
the air here that makes everyone take leave of their senses? Don't

look at me with that complacent face, Colonel. You may have flown ships once, but you're a disgrace to that uniform and an embarrassment to Milicorp Transnational. You can take it from me that you'll be replaced before the day is out."

Emner frowned at him with the expression of someone searching for words that he didn't expect would be easily understood. He replied, "What do you see us as running here, Mister Callen? Does your holy mission directive say anything about coming light-years to set up just another prison camp? Is that what I'm supposed to do? That's the first impression of our great and illustrious civilization that you want me to present to the Cyreneans? The model of the progressive culture that we bring them? The grand future vision that they should thank us for letting them become a part of?"

"I expect you to take whatever measures are necessary to manage a professional operation and keep it intact," Callen snapped.

Emner eased himself back in his chair and brought a hand up to cup his chin, contemplating Callen absently. "Ah, yes. Professional, professional. We must always be professional, mustn't we? Do you ever think of us as professional thieves? . . . Except, we're not even very professional at that, are we? Professional in the sense of being smart, I mean. We don't even steal for ourselves." He looked Callen up and down as if noticing a new side to him for the first time. "Tell me, do you like being a programmed robot, Mister Facilitator?"

"That's what the obsession with uniforms is all about, you know," Yannis came in. "Pride in the efficiency that you think it represents. But what it really represents is conditioned mindlessness to obey."

"Which in itself isn't necessarily a bad thing when there's need to defend yourself," Emner said. "But when you take a long look at *whom* it is we're obeying, and for what . . ." He shrugged and left it unfinished.

Callen had had enough. Besides everything else, he had been instructed to keep tabs on Shearer when Shearer made his anticipated move to join Wade. From the way things were looking, it seemed that something might happen very soon. Shearer was already in touch with Cyreneans, and they had given him a letter. The operative Dolphin had been placed in the same room as Shearer in the base, but it would be doubly important now to keep close watch on every move and not miss a thing. Callen couldn't afford any slack or risk further sloppiness at this juncture.

"As authorized under the emergency proviso in the operational directives, I'm assuming effective command of this base immediately," he declared. "This to be subject to confirmation by the requisite ratifying body of the mission's officers as specified. Officer Krieg here will stand as witness. I would like to think I can assume your acceptance and cooperation under the due posted procedures."

"Be my guest." Emner waved a hand. He seemed tired and not especially interested.

And Yannis could go at the same time, while they were at it, Callen decided. He would have them both taken up to the ship for a thorough medical and psychiatric examination. He took his phone from his jacket and activated a code to connect him to the orbiting *Tacoma.*

"Day Room Officer," a voice answered.

"This is Facilitator Callen, from Revo base."

"Sir!"

"Find Lieutenant General Delacey, and have him call me back. Tell him I want him down here on the surface as soon as he can make it."

Yes, Callen told himself as he returned the phone to his pocket and stared grimly at the two faces watching him indifferently. There were soon going to be some big changes around here.

CHAPTER FIFTEEN

Jerri awoke the next morning feeling strangely unsettled. It was the kind of feeling one had after experiencing a disturbing dream that was impossible to recall. It took a moment of staring at the unfamiliar ceiling that didn't belong to the cabin she had occupied for the past two months before she remembered where she was. This was her new room in Revo base. They were at Cyrene. But the nagging feeling of ill-ease wouldn't go away. She lay, letting the fragmented parts of consciousness come together and begin functioning again, and tried to analyze it.

Finding out whether or not Martha Lemwitz was still around, and taking up the anthropologist position that had been available was no longer of interest. Marc had come to Cyrene to rejoin his former partner, Wade, and Wade had departed from the Terran sphere of influence to live his own life independently, as they had suspected. After receiving the message via Korsofal, Marc had told her that he intended doing likewise as soon as he had a lead on how to locate Wade. And he had asked her to go with him. Whether because something in her had changed during the voyage and she saw the new world beckoning her to a new life, or because the rational, levelheaded, ever-cool Jerri Perlok was tottering on the brink of falling in love—or perhaps a little of both— she wasn't sure; but it had seemed the most natural thing in the world to say yes. But now, in the morning, there was something about the thought that disturbed her. It wasn't that she was changing her mind. Far from it—the prospect felt even more attractive and exciting than ever.

But a muted warning note was sounding somewhere around the fringes of her consciousness.

Korsofal and his family lived on what sounded like some kind of farm to the west, south of the city. Whether he owned it or managed it on behalf of other interests was unclear. Jerri and Marc had a standing invitation to come and see the place anytime they chose. All they could make of the story behind the letter was that it had found its way to Korsofal via someone who was in touch with Wade. Jerri was still suffering from a sense of unreality about conversing with alien beings of a world orbiting another star. Maybe the strangeness of it all had something to do with her not having slept soundly.

She rolled up onto an elbow and looked around. On his pad of foam rubber on the floor, Nim stirred, opened an eye, and yawned. Zoe was still fast asleep in the cot opposite. Jerri wondered if whoever allocated the rooms had put her in with Zoe because Zoe was a dog person too. If so, it was nice to know that something was working.

The flowers that she had put in water in a jug on top of the locker had changed color again. They had caught her eye when she and Marc were on their way back into the base enclosure, and she had stopped to pick some. They were like small orchids, delicately formed, with lilac petals hinting of white at the tips and turning to a pink blush at the base. They also had a dark, puffy collar encircling the stem immediately below the base of the petals, unlike anything Jerri had seen before. After putting them in her room, she had spent the rest of the day and early evening taking care of administrative chores and attending a social function staged after dinner. On returning to the room she found that the flowers had undergone a peculiar change. The lilac petals had curled inward and closed into buds, while the collars below had unfolded to reveal themselves as second sets of larger and finer petals of dark purple, effectively transforming into different flowers. Now, with morning, they had returned to their original form. Jerri leaned over to inhale the scent. It was delicate and subtle, like the textures and the colors, pervading and freshening the room.

Marc believed that the authorities were anxious to catch up with Wade too for some reason, and had formed the theory that his own clearance for the *Tacoma* had been rushed through in order to set him up as a lead. It was likely, then, that his movements were being watched. *That* was what was troubling her, Jerri realized suddenly. She had an inexplicable premonition that he shouldn't be seen approaching this Dr. Uberg, that Wade's letter had named. It would reveal Uberg as knowing things that the wrong people would want to find out. Jerri could maybe talk to Uberg instead—inconspicuously, without attracting attention. And suddenly, now that the source of her apprehensions had crystallized, she felt more at ease.

She got up, ran some fresh water for Nim, showered, and dressed. Then she clipped Nim's leash on and let herself out of the room quietly so as not to disturb Zoe. Once outside the hut, she used her phone to call Marc.

"Hey," she greeted.

"Hey."

"Where are you? I need to talk."

"I was just about to call you and say the same thing. I had break-fast early. I'm at the Rec Center. There's an open patio area outside, back of the cafeteria. Why don't I meet you there? We can sit in the sunshine. Remember that round yellow thing? Or here, I guess it's things."

"I'll be there in five minutes," Jerri said.

Jeff Lang, real name Michael Frazer, code name for the *Tacoma* mission, Dolphin, was originally from Minneapolis as his cover story maintained. He had joined the military at an early age, after discovering at high school that an ROTC uniform drew available teenage females like bugs to a UV zapper, and gone on to complete several tours in the Middle East as a rookie Marine, and later as a not-so-rookie Special Operations infiltrator in southern Asia. When the whole sordid act finally fell apart, he expressed his cynicism and disillusionment by moving between the independent militias and freebooter bands that emerged in the Midwest and mountain states during the period of anarchy before the political situation stabilized. When Occidena finally consolidated, his talents quickly earned him a natural place and a more secure living on the less visible and unpublicized side of the services provided by Milicorp.

Shearer hadn't gone to any great length in unpacking his belongings, which could mean that he was planning on making a move sometime soon. There had been no communication with him from Wade during the voyage—something Shearer had mentioned repeatedly. That seemed to indicate that information on how to find Wade would have to come either from outside the base, or from somebody within it. The log and taps on Shearer's phone showed no undue contact with anyone from the previous missions that it would have seemed odd for Shearer to have known. Lang had searched their room for the letter that Shearer had been given by the Cyrenean only hours after landing, but either Shearer had destroyed it or he was keeping it on his person. Lang could only go so far in shadowing Shearer's movements without making his continual presence grounds for suspicion. He was already aware of being an irritation.

He sat at a corner table inside the cafeteria, a news sheet spread in front of him, apparently playing idly with the buttons on his phone while he stared at its miniature screen. The phone held access codes to the security system, and he was able to keep an eye on Shearer via the cameras located around the base. Shearer was outside on the patio area, feeding tidbits to Jerri Perlok's dog and apparently teaching it to shake paws. She herself had left some time before, after evidently meeting Shearer so he could take over dog minding for a while and give her a break. At one point in his training Lang had been taught how to deal with attack dogs, and they still produced a negative reaction in him.

Callen's hope was that Shearer would make his move sooner rather than later. He had two conflicting considerations to deal with. On the one hand, the slackness and population shrinkage at Revo base were intolerable, and restrictions on movement needed to be imposed until more could be learned. The pretext would be that the missing people had gone down with a hitherto unrecognized alien infection that Terrans were susceptible to, and the base was being quarantined pending investigation. On the other hand, tracking down Wade was a high-priority item for reasons that were none of Lang's business, and shutting the base would mean penning Shearer in along with everyone else. And that would negate the whole purpose of bringing him here.

Callen had compromised by postponing the announcement on closing the base for a couple of days to give Shearer time to act on whatever was being prepared. Provided Shearer took advantage of his opportunity soon, that seemed fairly safe. The arrivals fresh in from Earth would be busy enough for a while before whatever had affected their predecessors started putting them in a mind to begin a new exodus of their own. In the meantime, there was little else to do but watch and wait.

A point of concern was that things didn't seem to be playing out as intended, however. In Lang's experience, if the letter had indeed given Shearer directions on how to proceed next, a person in Shearer's situation should be doing something visible to follow up. But Shearer wasn't showing much sign of it.

The Personnel Directory for the base listed Dr. Dominic Uberg as a botanist. Jerri found him in one of the prefabricated laboratory huts behind the Recreation Center, taking notes and photographs among a collection of plants and seedlings growing in lines of labeled boxes filling a glass-walled extension on one side. The place had a general air of being underutilized, with cartons, cans, bottles, and containers stacked in offices and workspaces where there should have been people, and piles of unsorted papers littering half-empty shelves. A girl was working at a microscope in a side room when Jerri entered, but apart from Uberg himself, there was no other sign of life. He was in his early forties, perhaps, fair-skinned with crinkly yellow hair and metal-rimmed glasses, wearing a white work coat, and greeted her cordially. When she said she had come on some possibly rather sensitive business, he rinsed his hands in a metal sink and led her back through the hut to a cluttered room with a desk, computer station, shelves of soil sample jars, and botanical wall charts, that was evidently his office.

"So," he said when she had explained the reason for her visit. "You are just down from the *Tacoma*, and I've never seen you before. You are representing this person Marc Shearer, who doesn't come here to speak for himself, and you think I might know how to find Evan Wade." His voice remained pleasant, but the eyes behind the lenses were amused and mildly mocking, as if he were hearing a good joke. He might almost have asked if she was selling any good bridges today too.

Jerri reached inside her jacket, pulled out a folded tissue, and opened it to reveal the pressed rose that had been inside the letter.

Uberg's expression changed when he saw it. "I understand that this should mean something to you, Doctor," she said.

He took it from her and examined it. "*Rosa spinosissima*," he murmured. "A variety of the Scotch rose. Rich and robust. It seems to have taken extraordinarily well. And in so short a time. Remarkable."

"You talk as if it's from Earth," Jerri said.

"Yes indeed," Uberg agreed. "Originally native to Europe, but since naturalized in North America."

Jerri wasn't following. "How could it be? We—that is, Marc and I—were only given it yesterday. From a Cyrenean."

Uberg got up from the desk and went around to make sure the door was firmly closed. "You see," he said as he came back and sat down again, "the seed it was grown from could only have come from one place: here. I myself gave some to Evan Wade before he left." He spread his hands on the desk and regarded her with a new candor. "Very well, Ms. Perlok. I believe you."

Jerri slumped back in her chair. At last she felt that she was talking to someone who knew something and would give straight answers. "Doctor Uberg, what's going on here?" she asked. All the pent-up strain and uncertainty of hearing nothing but evasion for months came out in the sudden weariness of her voice. "Wade sent a note—we burned it. It talked about incredible things happening here. What did he mean?"

"There, I think you might be even a little ahead of me," Uberg replied. "All I can tell you is that Cyrene does strange things to people. They start seeing themselves differently—reexamining values that they've never questioned, and thinking again about how they want to spend the rest of their lives." He shrugged and spread his hands. "It seems that many of them take the notion into their heads to make a fresh start somewhere else."

Jerri shook her head disbelievingly. "You mean they just walk out? From an operational base? Nobody stops them? It doesn't make sense."

"Cyrene does strange things to *everybody*," Uberg said. "Dreams that influence them deeply. Some claim uncanny premonitions. They start behaving in ways they wouldn't normally."

Jerri recalled the peculiar compulsion she had felt that morning to come here herself instead of Marc, and then dismissed it as a coincidence. There were no grounds to go jumping to conclusions and for her to start acting out of character already. "Does anyone have any idea what might be causing it?" she asked.

"There are some very peculiar botanical life-forms here," Uberg said. "Unlike anything from anywhere else that I've ever heard of— we're sending quantities back to Earth for study."

"On the freighter that's being loaded in orbit," Jerri asked.

"We sent an earlier one a few weeks ago. I had a hand in organizing it—a lot of seed and plant specimens." Uberg smiled briefly.

"Are they connected with whatever's going on?"

"An early thought was that it could be something chemical, but the lab analyses haven't turned up anything. I know that Wade is very interested in some of the varieties he's found here too. And he's a physicist. What the connection with physics is that intrigues him so much, I can't tell you. One of the secrets that I learned long ago for living a peaceful life in this utopian existence that we have created in our wisdom is not to ask questions about things I don't need to know."

It seemed about as much as Jerri was going to find out for now. "So, then, getting back to Wade . . ." she prompted.

Uberg gave her a teasing half-smile. "Are you sure that Shearer really wants to go tramping off already? I'm only a botanist, but I seem to have been drafted as something of a de-facto scientist-general for the base. I could use a physicist here."

Jerri shook her head. "Sorry, but . . . we're sure. Marc had his mind made up before we left Earth. He's dedicated to the work that he and Wade were involved with."

"Ah, well, one has to ask. . . . What's your field, out of curiosity?"

"Anthropology."

"Oh. Are you the one who was to work with Martha Lemwitz?"

"That's right."

Uberg nodded and stared thoughtfully at Jerri for a few seconds longer as if sizing her up. Then his manner became more serious. "Tonight, the Cyreneans are hosting a welcoming banquet for the leaders of the newly arrived Terran mission, that I shall be attending," he said. "It's to be held at the residence of this part of the world's head-of-state, on the other side of the lake."

"You mean Vattorix, the Yocalan king?"

"That's what it's translated as—but I don't think it quite means everything we understand by the term. I've been asked to nominate and bring a small group of scientific and commercial people to go along too. I gather the idea is to use the opportunity to suitably dazzle some of the influential Cyreneans who will be attending." Uberg's mouth twitched upward at the corners. "After all, we mustn't forget that the prime purpose of the mission is to assist their development, must we? The investors back home must be getting impatient." He paused. "I will arrange two places for yourself and Shearer. I can say that I needed a physicist, and this seemed a good way to get him involved and up to speed as quickly as possible."

"And what then?" Jerri asked.

"By the time you get there, appropriate arrangements will have been made, and you'll be advised accordingly," Uberg told her. "Do you have any bio monitors or other trackable implants?"

Jerri was struggling to absorb that this was really happening. She swallowed and shook her head. "No."

"And Shearer?"

"I don't think so."

"Make sure. Anything of that nature must be neutralized. Also, leave behind all phones, compads, locator tags, anything with com chips or active radiative electronics. Bring only personal items that can be carried inconspicuously in a small carrying bag. New clothes will be provided—you won't want ones advertising that you're Terrans anyway."

"I also have a dog," Jerri said. Uberg registered surprise and interrogated her silently for a moment. She held his eye unwaveringly, trying to muster an expression saying it would have to be all or nothing.

"A rarity," he commented. "In fact, I'm pretty sure we haven't had one here before. The Cyreneans would be fascinated. I can include that as an added attraction. That will give an excuse for bringing you along as well. I'm glad you mentioned it. Very well. . . ." He showed his hands to indicate that he was through. "You'll receive details on where to be and when, later today."

Jerri waited for a second or so and started to get up. It seemed an empty note to be leaving on. "I just want to say thanks," she told him.

Uberg just nodded, already attending to papers that were on the desk. She started for the door, then stopped and turned. "Why?" she asked. "If you feel the way you do, how come you're still here?"

Uberg looked up. "There was something I had to remain behind to do," he replied.

Jerri waited. When nothing more was forthcoming she asked, "What?"

"I wasn't sure. But I think this might have been it." Jerri stared back at him uncomprehendingly. "I told you, Cyrene does strange things to people," he said.

CHAPTER SIXTEEN

Gloria Bufort studied herself critically in the full-length mirror in the dressing room of one of the chalets fenced off from the regular accommodation blocks. No, she decided. The blue two-piece with the blouse and silk neckerchief was too businesslike for an interplanetary ambassadress. A banquet called for something more grandiloquent— especially in a setting that in terms of style and customs brought to mind ballrooms from *Gone with the Wind* more than the twenty-first-century stellar frontier.

"Betty!" she called petulantly over her shoulder. Her housemaid, who had accompanied her through the voyage, appeared in the doorway opening from the bedroom. "It's no good. This makes me look like a flight attendant. What else is out there?" Betty had been unpacking and putting away the things that had come in the first baggage delivery, which had arrived from the shuttle pad area the evening before.

"Pretty much just some practical things for the first few days, as I said, ma'am. I guess nobody expected anything elaborate so soon."

Gloria gave an exasperated sigh and began peeling off the blue two-piece. "You'd have thought this Vattorix and his people would have given us more time to settle in before staging something like this," she grumbled. Okay, so Myles had told the Cyreneans that he wanted to meet with them as early as possible to stress the urgency of the defection problem. But if they'd had any consideration they could have made just a person-to-person thing involving him and whoever else needed to be there, and left the formal business until later. How could she be expected to look her best when everything she needed was still up in the ship? "Lay me out something casual for now," she instructed. "Stretch pants and a windbreaker will do. I just want to go out for about half an hour." Betty nodded and withdrew.

She would talk to Myles, she decided. If he was in charge of things now, he should be able to make it a priority to get the rest of her things sent down. They still had all afternoon, and a shuttle could make it in twenty minutes. Leaving the clothes in a heap on the floor, she went through to the bedroom, where Betty held out some pants and a top from a closet she was partly through filling. While Gloria pulled them on, Betty indicated a full-length dress of orange lamé with taffeta and ribbon ornaments at the neck and sleeves, that she had smoothed out on the bed.

"If I may say so, ma'am, that mightn't be too bad at all. I did make sure there was one trunk with some more dressy things—in case there was a dinner at the base or something like that. The sheen could be quite appropriate."

Gloria lifted the hem, looked at it disdainfully for a moment or two, and then let it drop. She turned to sit on the edge of the bed and stretched out a foot for Betty to put on the shoe. "What about jewelry to go with it? This is a diplomatic occasion."

"We have your Italian emerald set," Betty replied as she tied the lace. She tightened the knot and reached for the other shoe.

"Oh, I'm tired of those. This is the first time after two months of being shut up inside that frisbee that I'm actually going out where people can see me. I want something I can wear with the Cartiers. A full, swirling gown in white—how about the backless one with puffed sleeves and the sequined waist? I was told it looks regal. That's the kind of thing I'm talking about."

Betty stood up and turned to take a hanger from the closet. "They haven't been sent down yet, I'm afraid," she said. "And I'm sure the ship has a busy schedule today. I'm not sure there's a lot we can do."

Gloria rose to her feet and took the proffered wind breaker. "We'll see about that," she said as she turned toward the door.

As she emerged from the chalet, the armed Milicorp corporal posted outside the door straightened up. Gloria hesitated for a second, intending to tell him to raise Myles on the phone, but then she changed her mind. "Do you know where the acting Director is right now?" she asked instead.

"I'm pretty sure he's in the Administration Building, ma'am. In the Director's office."

Gloria nodded. "We'll go there, then."

They passed through the security gate giving admittance to the roadway running alongside the residential huts and turned in the direction of the Administration Building. A number of people were about, some of whom turned to look at her curiously. One or two sent her a cautious nod or half raised a hand. A man in military fatigues took off his hat. Gloria ignored them. Two months of the ship had been bad enough, but this kind of proximity and familiarity was too much.

She noted as they walked how stark and utilitarian the surroundings were inside the base. Perhaps a more suitable residence outside could be arranged, she thought to herself—there were lots of big houses around the outskirts of the city. Maybe that was something she could bring up with the Cyreneans tonight. They might even be able to furnish her with a proper staff of domestics and keepers for the grounds, ones who knew their place and had never heard of Terran unions or labor laws. She could picture it featured in the news documentaries back home: "Gloria Bufort's ambassadorial mansion on Cyrene." Now wouldn't *that* be something! And Henry could play with his stock options and communications electronic whatsits for as long as it kept him contented.

They entered the Administration Building and took the elevator up to the top floor, where the executive offices were. A corridor brought them to a door bearing the sign DIRECTOR. Gloria told the guard to wait and let herself through. A young man in shirtsleeves at a desk flanked by a computer station looked up inquiringly. "Is Myles in?" Gloria asked, motioning with her eyes at the door leading to the inner office.

"Who wants to . . ." The clerk recognized who she was suddenly and straightened up. "Yes ma'am! He sure is." The clerk got up from the chair and went ahead of her to the door, raising his hand to knock, but she restrained him with a wave.

"It's all right. He won't mind."

The clerk deferred, inclining his head, and stood aside. Gloria eased the door open, stepped inside, and closed it softly behind her. Callen was at the desk with a panel of screens to one side, pen in hand, poring over some papers that he was holding. His expression didn't change when he looked up, catching the movement. Gloria thought she could have expected at least a sign of welcome. She felt piqued.

"Well, don't bother saying hello or anything, Myles," she cooed after a few seconds.

"Hello," Callen obliged.

"You might at least look pleased."

Callen's brow knitted for an instant. He made a short waving motion with the papers and compressed his mouth into a forced smile. "I'm sorry. . . . You caught me right in the middle of something."

"So what's it like to be the Director and have the entire base at your command?"

"Just the acting Director. It was necessary. Today has been hectic. What can I do for you?"

Gloria moved to the desk, kissed him on the forehead, ran a hand down the side of his face and along his shoulder, and then sank down onto one of the chairs on the far side. "This thing that Vattorix has sprung on us for tonight. . . . "

"It was at my request," Callen reminded her.

"Not a full formal banquet. You just wanted to talk business. A handful of you could have taken care of that. The other stuff could have been left until later."

Callen conceded the point by spreading his hands. "I would have thought you'd welcome the opportunity to display your person and form after so long," he said.

"Yes, well, that's the whole point. My stuff is all up in the ship. I can't go there looking like a woman who sells insurance or someone on her first graduation date."

"What do you mean, 'stuff'?"

Gloria motioned down at herself with both hands. "To wear. You know, like clothes? And the things that go with them. I'm the ambassador to this planet now, remember?"

"But you had a consignment brought down as a first priority yesterday. It should have arrived last night."

"None of it's suitable. That was casual stuff for the first few days. Nobody expected anything like this. The *real* stuff I need for something like this is still up there."

Callen opened his hands again. This time he was unable to suppress a hint of irritation. His eyes glanced involuntarily at the screens next to him, displaying items waiting for attention. "Well, I'm sorry. If we'd known sooner that Vattorix would respond in the way he did, we could have made arrangements accordingly. But this isn't exactly Buckingham Palace or the Presidential House in Beijing. I'm sure you'll be able to put something acceptable together from what you have. Now, it's lovely to see you, but I really am—"

"But that's not *good* enough, Myles! I've been shut up in the *Tacoma* for two months! This is the first time I'll be around new people. I want my best stuff. You're the new Director around here . . ." Gloria waved a hand. . . ."or acting, or whatever. What you say goes. You've got shuttles coming down all the time. All you have to do is tell someone up there to get it loaded, and the have it picked up at the other end."

Callen shook his head. "I'm sorry, but that's impossible. There's a complex unloading schedule in operation after a voyage like this, not to mention all kinds of system rundown procedures and checks to attend to. Everyone is stretched to the limit, and half the people who were supposed to be here to help have disappeared. I really do have other things that must take priority right now."

"What's the matter?" Gloria shot back. "Don't you want your dinner date tonight to look her best for the king of Yocala and all his court? I mean, I *am* the ambassadress, and the least I'd expect . . ." She caught the pained look on his face and stared at him probingly. "We *are* going together, I assume, aren't we?"

Callen looked away, bunched his mouth for several seconds; then he seemed to make his mind up about something and turned his face back. "We both have new responsibilities now," he said. "There are certain protocols and behaviors that don't mix. In view of our earlier . . . relationship, I don't think it would be appropriate."

Gloria's face whitened. "What are you telling me? That I'm okay as a screw to pass the time on the trip? Do I have to remind you who I am, Myles? Just who the hell do you think *you* are?"

Callen rubbed his brow tiredly in a way that said he'd known this was going to happen. "I'm just saying that these things have a way of telegraphing themselves. If the news found its way back, it wouldn't be in the best interests of either of us. Surely I don't have to spell it out. It's best that it were ended now, before anything like that happens, before any damage is done." His face softened a fraction. "Yes, and if it's any consolation, I'll miss it too. Okay?"

But Gloria was no longer listening. She uncoiled from the chair and was barely able to stop herself lashing out. "I don't need you to worry about my interests back home," she hissed. "What do you even know about them? We own the ship, and we own the base, and we own you. I could squash you and not get a hair out of place." She marched to the door and threw back before opening it, "Come to think of it, I might just enjoy that. There. That's something else on your schedule for you to sweat about."

She was unable to prevent herself from closing the door with a bang. The clerk in the outer office kept his eyes on the screen that he was working at and said nothing.

CHAPTER SEVENTEEN

The Cyreneans had proposed sending barges over to ferry the guests across the lake as a relaxing prelude to the evening and to give the newcomers some advance practice in getting to know them better. But impressing the natives with the wonders that Earth had to offer was higher on the mission's priority list, and the Directorate decided that the Terran delegation would arrive in style by air.

Nobody that Shearer talked to knew if it had been the intention all along, since nothing had been said during the voyage, but Gloria Bufort, who was apparently down at the base but quartered privately somewhere, would head the delegation as Earth's official representative to Vattorix. She showed herself briefly to be driven from the Administration Building to the open area inside the perimeter fence on the east side that served as a flight operating zone, where she embarked with a retinue of the more senior people and their staffs into a sleek, shiny VTOL personnel transporter from the base's complement of aircraft. Shearer, Jerri, and the remaining other ranks packed into two boxy sambot constructions configured into flyers. The accommodation was bare and simple by comparison—but, they had to admit, ingenious. Uberg traveled with his scientific group, although somebody said he had been offered a place in the VIP air-craft.

The flight across the lake took a matter of minutes. A good number of boats were visible below, some idling or maybe fishing, others making their way between Revo to the west and points farther inland. With their bright, multicolored sails, they looked like flowers floating on a pond. A biologist just in with the *Tacoma* thought that the effect could be deliberate. She had read that Cyreneans attached a lot of importance to flowers, and used floral designs and motifs extensively in their decorations and art.

Details of the opposite shore unfolded as the flyer drew nearer. It was hilly inland like the southern side, but with a generally neater and more cultivated appearance. The wilder, more open terrain of the south shore had no doubt been a factor in selecting the site for the base. The field boundaries cut a patchwork of irregular sizes and shapes among blotches of green and purple forest interspersed with outcrops of rock. There was a view of houses strung loosely along a roadway following the water's edge, some with barns and outbuildings forming small farms, and then the flyer began descending. It crossed the shoreline above the mouth of a small river with moored boats and houses clustered around the banks. Figures were standing and staring, while others came out of doors to watch the flight pass overhead.

A larger house became visible, standing alone some distance to the left among trees inside walled grounds. The flyer's nose began to swing around, and the house disappeared from view ahead. Moments later, the boundary wall was passing by underneath. A stretch of parkland followed, and then lawns and gardens laid out between terraced ponds. The engine nose rose to bring the flyer to a halt with a wing of the house visible on one side; it hovered for a few seconds, and then completed its descent vertically to touch down in a paved court. The view through a window opposite showed the VIP VTOL that had preceded them already on the ground. Moments later, the second sambot flyer came into view from above and landed on the far side of it.

Although there had been a briefing after assembly at the base, a woman called Marion Hersie, who had come with the first mission and knew enough of the language to be assigned as the party's interpreter, stood up at the front to repeat some of the salient points over the cabin speakers.

"I want everybody to remember that we're here thanks to Interworld Restructuring Consolidated. They've brought us here as part of the program of facilitating Cyrene's economic and political development. This will be for their own benefit as well as that of the corporation and its backers, and eventually all of Earth itself. It's important to present *every* aspect of our technologies, methods, and institutions in a positive light. This evening, whatever your nominal profession, you are firstly salespeople for Earth. The Cyreneans you meet will have heard various things from different sources, not all of them true. Take a tip from what your insurance companies tell you: Don't admit wrongs or failures; your information might not be as accurate as you think. Don't apologize. We want Earth's image to be one of confidence and strength that the rulers here on Cyrene will want to emulate. Let them see you using your communicators to talk to someone back at base, or better, up in the ship. Showing things like a shot of the city from orbit is good. Impress on them that all the stars are suns, and how far the ship has come. When their leaders start to think of that kind of capability in terms of weaponry and what it could do for them, that's when we get their attention." Whines and clunks sounded as the door behind her and another at the rear of the cabin hinged outward to transform into steps. "Enjoy your dinner. All items on the menu have been passed as Terran-friendly. We'll be assembling back here at the aircraft at twenty-one hours local time for departure. You'll get a reminder beep fifteen minutes in advance. Thank you."

Hersie signed off with a click. The cabin's occupants got up in ones and twos and merged into lines shuffling fore and aft toward the exits. Nim, who had lain by Jerri's feet through the flight, was all eyes, ears, and alertness. She gave his head a reassuring ruffle. "We're gonna meet some new people," she told him.

"Maybe they'll have some juicy bones," Shearer put in from just behind her. Nim thumped his tail against one of the seats trustingly. Uberg had told them to leave their things in a baggage compartment and tell the crew simply that they might be wanted later.

They climbed down into the yard, which lay to one side of the house. A reception committee of colorfully dressed Cyreneans was already before the doorway of the VIP craft, where the lead group of Terrans had emerged. Gloria Bufort, wearing a glittery white coat with silver fur trim over a dark business dress, was making a show with grandiose arm motions and postures of starring in the center. A smaller group of Cyreneans was moving forward toward the sambot flyer.

While the groups from the two exit doors merged back together and Hersie made her way through them to the front, Shearer took a look at the surroundings. A wall continued from the wing of the house bordering one side of the yard. Halfway along it was a wide, railed gate opening down to what looked like a flower garden, but with tiers of seats overlooking a sunken area in the middle. The wall ended at steps going up to a terrace enclosing a pond, beyond which were treetops of what could have been some kind of orchard. Behind the flyer, paths and sets of stone stairs ornamented with sculptures led down among more flower beds and screens of shrubbery to the lawns. In front and on the far side of the flyer stood the main body of the house itself.

It was elegant and reasonably spacious, but a somewhat modest affair for a head of state, Shearer thought, falling distinctly short of what most people would have visualized as "palatial." Perhaps the Terran habit of referring to Vattorix as "king" had raised his expectations unduly. His first impression was of mix of Gothic and Arabian styles. It had a projecting central section supporting a balcony over the main entrance, with parapets and staggered cornices above. The basic construction was thick-walled and robust, but like the architecture setting the tone of the city, echoing a theme of narrow, arched windows, pillars, and rising flutings that emphasized verticality and height. The central part boasted a steep, sloping roof ending in a square tower, while the wings made do with onionlike domes capped by cupolas. The stonework was embellished with colored inlays and foliar designs. Flowers stood in sprays of color in beds along the bases of the walls and planters beneath the windows, while more provided an edging to the roofline. The domes above the two wings carried branching ornamentations spiraling up the sides, making their profiles asymmetrical. Shearer couldn't decide if the intention was to impart a floral character to them too.

His attention came back to the mixed group of half-dozen-or-so Cyreneans who had drawn up before the arrivals. Their styles of dress varied from brightly embroidered frock coats that might almost have come from eighteenth-century Europe, worn with baggy Cossack-like pants gathered at the ankles, similar to those that Korsofal had worn the day before, to loose, ankle-length robes. Three were Cyrenean women, wearing gowns fastened with belts and

draped from one shoulder in the manner of togas, with long cloaks—
quite stately and becoming, Shearer thought. They wore their hair
high, held by bands and clasps decorated with flowers. One of them
holding a posy, which she carried forward, smiling, and presented to
Marion Hersie. The Cyreneans raised their voices in an odd ringing
sound that was part way between a cheer and a murmur but obviously signified approval. Unsure how to respond, a few of the Terrans
started clapping, and the rest followed. This seemed to delight the
Cyreneans, who promptly began imitating them.

There was a brief dialogue in Cyrenean between Hersie and a tall,
blond-haired man in a scarlet coat, evidently speaking for the group.
She introduced him as "Pada," which she translated as "Doctor,"
Gedatrize, who studied philosophy and natural laws, and summa-
rized their exchange in fairly standard form as a welcome message
and her response. Then Gedatrize asked her something. She gave an
answer that obviously meant "Of course," and gestured toward the
group from the flyer. Gedatrize turned his head from side to side to
take them all in. A mischievous smile flickered around his mouth for
a moment. Then he said, "And now I make the chance to practice the
English. But not yet as good as she speaks the Cyrenean. My welcome
it is to you. And when we have the end, maybe the English will be
more good a little. Is yes? Thank you very much." His gesture was
rewarded with an energetic round of applause. The combined group
waited until the VIP party from the aircraft in the center began moving, and then followed them into the house.

A vestibule with a tiled mosaic floor and alcoves on either side
brought them through a high arched doorway into an open hall area.
On the far side, a carved staircase led up to a broad landing from
which secondary flights ascended left and right through two more
arches toward the wings. The hall was apparently where the intro-
ductory socializing before dinner would take place. The decor was
bright and cheerful, the predominantly yellow walls set off by wood
paneling, friezes, and moldings, and the floor a magnificent pattern
of marquetry-like inlays. A fire burned in a large open hearth on one
side, and suites of variously fashioned chairs and couches arranged
around several window seats to leave an open central area completed
the atmosphere. As groups of hosts and aliens began mingling and
talking, awkwardly at first in some places but loosening up quickly,

stewards appeared with tall carts divided into shelved sections containing drinks in a variety of glasses and goblets, along with appetizers. Gloria Bufort and a select group were taken on through somewhere, presumably to meet Vattorix, who would be joining the gathering for dinner.

Nim was already attracting a circle of admirers and curious onlookers. A swarthy, squat-built Cyrenean with curly sideburns extended a hand warily. Nim's ears pricked, and his tail wagged. The Cyrenean withdrew the offer hastily. "It's okay," Jerri said, trying to make the point with gestures and a smile. "He's just being friendly."

"Use a drink?" Shearer asked her.

"You bet," she told him gratefully.

A woman had begun stroking Nim's neck and back, and seemed fascinated by the fur. Leaving Jerri striving valiantly to deal with the questions via signs and her smattering of Yocalan, he moved over to a steward who had stopped his cart a few feet away and cast an eye over the offerings. "Er, speak English? Terran?" he asked the steward, who was at least looking if he wanted to be helpful.

"No English. Sorry."

The Terrans had been given NIDA sets to experiment with, but Shearer didn't think this was really the time. He tried a line of Yocalan he thought would ask what would be good for a lady to drink, but all it evoked was an apologetic grin. Feeling mildly disconcerted, he looked over the shelves again, selected two stemmed goblets with wide, flat bowls like champagne glasses, containing a purplish drink, nodded to the steward, and carried them back over to Jerri.

"Dog," Jerri was saying to the Cyreneans, who had increased in numbers even while Shearer was away. "Name Nimrod." She went on in broken Yocalan to answer that yes, he was full grown and wouldn't get bigger; yes they were big teeth, but no, he didn't bite people—although no, that wasn't so of all dogs. Shearer handed her one of the goblets and tried a small sip from his own. It tasted sharp with a fruity edge, and then delivered a dry, subtle after-flavor a little like rum. He had no idea if it was alcoholic or had any comparable effects.

A Cyrenean who seemed to be the companion of a woman who was stooping to pat Nim's shoulder and uttering "Ooh-la-la" sounds turned toward him. He was fair skinned like Gedatrize, with brown hair tied at the back, and clad in an orange-brown coat with a velvetlike sheen. The front was embellished with gold brocade and turned back in wide, pointed lapels to reveal silky yellow lining and a white neckerchief knotted above a close-fitting body garment resembling a vest. "If okay, I will exercise English," he said.

"That's what we're here for," Shearer agreed. The Cyrenean's brow furrowed. Shearer grinned. "Sure. My name is Marc."

"Ah, yes. And mine is Sergelio. This house, the wood things . . . " he indicated the panelwork and carved rafters making an art form of the ceiling above, "long years back now, I design and make. Now other peoples I teach the . . . you would say is work?"

"A better word would be art," Shearer said, taking it in more closely.

"A-rit?"

"Art."

"Art."

"Good. It means very beautiful. With much care and skill."

"Ah, yes, we try. So you make me a compliment?"

"Very much," Shearer said, and meant it—although it did cross his mind fleetingly to wonder what someone he thought of as a tradesman should be doing at a head of state's reception.

Sergelio went on, "And I have now the time with music. Later this night we will hear some." He laughed. "But not yet is mine so good."

"It should be interesting," Shearer said.

Sergelio looked at him. "And you, Mr. Marc. What is it you do?"

"I'm what's called a physicist." The Cyreneans would have no equivalent word, and he explained, "One who studies and learns . . ." he glanced at Sergelio, who nodded, "The world. What it is made of—matter, substance. How things happen the way they do. Why things happen the way they do." He pointed to the fireplace, then up at the ornate lamps with oil reservoirs illuminating the room. "What is fire and heat? What is light?" He indicated his own mouth and ears. "What is sound?"

Sergelio followed, watching him intently, and seemed to understand. "Physi-cist," he repeated.

"Yes. Very good."

"And that is how you learn to make the bird-ships that fly across the water, and you sail in from the star?"

"Yes. You've got it."

"And the phone far-away talking-seeing." Sergelio looked about, then gestured at the compad on a nearby guest's wrist. Shearer had left his own behind as instructed. "Another Terran once showed it for me. This is a thing the physicist learning makes too?"

"Physicists gained the *knowledge*," Shearer said, trying to be helpful. "The knowledge makes it possible."

"Ah yes. I understand, I think so." Sergelio looked away for a moment at his wife or ladyfriend, but she was engrossed in an animated conversation with Jerri and some others. "The Terrans try to tell Vattorix he should want these things too," he said, turning back. "That they will provide. Teach Cyreneans to be physicists."

"Better lives for all his people," Shearer answered. "More food. Comfortable houses, warm on Henkyl's Day and cool on Longday, even in carbayis. Fast travel to many places. Fast communication—talking and seeing. Easy reading of any knowledge."

Sergelio nodded. "Yes, I understand how knowledge could make these things for all peoples. And this we would like to have. But is not what Terrans say to Vattorix. They talk of strong weapons to make wars. Physicist knowledge that makes . . . what is word for strong and frightening, so people must do as is decided by others, not do as they would wish?"

"Power?" Shearer offered.

"Yes, that is word I forget. Power for Vattorix to command peoples to obey. But this is not what Vattorix wants."

It sounded like a breath of fresh air to Shearer—a ruler who wasn't obsessed with personal aggrandizement and power? "So what does Vattorix want?" he asked.

Sergelio seemed surprised. "The things you just say—for all peoples. That is why he is put in the job that he does. If he does not do his work well, then he is taken away from job—the same as if my wood workings fall down."

"So what's Vattorix's pay-off?" Shearer couldn't help asking.

Sergelio looked puzzled. "What is pay-off?"

"His reason. What does *he* get back. Personal wealth? Many possessions?"

"Ah, yes, this I hear from Terrans before. But I still do not understand. Enough possessions to have is nice, yes. But why too many possessions? Is like too much food—more trouble than good."

"Power, then," Shearer tried. "So Vattorix has more things in life that others can't take away."

Sergelio needed to think about that for a while. "True, that will give him those things today, maybe tomorrow," he agreed finally. "But over longer time, will make pain and anger with many other peoples. Long-sight will tell him that this way are more bad things than good things, and so he knows."

"Long-sight?" Shearer repeated, frowning.

"That is what Terrans tell me is your word," Sergelio said. "It means the wise choices that come when everything sleeps and world is quiet and listens. That is how Cyreneans find . . . know-ledge." Shearer shook his head, not comprehending. Sergelio thought for a moment. "When you come out from bird-ship, you see the wall of bricks, and the wall has a door."

Shearer remembered the sunken flower garden with its tiers of seats. "Yes. but not a door, a gate," he replied.

"Okay, is gate. That is the place where Vattorix and the . . . what is people who talk with him to decide things?"

"Counselors. Advisors."

"Yes, good. That is where they meet at night to talk questions and agree."

"At night?"

"Yes. Is when the long-sight comes." Sergelio looked at Shearer curiously. "Is not the time when Earth peoples think of the important things that will mean good lives or bad lives?"

Shearer shrugged. "No. Most people just sleep."

"We say on Cyrene that the day deceives, but the night is true. Like the child that sees the nice things that it wants now." Sergelio gestured to indicate some candylike delicacies on a nearby serving cart. "That is the day-sight. But the bad things that come from you eat too many," he put a hand on his stomach and pulled a face of someone feeling sick, "he doesn't see. The grown man, he sees. That is the night-sight." Sergelio paused, eyeing Shearer dubiously for a response. Shearer didn't know what to make of it. "But then I should know, I was told," Sergelio said. "Terrans on Earth do not feel these things."

Marion Hersie appeared at that point and began rounding her charges together and ushering them toward another arched opening on one side of the stairway. As the general tide of movement began around them, Jerri looked around for some clue as to what she was supposed to do with Nim. Uberg materialized next to them as if from nowhere.

"Any idea what we do with the dog while we're having dinner?" Shearer asked him.

"Don't worry about that," Uberg answered. His eyes were moving rapidly and taking everything in, not looking at them directly. His voice was low and strangely tense. "Just stick close."

Beyond the arch was an anteroom where Gloria Bufort and her immediate party were in the process of being shown through a door to a large room where tables with places laid for eating were visible. Evidently they were to be seated first. With them was a group of Cyreneans with nothing obvious to distinguish them from the general company, but who had to be the principals. Shearer picked out Callen from Milicorp and Captain Portney, the *Tacoma*'s commander, who they had been told would be coming down from the ship to attend the event. Close behind Callen was a tough-looking, craggy-faced man with short-cropped hair that Shearer had seen once or twice at functions in the course of the voyage, but couldn't identify. He looked constrained and out of place in a formal suit. The broad, bearded figure walking beside Gloria, with a fierce mane of dark hair that could have belonged to a Corsair pirate, and wearing a dark blue coat over a white robe, Shearer recognized from shots shown at the briefing as Vattorix himself. As usual, Gloria was taking center stage.

"I'm not a head of state, but I live in a far bigger house than this," Shearer caught as they moved on into the dining room. "How would you like one five times this size?"

"Why? What would I do with it?" Vattorix asked.

"We also own one of the largest collections of contemporary art works on the West Coast. I'm told it's valued at a sum that would buy all the buildings in your city here."

"Very nice," Vattorix agreed, obviously wanting to be polite. "But what do you *do*?"

As the main group converged behind, slowing to allow a respectful interval before following, Uberg steered Shearer and Jerri away from them and toward a passageway at the rear and waved them through. It led to what looked like store rooms and a scullery off the kitchen. Two Cyreneans were waiting, one holding Shearer and Jerri's bags from the flyer. Without a word, they turned and led the way quickly through more passages and out to a yard which, if Shearer's sense of direction was accurate, lay beyond the wing that had flanked the sunken flower garden. An enclosed carriage harnessed to two Cyrenean horses was standing waiting, with a driver seated up front and a figure standing by the opened door, holding another bag. Shearer realized that his chest was pounding with a sudden adrenaline rush. This was it!

They hurried across to the carriage. Jerri sent Nim bounding in and then followed. Shearer threw in his bag, climbed a step to the dark interior, and turned to say an appropriate word to Uberg. But to his surprise, he found that Uberg was waiting to follow him, while the man who had been waiting stood behind, holding the door.

"I told you there was something I had to remain at the base to do," Uberg said. "It's done. I'm not sure exactly what my future has in store, but I do know that it will be somewhere out on Cyrene. When you've been here a while, you'll learn to feel these things."

CHAPTER EIGHTEEN

Myles Callen was angry. It was not the rush of violent anger that might flare in the face of an insult or a display of stupidity that went beyond the bounds of tolerance, and would just as quickly abate again. That kind could be controlled and contained; a big part of surviving in a deceitful and treacherous world lay in cultivating the ability to do so. It was the slow, gnawing kind of anger that fed upon itself and smoldered and grew, demanding action. The dispatch had already gone back to Borland; there had been no choice. In any case, covering up from his superiors wasn't Callen's style. Less than two days after taking command, he'd had to report a major failure of the security provisions. He wasn't accustomed to things like that.

He sat in the office that had been Emner's until yesterday, glowering at the desktop with its tidily arranged assortment of papers and accessories waiting to take on the look of work in progress, and the panel of monitor screens to one side. As a first measure to get the message out that things had changed and the days of Emner's ineffectiveness were over, he had given new orders to Delacey, who had replaced Yannis as security commander, for the gates to be closed to casual egress, and for rules to be drawn up governing the issue of passes to cover exceptions. The explanation of an unidentified sickness affecting Terrans who had left the base had been posted, and he would talk with the Chief Medical Officer later about spinning some plausible-sounding line to back it up.

Which left the problem of Shearer. Callen had left the cell door invitingly unlocked, and while he had been watching and waiting for

Shearer to make a move, Shearer had been smuggled out through the window. The speed with which it had been effected, he had to admit, had taken him by surprise. Uberg, who was also missing, had obviously been a part of it. Yet Dolphin had followed Shearer's every move, and Shearer hadn't been near Uberg; neither had they communicated electronically. It seemed, then, that Shearer was a shrewder operator than Callen had given him credit for. They must have set it up via a third party, probably the girl. So maybe scientists could be as smart, every once in a while, as most of them thought they were all the time, Callen conceded.

There had to be Cyrenean involvement in what had been going on; or at the very least, from the sheer number of people who had gone missing, the Cyreneans couldn't be unaware of it. A diplomatic approach to the ruling powers would normally be the first choice in such circumstances, but the diplomatic initiative in the case of this mission had been put in the hands of an airhead, and Callen wasn't prepared to risk another fiasco. That left force, which was certainly something that Callen was more at home with—and in comparison with anything the Cyreneans were capable of mustering, the mission's military contingent could pack a hefty punch. However, the conditions of overt native hostilities or militant rivalry that might lend themselves to exploitation, typically by giving some token support to one side and so forcing the other to seek a deal of some kind to redress the balance, didn't appear to offer themselves on Cyrene. And besides that, heavy-handed intervention of that kind, within days of Gloria Bufort's arrival in the role of ambassadress, had been ruled out by Earth.

Then it would have to be a compromise between the two—a representation to the Cyreneans, kept within the bounds of what was permissible, but with show of force to get the message across that the new management meant business and wanted answers. Yes, there would be an element of bluff in it; but the Cyreneans were smart—maybe too smart at times, Callen was beginning to think already. To get the message across clearly, the representation would need to be done with a military face, not the Gloria Bufort brand of bimbo diplomacy. But it would be unbecoming for him, as the new acting base Director, to make the first approach. Bigger guns were more properly held in reserve.

His mind made up, he leaned toward the desk touchpad and keyed in Krieg's number. Krieg's close-cropped head and craggy features appeared on the screen a few moments later. "I've got a job for you," Callen said. "We need to get this business out in the open and talk to our friends face-to-face. It should have been done long ago. Can you get over here to talk about it?"

For his mission, Krieg used one of the twelve-man RS-17P "Scout" military Survey & Reconnaissance Vehicles provided as part of the standard equipment inventory for rapid response and emergency situations. It carried four nose cannon and a pair of waist laser turrets for ground suppression and Landing Zone defense, as well as various underwing munitions packages. Although the precise functions of these devices would no doubt be lost on the Cyreneans, the overall nature of the craft could hardly be mistaken. The intention was to signal the kind of resorts that the Terrans had at their disposal, and to impress that the matter was serious. To this same end, it was decided to forgo the formality of making advance arrangement with the Cyreneans for a meeting. Krieg's force would simply drop in unannounced. And since it was close by, and one place that they knew for sure would give access to the local governing system, the place would be Vattorix's residence across the lake, the same place where they had been received the night before. The choice also represented a mild testing of limits as to how far they could push Cyreneans. If it turned out they had gone too far, it could be written off with apologies and the excuse of newcomers being unfamiliar with native customs.

A group of curious Cyreneans had already gathered outside the main entrance of the house by the time the Scout touched down. Krieg emerged in one of his rare concessions to wearing uniform, flanked by a lieutenant and preceded by a ten-man guard detail carrying weapons but not wearing combat gear, who fanned out on either side with parade-ground precision to present arms. A Cyrenean who introduced himself as Afan-Essya greeted them and stated himself to be a close helper of Vattorix and organizer of day-to-day affairs, which sounded pretty close to "Secretary." Krieg, assuming a due measure of propriety but at the same time injecting a no-nonsense note, conveyed that he was here representing the new

Terran administration in connection with a matter they considered highly important and wanted to take up with the highest levels of Yocalan authority.

It would have satisfied Krieg to deal with Afan-Essya at this juncture; or any other comparably placed official with whom a preliminary discussion would be appropriate. He was therefore surprised and momentarily thrown off balance when Afan-Essya, after a brief consultation with the others around him, suggested that the best person to take it up with would probably be Vattorix himself. But Krieg was if anything a pragmatist, not much given to standing on form, and he certainly wasn't about to miss an opportunity like this. Recovering quickly, he readily agreed. A messenger was dispatched into the house, and Krieg invited inside to wait. He followed, taking just the lieutenant with him—bringing a whole armed troop into Vattorix's house would have been pushing things too far, even for Krieg. For a few minutes he was indulged in small talk that revolved around his first impressions of Cyrene and various details of the art and decor in the front entrance hall, where the reception had taken place the previous evening. To Krieg's relief it turned out that Afan-Essya had acquired considerable proficiency as an interpreter. Then the messenger returned and announced that Vattorix could see the visitors at once.

Afan-Essya, with two others, conducted Krieg and the lieutenant up the central staircase and then via one of the secondary flights of stairs to a gallery lined by pointed windows and ledges of large flower vases along one side, and doors into a series of rooms on the other. They came to the last of these and entered a spacious, sunny room with walls of carved paneling and windows opening to a balcony overlooking the lawn and grounds falling away toward the lake. Vattorix was standing at an oval table near the windows, wearing what looked like casual dress—a plain tan tunic fastened by cord loops and metal clasps over Cyrenean Cossack-style trousers. He greeted the two Terrans affably, indicated two imposing chairs with high backs and wide arms, upholstered in a brown leathery material, on one side of the room, and seated himself on a matching couch facing them from the wall. Afan-Essya remained, while the other two Cyreneans who had accompanied them from below withdrew.

After a few minutes of opening pleasantries that Krieg managed to get through without giving vent to his rising impatience, Vattorix asked the reason for their visit. Despite his responsibilities, he had evidently devoted some effort to schooling in the language of the newcomers. His eyes were deep brown but with a strangely orange tint around the pupils. He regarded Krieg with a steady, penetrating gaze, his head tilted, causing his chin and beard to jut forward in a way that could have signified defiance or just simple curiosity. Never having had much need or bent for the fine art of reading subtleties in his fellow humans, let alone aliens that he had only met for the first time yesterday, Krieg decided that the best tack was simply to plunge in.

"Two ships from Earth came here before the *Tacoma*. . . ."

Vattorix looked questioningly at Afan-Essya, who held up a hand. "Can you explain *Tacoma*?" Afan-Essya said.

"That's the name of our ship—the one we came here in. Like my name is Krieg." Krieg wasn't in the habit of expressing himself simply for the convenience of foreigners. The conversation was going to have to rely heavily on Afan-Essya.

"Very well," Afan-Essya said, and conveyed it to Vattorix.

Krieg resumed, "A lot of the people from those ships have gone missing."

"How are we to understand 'missing'?" Afan-Essya asked.

"They're not at the base anymore."

Vattorix and Afan-Essya looked at each other in a way that said yes, they both followed that, and then back at Krieg expectantly. Krieg waited for them to figure the rest out for themselves, but they continued looking, apparently waiting for more from him. Eventually, Afan-Essya said, "So we take it they have chosen to live somewhere else."

"Yocala has many nice places," Vattorix put in. "I would go too if I were Terran, I think. The base with the fence around it is like living in . . . " he said something in Yocalan to Afan-Essya.

Afan-Essya turned back to Kreig. "Where you keep animals inside fences. Is it 'farm'?"

"Farm." Vattorix nodded. "Who would want to be an animal in the farm?"

They weren't getting it. "They don't have leave to quit the base," Krieg said. "There was never any official approval given."

The two Cyreneans frowned and exchanged some words between themselves. "Are you saying they are escaped?" Afan-Essya asked, looking back. "That they are crime persons? No, they couldn't be. Not so many of them."

"Maybe the reason for the fence?" Vattorix suggested.

"The base is not a prison, yes?" Afan-Essya checked with Krieg.

"No, no." Krieg glanced perplexedly at the lieutenant. "How can I put this? They come here on a contract. . . . Savvy? It's like a promise. They're brought here to do work for the corporation that runs the show. Like a government. The people who make the rules."

"It sounds like a prison," Afan-Essya commented. Vattorix nodded his head in agreement.

"Not at all. They're free to choose what they do," Krieg insisted.

"Then why can't they choose where they want to live?" Afan-Essya asked.

"I already told you, because they're under contract. They have a duty to the corporation."

Another brief dialogue between Afan-Essya and Vattorix ensued, punctuated by shrugs and rubbings of chins, and ending in an exchange of nods signifying agreement. "Then that is a matter between your corporation and its prisoners," Afan-Essya told Krieg. "It seems a strange organization for living. But it is not our affair to question the ways of others."

"I cannot be surprised that they wanted to leave their farm," Vattorix remarked. He gave the two Terrans a long, dubious look, as if to say that they really ought to try thinking it through.

"Right, it's our business," Krieg agreed. Now they seemed to be getting somewhere. "But, as I don't have to tell you, Cyrene is kind of a big place. It's a question of finding them."

"They have the bird-ships and the talking-seeing glasses," Vattorix said, speaking to Afan-Essya. "I suppose so they must do their own way." He made it sound like a fact of life that they had to live with, but not a thought that he found appealing.

"But this is where we think you can help," Krieg said. Callen had briefed him not to make any direct or implied accusation that the Cyreneans might have played an active part in spiriting Terrans away. "There can only be so many places where someone can go.

Many of your people must know where the Terrans are. They can't be living out there invisibly."

Afan-Essya shrugged as if agreeing the obvious. "Well, yes, I'm sure that's true," he replied.

"Then there you are!" Krieg sat back and regarded them triumphantly. This was the key admission that he had been after. He'd had no idea that eliciting it would be so easy. "What we need is your cooperation in tracking them down. The directors of the corporation would be very appreciative."

Vattorix, however, frowned and said something to Afan-Essya in the unmistakable tone of one asking if he had understood correctly. The Secretary nodded and replied at some length in a worried voice. Vattorix's expression darkened beneath his shaggy mane of hair, and for a moment he looked as if he might explode in anger. Krieg's smile faded as the realization seeped in that perhaps this wasn't going to be so easy.

Afan-Essya cautioned, "You are telling Vattorix that his nation is a prison, of which he is the . . . " he sought for a suitable word, "director."

"No, you've got it wrong," Krieg protested. "I'm talking about cooperation between authorities that have interests in common. The Directorate at the base; your government in Yocala. We want to see a future relationship that will benefit all of us. Right?"

Vattorix raised a restraining hand before Afan-Essya could answer. He wanted to take this one himself. "Yes, we are the government in Yocala. So what does this mean? It means that our . . . what was the word you said, 'duty'?" Krieg nodded. "Our duty is to serve the people of Yocala. What is serve? Serve means we protect their right to decide how they will live. The Terrans from your base choose that they will live as Yocalans. This means they are my people now. My duty is to protect their right to say where they will live. It is not to serve your corporation." Afan-Essya made to interject something, but Vattorix waved him down and went on, "But you would use your weapons to make the people serve government. Is wrong way up, like house with roof built under bottom. If is so on Earth, then okay, your business. But here, Terrans from base are our people now. So we should protect *their* right against *you!*"

"But they're in breach of contract," Krieg retorted.

"Is contract with you, not with us," Vattorix answered.

"Don't governments here enforce contracts? Isn't that supposed to be a big part of any government's job?"

Afan-Essya took a few moments to communicate the gist to Vattorix. "One that was made here, on Cyrene, yes," Afan-Essya agreed when he turned back. "But this was made on Earth. No contract like the one you describe would ever be agreed on Cyrene."

There was an odd look on the Cyrenean's face that Krieg found puzzling. "How can you be so sure?" he demanded.

"Until you learn to know, there is no way I can tell you," Afan-Essya replied. "And when you have learned, there will be no need to tell you."

Callen sat in his office listening sourly to Kreig's conversation as recorded by the compad that the lieutenant had been carrying in his breast pocket. When it was finished, he replayed a few salient parts and then sat staring vexedly at an image of the center of Revo city on one of the side-panel screens, coming in from a reconnaissance drone. No signatures were being returned by electronic ID or tracking devices. Without help on the ground, there was no way they would ever get a lead in that tangle of streets and alleyways, markets and squares, all teeming with people. And there was no guarantee that Shearer had gone into the city anyhow. With a reception organized and waiting, he could have been whisked away in any direction up or down the coast, inland, or even westward and out to sea.

Very well. So the Cyreneans weren't going to help. The time would come later when they would regret that decision. But in the meantime Callen had to consider his other options. He thought for a while longer, then touched in a code that would alert Dolphin to call him back when it was safe to do so. The call tone sounded less than a minute later, and the screen presented the face of Dolphin, real name Michael Frazer, current field name Jeffrey Lang.

"Seven this evening," Callen told him. It meant they were to meet then in a storeroom by the staff kitchen at the rear of the Administration Building. They never let themselves be seen together openly. "There's going be another defection to the Cyreneans. But this time we'll be the ones arranging it."

"Who this time?" Dolphin asked, looking puzzled.

"You," Callen said. "Lang wants to follow after his friends. We already have you set up with a temperament that will make it believable. I want you to go out there and pick up the trail. There has to be some kind of contact or network among the Cyreneans that knows which way they went. I'll have an operational profile put together by the time we talk."

CHAPTER NINETEEN

The apartment on the top floor above the drapery store looked out over a busy square in the center of Revo. On the far side, steep-roofed buildings of typically Cyrenean solid appearance and vertical accentuation stood over an arched, cloisterlike walkway extending the width of the block, lined with street vendors' stalls and tables. Apparently the steep roofs were for throwing off the heavy snows when winter came. The upper parts of the structures were staggered back into terraces somewhat like ancient Sumerian ziggurats but with less regularity and symmetry, with many balconies displaying the ubiquitous profusion of plants and flowers. In some places, bridges at various levels connected across the side streets entering the square.

The place belonged to a Cyrenean called Soliki, who was at present attending to his business downstairs. Shearer and his companions had been brought there late the previous night. The Cyrenean who had been waiting with Uberg's bag by the carriage had traveled with them and seemed to have been assigned as a guide. His name was Chev. He had left again after delivering them to Soliki's, and said he would be back the next day, when he had further information on the "arrangements."

While Shearer stood at the window in the spacious kitchen and stared out at the town, Soliki's wife, Antara, clattered around the wood-fueled range, preparing a stew-and-pastry dish of some kind. She was a buxom woman with a reddish, chubby face, and wore an open loose, vestlike bodice over a loose white shirt, and a full calf-length skirt. At the large table occupying the center, their daughter

Evassanie, who looked to be in her early-to-mid teens, was kneading bread dough. In addition to a loose single-piece garment hanging to the knee and open sandals, she was wearing one of the Terran NIDA mesh caps on her head. She had become instantly fascinated with it, and hadn't taken it off since Uberg invited her to try it out an hour or more previously. To let her explore her newfound interest, the three Terrans were still wearing theirs too. Jerri was seated at the other side of the table, cleaning and slicing a mix of vegetables that she had offered to help with, and Uberg on a seat by the wall next to a wooden dresser filled with dishes and knickknacks. Nim had found a spot on a rug near the range and was dozing, chin on paws, every now and again opening an eye and moving it from side to side to keep check on the unfamiliar surroundings.

Shearer's general impression confirmed what he had read and heard about Yocalan culture being at a stage roughly comparable to Europe in the eighteenth century. Jeff said it was estimated to have taken only somewhere around the equivalent of two hundred years to progress from the Cyrenean counterparts of Aristotle. And yet the remarkable thing about it was that, as far as Shearer had been able to make out, anyway, the Cyreneans didn't seem to posses any marked aptitude for analytical thought or what would normally be viewed as "scientific" thinking. It seemed an odd contradiction. He commented on it again to Uberg as he stared absently out at the town skyline with its towers and domes rising behind the facade opposite,

"That's true," Uberg agreed. "You won't find elaborately developed systems of formal logic like the ones the medieval Scholastics wrestled with. But it also means that the Cyreneans didn't spend a thousand years splitting hairs before realizing that deductive arguments are only as good as the assumptions and can't tell you anything about reality."

"Excuse me, what does law-abiding numbers mean?" Evassanie broke in. "I can't make anything of it."

Or at least, that was how Shearer's NIDA set translated it. By now, he thought he knew what had happened. "Formal," in the mind of someone like Uberg, in the sense he had meant it, would have a strong association with rigid systems of rules as pertaining to logical and mathematical derivations. In a Cyrenean mind, however, the notion of sets of rules would more naturally connect to civic laws regulating personal behavior. So what Shearer had heard was the net result of Uberg's utterance being processed twice through the NIDA loop: from Uberg into whatever Evassanie had heard, and from that back into an interpretation in Shearer's own style of English. All things considered, it didn't do a bad job at all, he had decided. But the system developers back on Earth still had some work to do.

There was also a problem with proper nouns, they had discovered, so he didn't know how "Scholastics" would fare. Earlier, Evassanie had mentioned Cyrene's moon, Calypso, which Shearer's NIDA had translated as "Rumba," and the misunderstanding had taken several minutes to clear up. Jerri's and Uberg's units had given them no problem. All they could think of as an explanation was that Shearer had gone through a dance-craze phase as a student in Florida, and somehow it had left him with different neural associations and connotations. Even more interestingly, when Shearer tried to replay and follow more closely what he had experienced, he realized that he had not actually *heard* the NIDA "ghost" voice saying "Rumba" at all, but hadn't *seen* a glimpse of his former dance teacher demonstrating it. So it seemed that when unfamiliar patterns of alien conceptual linking prevented the NIDA system from finding an appropriate audio match, it was somehow able to compensate by stimulating a visual association instead.

While Jerri entered into an exchange with Evassanie to answer her question, Uberg went on, "On the other hand, Cyreneans have an uncanny ability when it comes to intuition. Where we would spend hours, days, or who-knows-how-long arguing and analyzing all the incidentals and details of an issue, they have an instinct for going straight to the heart of it and knowing what to do. I can't explain it. It's not an intellectual process as we know it. Maybe there's the answer to your question."

"Is this what you people who have been here for a while keep telling us?" Shearer asked. "That you say people have to find out in their own time?"

"I'm pretty sure it is," Uberg replied. "As I told you before, I long ago developed a premonition that I should remain behind at the base, even though I was feeling the same things as those who were leaving—we talked about things like that of course. But I had no real idea why. Now, all of a sudden, I'm pretty sure it was to help you find

Wade. Why should that should be so important? Once again I have no idea. I just know that it is. Not think—*know*. That's the way it works."

Shearer frowned. This went against everything he had been taught to think as a physicist. He was about to object, when Evassanie, evidently catching part of what they had been saying, told them, "You have to learn to listen to the flowers."

It sounded like another crazy NIDA translation, but Jerri saved them from being diverted off into another lengthy round of explanation by observing, "Aren't the flowers here gorgeous? Do you remember those ones I picked outside the base when we met Korsofal and the others, Marc? They were the same as those over there next to you." She motioned with the vegetable knife that she was using to indicate the planter on the window sill by where Shearer was standing. He looked down at it.

"Were they?" It contained several kinds of blooms. "Which ones?"

"Guys," Jerri sighed. "The pinky-lilac ones . . . with the white at the tips and the dark kind of collar at the base. . . . Yes, those. I'm pretty sure they were the same."

Uberg got up from his chair and came across to inspect them. "Yes, I'm familiar with this type," he informed them. "The collar, as you call it, is actually a secondary set of petals that open at night."

"Yes, I saw that," Jerri said. "The lilac ones close down into a bud inside."

"It's called the moon flower," Evassanie said, following them. "It is one of those that speaks the most clearly. You listen to it at night."

Shearer was about to say something, and then he remembered the sunken flower garden at Vattorix's house, and what Sergelio had said about it being where Vattorix and his advisors debated issues of state and arrived at their decisions. At night. Sergelio had said that was when "long-sight" came: the time for people to ponder upon what choices would mean living good lives or bad lives. Shearer was still trying to make sense of it, when Nim stirred suddenly, opened his eyes, and sat up.

Moments later, they heard the door open on the far side of the hallway outside; footsteps crossed to the open doorway into the kitchen, and then Soliki appeared. He was lean and lined of face, with a pointed chin, thin, high-bridged nose, wispy graying hair, but with a jovial manner that showed itself in a tight mouth with natural upturns at the corners, and bright gray eyes twinkling behind a pair of oval-framed spectacles. He wore a splendid purple coat with breeches cut more tightly than the baggy Yocalan norm, and an orange shirt with frills and ruffs. He took the coat off and placed it carefully on a hanger near the door while exchanging some words with his wife and daughter. Evassanie's replies came through Shearer's NIDA as "Of course. Aren't they our guests?" and, "No, he's been wonderful, just lying by the stove. Do you think the Terrans could bring me one? . . . Oh, Daddy, what a thing to say!"

Soliki sat down in front of a dish that had been set at one end of the table containing a cold salad preparation with fruit and some bread on the side, and Antara came across to fill the cup next to it from an earthenware jug with a spout. His knowledge of English was nil. He had laughingly shown an interest in the NIDA system earlier, but declined to persevere with it. They would have to rely on Uberg's limited Yocalan, plus whatever Evassanie's NIDA could add. Soliki smiled at the three Terrans as he drank from his cup, and said something to them.

"He asks if we are refreshed now, and ready for whatever happens next," Uberg told the other two.

"Does he know what happens next?" Shearer asked.

"He has no idea. . . ." Uberg listened, checked something with Soliki, and nodded. "Whoever is in charge of the arrangements is not telling people more than they need to know. It seems strange to him, but it's none of his business." Uberg's voice dropped to add his own aside. "I think he thinks it's so nobody will say anything wrong if other Terrans come asking questions, but he's too polite to say so. They think that in some ways we're a strange lot."

"Maybe we'll hear more when Chev comes back," Evassanie said.

"That's a nice coat," Shearer commented, noting the care that Soliki had taken with it and wanting to be sociable.

"Marc is admiring your coat, Father," Evassanie told Soliki.

Soliki looked pleased and beamed as he prepared to attack his salad and answered with evident pride.

"Father is pleased that you think so," Evassanie said. "He made it himself. A daring voyage over unknown oceans." Presumably some

Cyrenean metaphor that didn't quite tie with anything, but the meaning was clear enough. Antara added something that sounded complimentary.

"I didn't know he was a tailor. It looks more of a drapery shop," Jerri commented.

Evassanie passed it on with a little help from Uberg. Soliki looked a little bashful, replied at some length, and pulled a face. "Yes it's true, Father says. We are only running a business here. It has provided for us, and we have a large staff and pay them well. But he has been studying and learning, and one day he will be a qualified tailor and make suits that become famous." Evassanie sounded proud as she spoke. Antara came back to refill Soliki's cup and patted him encouragingly on the shoulder.

Shearer and Jerri looked at each other with mildly puzzled expressions. Uberg seemed to be expecting it, and explained, "Things here aren't the way we're used to. The artisans and the craftsmen are the ones who are valued and respected—those who can create things of quality and beauty. Commerce is considered an activity of secondary importance." He shrugged and rubbed his nose with a knuckle. "It does make a certain kind of sense, I suppose. I mean, you can get by without the buyers and sellers. Producers will always have a market. People have to eat, dress in something, and have somewhere to live."

Shearer cocked his head curiously as he remembered something else."Did you talk to a character called Sergelio at the dinner last night, by any chance?" he asked Uberg.

"No—I was rather busy behind the scenes from the moment we arrived. But I've met him before. He's what we'd call a master carpenter."

"That was what I meant. He showed me some of the work he'd done on the house. I thought it was odd for a carpenter to be at an event like that. Now, I think, maybe you've explained it."

"Exactly. People like that are the nobility here."

A lot more was suddenly falling into place. Shearer recalled the question he had overheard Vattorix putting to Gloria Bufort as they went into the banquet room: "Very nice, but what do you *do*?"

Since Uberg was wearing a NIDA, Evassanie had been following and relaying his meaning to Soliki and Antara. Soliki seemed intrigued, but at the same time puzzled. Evassanie translated: "Father has met other Terrans who left your . . ."—there seemed to be a hiatus as Shearer's NIDA sought for a word, and then he had a momentary vision of a sheep pen. "He says they told him that on Earth it is different. The people who make everything enjoy very little because people who do nothing take it away from them and sell it for much more than they have to pay. Is that so?" Antara, who had moved to the dresser to take down a container of something, clicked her tongue and shook her head as she listened.

Uberg shot a quick, baffled glance at Shearer before answering. "Well, I've never heard it said quite that way before, but yes . . ." He nodded. "I suppose that about sums up the way things are."

Now Evassanie looked puzzled as well. "But why do the people who make the things do it? Why do they let the people who do nothing take away what they have produced?"

Jerri had been catching Shearer's eye and nodding emphatically as if to say, *Listen!* It was exactly the point she herself had made several times in their conversations during the voyage. She turned her head toward Evassanie and answered, "Because the ones who do nothing worthwhile have accumulated enough money to pay people with weapons to take it for them."

Evassanie looked shocked. "Your king allows this?" she asked, speaking for herself now.

"It's the basis of our system of law," Jerri said. "The king enforces it. He has the weapons."

For a few seconds Evassanie just stared at her incredulously. Antara had to intervene with a question that obviously meant *What did he say?* Evassanie told them.

Antara turned her face toward Soliki, who had stopped eating and was looking speechless. She muttered something and went back to the stove to set the container down on a work top to one side.

"Their king is a criminal," Evassanie translated.

Soliki continued regarding the Terrans with something close to an astonished expression, then said something in a dismissive tone and returned to his eating. They looked at Evassanie inquiringly.

"My father says, it's no wonder that the Terrans all want to leave the"—flash of a   sheep pen again—"and come to live with us instead," she told them.

❧◖❦◗❧

Chev returned shortly afterward. His news was that they would
be spending a little time with some Cyreneans who were very eager
to meet the Terran "scientist," and that he thought they would find
interesting: people like themselves, who were curious about how the
world worked and what it was made of. The ones he had talked to
would be riding ahead today to tell the others. The three Terrans
would leave first thing next morning, and he would be traveling with
them.

CHAPTER TWENTY

Chev had taken the apartment's spare room, which could sleep only one person. For Shearer and Uberg, Antara had swept out an attic and cleared enough space between the boxes and bales of cloth that had been stored there to lay two mattresses on the floor. Jerri had done a little better, taking a spare bed in Evassanie's room. This arrangement delighted Evassanie, for besides having the Terran lady to herself to interrogate with endless questions about Earth and its peculiar ways after the household had finished supper and retired for bed, it meant that she had Nim in there with them too.

The room was rich with life and color, testifying to a busy mind with many interests and expressing the emerging individuality of young teenagers' personalized pads just about anywhere. Embroidered cushions with tassels and fringes lay scattered on the beds, lined the window seat, and filled a small armchair standing by a worktable beneath a wall covered with shelves and cabinets. A tailor's dummy stood in one corner, draped with a partly made garment; a narrow table beside it carried a litter of bowls, implements, and pieces of what looked like sculpture or pottery; and the walls were covered in tapestries and paintings, some framed, others just attached with pins, amid a miscellany of notes, ribbons, a couple of hats, and other ornaments. The shelves bore numerous books, along with an assortment of pots and vases, decorated boxes, and several dolls evidently carried over from childhood.

Evassanie's fascination with the NIDA hadn't abated, and she insisted on showing Jerri her collections of jewelry and spice bottles, favorite dresses in the hanging closet, selected books, contents of her needlework basket, and other treasures. Her ambition, she confided, was to paint landscapes and outdoor scenes, which offered endless scope in all kinds of decorative fields, making it an "honored" profession. Jerri would have liked to let her see some scenes of Earth from the ship's library through broad-field phone spectacles, but they had left all their trackable electronic devices behind. Then came the inevitable question of, "What do you do?"

Jerri did her best to describe the functions of an anthropologist. Evassanie listened with evident interest. A profession devoted to the study of people's origins and how different societies behaved and lived was a new concept to her. Earlier Terran researchers had reported on the conspicuous absence of much in the way of religious conviction among the Cyreneans, contrasting sharply with its universality on Earth. Evassanie didn't appear to find it a subject of great importance when Jerri asked her about it. The general Cyrenean view seemed to be that life and the universe were expressions of a powerful creative principle that was echoed in individual vision and inventive abilities, but what and why were not matters that they felt equipped to furnish answers on—and so didn't try to.

It was the same disinclination to bind themselves to chains of reasoning derived from assumptions that might be questionable, that Uberg had described. The Cyreneans trusted their intuition, and if it drew them in a particular direction, they followed it confidently. If it didn't, they made no attempt to second-guess the issue. Were it not for the results, everything that Jerri had learned and practiced as a scientist would have led her to expect the Cyrenean way to be inferior—a reliance on the kind of superstition and belief in dreams and "signs" that Earth had been outgrowing for centuries. It was galling—not to say more than a little humbling. Evassanie didn't help matters either by observing, when they had been discussing the subject for a while, "I suppose you need to study how different people live to see if you can find a better way than the one you've got." After a second of further reflection she added, "Is that why Terrans send ships out and build bases on all those other worlds at other stars?"

The suggestion was preposterous, but Jerri couldn't argue. By the standards that she herself had been defending for years, the Cyreneans were getting a lot of things right that cultures on Earth had sometimes aspired to and now were all but forgotten. It reminded her of something that Evassanie had said earlier.

"When you were talking about your father's shop downstairs, you said that he has a large staff of helpers and pays them well," she said.

"Right." Evassanie nodded.

"You made it sound like something people would approve of— the right way to run a business."

"Well, yes," Evassanie agreed, hesitating for a moment, as if it should have been obvious. "It pays the debt we owe to those who provide for us."

Jerri gave a quick frown and tossed up a hand. "But wouldn't there be more for him if he had fewer helpers and paid them less?" she said.

"Is that how they do it on Earth?"

"That's what they aim at, sure. Being efficient."

Jerri had to pause and think about that. "Then their ideal should be to employ nobody at all and pay nothing," she said finally. "If everyone did that, then nobody would be able to buy anything. Every business's workers are other businesses' customers. They'd all have no business. That doesn't sound very efficient."

They treated each other decently, Jerri told herself—not through fear of some insane, vengeful god, or to earn favors for personal gain, but because in the longer term it added up to a life that was better for everyone. Were all of them smart enough to have figured that out? Jerri didn't think so. For one thing, as Uberg had said, they didn't do much figuring out about anything. And for another, the problem had been subjected to several centuries of logical analysis beyond the point of exhaustion on Earth, and the inevitable verdict had always been that survival in the short term demanded selfishness, and if that reality of life was not heeded, whatever might or might not happen in the longer term didn't matter. So it had to be the "uncanny intuition" that Uberg had alluded to that enabled them to see further. Somehow the Cyreneans just *knew* when more immediately apparent benefits were illusory, and what would be genuinely better for them in the long run. Deferred gratification. Being able to recognize and act on it was supposed to be an indicator of intelligence. If so, the Cyrenean brand didn't correlate with any of the measures of intelligence that Jerri was familiar with. But it seemed to be fearsomely effective. She was glad she wasn't a con-artist trying to make a living among these people, she decided.

Later, when Evassanie had finally settled down and become still, Jerri stood at the window of the darkened room, staring out over the sleeping town. Its daytime lines had blended into blocks of shadow broken by scattered lighted windows and orange lamps in the streets and under the arches, and disconnected highlights and outlines cast by the paler light of Calypso emerging above clouds to the east. Nim, too, was unusually alert, sitting on his haunches on the window seat, tongue lolling and eyes wide, sharing her contemplation of the scene and absorbed in dog thoughts. Above the seat back, extending the width of the window outside, was a planter box containing a mixture of leafy growths and maybe a dozen blooms that Jerri had recognized earlier in the day as moon flowers. They stood now in their nocturnal regalia of large dark petals fully opened, reduced to eerie silhouettes in the moonlight, throwing distorted shadows on the glass.

What the Cyreneans called "long-sight" seemed to have its effects also in their history. Although, to be sure, there had been occasions when differences got out of hand or a local squabble boiled over to the point of people getting violent, they were rare. Cyrene had known nothing like the orgies of mass bloodletting and cruelties that Earth had known. The Cyreneans simply wouldn't follow leaders who would bring about such things, Jerri was beginning to realize. They sensed insincerity. They knew when the line they were being spun was for the spinner's ultimate benefit, not theirs.

She thought of the untold millions on Earth who had marched and cheered and hated, fought and bled, hacked each other to shreds, blown each other to pieces, rotted in jails, seen themselves and their families starve . . . all, at the end of it, for the enrichment and greater security of others, and to expand other people's authority and power. It couldn't happen on Cyrene. She was looking out at a whole world that would never let it, of people who would never be a part of it.

Just as surely, she found herself becoming aware with a strange clarity of mind that she couldn't remember ever experiencing before, yet not for a specific reason that she was able to pinpoint, that her future now lay here, on Cyrene. She felt as if she had never been completely alive until this moment and was knowing for the first time what it was to be fully conscious. Earth, even with all its memories and associations, seemed like a dream already fading, that had left impressions and fragmented images but no longer held anything of great consequence for her. She had no explanation, but crazy as it was, after a mere few days she had never felt more certain of anything in her life than that she *belonged* here.

She thought back to the Terran base that she had stayed in for precisely one night. The impression that came back to her was of a prison, with connotations of fear and degradation that were vivid emotionally but featureless in terms of anything definite that she could identify. She just *knew*.

Had she been there now, she realized, her only impulse would have been to get away.

CHAPTER TWENTY-ONE

Chev put Shearer in mind of brigands and buccaneers, or swash-bucklers from a Dumas novel. He was sturdily built, with brawny arms and shoulders, wavy black, neck-length hair, dark eyes, and a tanned, roguish face that carried a small, pointy beard and split into laughter at the least provocation. He had gone out by the time the three Terrans rose the next morning, but reappeared shortly after, wearing a short-sleeved leather jacket over a loose yellow shirt, voluminous pants tucked into calf-length, turned-over boots, and a jaunty hat. Although evidently thinking it to be an odd requirement, Soliki had procured Cyrenean clothes for the other three who were leaving. After making sure that they had all their things, Chev led them downstairs and out to the same carriage that brought them from Vattorix's residence. This time, however, Chev would be driving it himself. Antara and Soliki came out from the shop to see them off, and Antara gave Jerri a bag containing bread, cheese, fruits, and some Cyrenean wine for their journey, along with some scraps and a bone for Nim.

The drive through the town afforded more spectacle and novelty than they were able to take in. The usual Cyrenean extravaganzas of color and botany proliferated everywhere, with banks of shrubs and greenery fronting the buildings and finding their way into the alley-ways between, and trees lining the centers of the wider streets. Life thronged and bustled on every side. Small shops with gaily painted shutters beneath strangely scripted signs displayed wares ranging from foods, fabrics, and apparel, to pottery, metal goods, and art works. Arcades of stalls huddled beneath terraces of windowed apartments and roof gardens, and dark bazaars wound away out of sight among the archways and buildings. There were street entertainers drawing small crowds, performers dancing and reciting to peculiar music following an unfamiliar scale, strange odors and cooking scents. In one place a strong man was demonstrating his prowess; in another, an audience of children shrieked with mirth at some kind of mime and puppet show. Nim was transfixed with his head hanging out of the carriage window, paws on the ledge, several times getting involved in growling and barking exchanges with a number of lithe-limbed woolly creatures loose on the streets that hissed and appeared to be more a mixture of feline and ursine characteristics than canine, but seemed to fit into much the same niche.

There were the negative aspects too. The municipal trash collection department could have done with some improvement, and a minor river that they crossed via a bridge and then followed upstream for a short distance—from its direction, a tributary flowing into the channel that connected the lake to the bay—was oily and sluggish with discharges from dye works, tanneries, abattoirs, and innumerable other trades shops and yards. They seemed to have been mixed indiscriminately with the dwellings and amenities as circumstances and expedience dictated. The situation was not helped by the reliance on animal traffic, which inevitably left its mark everywhere as piles of dung shoveled aside to await removal, and in several places, foul-smelling gutters overflowing from blocked drains.

These were all things that were fixable, and in the fullness of time no doubt would be fixed. But as Jerri pointed out, they were just superficialities. More important, the underlying social bedrock, upon which the emerging culture was founded, was right. They didn't alienate themselves with delusions of independence, and turn competition into an obsession that made nastiness a virtue and brutality venerable. Apologists for the system back on Earth taught all the reasons why it couldn't be different, but somehow the Cyreneans had stumbled on a way whereby it could. And with the coming material abundance to be expected from the technologies that showed every sign of being imminent, things could surely only get better. The benefits would naturally find fair distribution without need of strife and struggle between each and all to fight for them. Jerri seemed to have undergone something akin to a sudden enlightenment, and had been enthusing about things Cyrenean all morning.

"Have you heard their story of why there are hes and shes, and why they pair up?" she asked the other two. She had on a knee-length belted tunic that reminded Shearer of Diana the Huntress, and over it a long, heavy, hooded cloak. They were coming into the outskirts of the town, with houses more spaced out among gardens, orchards, and tracts of open land. On one side, a small, festively dressed crowd suggestive of a wedding party were gathered outside a curvy building with a pointed dome.

"No," Shearer said, looking away from the carriage window. "What is it?"

"Evassanie told me last night. Originally, Nature had planned a totally competent, all-round capable being to inhabit the world, that would know everything and could do anything."

"That sounds like me when I was as teenager," Uberg commented. "I find myself going around saying what everyone does: Oh to be young again, knowing what I know now. But I'm beginning to suspect it's the wrong way around: Better to be the age I am, and knowing what I *thought* I knew then. Which was everything."

Shearer smiled. Jerri went on, "But it was too complicated, and so many things about it were irreconcilable with each other that it could never work. So what Nature did was split it into two individuals. So to recover the complete person, you have to join them together again. And that's why families have two parents. It needs both to *raise* kids. If it was just about making them, there are lots of other ways."

"I like it," Shearer said.

"So why does it take two with bugs, plants, and fish that just lay their eggs and swim away?" Uberg challenged. He meant it light-heartedly. In a dark green frock coat, cornered hat, and with his metal-rimmed spectacles, he looked like a character from light comic opera.

Jerri thought for a second, then shrugged. "Nature was practicing getting the machinery right." She looked back to take in Shearer as well. "But it doesn't stop with families. They see all of their society in the same kind of way—as a complex superorganism that needs all of them working togther to function. So is it surprising that things like wars and destructive rivalries never became a major problem?"

The daytime period at this time of year came in three phases. First was a Yocalan word derived from Goruno, the Yocalan word for Ra Beta, denoting the period of redder, lesser light brought by the rising of the more distant companion star, which commenced before most people were awake. Then there followed the brilliant "Two Kings," translated by Terrans as "full morning," that began with the rising of Ra Alpha and lasted for as long as both stars were visible in the sky. The final and also the longest phase was "Henkyl's Day," or simply "day," which lasted from the setting of Ra Beta in the west to when Ra Alpha followed. This was the beginning of the current four hours of darkness that completed the planet's twenty-eight hour rotational cycle. Since the onset of full morning was the normal time for getting up, the earlier part of the waking day was hottest. Therefore Cyreneans in general tended to begin their day slowly with social and more leisurely activities, and get down to their heavier business later.

The carriage emerged into open country on the north side of the town, where the road began winding its way upward between craggy folds of rocks, and ravines carved by fast-flowing streams. Among them, clumps of strange trees with thick, rounded boles and broad, bluish fronds stood above tangles of vines and brush. At the top of the climb the terrain leveled out into a vista of broad, rounded slopes extending away to the north. Little changed for what must have been several hours, and then they came to a settlement of houses and out-lying farms that Chev informed them was known as Vigagawly.

It had one or two stores and a staging post, where they stopped to change horses. While a groom took the carriage around to the stable, Chev brought his charges inside to meet the proprietor, who was evidently an old acquaintance. He produced a hot brew and a dish of something like quiche with spinach to supplement the food that Antara had provided. Meanwhile, word of the Earth aliens' arrival had traveled quickly, and before they had finished their meal they found themselves being investigated by a deputation of children from the village, while curious adults in an assortment of smocks and trousered work outfits hovered in the background. Chev had no time for such mincing uncertainty, and bellowed at the children to come and introduce themselves and not just stand there. Some at once complied rambunctiously, while others were more shy and hung back. The more forward among them proceeded eagerly to show off their mastery of such phrases as, "Hello," "Goodbye," and "What is your name?" Evidently, other Terrans had passed this way before. Interesting, Shearer thought.

The children were also accompanied by a couple of domestic bear-cat creatures like the ones in town, one with spiky orange fur and black markings, the other smoother and a uniform tan color. After the ritual exchange of suspicious hisses and growls, with encouragement from their respective owners they and Nim seemed to accept each other and settle down. Shearer's NIDA was unable to find a word for them and kept evoking images of dogs, which would be of no use when he was talking to a Cyrenean and wanted to refer to one or the other. Overriding the associative function, he touched the button on the control unit attached to his belt—it didn't emit a tracking signal that Terran satellites could pick up—to ask the system for the nearest phonetic rendering of the Yocalan word.

"*Glok*," the vocalization in his head supplied. Shearer confirmed the option to use it. And *glok* it would henceforth be.

By the time they were ready to set off again, Ra Beta had set in the west, ushering in the start of what Shearer thought of as a normal day with one sun in the sky. Jerri and Uberg had gotten into a debate about Cyrenean social values and customs that sounded likely to continue. So leaving them to it, Shearer elected to ride up on the driver's box with Chev.

It was not open in the style of coaches from a comparable period on Earth, but had its own shade roof, along with side and rear shutters that could be opened in fine weather or for better all-round view. The vehicle body was carried above a chassis and axles on a system of U-shaped springs resembling huge tuning forks, and the wheels had tires of a resilient tubular material that looked like power cable, but which Chev said was a toughened and processed variety of vine. He showed Shearer a length carried in the trunk for on-the-road repairs. It had a leathery outer skin and cellular interior composition somewhat like sponge.

Beyond the village, the road continued as little more than a track meandering to follow the contours across more rolling country of grassy hills and hollows. Scattered along the way, standing alone or in small groves, were plants ten to twenty feet high with wide stalks flaring at their tops into crowns of rounded yellow and green knobs, looking like giant broccoli. Birds of many kinds screeched and chattered among them, or circled in flocks above, and several breeds of apparently domesticated animals browsed in the lusher areas of grass, indifferent to the passing carriage. From time to time they encountered some that had wandered onto the road ahead, forcing Chev to yell them into moving, or else make cautious detours with wheels going up on the verges. And yes!—Shearer thumped the roof of the passenger compartment to draw the attention of the two inside. "Look . . . over there!" he called to them. A group of four or five that had central horns on their heads, although curved forward rather than straight. "Real unicorns!"

Except that the rest of them was decidedly more piglike than horselike.

Evassanie had shown Chev the wonders of her NIDA set, and after experimenting a little and being astonished at the results, he had become eager to try it out at greater length. His knowledge of English otherwise was very slight. When Shearer produced one, Chev donned it in the normal way and then put his hat back on top of it. They found that its operation was unimpaired.

"You know," Shearer said, drinking in the openness and isolation, and drawing a long breath of the subtly scented air, "A lot of people back on Earth would give up all their machines and electronic toys to live somewhere like this if they had the choice. It would be their ideal."

Chev snorted and laughed. "It's easy to think things like that when you have a choice. When it's what you have to do, maybe it's not so ideal. Maybe they should be up here in the middle of a winter in the hard years. Ask the farmers back there that we just saw in Vigagawly. They know."

"Some people on Earth think we have too many machines."

Chev thought about it for a while, as if trying to see what the problem was. "Well, you can eat too much food too. That doesn't mean there's something wrong with food. You just stop when you've had enough. Don't they know when they've got enough machines?"

"There are whole industries with huge numbers of people telling them all the time they need more," Shearer replied. "They put a model picture inside your mind, of how you should live, and what it takes to live that way. Then, when you look at what you've got and compared it with what they've made you think you ought to have, you're never satisfied or content. And that's the idea."

Chev shook his head and made a face that seemed to ask how that could happen. "So are the people who chase after these pictures like seeds drifting with the wind—blown this way or that way by something outside themselves? Have they nothing inside to give them direction?" He released a hand from the reins and jerked a thumb several times at his chest. "I am the only person who knows who I am and what I want to be. How can anyone else tell me?"

"So who are you?" Shearer asked, glad to get away from Terran politics. "Tell me then, Chev, what do you do?" It was a change to be asking the question of a Cyrenean.

"Me?" Chev laughed loudly. "I am different people at different times. I change as the seasons change. When the harder winters come, and Goruno has disappeared from the sky, I am a citizen of the town. It might be Revo. Or maybe it is somewhere else. It depends where I've ended up. That is when I put in my due."

"How?" Shearer asked.

Chev let go the reins to close an imaginary pair of tongs, then held them with one hand while swinging a hammer with the other, at the same time making loud clanging and banging noises. "I tame the shiny metals that the rocks shed as tears, and shape them into beautiful things. Useful things . . . Beautiful useful things. What is the difference? Tools for craftsmen and farmers; gates for gardens, and pots for kitchens; hinges, bolts, handles, and chains; knives, reapers, axes, swords. . . . I can make you anything."

"Sounds like a good way of keeping warm in winter," Shearer agreed.

"Then in the long, mild seasons, when Goruno has reappeared near Henkyl again, and they begin the long dance that will take them away from each other to their own halves of the sky, or after the summer, when they are moving together again . . ."

"Where we are right now," Shearer interjected.

"Yes. Most years I become a sailor and go to foreign lands. But this year I am a king's agent. Having the Terrans here means that

Vattorix and his counselors have more things to take care of and need extra help." Chev shrugged. "So I do whatever is wanted. "Sail a boat. Drive a carriage. Deliver things to places. . . ."

Smuggle disillusioned Terrans away, Shearer thought to himself. Perhaps not the most tactful of subjects to pursue. "So what about the summers?" he asked instead.

"Ah, when each sun has its own day. Those are the times of my life for relaxation, reflection, and the finer things." Chev emitted another laugh. It seemed to be a huge joke that Shearer didn't quite get. "Then we have the me of the many faces." He turned sideways and doubled over in his seat to make an exaggerated bow, doffing his hat at the same time, then sat up and turned it over as if begging; he clapped a hand to his chest with a suddenly fierce expression, and then made an imbecilic face and tittered inanely.

"An actor," Shearer realized suddenly. "It's when you socialize and entertain others."

"Not just an actor." Chev burst into song, delivered as several bars of resonant baritone. The NIDA rendered them rhymelessly as:

"When the two kings rule high, and the night fades and dies,
The body seeks rest and cool water's delights,
But the soul has its wine and the pretty girls-O"

He glanced sideways, mouthing a silent "Ow" that Shearer took to be the Cyrenean equivalent of a wink.

"Is that a Yocalan song?" Shearer asked.

"From an island called Quoselt—three days sailing west from Revo. They have some pretty girls there, all right."

"Are their ways and customs like yours here—in Yocala?" Shearer asked.

"Oh, very similar," Chev said. "We are the same culture." A NIDA-injected comment cautioned Shearer that "race" might have been meant. "But they are close to us. In farther parts of the world—months of sailing, maybe—you find others that are different."

"Don't you ever end up fighting with each other?" Shearer asked. "Are there never wars?" The NIDA apparently had difficulty finding an association for the word, and presumably failed to activate any suitable concept in Chev visually. Shearer had to supplement it with an explanation. Chev seemed astounded and unable to see how it could achieve any worthwhile aim. "Whatever the problem is about, fighting over it will always end up costing everybody more than it would have taken to solve it," he opined.

That was a sentiment with which Shearer agreed totally, and had been arguing—usually in vain—for a good part of his life. But he was still curious as to how they managed to avoid such things on Cyrene. "How do you stop both sides from plunging into it, each one thinking they're going to gain?" he asked.

"They would both be wrong," Chev said.

"True. But getting them to understand it up front is another matter. And even after they've learned, they'll forget, and do the same thing all over again next time."

"That's how it is on Earth?" Chev queried.

"All the time. Our whole history."

"Yes. So I have heard."

"But it doesn't happen like that here?"

Chev shook his head. "No. It wouldn't happen that way on Cyrene."

"How do you prevent it?"

"Cyreneans would never believe they could gain from something like that. They would know."

Shearer sat back on the seat nonplussed. Just when he'd thought he was about to get a straight answer at last, once again there was no attempt at an explanation or reasoning to justify the assertion. Just this eternal, impervious Cyrenean falling back on gut-feel intuition again, which told him nothing.

He tried another angle. "You said that you make swords."

"The best," Chev agreed.

"We met a Cyrenean the day we landed at the base. A man called Korsofal. He lives south from the city somewhere."

Chev shook his head. "I do not know him."

"He was carrying one. It was hanging from his saddle. Why would he need it if you don't resort to force?"

"I didn't say that," Chev replied. "I said that whole peoples don't take to slaughtering each other and destroying each other's lands in the ways you described. Because no good could come of it, and they would know." He tossed up a hand, the reins draping over it loosely.

"But some people will always exist who would live by taking for themselves what others create, and returning nothing. And who can only be restrained from doing so by force."

"Criminals, you mean?"

"Yes, exactly. So it is a wise thing to have weapons."

"For defense," Shearer said. He didn't have much argument with that. But to his surprise he saw that Chev was frowning as if not fully agreeing with him.

"It's more than that," Chev said at last. "If you have to use it, then its purpose has already been defeated."

"You mean it's a deterrent," Shearer said, getting the point . . . he thought.

But Chev continued frowning. "More than even that. A deterrent would discourage a criminal from committing a criminal act. What I'm talking about is stopping the criminal from becoming a criminal in the first place."

This time it was Shearer's turn to frown. "I'm not sure what you mean. How could that work?"

"Well, I'll put it this way. If it was in your nature to try and make your living that way, in which kind of a society would you be more likely to prosper if you were to act on it and become a robber, and in which kind would you be more likely to prosper and live longer if you decided on an honest job? One that had swords, or one that didn't have swords?"

"Okay." Shearer held up a hand and nodded. "I take your point. Its just that . . ." He hated being negative, but he had to shake his head. "Can you really expect to rely on the kind of people who become criminals to figure out something like that?"

"On Earth, maybe. Yes, from what I've heard that's probably very true."

"So why should it be any different here?" Shearer asked.

"Oh, here we're not much good at figuring out anything," Chev replied. "A Cyrenean would just *know*."

Shearer gave up and returned to contemplating the view.

CHAPTER TWENTY-TWO

As part of his specialty training for the Cyrene mission, Dolphin, currently operating as Jeff Lang, had undergone a speed course to familiarize him with the basics of the Yocalan language—as much as could be gleaned in the brief period of human contact, anyway. Even though the mission had been thrown together at short notice, he found it was sufficient to get by.

Dressed native-fashion in a hooded cloak, cord-tied tunic, and baggy pants with boots to add plausibility to his story, he sat at a table in an alcove near the serving counter of an inn near the waterfront on the northern side of the river dividing Revo town. The day had cooled after the fierce morning period, and people were beginning to leave and go about their business. A young waitress with fair hair tied in two long tails, and wearing a full, ankle-length skirt was bringing trays loaded with dishes of food through from a room at the rear. The brew in the earthenware mug in front of him tasted malty and nutty with a slightly sour edge—not bad, but on the warm side for his taste. His injection into Cyrenean society had happened a lot more suddenly than anyone had anticipated. It was too soon yet for him to have formed any firm impressions of it.

The innkeeper, whom Lang had spoken with earlier, got up from where he had been talking to three men at a bench beneath the window and came over. "Would they have 'ad an animal with 'em?" he inquired, lowering himself to rest against one of the stools. "A black one with a long face. Makes a funny noise like a stuck door scrapin'."

"That sounds like them," Lang said, straightening up.

The innkeeper turned his head back toward the group he had just left. "'E says it might be. 'Ow many was they, Orban?" He looked at Lang. "Two men an' a girl, was it yer said?"

"Right."

"Two men an' a girl, we're looking for," the innkeeper called over.

"Well, I don't know how many were in there . . ." one of the three answered, followed by something Lang didn't catch.

"Come over 'ere and tell 'em, then." The innkeeper waved an arm. A thin, dark headed man in a blue smock and short black jacket, who was presumably Orban, got up and shuffled over. The innkeeper gestured at Lang. "'E's another one of 'em that's wants out. 'E was supposed to meet up with some others, 'e says, but 'e missed 'em some'ow an' thinks they might be in the town. Two men an' a girl, 'e says they are."

"Well, I never actually saw them myself . . ."

"Tell '*im*, not me."

Orban turned his face toward Lang. "I didn't see them myself. But there was a carriage that went along the Corn Market Street that caused a bit of a stir. It had this black animal sticking its head out the window and making a noise, starting all the *gloks* off. And one boy I heard who was there said there was a woman in it too. Dark hair, kind of red."

"That's them," Lang said, nodding.

"An' you said they were comin' from Soliki's?" the innkeeper checked.

"Well, I don't know that for sure. But I did hear tell this morning that some Terrans were staying with Soliki these last two nights."

The innkeeper looked at Lang. "Soliki the draper's. In the square where the monument is. You know it?"

Lang spread his hands. "I only got here a few days ago."

"'E don't know where it is," the innkeeper relayed to Orban.

Orban scratched his chin. "A few days? Why are they in such a rush to leave?"

"'E don't know where Soliki's is," the innkeeper said again.

"Do you think we'll have a whole world of them coming here?"

Lang took a Cyrenean coin from a pocket in his tunic and slid it along the table to the innkeeper. "That's to cover one for him, on me, when he gets back," he said.

Orban looked mildly grieved. "Oh, I'll take you to Soliki's," he said. "You didn't have to do that, sir. But I don't mind if I do. Thank you very much."

CHAPTER TWENTY-THREE

The name of the place the carriage arrived at late in the day after descending into a steep-sided valley was Doriden. It consisted of four main stone buildings situated around a central quadrangle, standing beside a deeply cut stream, and several smaller buildings around the outside and across the stream, that appeared to have been added later. Two bridges spanned the stream to connect the two parts of the institution, and standing between them on the opposite bank was a mill house with a waterwheel. Beyond the outbuildings on the far side were vegetable plots, a fruit orchard, and paddocks with various types of animals. The hillside above was planted with rows of plants that could have been some kind of corn or vine.

Shearer's NIDA translated its function as a "monastery of learning." From what he could make of the answers he got from Chev, it didn't confer diplomas or degrees, and so probably didn't qualify as a "university," but nevertheless had sufficiently strong connotations with more than just the process of learning to be let off as an "academy" or a "college." The NIDA's choice of "monastery" seemed odd, since Cyrene—or at least, the Yocalan part of it—didn't boast much to speak of in the way of structured religion. More questioning by Shearer produced the impression that what the NIDA had latched on to was the concept of dedication to seeking truth and understanding to help make the world a better place.

This was reinforced later in the evening, when the four arrivals sat down at one of the long tables in the communal dining hall for dinner with a member of the staff called Blanborel, who had greeted

them, and several others. The guests had been expected as a result of
Chev's talking with the people from Doriden who had ridden ahead
the previous day, and had found rooms prepared and baths heated
for them to clean up after their day of traveling.

"Other people produced this food I'm eating and the clothes I'm
wearing," Blanborel explained. "And then there are those who can
make a house that stays up or a boat that doesn't leak. And those are
not the kinds of things I'm best at or have any great fondness for, to
be honest. But those things all require work. And through better
understanding of how the world works . . ." he made a sweeping gesture that took in Shearer, Jerri, and Uberg, "which Chev tells us is
what you do in life, we try to find ways in which work can achieve
better results. So that is our claim to worth and respect." Blanborel
made the silent "Ow" that was the Cyrenean equivalent of a wink and
lowered his voice behind a raised hand. "At least, that is what we
have to say. And it's true as far as it goes. But if you really want to
know the truth, sheer curiosity plays as big a part. It does for me,
anyway. I just *have* to know. Isn't it the same for you Terrans? I
mean, really—deep down inside. Eh?"

He was large and rotund, with a fleshy, ruddy face, graying beard,
and shaggy hair. After the NIDA's determination of "monastery,"
Shearer couldn't help thinking of him as the Abbot. He even had a
cowl-like hood thrown back from the long jacket that he was wearing.

"That wouldn't do for me," Chev, eating heartily, told the table.

"Different people everywhere think in their own way," Uberg
said. Since there were only enough NIDA sets to equip Chev,
Blanborel, and a colleague of Blanborel's called Zek, the Terrans
either spoke through them, or else slowly in pidgin sentences that
mixed in bits of Yocalan. In addition, some of them had a grasp of
rudimentary English, perhaps picked up from other travelers.

Darco, a young man sitting next to Blanborel, who could have
been some kind of student and had been listening intently, leaned
forward to address the Terrans. "Tell me, is it true," he said. "The far
distance stars like from where you are come from." He used the point
of the knife that he was eating with to separate out a seed grain
suspended in a smear of sauce on the edge of his plate. "There is your
Earth star, yes? Or is maybe like Henkyl. Because is said Henkyl star
also. Just more near. "

"Okay," Shearer agreed.

"Then next near other star same size is where Revo city. True is this, yes?"

"That's about it." Shearer nodded.

"But Earth star is not next near. Is far away very more. Maybe like other side Yocala. True is this, yes?"

"Right on." Shearer nodded again.

"Amazing," Blanborel said, shaking his head..

"Don't worry about it. It still amazes us too," Jerri told him. Darco sat back and exchanged mystified looks with colleagues who had been helping each other to follow.

One of them put a question to Blanborel, who relayed, "You come here in ships that are bigger than the bird-ships that land at your camp by Revokanta." That was the name of the lake east of Revo city.

"You can see them crossing the sky at night," Chev put in.

"They don't have sails like ships or wings like birds. And anyway, they must travel much faster than sails or wings could make. So what do they have?"

Shearer and Uberg looked at each other helplessly. How did one begin explaining a Heim drive? Then Shearer remembered the stream outside, that flowed through the middle of Doriden. "Imagine that the space between the stars . . . the whole universe that you see . . . is like the water that a fish in the stream down by the mill swims in," he said. They all watched him intently. "The fish only knows the water. That is its universe. To get to, let's say Revokanta, it would have to swim down, out to the ocean, and around through all the water that exists between Doriden and there. But now think of the bird who can rise above that universe and fly there outside the water. . . . Our ship is like the bird." He looked around, but it didn't seem he had quite got the point across. The questions were not exactly pouring back in a flood.

Darco came in. "I think the question was more what makes the . . ." He looked around, asking for the word.

"Force," Blanborel supplied.

"Okay, the force that pushes the ships." Darco held up a cupped hand and blew into it, at the same time moving it away. "Like with the sail ship, is the wind. Because you don't have bird-horses, no?" He grinned and the others laughed.

"It's an invisible force," Uberg tried. He picked up a bread bowl from the table and rocked it up and down on the palm of a hand as if weighing it. "Like the force that you can feel pulling things down toward the ground. But the one we produce is a lot stronger."

"Do you mean electricity?" Zek asked. Shearer blinked in surprise. Zek looked at Blanborel, and then both of them beamed at the Terrans proudly, as if it had been a secret that they had been waiting for the right moment to reveal.

"Oh yes, we are familiar with it here," Blanborel said. "It's not all wind, water, and animals, you know."

"Well, yes, electrical forces do come into it," Shearer said. He hoped he wasn't going to be asked just how strong they were. He had once calculated the relative strengths of the gravitational and electrical forces—thirty-nine orders of magnitude—was about the same as a millionth of a millimeter to a hundred thousand times the size of the known universe.

However, Zek went on, "Although I admit we haven't worked out how to put it to much practical use yet. But I'm sure that will all come in its own time."

Blanborel took in the expressions on the faces of his three alien guests with evident satisfaction. "We had intended to show you around tomorrow to see some of the things we're doing here," he informed them. "But since you seem interested, we could make it this evening, after we finish eating, if you wish."

They interrogated each other silently, each nodding in turn. "Yes," Uberg answered for all of them. "I think we'd like that very much."

"Well, let's eat up, then," Blanborel said, waving at the table.

Zek turned his head to the students who were with them. "And any of you can join us too," he told them. "I'd recommend it. This isn't a chance that you get every day. And it might be some of the best education you'll get this year."

CHAPTER TWENTY-FOUR

The mixed party of Cyreneans and Terrans crossed the stream via one of the bridges and followed a path to the entrance of a long, low building of adobe-like walls with a peculiarly curved sloping roof, one end of which abutted the mill house. Nim had already found new admirers and was being entertained elsewhere. Inside, the stone floors, heavy timber framing, and large spaces connecting through wide openings gave a first impression of a large stable or farm building. But the rooms they passed through turned out to be workshops, with tool racks, benches fitted with vises, shelves of jars and bottles, tables with burners and assorted glassware, and a number of ovens and furnaces. Shearer was able to identify several hydraulic devices and a piece of clockwork of some kind that seemed to be experimental setups. In addition there were various systems of levers and pulleys, a crank-driven piston and cylinder that looked like a pump, and other mechanisms whose function was not immediately apparent. Although quiet now, the place had the look about it of being busy during the day. It was a long way from Berkeley and belonged to another age, but Shearer had a feeling of being at home.

Zek led the way through to the mill house at the end of the building. It contained not a mill as such, they could now see, but a power plant. The main shaft from the waterwheel drove an open system of metal and wooden gearing, from which belts running on pulleys turned three secondary shafts. The secondary shafts were running faster than the input shaft and connected to drum assemblies sprouting levers and screw adjusters that were clearly clutches, each having an output shaft that was at present stationary.

One of the output shafts went to a set of vertical slides ten feet or so high constraining a cylindrical weight to drop onto an anvil—a powered drop hammer. Another drove a reciprocating saw moved by a crank. But the setup that Zek led the group to stood apart to one side. It was in the form of a circular metal yoke three feet or so in diameter, standing on a sturdy wooden plinth. Four squat pole pieces at right angles projected inward from the yoke, their inner faces concave so that together they defined a circular central space. Inside the space was a rotor mounted on bearings, separated from the pole pieces by a narrow gap. The pole pieces and the rotor were wound with thick metal turns that looked like copper. Nearby was a wooden board mounting hefty brass terminals and copper breaker switches. Zek and Blanborel looked at the visitors inquiringly. Shearer smiled in undisguised delight and admiration.

"I suppose you know what it is?" Jerri said to him.

"Almost out of a Faraday museum. A basic DC dynamo—or a motor if you run it backward."

Inwardly, Shearer was surprised at just how familiar it seemed, and by its advancement conceptually. He had a suspicion there was more than a little Terran influence here. The space beyond where the machine stood was an entire electrical lab, with large earthenware and glass pots containing metal forms immersed in liquids—obviously primitive storage cells—more windings and mechanisms, and a bench with wires, springs, gauges, and a balance, on which some kind of measurements seemed to be in progress. Muttering had broken out among the students. A few who were evidently conversant with the work were explaining things to the others—and evidently enjoying the opportunity to show off a little.

"My talking hat didn't understand the name you used," Blanborel told Shearer. "I assume it was a Terran."

"A famous person in our history," Shearer replied. "He discovered similar things."

"You mean concerning electricity?"

"Yes."

"How long ago would that have been?"

Shearer did a quick mental calculation. "Between a hundred and a hundred-twenty of your years."

"Fascinating!"

"Are you going to get it going for us?" Uberg asked.

"Of course," Blanborel replied. "But that's Zek's department. . . . Zek?"

Zek was already moving forward. "I was afraid they weren't going to ask," he said.

Chev, looking mystified, gestured at Shearer appealingly. "The shaft from the wheel outside turns those wheels, and they work the hammer and the saw. That, I can see. And yes it's very ingenious. But you're more interested in this bird cage thing." He waved at the dynamo. "I don't understand what it is."

Before Shearer could answer, Zek worked a couple of levers on the clutch controlling the dynamo drive shaft. To the accompaniment of clunking and whirring, the rotor of the dynamo began turning. As Zek eased one of the levers forward, the rotor gained speed until it was turning as fast as the input shaft to the clutch. The knowledgeable students were giving a commentary in Yocalan to the others and seemed to be coaxing them to come closer, but the neophytes to this arcane art appeared less sure.

"So what is it supposed to do?" Chev hissed again at Shearer as Zek moved over to the switchboard. Shearer raised a hand saying he would see in a moment.

Zek stood facing his audience for a moment, rubbing his hands together and showing his teeth like a conjuror about to deliver his finale. Then he turned, closed a circuit, and began moving a sliding knob, at the same time watching a pointer moving in a slot on a vertical graduation like a thermometer scale. Astonished gasps erupted from the onlookers. Some of the more trusting who had begun edging forward withdrew hastily again.

A glass tube clamped in a stand on the bench had begun to glow with a reddish light at one end. As Zek continued moving the slider, the glow extended along the tube, at the same time intensifying until it had become pale, shimmering orange. A reverent silence fell for what seemed a long time as the company took in the sight. Then, gradually, they came back to life again one by one, and questions began coming from all sides. Leaving one of his acolytes to deal with them and another to watch the switchboard, Zek came over to where the visitors were standing.

"So," Zek pronounced. "What do you think? Will we be traveling to the stars a hundred years from now? Coming to visit you at Earth, maybe?"

"It could be a lot sooner, from some of the things I've heard," Uberg said.

"Would your Faraday have approved of our efforts?" Zek had obviously straightened the name out with his NIDA unit.

"You'd need to ask Marc," Uberg said, indicating Shearer. "My business is flowers and trees."

"Apart from making light in a bottle, what use is it?" Chev asked.

"Faraday was asked that question too," Shearer said. "His answer was, What use is a newborn baby?"

"Oh, excellent!" Zek exclaimed. "I must remember that. I intend, shamelessly, to steal it."

"I'm sure he won't mind," Shearer said

"Marc!" Jerri gave him a reproachful nudge.

The acolyte at the switchboard, having satisfied himself that all was well there for the time being, moved across to the dynamo, picked up an oil can that looked like an Aladdin lamp with a long spout, and proceeded to administer doses of the contents to holes above the rotor and clutch bearings. Zek ushered the others to the end of the bench and indicated a coil surrounding a metal core, held vertically in a frame. Several inches below it on the bench was a slab of metal the size of a typical book. When Zek closed a switch, it leaped up to attach itself to the end of the core with a loud *clack*.

"It can move things," Zek said, looking at Chev and answering the question he had asked Shearer. "You look like a pretty strong fellow, Chev. All the same, I'll bet you anything you care to name that we can rig up a lifter that you couldn't beat." Chev replied with a dip of his head and made an exaggerated gesture of conceding. Zek turned to Shearer. "We're not sure yet exactly what the law is that describes the process. But the inspiration for the way to find out will doubtless come in its own time." He looked at Uberg and grinned. "Do you know which flowers Faraday listened to?"

Shearer was still puzzling over this odd remark, when Blanborel remarked. "The magnet doesn't have to be in the same place as the generator." Shearer's NIDA was pulling the terms from his own vocabulary. "We're stringing a wire across to my room on the other side. Zek can get it to make a click at one end when a switch is pressed at the other end. We're working out a code that will enable us to talk to each other." He gave Zek a doubtful look, as if worried about him, and then confided in a stage whisper, "He thinks we'll be able to talk to people in Revo one day, too. But I think that might be a bit far-fetched. Don't you?"

"Well, don't go too crazy with the bets," Shearer advised. "We talk to people back on Earth."

That seemed to be all there was to see. But then Zek, beckoning, led the way over to a door in the rear wall and turned an iron ring to open it. Beyond was large open space with windows high in the wall on the far side and a rectangular pit several feet deep excavated in the floor, apparently in the process of being prepared for something.

"The water mill is all right up to a point," Zek said, standing aside as they came through to look. "But it can be erratic. When there hasn't been much rain up in the mountains, we know that things are going to get slow here—maybe even come to a standstill. But there is another land north of Yocala, called Ibennis . . ."

"We know of it," Jerri confirmed.

"And a man there called Wolaxal has made engines that turn by steam. They use them there to pump water for the fields. He's going to come to stay in Doriden for a while, and build one for us here." As Zek spoke, he watched the faces of the Terrans carefully, as if looking for a reaction. He waited a few seconds and then asked, "Do you think that would be a good idea?"

"Splendid!" Shearer said without hesitation. This was the equivalent of two hundred years after Aristotle? At this rate they'd be flying while Zek was still alive.

"Why? Do you not think so?" Uberg asked Zek.

"We're not sure," Zek replied. He paused and seemed to think for a moment. "The Terrans who were here before seemed to think there were better ways."

So Shearer's suspicion had been correct. They weren't the first Terrans to have come to Doriden. "Better ways?" he repeated.

Zek looked at Blanborel, who explained, "They had been to faraway parts of Cyrene that even we have never seen. They told us that there exist in such places vast underground lakes of substances like plant and animal oils, but more powerful. And we could build better engines that use these."

"Without the furnaces and boilers that Wolaxal's engines need," Zek said.

Shearer thought about it and looked dubious. The two Cyreneans eyed each other meaningfully, as if it confirmed something they had suspected. "You don't seem so happy at the idea," Blanborel remarked.

Shearer wasn't quite sure where to begin. "I know what they're talking about," he said. "And it's not that the idea it isn't a good one. But the technology to use such fuels isn't something that can just stand on its own. It's part of a bigger picture that all has to go together. It needs . . ." he gestured back in the direction of the door they had come through, "a developed science of electricity; machining and measurement precision much finer than what you can get away with using steam; a whole supporting industry of extraction and refining methods that you don't have yet. . . . It would be like trying to build a carriage before you have mastered carpentry. Surely whoever proposed the idea would have known this."

"They weren't suggesting that we do it ourselves," Blanborel said. "They said they would provide all the support. It would make Yocala all-powerful among the nations of Cyrene, and Vattorix would become an invincible conqueror, able to impose his will every-where." Jerri threw Shearer a look that said *now* it was starting to make sense. Blanborel concluded, "Why they thought that we or Vattorix would wish such things, I do not know."

"So what was in it for them?" Shearer asked resignedly. The Cyreneans looked uncertainly at each other.

"What did they want?" Jerri said.

"Oh, I see. . . ." Blanborel nodded. "They would be entitled to appoint an advisor to sit on Vattorix's forum of counselors. Also, they would retain the ownership rights for supply elsewhere on Cyrene once the means to produce the fuel were set up in the regions where the underground lakes exist."

The Terrans received the information with ominous looks. "And what happened?" Uberg asked. "Did Vattorix make any such agreement?"

Blanborel shook his head. "No. As I said, he could not under-stand their reasons. And then after a while, we stopped hearing any more about it. I think the Terrans started having other problems."

"That's nice to know, anyway," Shearer said, sounding relieved.

"You wouldn't have approved?"

"It's a long story," Shearer answered. "But let's just say that things our leaders do are not always things we agree with. That's why a lot of Terrans have been leaving." He hoped he wasn't going to be called upon to give a long explanation. Again, there was an exchange of questioning looks between Blanborel and Zek. Finally, Blanborel gave Zek a quiet nod.

Zek turned toward the Terrans. "We must confess to you that this is not the first time we have heard the things you have just told us. But there seem to be two kinds of Terrans. Some want to go their own way and live among us. But they have to hide their movements from others who would try to prevent them. We needed to be sure which kind you were."

Uberg looked surprised. "I thought Chev would already have told you. We are on our way to join another Terran who left earlier. His name is Wade. Chev is escorting us—I believe, acting on Vattorix's behalf."

"Oh, yes, we know about that," Blanborel agreed, smiling faintly. "But we couldn't know what happened to Wade's communications inside the Terran camp. You could have been someone pretending to be Uberg, sent to find out where he went."

"He's got a point," Shearer murmured, nodding at Uberg and Jerri.

"And what Marc said about energy technologies convinced you?" Jerri said, looking puzzled. "I don't understand."

"It was not what the Terrans who tried to tempt Vattorix said," Zek explained. "They wanted to supply and control everything for us, so that we would be forced to follow their policies. But it was exactly what we were told by another Terran, whom we do trust completely."

"Who?" Shearer asked.

"Your Professor Wade!" Zek answered. Blanborel grinned as if it were a huge joke.

"He was here?"

"Oh yes. We learned much from him." Zek inclined his head toward the doorway, just as a burst of crackling—unmistakably a spark discharge—came from the other side, along with alarmed shouts. "He gave us a lot of advice on building the dynamo. I won't pretend it was all our own doing."

"The clicking telegraph was his suggestion too," Blanborel put in.

So everything was going fine, and they were already en route to wherever Wade was. Chev had presumably not said so back at Soliki's to avoid giving clues as to their destination that could find their way back to the wrong place.

Jerri, however, seemed unsure about something. "But is holding back from a more effective technology really in your better interests?" she asked Blanborel. "Especially if you've got Terran interference to think about too. I don't know . . ." She looked questioningly at Shearer.

"No, that wasn't what I meant," Blanborel said. "Professor Wade told us that trying to go straight to oil would be impractical for all the reasons that Marc just said. He saw steam as a necessary intermediate step—to be got through quickly. The main thing he cautioned against was surrendering any rights and ownership. He urged us to be patient and wait a little to develop technologies we understood and that would be our own, rather than be rushed into something the Terrans would control. And I'm pretty sure he persuaded Vattorix."

Shearer stared at him thoughtfully. Now he thought he was beginning to see why Interworld were so anxious to track Wade down and rein him in. If this was the kind of thing he had been spreading, it could put the corporation's plans back years—maybe put paid to them permanently. Back in Berkeley, Shearer had heard him remonstrate on how the system of exploitation was too firmly in place and universal for its hold to be broken now. It seemed as if he might have embarked on a personal mission to make sure the same thing didn't happen on Cyrene. That sounded like Wade, all right.

"It wouldn't have happened anyway," Zek said. "Now I know why I went ahead and sent the invitation to Wolaxal to have him build us one of his engines."

Shearer stared at him perplexedly. It was the crazy Cyrenean inversion of logic—or lack of it—again. How could Zek have made such a decision with seeming confidence, and only now know why? He was determined to get to the bottom of this.

"Why didn't you think the Terran deal would go through?" he asked Zek. "Did you talk with some of Vattorix's people who had debated it?"

Zek shook his head. "I'm not sure if anyone debated it," he said. "It just didn't feel good."

"I'd have thought you would understand," Blanborel said to Uberg. "Didn't you say you know about flowers?" Uberg could only return a baffled look. The two Cyreneans nodded to each other in a way that said they had seen this before.

"Don't tell me. On Cyrene, you just get to know these things," Shearer said for them.

CHAPTER TWENTY-FIVE

Orban, the thin man whom the innkeeper had introduced the day previously, took Lang along a cobbled alley and into a narrow street that led past a feed merchant's yard and a shop displaying saddlery and horse harnessware. The day was into the later part of the cooler period that came after the first sun's setting. The draper had been able tell them only that the fugitives had left with somebody called Chev to spend a day or two with people who wanted to meet the Terran "scientists." He didn't know how far away or in which direction. One of the several stable owners that Orban and Lang talked to had told them he might have some news later today.

Orban had also taken Lang to meet some of the departed Terrans who had chosen to remain close to the base and gone to ground in various parts of the town. One was teaching algebra and geometry; a couple who had moved into rooms near the docks were running a bar, into which they had introduced darts, checkers, and a pool table that they had commissioned a local carpenter to build, and were doing quite a trade; an ex-Milicorp trooper had moved in with a Cyrenean girl and become foreman for a construction crew. But none of them had heard anything about a recently arrived party matching the description of Shearer and his companions.

"I thought about it this morning after I woke up, but if you don't mind, sir, I'll give it a pass," Orban said. "Collecting and delivering things around the town is what I do, and there's reason enough to be content in that. But thanking you kindly, all the same."

"We'd pay you a lot more than you'll ever make collecting and delivering," Lang answered. "It would be a highly valued service to us. One day the Terrans will be strong allies of Vattorix and an important influence in Yocalan affairs. Your help would not be forgotten. As an officer on our payroll you could do very well." An informer in the town would be an invaluable asset, and somebody like Orban, who moved around and talked to everybody, would make an ideal recruit. But Lang had been unable to come up with a line that he would buy.

Orban's brow knitted in the way of someone who had made up his mind but didn't want to offend. "Very kind, I'm sure. But what would an officer like that *do*, exactly? I don't get the feeling it would be the right thing."

This infuriating Cyrenean recourse to feelings again. Why couldn't they ever give a plain, simple *reason* for deciding the way they did? "How could you know enough to feel anything at this stage?" Lang asked. "All I'm saying is stay in touch after today. I can give you a device that will let you communicate with us at any time."

"As I told you, sir, I thought about it when I woke up this morning. . . . Anyway, here we are. Let's see if anything's come up."

They entered the rear gate of the yard and walked between heaps of straw, stacked sacks, and stable buildings where a couple of grooms were cleaning out stalls. The owner that they had talked to earlier was at the far end, at the back of the building facing onto the street, washing down one of several Cyrenean horses with moist and muddied flanks, recently in from the road. "Any luck, squire?" Orban inquired as they approached. This was the third stabling house that they had visited. They had been told that early the previous morning, it had provided two sturdy horses for a carriage driven by a man matching Chev's description.

The stable owner looked over his shoulder. "Yes, I think so," he said, without stopping what he was doing. "Those two there." He motioned with the sponge he was holding, indicating a patchy brown and a gray-and-white that were already dried and eating from a manger. "That's them. They were turned in about half an hour ago. So they wouldn't have gone more than about thirty, say forty miles at the most."

"Does you know where they was turned in from?" Oban asked him.

"Just a moment. Yem inside should know. . . ." The owner looked toward the door at the back of the building. "YEM!" A Cyrenean shuffled out, clad in a loose shirt and jerkin. "Those two there that I asked you to keep an eye out for. Who was it turned them in?"

"A gentleman an' a lady riders, it was. They said they got 'em at Vigagawly, up in the 'ills."

"Vigagawly," the stable owner repeated, looking back at Orban and Lang.

"Where's that?" Lang asked.

"A hill hamlet to the north from here—about half a day by carriage this time of year with the weather we've been having."

Lang looked uncertainly from him to Orban. "What goes on there?"

"Oh, nothing that the friends you're trying to catch up with would be very interested in," the stable owner said, rinsing out the sponge and returning to his work. "Sleepy little place. They'd just have been changing horses and carrying on."

"What's past there?" Lang asked.

The owner stopped to scratch his head. "Depends which way they went. There's several roads you could take north of Vigagawly. There's the road inland through Trif and across the marshes. Another west toward the coast. And then there's the road north over the top and on, that could take you across into Ibennis."

"Maybe they'd know which way they went at this hamlet that you mentioned," Lang said.

"Oh yes, they'll know." The stable owner laughed. "Everything that happens in a place like that is news."

"How can I get there?" Lang asked. "I don't need a carriage. I can ride."

"You might be talking about a couple of days or more."

"No problem."

That was another thing covered in training. Traveling to other worlds in Heim-drive ships, communicating and navigating by satellite grids, and being able to use a compact machine pistol like the one concealed under Lang's tunic was all very fine, but it was surprising how many more basic skills were often better suited to the kinds of world they were discovering.

"We can fit you out, all right," the owner said. "It's a bit late in the day now to be starting out, though. Maybe first thing tomorrow. And it would give you time to find yourself a guide. I wouldn't recommend a stranger to these parts to be going up there alone."

Lang looked at Orban. "Are you a riding man too? I'd make it well worth your while. And we could talk some more about the other business that I mentioned."

Orban shook his head with the kind of smile one gives to somebody who doesn't give up. "Very kind of you, I'm sure, but my business is around the town. This man will know plenty of people around here who'd be able to take you, I'm sure."

"YEM!" the stable owner bellowed in the direction of the door. The same figure as before shuffled out again. "Feller here needs a guide to take him up past Vigagawly. Who do we know that might be free?"

"I don't know my way around this town yet." Lang cautioned.

"If they give us a few names, I can take you to them," Orban said. "At least I'll be able to do that much for you."

It sounded as if once that was taken care of, Lang would have the rest of the evening free. "You probably have a lot of other local information that I could use," he said to Orban. "I could stand you another couple of flagons at the inn later if you'd like to talk about it."

"Oh, there's no need to do that," Orban said. "But thank you very much, sir. I don't mind if I do."

CHAPTER TWENTY-SIX

Chev's instructions had been simply to bring them to Doriden. Neither he nor Uberg had been made aware of where the trail led beyond there. Now that Blanborel was satisfied that Uberg was Uberg, and Shearer was indeed the person that Wade was expecting, he revealed that the way ahead for them was to continue north for a further two days. It would mean going back up into the high country and following the road over the top and down into the valley of a river called the Geevar. It was a bit bare and desolate up there, but at this time of year the road was passable. Beyond the Geevar they would enter a region of forest and mountains known as the Harzonne, bordering the land of the Ibennisians. Exactly where to head for then, Blanborel couldn't tell them. "But don't worry," he told his guests. "Wade's friends will come to you. They'll know you are there."

Finding much to interest them, they decided to stay at Doriden the following night as well. At the same time, naturally, they had an invaluable stock of Terran knowledge to share with their hosts and the students. In the evening, after dinner, out of curiosity Shearer introduced a group of the students to the nuts game. They used a bowl of dried seedpods gathered from dishes set on the dining-room tables.

The result was totally different from every instance he had witnessed on Earth. Upon his announcement of "Go!" the four players sat looking at each other with expressions of quiet and confident trust. After the stipulated ten seconds, none of them had made a move. They watched while Shearer doubled—approximately, judging by eye—the number of pods he had placed in the bowl to start with, which brought it to about half full. They did the same thing for the second period, and the bowl was full. At that point one of them assumed the lead and took a portion that looked to be around an eighth. The other three followed suit, reducing the content to half again, after which Shearer once more topped it up. Seeing that Shearer's stock was by this time getting depleted and that he and his colleagues had plenty, the leader obligingly returned a few. The others did likewise. The cycle could obviously have repeated forever.

The next morning, the three Terrans were still discussing the experience as the carriage bumped and swayed on its way along the narrow road away from Doriden, with Nim standing with paws on the window ledge, missing nothing. Uberg hadn't seen the nuts game before.

"It reminds me of a problem called the Prisoner's Dilemma that we studied when I took a philosophy course years ago," he said.

Shearer nodded. "That's what it's based on."

"What's the Prisoner's Dilemma?" Jerri asked.

"Two suspected accomplices in a crime are interrogated in separate rooms," Uberg replied. "Each is given an offer, and is made aware that the other has been told the same. He can betray the other by confessing, and in return receive a reduced sentence. But if both confess, each confession is less valuable and the sentences will be harsher. However, if they cooperate with each other by refusing to confess, the prosecutor will only be able to convict them on a minor charge."

"Okay, I think I've heard of it," Jerri said. "Something like it, any-way."

Uberg went on, "If there is no trust between them, it is to both their immediate advantage to betray the other first. They would both fare better if they refuse, but it requires equal nerve and trust in the other by both of them to act on that conclusion."

"And that was exactly what we saw with those guys last night," Shearer said. It was the old problem that logicians and students of human behavior had been debating since the times of the Ancient Greeks and probably before then. In the long run, everybody in a society would do better if they cooperated with each, but it only worked when *everybody* played the game. As soon as a few realized that they could gain a short-term advantage for themselves by exploiting the misplaced trust of others, then the only workable strategy for the remainder would be either to adopt the same predatory tactics to survive, or else be eaten. Once the slide started there was no way to stop it, and that was what had happened to Earth.

But on Cyrene a different principle was in control, and somehow it was able to endure. Wade had realized it too, and was determined to help the Cyreneans develop and build what would eventually be a star-going civilization around it. When that happened, the days of what Earth's diseased political and economic carcass would have become would be over. No wonder Interworld were going all-out to stop him.

The guide that the stable owner in Revo had found for Lang was called Xorin. They had ridden to the hill hamlet of Vigagawly the next morning, but while everyone they talked to could confirm that the carriage had stopped there and describe its occupants, none was able to say where it had been heading. Scouting around among the farms lying to the north, where the several roads diverged, Lang and his companion stopped to interrogate an old man and a youth that they came across, driving a cart filled with purple turniplike vegetables.

"I 'eard about 'em, right enough, but meself I never seen 'em," the old man said. "What kind of people are they, these Earth ones that yer friend 'ere's lookin' for? What do they do?"

"They're people who want to find out about things," Xorin told him.

"Learnin' an' such," the old man said. He gave the impression that he approved, even if not really seeing the point.

"Isn't there a place somewhere up along the Harzonne road where people do things like that?" the youth said. "Lads like me go to get taught about numbers and measuring; how to make mechanisms. Things like that."

"You mean Doriden?"

"Doriden, that's it," the youth affirmed. He looked at Xorin. "Some Ibennisians came through here a while ago on their way there. The smith in Vigagawly says they're going to build some kind of engine there. One that runs on steam. It will do the work of twenty horses."

"Which way is Doriden?" Xorin asked.

"Go back to the bridge that you came over. Carry on north about four miles from there and take the left road. . . ."

"*Goddamn woman!*" Myles Callen stabbed savagely with a finger to delete the missive from Earth and glowered at the option boxes left on the screen. He had fallen into bad favor among Milicorp's higher echelons, and Rath Borland, true to form, was distancing himself and keeping his head below the parapet. Athough the reasons hadn't been spelled out, from some of the allusions and wording, Callen had a pretty good idea of what had happened.

The stupid bitch just *had* to find a way of ensuring that gutless-wonder Henry would get to know. Henry had whined to Joseph Corbel, the tribal chief, who had conveyed to his corporate ministers at Interworld that maybe their choice of security contractor left something to be desired. Now Milicorp were rolling out the damage control team to assure them it was one overstressed Facilitator who had declined taking therapeutic leave and was out of line. No prizes for guessing who wouldn't be likely to be around much longer after he got back.

The galling thing was that he couldn't really argue. That he had sampled the forbidden fruits of such rareified strata, he had no regret; bringing a little much-needed equalization into the world was gratifying, and if he started repenting now it would mean denying himself and writing off a good part of what made life challenging. But he had to admit that this time he could have used better judgment. It was all very well for the asses that warmed chairs at HQ to talk about overstress and therapeutic leave. They should try a few weeks in the field, or being shut up in something like the *Tacoma* for a couple of months sometime.

He was still fuming and brooding over what to do about it, when a call alert sounded on a secure personal channel. He acknowledged, and a code appeared announcing the caller as Dolphin. Callen cleared the call and directed it to a vacant screen, which illuminated to show the face of Dolphin, looking sun-flushed and dusty, with the top part of a hood thrown back over his shoulders.

"Well?" Callen asked without preamble.

Dolphin answered in a low voice, at the same time scanning with his eyes as if to make sure he wouldn't be overheard or interrupted. "I'm at a place called Doriden, a day's ride north from Revo. As best I can make out, it's a kind of technical academy. They were here for two nights and left this morning, heading for the area called the Harzonne. They don't seem to have had any definite destination there, but they are on their way to join Wade. It sounds as if the Cyreneans he's with there will know they're coming. Local tom-toms, I guess."

Callen nodded. Something seemed to be working out, anyway. "How are they traveling?" he asked.

"An enclosed coach with a driver's shade, dark brown with yellow ornaments and flashes. Two horses that they got from a place along the way called Vigagawly. One black and brown, the other plain black. All three targets positively identified. Also, a Cyrenaen who goes by the name of Chev, exact function uncertain."

"Keep after them. Plan unchanged. Any more?"

"That's it."

Callen nodded. "Out."

He called a map onto the screen, used an index compiled by the earlier missions to locate Doriden, and identified the Harzonne as a region of forested, hilly country on the border of Yocala and the land to the north, which was called Ibennis. For several minutes, he sat mulling. Then he got up abruptly and went a floor down from his office to the Communications Section.

The Duty Supervisor led him through to a room filled with consoles and monitor stations, from where surveillance operations around Cyrene and communications with the ship were coordinated. An operator brought up a screen showing the area inside a hundred-mile radius from the center of Revo. Scattered over it were numerous icons and codes indicating boats, conveyances, and other possibly connected activities that were being tracked. Callen extended a hand to point at the area he had studied upstairs. "Concentrate on here— somewhere along that route, between there and the Harzonne region. We're looking for a brown, enclosed carriage with two horses, one black, one black and brown. Low priority on other categories. Discontinue other areas."

So Wade was threatening to subvert the whole operation, and Interworld wanted him back, did they? Try persuasion first, but use as much force as necessary if that fails, Borland had said. Callen wasn't in a mood to pussyfoot around asking favors or trying to persuade anyone. If he was going after Wade, he was going in hard, he told himself. He'd deliver to them what they'd asked for, with no nonsense and professionally—the way he knew how. And then they could all do what the hell they liked.

CHAPTER TWENTY-SEVEN

Chev was not familiar with the region they were now entering. After climbing back up to the highlands beyond Doriden, the road reduced to little more than ruts in places, with occasional piles of gravel that were apparently left for filling in the muddy stretches in poor weather. The land became more open and rugged, with rocky crags and ridges of grass and shale slopes rising among between flat basins of bog land and shallow lakes hemmed in by rushes and reeds. Trees gave way to lower growths of brush and scrub inhabited by noisy populations of birds and various other small creatures that could be seen from a distance but vanished at the carriage's approach. Jerri let Nim out to meander from side to side around the carriage, every now and again running ahead to investigate something he had seen.

Of course, there were the inevitable proliferations of flora. Chev stopped the carriage to point out a clump of huge lilac blooms growing twenty yards or so from the road that must have measured three feet across. Uberg insisted on walking across to have a look at them and said they belonged to the same group as the moon flowers, possessing the characteristic collar of secondary petals that closed during the day. Chev told them it was known as the "Oracle Rose"— at least, that was what Shearer's NIAD made of it. It seemed to play a similar role in folk lore and mythology as crystal balls did on Earth, and was credited with the ability to instill visions of the future.

From the directions they had been given at Doriden, they would drop down into the valley of a west-flowing river called the Geevar before ascending again on the far side into the mountains of the

Harzonne. There were settlements along the Geevar valley, and the hope had been to find accommodation of some kind there for the night. However, as late afternoon came, and they were forced to make a detour to find a ford across a stream on account of a bridge being partly down, it became clear that they were not going to make it down into the valley before dark.

It was the time of month when there was no moon, and the broken nature of the ground they were passing over, with steep drops falling away from the roadside in places, made it too treacherous to think of continuing. As Ra Alpha reddened and sank in the west, Chev decided on a ravine sheltered by rock walls as a suitable place to call a halt. A stream flowed through the bottom that would provide fresh water, and there was grass for the horses and brushwood that would make a fire to cook supper on and keep them warm through the short but intense night. The front boot of the carriage below the driver's box held a stock of blankets, pots, and utensils, and they had picked up provisions at Doriden sufficient to rustle up a stew with bread followed by fruits and cakes, and supplemented by a couple of flasks of Doriden's home-produced wine.

The fire attracted peculiar insects, and here and there pairs of eyes out in the darkness threw back reflections—but without whatever they belonged to venturing too close. Chev said he didn't think there would be any animals in these parts to be concerned about. Nevertheless, it would do no harm to take turns at standing watch, even though, from what he had seen, Nim would let them know soon enough of any intruders.

After they had eaten, Chev entertained for a while with tales from his seafaring interludes. Then Jerri brought up the question that had been going around in Shearer's mind earlier: How did Cyreneans feel about the thought of one day possessing the kinds of technology that the Terrans had?

Chev didn't answer at once, but seemed to think it over while using a stick to retrieve some pieces of meat that he had set by the side of the fire, and then flipping them to Nim, who was alert and restless, no doubt because of the proximity of other strange animals. Finally he replied, "Yes we think such things are all very wonderful: Go to other worlds; see and talk across any distance; build machines to do lots of work." He tapped the NIDA unit that he was wearing.

"And this! A hat that hears other tongues and makes voices that speak in your head. I would have said it has to be magic. But the scholars back at Doriden tell me no. So maybe one day I will understand." He looked around at the three Terrans. The boisterousness and playacting that had attended his sailing yarns had gone, and been replaced by a seriousness that Shearer hadn't seen in him before.

"Cyreneans admire the knowledge and ability that it takes to do such things," Chev went on. "To become capable of them too would make us proud and earn much respect. But your question did not ask how we would feel about *doing* or *being* anything. It asked how we would feel about *possessing* the results of work performed by others." Chev shook his head. "I have heard this before about Terran ways, from people who work with Vattorix, and I still do not understand it. Is it true that simply the amount of possessions decides how the worth of a person is measured where you come from? And that people sell their freedom, even their whole lives, to outperform others in amassing possessions that they don't need?" He half-turned to wave a hand toward the two horses at the edge of the circle of light from the fire, munching from a pile of grain that he had poured out of a sack to supplement the grass. "Look there. The horses are consuming feed that was planted and grown and harvested and threshed by our friends back at Doriden, or maybe a nearby farmer. And it is right that I should respect the farmer for that. But your system would have me honor the horse!"

Shearer's eyes widened as he listened. This was what he had thought his whole life, but he'd had to travel to another star to hear an alien put it into such succinct words.

Chev paused. The Terrans looked at each other questioningly, but they remained silent. "Forgive me if I am being offensive," he said.

Uberg shook his head hastily. "No, not at all. What you say is right. Don't imagine that all of us agree with the way things are on Earth." He waved a hand. "Please. . . . Carry on."

"The morning that we left Soliki's," Chev said. "Before I collected the carriage, I had breakfast with some people who had been at Vattorix's the evening before, at the dinner."

"Okay." Shearer nodded.

"There was a woman there who had just arrived from Earth with the new ship in the sky. She was said to represent Earth. The principal guest sent to meet Vattorix."

"Gloria Bufort," Jerri put in. She caught Shearer's eye and rolled her own upward momentarily.

"That is she," Chev said. "She asked nothing of what Vattorix has done to earn the trust and respect that we hold for him. Neither did anyone tell of what she had done to be so exalted among Terrans. But it was implied that her status is superior to his because she occupies a larger house. How can this be? If the quality of houses is to be the measure of who should represent Earth, then why was she there and not the craftsmen who built it?" Chev opened his hands in a way that said it made no sense, and inviting an explanation if anybody had one. Evidently no-one did. "She described at some length how she and her husband own many paintings by artists who are highly regarded on Earth," Chev went on. "And it is right that fine works of art should be valued, and the artists who have the talent to produced them duly honored." He shook his head, again with the look of incomprehension. "But none of the artists were present, and nothing was said in their honor. Instead, she, who has no talent, was honored for possessing them. If mere possession of goods is to be the measure of who should represent Earth, why did you not send a thief? "

A long silence persisted. Chev leaned forward to toss some more wood onto the fire. Shearer and Jerri watched the new flames brightening. Finally Uberg looked across at them from the far side. "I think we've answered the question of what kind of government they have here, anyway," he said. "It is an aristocracy. But an aristocracy based on ability. It's an aristocracy because those of inadequate talent or character are excluded from the higher ranks. But it avoids the evils that follow from the use of force to acquire material wealth, because the Cyrenean form of wealth can't be acquired that way. Neither can it be stolen. And customs and laws aren't necessary to exclude those who don't measure up. They automatically exclude themselves."

Since there were only four hours or so of full darkness at this time of year before the rising of the first sun, and neither of them was especially sleepy, Shearer and Jerri decided to share the first watch together and make it double length, which would let Uberg and Chev benefit from the most restful period. Chev fashioned a cocoon from blankets and skins, and was soon stretched out by the fire, his hat over his face, while Uberg, feeling the chill more, made up a bed for himself in the carriage. Nim, with the uncanny guarding instinct of his species, settled down on the outer side of the fire, positioning himself between his charges and the great unknown beyond. Shearer and Jerri found themselves a niche among some boulders to the side and snuggled up together under their blankets. It was practically the first private moment that they'd had together since leaving the ship. The ship seemed like another world that they had lived in a long time ago—which in many ways it was.

Shearer leaned his head back on the folded coat that he had spread on the rock behind them. It was a clear night, with myriads of unfamiliar stars shining brilliantly. The sight reminded him of Jerri's interest in ancient mythology. "Do you recognize any of your con- stellations?" he asked her curiously. It was not a subject that he'd spent much time on himself. He knew Venus, low near the setting Sun when it was the only other light in the sky, but would have been unable to pick out any of the other planets.

"No," she said. "I've looked, but they're all different from here. I haven't even learned where our sun is yet."

"Do you think they had events in their skies here too—like the ones you told me about, when the poles shifted and different gods moved to the center?"

"I don't know. I guess we'd need to know more about old Cyrenean myths."

"What caused them? . . . Back on Earth, I mean."

Jerri shrugged and leaned her head on Shearer's outstretched arm to gaze upward along with him. "It would have to be encounters with other bodies. According to some theories, Venus and Mars were involved. There's not much doubt now that Venus is a relatively young object, still hot. Astronomers used to think that the Solar System has been pretty much the way we see it billions of years, but nobody really believes that anymore. Violent changes have happened within recorded human history. And with electrical discharges between them on that kind of scale, the kinds of plasma discharge effects you'd get in the sky would be awesome—colossal, eerie, terrifying."

Shearer had come across some of that. In keeping with the

behavior of charged bodies immersed in a plasma—in this case the heliosphere, or plasma environment extending around the sun—the planets formed isolating sheaths around themselves, which in the normal course of events shielded them from each other's electrical effects and resulted in regular, repeating, quiescent conditions determined only by gravity. But if instabilities were introduced sufficient for the sheaths to come into contact, powerful electrical forces would suddenly come into play, and the well-behaved models based on neutral bodies moving in a vacuum that had been blithely assumed since the times of Newton and Laplace would cease to apply.

After continuing to stare upward in silence for a while, Jerri went on, "I sometimes think that was where religions came from—the original ideas of gods battling each other in the sky, and sending thunderbolts and vengeance down on Earth. Maybe you're right. Maybe nothing like that happened here, and that's why the Cyreneans seem to be able to get along well enough without."

"Without what? You mean religion?"

"Uh-huh. Well, it's a thought. . . ." She shook her head as if that still didn't explain everything. "But, oh, I don't know . . . We've already said it. They might be just into steam engines, but they get the important things right: truth, honesty, justice, kindness—the things that will make a better world in the long run. Something gives them the moral guidance and lets them see through scams and phony short-term fixes. But it doesn't have to be forced. It comes from inside."

"It's the only place that kind of restraint can come from and be effective," Shearer said. "It can't be imposed from the outside."

Jerri turned her head to look at him in the starlight and the glow from the fire. "So what is it?" Shearer could only shake his head. "Is it something about this planet, about Cyrene? . . . Tell me something, Marc. Can you feel it, just sitting out here right now? Something different. Like being more alive, somehow. As if you were a complete person for the first time in your life."

Shearer nodded slowly. "Yes. I know what you mean. I've noticed it too." He hadn't said anything about it because he had wondered if it was his imagination, or maybe a reaction to strange surroundings and the knowledge of being so remote from everything that was familiar.

"You have? Really?" Jerri said.

He nodded. "It happens at night. I think of it as being more 'in touch' with the universe."

"I felt it the first night we were at Soliki's—just looking out over the town after Evassanie was asleep. It was so strange, as if Earth and everything about it was a million years ago, fading into a fog, and only Cyrene existed in the future. It sounds crazy, but we'd only been here a matter of days, and it felt like home already. . . . I felt I didn't want to go back."

It was uncanny. "I know," he said.

"You too?"

He watched her face for a moment, the silent pleading written across it. "Yes."

"You could stay here and make a new life? Find a home?"

He tightened his arm around her shoulder, drew her closer, and grinned. "Sure. But it would have to have a dog in it," he told her.

The mini sambot hidden in the darkness under the fernlike plants growing a few yards away was about the size of a human hand and configured as a six-legged spider. It had made its way from the reconnaissance drone that had landed with a whisper a quarter of a mile away soon after darkness fell. As it listened, it interspersed periodic images with the transmission that it was sending back. When Shearer and Jerri finally got up and went to the carriage to awaken Uberg, the robot followed them. When they moved away, it scurried up one of the wheels, reconfigured two of its legs into longer grasping appendages, and found itself a lodgement among the axle and suspension.

CHAPTER TWENTY-EIGHT

The first dawn was cloudy and misty with some light rain, but it broke up with the second rising, and by the time they set off again the skies were partly sunny and brightening. Soon they found themselves passing between two high, rocky shoulders at the head of a gorge, with the valley of the Geevar spread out below as a carpet of trees, and the ribbon of river winding along the bottom. Hills rose again on the far side, and from their elevated situation they could see higher land beyond, which had to be the Harzonne region.

As they descended, the wind that had been noticeable higher up died away. Trees reappeared and became thicker, and the land grew greener. Occasional huts and groups of domesticated animals starting to put in appearances, and the rutted track gradually transformed into a reasonably kept road.

It took until the middle part of the day to reach the valley floor and get to the river. The trees had been cleared in places for fields and small farms, and the houses in some places were quite numerous—although with nothing that could really be described as a village. Eventually they stopped at a house with a large animal shed and some outbuildings, where a woman attended by a bevy of small children made them welcome and provided soup with bread, in exchange for which Chev gave her some provisions from Doriden. The dialect was different from that around Revo, and for the most part the Terrans had to rely on Chev with his NIDA to follow what was being said. Her husband was working with neighbors a short distance away along the valley, digging ditches. She was clearly fascinated to meet some of the aliens that she had heard of but so far never seen. It seemed odd to her that they could fly from other stars and yet were traveling in a carriage—but who was she to question the ways of people of whom she knew nothing? The children, as usual, became instant fans of Nim.

They crossed the Geevar river by a ford a couple of miles farther on that the woman directed them to, where the water widened into shallow sand and pebble beds in a steeply banked glade overhung by enormous trees. On the far side they turned right to follow the river back upstream toward the east, which would bring them to the only way within many miles of continuing northward to the Harzonne. The road was soon engulfed on all sides by dense forest, which closed overhead, sometimes for miles at a time, to form an unbroken canopy. Uberg expressed feelings of relief. He had been concerned about their exposure on the higher, open ground for the last two days, and the risk of being spotted by Terran satellites and other surveillance.

"Why would they take any particular interest in this carriage?" Jerri asked. "There must be hundreds of things going on in every direction around Revo."

Uberg sook his head and didn't seem reassured. "You just never know with those people," he said.

"Maybe that was why Wade chose an area like this to hole up in," Shearer suggested.

"That would make sense, I suppose," Uberg agreed.

With the onset of the double-sun period of the day, the air in the forest became heavy and humid. There was little to see but immense trunks, curtains of hanging creepers, and tangles of undergrowth receding into shadows. Opening the windows of the carriage let in annoying, buzzing insects; closing them again made it hot and oppressive inside. Uberg took of his jacket, loosened his shirt, and arranged some cushions around himself, among which he sank into a doze. On the seat opposite, Jerri lay back to rest her head on Shearer's shoulder. At least the road now was covered in needles and leaf mold, a lot smoother than the bumpy ride down from the heights earlier that morning.

"That woman back there," Jerri said absently after a while. "The soup was probably for her kids."

"I'm sure they'll enjoy the fish and the bird that Chev gave them," Shearer said.

"Yes, I know. But even before he said anything about that, we just show up and she's ladling out dishes. . . . It reminds me of a lot of places I've seen on Earth that people where we come from would think of as a bit backward."

"In your field work you mean?"

"Yes. Parts of southeast Europe, where they've always had trouble of some kind or another going on. Places in South America. It's always the people who have the least who are the most generous. They'll share their last bowl of soup with you—the way she did. The ones who have the most are the meanest. You'd think it would be the other way around."

Shearer wasn't sure he felt like getting into another philosophical debate. He was on the point of dropping off to sleep himself. "That's probably how you come to have the most to begin with," he said, shrugging.

She dug him in the ribs with an elbow. "Cynic."

"Maybe it's because people here have never had to listen to four-hundred-pound armchair generals who've never been in anything riskier than a computer game talking tough about how you have to be mean to survive," Shearer said. "You've seen how Cyreneans played the nuts game.

"Cyreneans wouldn't. It's the way Darco said back at Doriden. They don't need something outside to give them direction. Somehow they find it inside. . . ." Shearer stopped speaking as the carriage halted. A moment later there was a rap on the side from up above, and Chev's voice called down.

"We've got company." Jerri sat up, and Shearer leaned past her to open a window and look out. A hundred yards or so ahead was a small clearing among the trees, from which roads went two ways. A figure on a horse was sitting motionless at the fork.

"Any idea what it means?" Shearer called back to Chev.

"Your guess is as good as mine."

"Could it mean trouble, do you think?"

"Well, I can't say it never happens."

Shearer remembered Korsofal, the first Cyrenean they had met outside the base on the day they landed, and how he had carried a sword slung from his saddle. He had asked himself several times if they should have made some such provision before leaving Revo—not that he would have had much idea how to use such weapons. Chev had a sword and a crossbow-style device that he carried up on the driver's box. If this did bode some kind of trouble, they were all in his hands now. Behind Shearer in the carriage, Jerri was shaking Uberg awake.

"How does Nim measure up in situations like this?" Shearer asked her, turning his head.

"He can do his share if he has to," she said. As if on cue, Nim had pushed himself into the window alongside Shearer to take in the scene, and was emitting low growling sounds from deep in his throat. Shearer put a restraining hand on his collar.

"Well, we can't turn around, and we can't stay here," Shearer said up to Chev. "Just carry on easy, and see what happens."

Chev urged the horses into motion again at a slow walking pace. A second mounted figure became visible a short distance back behind the first, in the shade. As the carriage drew nearer, the second horseman moved forward and up beside the first. Chev stopped again when they were about ten yards away.

Nothing happened for five, maybe ten seconds. Then the one whom Shearer had seen initially eased his mount forward, the other following. He wore a wide-brimmed hat turned upward on both sides, and an open coat gathered at the waist, with huge epaulettes standing out to exaggerate the shoulders. The hat was a jaunty affair with a large, curling feather gracing one side. His face, now visible under the brim had a pointy beard with mustachios that echoed the rakishness of his hat. Rembrandt on horseback.

An exchange in Yocalan with Chev followed. Since Chev was still wearing his NIDA, his side of it came back through Shearer's unit as, "We are, indeed. Cheveka Tivenius, at your service. At present on business of the esteemed Vattorix himself, no less. And who might I have the honor of addressing? . . . Indeed? . . . And this gentlemen is? . . . None at all. The journey went smoothly. . . . We did, and they are all well. . . . Yes, they are, and with another. . . . None, I'm sure. . . . Oh yes, ha-ha! A Terran *glok*. . . . All the way from Earth. . . . No, it's very friendly. But I don't think I'd want to find out what happens if you tease it too much. But let me introduce you."

Shearer had by this time climbed down and was helping Jerri out, while Uberg waited to follow her. The horseman swung down from his saddle and doffed his enormous hat. "My friends," Chev said from his perch up on the box, "meet Carsio Eckelan, who tells us he was a designer and builder of ships up in Ibennis, and is now honored to work with the Terran Wade, whom you seek." He gestured and looked at Eckelan. "These are Marc Shearer, the inquirer into nature, and Dominic Uberg, the authority on flowers and plants, that you were sent to meet. And with them is Jerri Perlok, who studies people and how they live . . ." Chev glanced at Jerri questioningly, as if inviting her to agree. She nodded.

Eckelan then said something to Chev, but all the time looking at Uberg. Chev translated: "He says then maybe Dr. Uberg is the one he should address. These appear to be times of strange dealings among Terrans, when words are not believed and appearances are not trusted. He has been told by Evan Wade that if you are indeed the ones he has been expecting, you will be carrying a token from him that he would be able to identify."

The Terrans looked at each other in puzzlement for a few seconds, and the Shearer murmured, "The rose."

"Ah, oh yes, of course." Uberg reached inside his coat and drew out a wallet, from which he extracted an envelope. He opened the envelope and handed Eckelan the pressed, dried specimen of *Rosa spinosissima* that Korsofal had delivered with the letter from Wade.

Eckelan nodded, satisfied, and returned it, then nodded up at his companion. "It is they."

Shearer looked up at the other, still sitting on his horse, who was now grinning. He had an unusually fair face for a Cyrenean, with blond curly hair showing beneath a low cap, and eyes that could have been blue. It seemed a good time to return the courtesy of the aliens always seemingly making the effort to communicate in English. Shearer offered haltingly in the best Yocalan he could muster, "Greetings. The plea-sure is ours. We come in friend-li-ness to your land."

The other's grin broadened. "Never mind all that crap, mate." The twang was natural Australian. "You're the fella that Evan's been waiting for, right? Glad ta meetcha. The name's Nick Parker."

Parker climbed down to join Eckelan, and in the ensuing round of handshakes he introduced himself as a medical physician from the first manned mission. Eventually, he said, so many Terrans had left the base that he decided he'd be of more service to them on the outside than by staying in. Formalities being completed, Eckelan stepped forward to hold open the carriage door and gestured. "Please. . . . We will take you to Wade."

The two horsemen remounted, turned, and moved ahead along the road branching to the right. Chev started the carriage again to follow. From the window Shearer made out two more mounted figures leading, who must have been stationed farther back. And then four more emerged from the trees behind where the carriage had stopped. The reception party had certainly not meant to take chances.

For a while the road continued winding its way upward through convoluted country of valleys and hills, but the dense covering of greenery remained. Then, from a high point it began descending again. They seemed to have left the valley that they had followed from the Geevar, and were now dropping down into another basin lying to the north of it. The last light from Ra Alpha was barely filtering through the trees to the west by the time they rounded a bend to be suddenly confronted by a large, gray, stone building standing on the far side of a a fenced paddock and one or two small fields. A smaller cottage stood close by, along with a number of sheds and storehouses. The main house was almost hidden, visible mainly as a collection of gables and parapets poking above the orange and green treetops. It could have been a remote mansion built by some recluse; the seat of something resembling a monastic order, or body given to contemplation and study, maybe. Perhaps it had been built as some kind of castle or defensive post.

A track from the gateway opening onto the road led around the house to the main entrance, where a group of figures was standing, obviously waiting. Presumably they had been alerted by a scout sent out to watch, or by somebody who had ridden on ahead. As the carriage halted, a tall, broad figure in the center, wearing a bush shirt with jeans and a padded sleeveless vest, came forward, his teeth flashing in the gathering darkness as he smiled. His hair was wilder than when Shearer had last seen it, his face darker and more weathered, and he had acquired a shaggy beard streaked with gray. But his voice was as hearty as ever as Shearer came tumbling down from the carriage to receive a hefty clap across the shoulder.

"Well, hey, you finally made it, eh? Welcome to Cyrene!"

"Hello, Evan," Shearer said.

CHAPTER TWENTY-NINE

The name of the place was Linzava. They had come to it via its rear approach, as it were, over the divide from the Geevar valley to the south. The main access route was via the valley leading north, which they had entered from its top end. It carried a tributary of the river called the Woohosey that Blanborel had described, bigger than the Geevar, that formed the border with Ibennis on the far side to the north.

As at Doriden, the first thing after their arrival and being shown their quarters was some refreshment to reinvigorate them after the day's travel, starting off with a jug of *pikoe*, a hot herb brew apparently drunk universally in these parts. It was less formal affair this time, in a room of timber beams and mullioned windows enlivened by long, bannerlike wall tapestries. One more person joined them in addition to Eckelan and Nick: a woman of Asiatic appearance that Wade introduced as Elena Hukishido, a biophysicist whose background was in cellular photons—the field that had led Wade into the study of quantum processes. She was from Seattle originally, of mixed parentage, and had come out to Cyrene on the first manned mission—the same one as Wade. She was dressed Terran style in a traditional high-neck dress with slits that revealed shapely legs to good effect. Shearer put her at around thirty-five. They could meet more faces in the days ahead, after they had rested, Wade said. As the company began tucking in to a selection of ribs, roasts, and finger food, he described some of Linzava's background.

The original house had been built a century or more before by an architect-builder as a hunting retreat, intended later to become a secluded home for his retirement. After he died, his children had added extensions of various kinds and styles over the years, giving the place a something of a haphazard appearance, and then vacated it as the urge overcame them to see more of the world and its life. In later years it was likely that they in their turn would come back, if only to spend intervals away from homes they had found elsewhere. In the meantime, the premises were available for use by other enterprises. And just at the moment, that meant Wade and somewhere between one and two dozen other Terrans from the first and second missions—not all of whom were present at this particular time—and the small but dedicated band of somewhat exceptional Cyreneans who in one way or another had come together around them.

The connection with Doriden was stronger than had been apparent, but the fact was kept obscure to avoid inviting attention from the Terran authorities. With its emphasis on training students, and experimenting with rudimentary technologies, Doriden, in a way, served as a front to disguise the extent of what the Cyreneans were really learning from their Terran contacts.

The plans that Wade hinted at went far beyond Vattorix and Yocala, Ibennis to the north, and other neighboring or nearby states. Zek's steam-engine project at Doriden was seen as an interim measure to provide the experience and acquaint an initial cadre of students with the concepts involved. Beyond that, moves to develop a pioneer oil-producing operation on a modest scale were already progressing more rapidly than Zek and Blanborel at Doriden had revealed. But it would require all the essentials of a higher-quality engineering base as Shearer had pointed out, along with means for drilling, refining, and transportation, much of which would depend on the cooperation of people and their rulers in distant places. Such contacts were being cultivated right now in various parts of Cyrene. That was why many of the Terrans who had come to Linzava were currently absent.

"I don't want to sound negative," Jerri said when Wade had gotten that far. "But can you be sure it will stay as simple as that? I mean, look at the kind of thing that happened with us. It sounds like a recipe for colonial wars. Despite all their history, how certain can you be that it won't provoke the same kind of thing here?"

Wade banged the table with the palm of his hand and gestured at her as if inviting all of them to witness. "Jerri's got it, right on! That's the whole point. The leaders we're so expert at ending up with would see no other way than to fight over who gets to own what. The Cyreneans won't. They'll do it the way they do everything else—which you must have seen by now. They'll work together for what they know will be better for all of them in the end."

"Which is all a good reason for keeping the jolly folks back home out of it," Nick put in from beside Wade. "We all know what their stake is. The Cyreneans don't want to end up as the work-horses on somebody else's plantation. They'll run their own show—the way it should be run."

"Do you remember how we used to talk about what a different place Earth might have been if Europe had actually practiced the Christian ethics that it talked about, and initiated an industrial era that preserved them?" Wade said, singling out Shearer. He threw out an arm expansively. "Well, this is it, Marc! It's all happening out there. If we can just get them through the early stages without Earth interfering."

Eckelan, who had removed his hat to reveal brown, shoulder-length waves and was sitting with Shearer and Uberg, elaborated, using the spare NIDA. Wade hadn't seen one of the devices before and was impressed. "We are aware of the need to move on to other things than relying on animals. You have seen the sewer they make of Revo. Over half the land that we farm is to grow feed for them. Your friends have told us how it was on Earth."

As he listened, Shearer began to realize the full enormity of the threat that Wade and this group represented to the designs of Interworld and the interests that it acted for. This world would stand together to resist economic imperialism. The people would refuse to be divided by false promises and accusations, and their leaders would never sell out or betray them. None of the usual methods of creating dependence and then asserting control would work here. The investment in three missions and any prospects for subsequent earnings would have to be written off. Uberg was looking mildly stunned. It seemed to be the first time that he had fully seen all the ramifications too.

Jerri broke the silence that the newcomers had lapsed into. "It's this business about them just somehow . . . *knowing*, isn't it?" She looked at Wade, as if finally hoping for an answer. "How do they work these things out? They're really not very analytical."

Wade's eyes twinkled as he answered. "I'd say they have things in proportion."

"This wonderful intellect that we thought was going to be the answer to everything is good only as far as it goes," Nick said.

"And what's that?" Uberg asked.

"Making machines that work," Wade replied.

"And that's it?"

"Pretty much."

"So what about all the other things?" Jerri asked.

"Such as?"

She shrugged. "Life, the universe, and what it all means. Where it all came from."

Wade turned up his palms. "Nothing's repeatable, testable, or really falsifiable. They're not matters that are accessible to science. But science has gotten away with pretending that they are by claiming false credit through association that rubs off from technology. See, with engineering you're nailed to a reality check every inch of the way. If your design's flawed or what you think you know is wrong, your plane won't fly and there's no way to hide it. But with the things you're talking about, nobody knows. All the stuff you hear is more ideology than anything else. A person can go from undergraduate through to retirement and have a comfortable career based on some theory about cosmology or biology that's totally wrong, and it doesn't make any difference." Wade looked from side to side to take in all three of the new faces. On Jerri's other side, Chev continued eating casually in a way that seemed to say none of this was new. "But as Jerri said, Cyreneans don't try to analyze what life's all about. And yet they get it right. The basic things that matter, anyway. The rest will follow."

"And it isn't religion," Uberg put in.

Wade shook his head. "They don't have any religious ideas here of the kind we know. They have some extraordinary insights to the workings of mind and living processes, and they feel a strong affinity with what you might call a cosmic consciousness that pervades all life. But they don't try to analyze or reduce it to everyday terms. They just accept what they feel, and are satisfied to follow it as their guide for living." He looked around again. "And they manage to do remarkably well, don't they?"

"What they *feel*," Shearer came in. "I've been hearing it all the time, and I still can't make any sense out of it."

"You won't," Nick promised. "Don't worry about it."

"You do feel strange, intuitive things here," Jerri agreed. "Dominic told us we would, and it's true. Marc and I have both experienced it."

Uberg was looking with a faraway expression at no one in particular. "Blanborel back at Doriden said that I should understand it better than anyone, because I'm a botanist. . . . Could it have something to do with the richness of the biosphere on Cyrene? I've seen places that make our tropics look meager in comparison."

Wade looked at him mysteriously for a moment or two. "You know, Dominic, you're a lot closer than you think," he said.

"You sound as if you know the answer," Uberg answered.

"Oh, yes, I do," Wade assured him.

They waited. "Well, tell us, then," Shearer demanded finally.

"Where, oh where to begin? . . ." Wade sighed and leaned back in his chair. He turned to Elena, who had said little so far. "Do you want to take it?"

Elena finished what she was eating without hurrying and looked around. "Okay, I'll throw it back. Before we can talk about what's going on here on Cyrene, we need to go ask that old question about living and non-living things. We use the words all the time, and everybody knows what we mean. So what is the crucial difference that distinguishes them? Does anyone have any ideas?"

It was a frequently heard question, and anyone familiar with it would know that the first answers that people tended to come up with were easily disposed of. Crystals "grew"; explosions, chain reactions, and autocatalytic processes "grew exponentially"; and the synthesis of biological molecules was long past the point where the chemistry that occurred in living things could be claimed as unique. Shearer guessed that Elena had something special in mind and decided to stay out of it.

"Life reproduces itself," Jerri offered.

Nick responded. "We're a bit out of touch here because electronic communication's a no-no. But even before I left Earth they had sambot systems assembling modules the same as the ones they were constructed from, and then passing on their own programs. Wouldn't that qualify?"

Jerri looked at Shearer. He shrugged. "Okay, I'll concede it," she said.

"Let me try refining it a little," Uberg came in. "A living system *selects* materials from its environment that it builds into *more complex* components, from which it manufactures a replica of itself. How would that do?"

"I'd say that what Nick just mentioned is borderline," Wade answered. "And there are already designs for self-replicating sambot-factory combinations that will go all the way from raw materials extraction, on up. That would have to make them living, by your definition, wouldn't it?"

Uberg thought about it and nodded glumly. "I suppose it would," he admitted. "Although I can't say I like it." He looked back at Elena. "Very well. You tell us," he invited.

Everybody was listening intently by now, although in the case of the two Cyreneans more out of fascinated curiosity, since the concepts involved were unfamiliar to Chev and still relatively new to Eckelan. "We're agreed that all plausible futures exist and possess equal attributes of reality?" Elena checked.

"Okay." Shearer acknowledged. The others nodded.

It was one of the implications that fell out of the multiple dimensions of Heim physics, and connected with the earlier "many worlds" interpretation of quantum mechanics. All the futures that might be experienced actually existed "somewhere"—in a way, somewhat like the superimposed images of a composite hologram, but of stupefyingly greater complexity. Exactly how was still the subject of endless debates among philosophers and physicists. Although the mathematical formalism permitted all possible configurations of matter that were compatible with physics, it was generally acknowledged that not every reality that it was possible to construct in theory was necessarily represented. It was inconceivable, for example, that the inhabitants of any reality would spend their lives exchanging meaningless noises instead of conversing, or fill their bookshelves with volumes of blank pages, or one would exist in which birds built their nests upside down. This was what Elena had meant by "plausible."

Elena went on, "Then here's my proposition. What makes living and nonliving objects different is the way in which they come to experience the particular futures that they do. The future that, say, a rock lying on a hill gets to experience is determined totally by chance and forces external to itself. It's like the hero of a Greek tragedy—resigned to enjoy or endure whatever the gods choose to inflict.

"But a living organism, while still subject to those factors, is able in addition, by *altering its behavior*, to change the probabilities of what would otherwise have happened. In many-worlds terms, you can think of it as being able to *steer itself* toward futures that it senses as being more 'desirable' as determined by some criterion." She looked around just a Shearer raised a hand to stop her there.

"I could show you lots of automatic devices that take some kind of action to avoid hazards or gain a benefit," he said. "A boiler safety valve. The soft-landing system of a space probe. Are you telling me they're alive?"

Elena nodded as if she had expected it. "Two points against. First, you're projecting your subjective ideas of what constitutes a hazard or a benefit into those mechanisms. Survival or destruction have no inherent value or meaning to them. Their behavior is imparted by the designers. Therefore it qualifies as an external force that they're subjected to."

"Hm, hm. . . ." Shearer made a to-and-fro motion with his hand and rocked his head, saying that he'd have to think about that.

"It doesn't arise from the inside," Uberg said. "I agree."

Elena continued, "And the second point has to do with *how* the steering toward a more desirable future comes about. Western tradition explains the world in terms of one-way cause-and-effect relationships propagating forward through time." Suddenly Shearer was all attention. This sounded as if it had some bearing on his work at Berkeley. Work that Wade had been involved in. Elena nodded at him, as if she could almost read his thoughts. "And it works well in describing the mechanical world of energy, particles, rocks, boiler valves, and space robots. But it falls short when it comes to accounting for processes that are inwardly directed toward a purpose. To work toward a goal, you are seeking to attain some condition that hasn't yet come about, but which exists in the future—are you not?"

"Aristotle's final cause," Uberg murmured.

Jerri shook her head. "Sorry. What's that?"

"I'm not much up on Aristotle," Elena confessed.

"He distinguished various 'causes' that bring an event about," Uberg explained. "What he called the final cause is the result that it's aimed at." Jerri looked little the wiser. Uberg sought around for an example. "In the immediate sense, what causes a house to be built is people laying bricks. But you could also say that what 'causes' them to lay the bricks is the desirability in their minds of the benefits they stand to enjoy from the end product."

"Hence, you could think of the future as affecting their present behavior," Elena completed.

Wade had been containing himself for long enough. "Or to put it another way, organisms working toward some desired end are sensitive to an influence traveling backward in time," he suggested. "Because isn't that what 'affecting present behavior' means?" He sat back and regarded Shearer challengingly.

"Are we talking advanced quantum waves here?" Shearer asked. "A-Waves?" Wade nodded. By now there was no need to spell out for Jerri or Uberg what they meant.

Shearer jerked his head to look back at Elena. The pieces were starting to come together. Wade had said she was a specialist in biophotonics—which involved the sensitivity of living organisms to radiation.

"Wait a minute, wait a minute. Please. . . ." Uberg put a hand to his brow as if making sure that he was hearing correctly. "Marc has told me about these impossible waves that are supposed to travel back in time."

"Oh, they're real," Wade assured him.

"From the things I hear about the experiments at Berkeley, I don't see how you can sound so confident."

"Things have been happening that Marc and I haven't had a chance to talk about yet," Wade replied. He turned his head toward Shearer. "I said in my letter that more incredible things have been going on here than anyone ever imagined."

"I haven't forgotten," Shearer said.

Uberg was staring disbelievingly. "Are you telling us that living systems are sensitive to these waves somehow? That they respond to them?"

"Exactly so," Elena came in again. "A purposeful organism needs a means of steering toward futures that it senses as being more desirable—a 'compass,' if you like. The subjective experience of such influences might be described by words so commonplace that we don't think twice about them: 'imagination'; 'vision'; 'apprehension'; 'instinct.' But the mere fact that these words exist in the language is significant in itself. The choices that an organism faces have meaning because it 'feels' such motivations. A rock does not."

A long silence ensued while the newcomers absorbed this proposition. Shearer's excitement at what he thought he was hearing must have showed. Did it mean that the work he had once dedicated himself to, and then had to resign himself to seeing written off as a lost cause, was resurrected? Wade's confidence couldn't have arisen from anything that had taken place at Berkeley.

Jerri seemed to be grappling with the implications and looked as if she was going to need time to come to terms with it. Uberg, whose field was the most directly impacted, was looking incredulous, while the two Cyreneans just shrugged at each other with baffled grins.

At last, Uberg, after staring at Wade fixedly for several seconds as if searching for a catch, said again, "Living organisms respond to waves propagating backward through time."

"Yes," Wade confirmed simply.

"Then could you explain how this is possible?"

"Better than that. I'll show you," Wade replied. "But we'll need to wait a few more hours. And I refuse to talk any more about it while we're eating."

"But we want to know!" Chev protested.

"Oh, you already know what Evan's talking about," Nick told him. "All Cyreneans do. It's just that you don't know how it works yet."

"Enough for now," Wade pronounced in a tone of finality. "We should be getting to know one another. Marc, tell us about how you got across from Florida to California while the Breakup was going on. It's quite a story. That was when he and I first met, you know...."

CHAPTER THIRTY

It was well into the period of full darkness after Ra Alpha's setting, which on Cyrene at this time of year equated to the small hours of the morning, when Wade led the way through to the rear portion of the house. Shallow steps descended through a connecting passageway to an adjoining structure. An Ibennisian from the north, called Dijen, had joined the party that had eaten earlier. He had experimented in chemistry over the years and was at Linzava learning something of the underlying physics.

The talk had turned back to the subject of biological systems being sensitive to A-waves. However, as Wade and Elena had pointed out using Uberg's earlier analogy, simply drawing up the plans and embarking on the building of a house doesn't guarantee that the goal will be achieved. All kinds of chance factors will affect the outcome, as well as the actions of others pursuing goals of their own that might conflict. As with bacteria attracted toward sunshine in a pond, all that could be "sensed" were changing patterns of relative light and dark in a fog of the various futures that might come about. And this was precisely what the mathematical formalism of quantum physics described. The traditional Copenhagen interpretation saw the actualizing of one possibility out of many as the collapse of a wave function, while the later many-worlds view held it to be the experiencing of one universe out of an ensemble, all equally real. This is why the past is remembered but not the future: What has been experienced is clear and unambiguous, whereas the future is still a haze of unrealized possibilities.

Wade had long maintained that the proper context for describing biological processes—from their ability to manipulate single entities like electrons and ions—was quantum physics, not classical physics. This had led him to seek guidelines for the design of an A-wave detector in the realm of biological emitter-absorber molecules. It was clear now how Elena's work dovetailed in. But the work at Berkeley had never yielded a satisfactory demonstration. Now it sounded as if Wade was promising to deliver just that. So what did it mean?

Wade opened one of a set of double doors at the end of the passage and stepped through. A moment later he clicked a switch and the lights came on.

Electric?

Chev jumped back from the doorway with a cry of alarm and raised his arms protectively. Shearer, Jerri, and Uberg stared, stupefied, and then turned together toward Wade with looks that demanded an explanation. He smirked back at them unapologetically. Eckelen said something to Chev in Yocalan that sounded reassuring. Chev, looking slightly sheepish, came inside, shifting his gaze warily up and down and from side to side.

"Well, we could hardly get on with our work without some of the technical necessities from home," Wade explained. "Might as well throw in a few comforts as well, eh?" He was evidently enjoying having kept this as a little secret.

"So where are you getting it from?" Shearer asked, still not recovered from his astonishment.

"We, er, borrowed one of the fission modules that they use back at the base," Wade replied. "With our rate of usage, it should keep us going for years. But we'll let them have it back then, I promise. It's in a little building out back."

"The ones we saw," Shearer said to Jerri, who was looking at him inquiringly. "About garbage-can size."

"They must still weigh a few hundred pounds," Uberg said. "Don't tell me you brought it over from Revo, the way we came."

"Around by sea," Wade answered. "The Woohosey is navigable all the way up to Ulla, which is the town at the bottom of this valley. The road from there is not too bad. . . . Actually, it was here before I was. Elena was the one who masterminded that, if you really want to know."

"Well, I grew up surrounded by water," she said, meaning Seattle.

Shearer wasn't sure if they were in a laboratory or a flower garden. The area inside the door was familiar enough in a general kind of way, with several long tables serving as benches, and shelves of boxes and equipment—even a couple of computer stations. But the far end of the room resembled more a greenhouse. Banks of flowers of all sizes and colors stood in boxes beneath large glass panes forming a sloping roof. For a moment he was puzzled as to why the view past them should be dark, since it had been a clear evening when they arrived. Then he realized that the outsides were covered by shutters. Of course—Terran surveillance satellites.

The middle part of the room was a mixture of both. There were pieces of Terran equipment and instrumentation, including a couple of microscopes, electrical meters, and an oscilloscope, clustered in what looked like experimental setups; also things like vessels, glassware, wire, and terminals that appeared to be of local origin. But intermingled among it all were more flowers, some standing in pots, others attached to wires, probes, and other apparatus, or immersed in fluids, while some lay scattered on work tops and in dishes, exhibiting various stages of dissection.

"Moon flowers," Jerri said, picking out a row along by the far wall. They were dark red, their nocturnal petals fully open.

"You know them already," Elena commented.

"Oh yes. They're everywhere. The Cyreneans associate them with wisdom and good fortune," Jerri answered.

"They have good reason to," Elena said.

There were also animal cages, emitting scratching and mewling noises from occupants awakened by the intrusion. Shearer turned to Wade with a baffled expression. Wade ignored the question written across his face said to Nick, "Do you think Brutus will mind if we disturb him?"

"When did Brutus ever mind getting some attention?" As he spoke, Nick made his way over to one of the cages and undid the catch of the door. An excited flurry of activity greeted him as he reached inside. "Hey, fella, how's it going? Got some friends here who've come a long way to say hello. Want a *crel* nut? Here."

Smiling, Wade led the others over to one of the display stations. It was a peculiar arrangement, with a small benchlike seat facing the screen, and a simple layout of a few large buttons, somewhat like a child's play panel.

Nick rejoined them a few seconds later. Perched on the crook of his arm and clasping his shirt with fingered hands was an orange-furred animal about the size of a large cat, with a flat face, enormous round eyes, and a button nose. It was chewing something with evident relish and accepted another while it regarded the newcomers curiously. It supplemented its facial expressions with semaphorelike changes of the long ears protruding from the sides of its head, which it was able to move independently.

"An extraordinary species," Wade remarked as Nick set the creature down in the seat and secured it with a restraining harness. "Arboreal for most of the time. They build themselves tree houses out of branches and leaves—like nests, but more elaborate and with roofs. Then every nine years, when the hottest period comes with Cyrene between the two suns and at its closest to the primary, it becomes aquatic for about six months."

"Oz genes," Nick said over his shoulder. "A natural yen for beaches."

Brutus obviously knew the routine and was fiddling with the buttons on the panel. "This is a demonstration of responses to emotionally significant stimuli," Wade told his listeners. "A pretty standard kind of routine . . . you would think. But this has a very unusual aspect to it, as you will see."

Nick moved back to enter some codes into a pad connected to the panel, while Wade continued, "We present Brutus with pictures taken from two categories: Things that he likes . . ." Frames appeared in turn of baby individuals of the same species; another that was presumably an adult female in an unmistakably available pose; a selection of fruits and nuts; and something that looked like a cuddly toy. Brutus greeted each with a series of whooping and chattering sounds that were clearly approving. "And some things that he doesn't." There was a quick flash of an ugly, black, eellike form on scorpion legs with a gaping mouth showing ferocious fangs. Brutus yelped in terror and would have leaped out of the seat had it not been for the restraint. A multi-legged spider form crouching in the fork of a tree produced a similar reaction.

"We don't show him too many of those," Nick commented.

"Now we're going to show him a series selected by a randomizer," Wade said. "Brutus has two buttons. One prolongs the exposure. The other reduces it to a brief glimpse. A red light will come on when the randomizer has made its choice. Now watch." A green light came on at the top of the panel. "That means we're into a live run," Wade commented, gesturing. The red light showed, followed an instant later by sunshine and trees. Brutus held and admired the scene until a timer extinguished it. Next, after a short pause, was the alluring female, who received a similar rating. . . . As did the cuddly toy. Then came the legged eel-snake. Brutus yipped and hit the other button to cut it off.

But already, Shearer had noticed something very strange. He checked it again, when the screen showed the face of Elena smiling, which Brutus prolonged. He had been right. Brutus was making his choice *before* the red light come on! Before the randomizer had even decided which category would be used.

Jerri and Uberg had seen it too, but Chev seemed to be missing the point—no doubt because the concepts were unfamiliar, and he didn't know what to look for. Uberg's mouth was hanging half open speechlessly. Nick lengthened the delay between the light and the display, so there could be no mistaking what was happening. Jerri looked from Shearer, to Elena, and then at Wade. "He *knows!*" she whispered. "You don't need electronics to time anything. There's no way you can mistake it. He's pushing the buttons before the picture comes up."

"More than that," Shearer said, his voice strained. "Even before the type of picture is determined. He knows which emotional state will be produced."

Wade nodded to Nick, who stopped the run. Nick came back to the seat, released Brutus, and hoisted him onto an arm, at the same time pulling more nuts from his pocket. "No more of that tonight, eh? You did good, cobber. Makes yer old uncle Nick right proud, it does. . . ."

"This is what you told us," Uberg said, finally finding his voice. "Information propagating backward in time. The animal was reacting to it."

"*All* living organisms do," Elena reminded him. "That was the point I was making earlier. They can alter their behavior according to what they sense is going to happen—or is more likely to happen. That's how they do it: by reacting to A-waves."

While Nick moved away to return Brutus to the cage, Wade turned aside to take something from a piece of apparatus on one of the benches.

Uberg was rubbing his brow perplexedly. "All living organisms," he repeated.

"Yes," Elena said.

"Including our own—on Earth?"

"But of course. Aren't things that are alive there distinguished just as much from things that aren't?"

Uberg pointed at the screen they had just been looking at. "But you'd never see a demonstration like that on Earth."

"True," Wade agreed. "But that isn't because life on Earth is less responsive to any great degree. It's because there's less there for it to respond to. The A-radiation environment is weaker. Cyrene is a lot more fortunate." Wade glanced around to make sure he had everyone's attention. They seemed to be at the crucial part that it had all been leading up to. He paused for a second to choose his words, and then cocked his head to single out Shearer. "Elena and I had corresponded for some time before we came out to Cyrene with the first mission. She left the base first, and later got in touch asking me to join her to look more deeply into something she thought she'd discovered here."

Wade held out the object he had taken from the bench and let Shearer take it. It was a silver metal cylinder about the size of a coffee mug, with a bundle of wires coming out from one end to terminate in a connector, and a thin glass cap covering the other, inside which was an intricate arrangement of insulating struts and filaments supporting what looked like a small crystal bead. "There's an adtenna that works," he said. "I'll show you some tests with it tomorrow. The results are indisputable. Even Ellis would be convinced. But it needs the stronger signal conditions that exist here. On Earth, the information gets drowned in all the noise and fuzz."

Shearer handed the device back almost reverently. All eyes remained fixed on Wade. There was no need for anyone to speak. So what made the difference between Earth and Cyrene?

Wade replaced the detector in the apparatus that he had taken it from. As he turned to face the others again, he stopped to peer at a moon flower standing in a glass flask alongside and ran one of the opened red petals lightly between his thumb and a finger. "This will interest you, Doctor Uberg," he said, sounding almost casual. "The botany on Cyrene is very unusual—unusual to us, anyway. But I'm beginning to suspect that as far as the rest of the universe goes, it might be Earth that is unusual." He released the petal and carefully rearranged it back the way it had been. "I'm sure you're all aware that plants absorb radiation at some wavelength and reemit it at others. That's how they get their energy, and what gives them their coloring. However, some of the plants on Cyrene have a very remarkable property. They reemit not only electromagnetic radiation, but also the radiation we've been talking about—which we said all living things react to. The moon flower and its relatives are particularly good examples. The effect is greatest at night, when other disturbances that tend to swamp it are absent. The result is to amplify the natural A-wave background. So living things here feel the effects more strongly than living things on Earth do. They see farther into the fog."

Wade directed a challenging look around his listeners, as if inviting them to make of it what they would. "They have a sharper sense of consequences, and *know* what will be better for them. That's why you'll have trouble trying to sell them on a lousy deal that will ultimately prove self-destructive, and why they prefer to do most of their important thinking at night."

CHAPTER THIRTY-ONE

Lang had not slept well. It wasn't so much a case of inability to sleep—the long ride over the high country from Doriden, followed by the winding descent into the Geevar valley, had been tiring by any standards—or of a night's tossing and restless sleep. If anything, he had slept unusually deeply. But he awoke beset by disturbing feelings of a kind he couldn't recall experiencing before.

He and Xorin, his guide from Revo, had stayed the night in a house by the river with a ferryman by the name of Ayano and his wife, Fiera. They had a son called Mutu, whom Lang put at around twelve, as well as two younger children who were at present spending a couple of weeks with friends farther along the valley. Besides the ferry, Ayano also worked a smallholding of a few fields that rotated between grain, vegetables, and pasture, and managed a mixed herd of animals. Their house was one of two standing close together. The other, with its adjoining shed and forge, belonged to a smith.

Lang was still withdrawn after getting up, trying to analyze what was troubling him, while the others exchanged local gossip over a pot of *pikoe*. He was out of training for horseback riding, too, he realized. After two months of forced inactivity aboard the *Tacoma*, the days of hard travel from Revo had left him decidedly stiff and sore. Perhaps from observing Lang's movements, Xorin announced that he would leave him to rest for a few hours and scout around the area on his own for news concerning the carriage. Lang couldn't summon much inclination to disagree. Maybe it would give him some time to untangle his confused thoughts, he told himself.

Ayano and Fiera announced that they would be leaving shortly to check on a sick neighbor and take her some food. After Xorin departed and while Fiera was tending to the animals and collecting eggs, Ayano and Mutu went out to the stable to hitch up the wagon. Lang used the sink in the kitchen to wash. It was fed by a hand pump that seemed to fascinate Mutu, and which Ayano said had come from an Ibennisian town somewhere along the coast. The water was clear and refreshing. As Lang scooped it over his face and through his hair, letting it run down over his bare chest, he looked out through the window at the river and the leafy canopy of the forest beyond, and his movements slowed. He had never before experienced such vivid sensations color of and texture . . . and the feeling of harmony that it all went together to create. The moving river seemed to have come alive; and it was filled with life. Every tree was a miracle forming part of a larger whole, for which the planet beneath was merely a support. All of it was there to enable some underlying message to express itself.

Lang blinked and shook his head, and reached for the towel to wipe his eyes. He was an intelligence operative and had sometimes killed people. He didn't think this way. The only purpose in the whole sick mess was to stick with it for as long as it took to make enough to get out, and make sure that the ones who had scores to settle wouldn't track you down. Was this place starting to get to him already, the way he'd heard people say? Some thought it had to do with chemicals in the air, but the labs hadn't found anything.

He dried his face and went out through the kitchen door to the small garden at the rear by the river's bank. As he stood toweling his arms and body, the feeling came over him again more intensely, in waves. The pale reddish light of first morning was giving way to the full dawn, with the primary star just beginning to rise. Across the river, the trees stood in rounded green, yellow, orange, and brown banks, their arms extended in rapture to greet their sun god. He turned slowly one way, then the other, awed and uncomprehending. The branches above and around the house, the flowers lining the wall and coloring the water's edge, a new shoot prying its way up through the gravel of the pathway . . . every leaf, every insect teeming among them, even the specks of life invisible in the ground beneath, were parts of the same vibrant wholeness that he could feel.

A world of sound that he had been deaf to engulfed him: the pulsing rhythms and subtle undertones that formed the voice of the river; the rustles of the wind dancing among the trees; the nearby birds and the answering choruses from the far bank; an insect hovering around a plant by the door. He was immersed in an ocean of life that he had never realized existed. In some strange way, even though he had set foot on this world for the first time just a week before, the feeling of belonging, of being a part of it all, was stronger than any he had known through all his years on Earth.

And all of a sudden, out of nowhere, the thought of returning there felt somehow dismal and empty. He had no clear idea why. Pictures came into his mind of the people who had befriended him, whom he had deceived, and the prospect that lay ahead of fulfilling the mission that had brought him here. And he was overcome by revulsion.

"It's nice out here early in the morning," Ayano's voice said from behind him. Lang turned to find him and Fiera standing inside the gate from the yard to the side of the house. "We're away, then. We'll eat breakfast with Rannie when we get there. Mutu will fix you something if you get hungry."

"He's not going with you?"

"Oh, someone has to stay to take charge of the ferry. He's man enough now. There's a little bit of work to be done at Rannie's that I'll take care of, so we might not be back until later today."

Lang stepped forward and extended a hand to shake with each of them. "Well, we'll probably be gone by the time you get back. Thanks for everything."

"Ah, you're welcome any time, Jeff Lang from Earth. What else are friends for, eh?"

"Have a safe trip to wherever you end up heading," Fiera said. "You'll have good weather anyway."

Lang moved to the gate and watched Ayano help his wife up onto the wagon, then walk around and climb up onto the driver's seat. As they clattered out onto the roadway, he found himself feeling closer in some strange way to these simple, honest people that he'd met only yesterday than he had to almost anyone that he could remember. They seemed more alive, more real. It was as if he had been only half awake all his life, and the people that he had encountered in the course of it, shells and shadows—figments of a dream that was already fading. He shook his head and went back inside the house.

Mutu came back in when Lang had finished dressing and was pulling on his boots. He was strong and agile, with a lean, tanned face topped by a mop of yellow hair, and alert, lively eyes that were curious about everything and missed nothing. "Your horse is watered and fed, Jeff," he said. "And I've brushed him down, and his feet look fine."

"That was good of you."

"Father asked me to take care of him for you."

"I appreciate it."

Mutu made a show of being in charge of the house, clearing the table and putting things back in the cupboard and hanging others in their place. "He also asked me to prepare a meal for you before you leave, if you want one. Are you hungry, Jeff?"

"Well, that was a good supper last night. But something small maybe, since we'll be traveling."

"I could do some eggs and sausage with bread."

"Sounds good. Need a hand?"

Mutu added some wood to the range and put a pan on to heat. "Just hand me the *pikoe* and I'll warm it up." Lang passed him the pot, then took some clean dishes from the dresser and sat down at the table while Mutu gathered the things he needed.

For some reason, watching him evoked a sense of well-being and optimism that Lang was unable to pin down. Feelings came to him of Mutu being able to look forward to a worthwhile and rewarding life on this world, with connotations of warmth and security, a life of meaning . . . none of which made any sense, because Lang had no knowledge or experience of Cyrene upon which to base such notions. He recalled images of the remains of children he'd seen in combat theaters in Africa and Asia who had been shredded or dismembered by fragmentation munitions, or turned into blackened heaps barely recognizable as human by incendiary. He had seen boys of Mutu's age who had been taught to attach bombs beneath cars and lay mines, others screaming and bloodied under electric shock interrogation. What kind of a world treated its young people, who trusted and believed that a better world could come of it one day, in such ways? Mutu turned from the range to deliver the food from the pan.

Lang reached for the pot of rewarmed *pikoe*, filled their mugs, and banished such thoughts from his mind.

"I heard that Terrans have carriages that fly through the sky like birds," Mutu said, sitting down to join him. "But I'm not sure I believe it."

"That's right," Lang told him. "Why don't you believe it?"

"Then why are the other Terrans that you're looking for traveling in an ordinary carriage? And why did you come here on a horse?"

"Sometimes when you're in somebody else's world, it's better to just fit in and do things the way they do," Lang said. "Our flying ships are big and noisy. I don't think you'd want them coming down all over the place. You need places that are built for that kind of thing."

"We had a traveler cross the river here on the ferry about a week ago, who said it was just a tale," Mutu said. "He said he was a professor, and that it was impossible for anything heavier than air to fly."

"Birds fly, don't they?" Lang pointed out.

Mutu scratched his head and looked perplexed. "Yes, that was what I thought too. I suppose he meant things that aren't alive, and are heavier than air."

"Why should it make a difference?"

"I don't know. . . . So how do you do it?"

Lang thought for a moment, then picked up a knife, held it a foot or so above the table for a second, and then let it drop. "First, ask yourself why things fall down," he said. The way of thinking was obviously new, and Mutu had no ready answer. Lang reached out and gave him a short but firm shove on the shoulder, causing him to move sideways. "Feel that? It's called a force, right? When you apply a force to something, it moves—just as you did." He picked up the knife again. "So here it is not moving. I let go of it . . ." He repeated what he had done before. "And it moves. So it must have felt a force." He picked the knife up again and held it out, inducing Mutu to take it. "See, you can feel that force yourself. It's what's called weight."

"So where does it come from?" Mutu asked. Lang thought that maybe he was beginning to understand why Dad had taken a break. He pointed downward at the floor. "The ground does it?" Mutu said.

"Everything. The whole world underneath it. All of Cyrene. It draws things to itself. Did you ever see a magnet?" Mutu nodded. "Same kind of thing."

"How does it do that?"

"I don't think anyone really knows." In any case, Lang didn't.

Mutu ate in silence for a minute or so. Lang let him think about it. The eggs had something of a fishy taste but were okay. The sausage was strong and spicy. Lang had watched Fiera making it herself the evening before.

"It still doesn't tell me how you make something fly," Mutu said finally.

"We said that Cyrene exerts a force on things that pulls them down, right? Well, then all you have to do is find a way of creating another force, acting up, that's stronger." Lang showed the knife, tossed it upward a few inches from his palm and caught it again. "See, I did it right there."

"But it fell down again. You'd need something that acted all the time," Mutu pointed out.

"Well, that's what you have to figure out," Lang said. "Birds did." He took another mouthful of his meal while Mutu thought some more, and then added, "Here's a piece of advice. Never look at a problem and say, 'It *can't* be solved *because* . . .' Like, 'You can't make it fly, because it needs a force pushing it up all the time.' That's negative. Instead, you need to say, 'It *could* be solved *if* . . .' So, 'Hey, we could make it fly if we found a way to produce a steady force that pushes up.' That's positive. Get it? . . . So there's something to tell your professor if he ever comes back this way again."

Mutu seemed to decide that it was enough deep thinking for the time being. "So is that what you do, Jeff?" he asked. "Make bird carriages?"

Lang shook his head. "No. That was just something I picked up."

"So what do you do?"

Lang rubbed his eyebrow with a thumbnail, unsure how to answer. "I help protect people from others who might try to damage their work or steal it," he said finally.

"You mean like a guard?"

"Close enough," Lang said, and let it go at that.

After they had finished eating, Mutu insisted on taking Lang to the nearby house to meet Holgath, the smith. He said Holgath made tools and implements and knew all about forces, and Mutu was sure he would be interested in the things Lang had said. Lang suspected it was more to show off the alien guest from Earth; or maybe Mutu thought Lang would tell Holgath how to make a flying carriage. In any case, Lang was happy enough to go along.

They found Holgath at work in the forge, thick-armed and brawny, clad in a leather apron and wearing a headband stained with soot and sweat. Although he looked the image of a smith and could almost have been taken from a Terran history book, his house and the general condition of the workshop and its fittings didn't quite fit. Like other artisans, the blacksmiths of Terran history books and folk-tales eked a meager existence typically on the borderline of poverty, and lived in surroundings to suit. While unpretentious, Holgath's house looked solid, comfortable, and well maintained. His shop was well built and contained ample equipment of good quality. Cyreneans didn't try to gouge each other or profit excessively at the cost of another's ruin, Lang had learned from Orban during his short stay in Revo. How anything like that could be made to work, he had yet to comprehend.

Since he had time to kill until Xorin returned, he offered to lend a hand. Holgath gave him some long tongs to hold several heavy work pieces on the anvil while Holgath hammered a punch to make holes through the heated sections. Mutu worked the bellows and demonstrated other skills that he had doubtless picked up as a part-time apprentice. Lang used the opportunity to try and find out more from Holgath about how the system on Cyrene worked. Before Holgath could really understand the questions, Lang had to outline to him the basics of business dealings on Earth. Holgath took a swig from a leather water bottle hanging to one side, mopped his face with a cloth, and looked dubious.

"Everybody tries to take as much as they can get from everyone else, and give as little in return as they can get away with," he said, summarizing his understanding of what Lang had told him.

Put that way, it didn't make Lang feel too comfortable. "To maximize their self-interest," he confirmed.

"But what about the interests of everybody—the world as a whole?"

"The theory is that if everyone takes care of their own part of it, then the best deal that you're probably going to get will emerge out of it all," Lang said.

Holgath thought about it while he replaced the stopper and hung the bottle back up. "How can that be?" he asked at last. "Everybody cannot gain. There must be some who lose—who receive less than what they produce is worth."

Lang shrugged. "There's no way to avoid that."

"But then why should they want to do anything at all—unless they are made to? You would have to force them through violence. The only other way would be to take over all the property and leave them owning nothing but their labor, so that unless they work on your terms, they will starve." Mutu had stopped what he was doing and was listening with horrified expression. Lang could only shrug again. "Is that really how it is on Earth?" Holgath asked.

"Well, how is it here on Cyrene?" Lang replied, deflecting the question. It wasn't as if he had ever given much thought to such things himself.

Holgath frowned. It seemed to be something that he had always accepted and never had to put into words before. "A man works because it is in his nature to want to be useful and respected," he replied finally. "Is it not natural that I should look for a way to repay what the world provides for me, and find a place in it that I am respected for? I wish for my neighbors to live well and be friends, and they wish the same for me."

"Even to the point of not getting the most for yourself that you can?" Lang wasn't sure he could buy this.

Holgath shook his head. "To glorify myself and deprive another of his living? No." He picked up his hammer and punch to resume.

"You're saying that people here will work for the satisfaction of it? Simply out of some sense of . . . of gratitude? A kind of social obligation?"

"Yes. It's how they make their contribution to creating a better life for everyone."

Lang looked at Holgath skeptically. "I think Terran nature must be a bit different," he said.

Holgath waved the hammer at the work piece that Lang was positioning with the tongs. "Then why are you helping me with this, what we are doing right now?"

"This is a personal thing," Lang said. "But how do you get a whole world to think that way?"

"What do you mean, 'get them to think that way'? It isn't something you have to explain. Do you have to tell people how to breathe? It's something that everyone feels."

"Not on Earth, apparently," Lang said.

"Well, I don't know anything about that. It sounds as if something is missing from Earth." Holgath positioned the punch and measured the swing with his eye. "But on Cyrene it is something you would know."

Xorin returned shortly before midday with the news that the carriage had stopped the day before at a house some miles downstream and crossed the river via a ford. It was heading for the road that led north into the Harzonne region. The shortest way to follow it would be to cross on the ferry here and go west, which would bring them to the same road but from the opposite direction.

They walked the two horses onto the flat-bottomed craft, and Mutu made a fine show of his prowess in poling them out from the shallows and then sculling across the deep portion in the river's center. While Xorin was chatting with Mutu in the stern, Lang made his way forward past the horses to stand brooding to himself at the prow. He looked again at the forest, the hills, and the wide, flowing body of the river. He thought of Marc and Jerri somewhere ahead of him, that he had joked with, listened to, shared stories with all the way from Earth, and the kind of life that they had struck out to try and find for themselves in this new world where so much felt oddly "right," and yet was filled with such strangeness and wonder. And he thought of the people behind him who had sent him on his mission, and the world and everything about it that they represented.

Something deeper down inside than the person he normally thought of himself as being seemed to be taking control. He slid his hand inside his tunic, drew out his compad, and stared at it. There was really nothing to decide or think about. The decision was already made. He dropped it over the side. Perhaps it was a lingering preservation instinct that made him hesitate a little longer over the machine pistol. There was no telling where he might find himself well-served by something like that on an unknown world full of who-knew-what kinds of unsuspected perils.

But already another instinct was telling him that if he was going to begin a new life, the only way was to do it with total commitment and completely, without hedging bets or a precautionary foot left planted in the world that he was leaving.

He let the weapon go, and watched it disappear beneath the slow, black waters.

CHAPTER THIRTY-TWO

It was decided that Chev would stay for a few days at Linzava before departing back for Revo to return the carriage and resume his duties in the service of Vattorix. Eckelan and two others would travel with him as far as Doriden, where they wanted to study Wolaxal's steam-engine project. In the meantime, a priority for the three Terrans whom he had brought to Linzava would be learning to ride. They couldn't expect carriages to be made available every time they needed to travel any distance, and so the sooner they were able to become independent in this respect, the better.

After all the traveling and then staying up into the night to see Wade's demonstration, it was late morning by the time they were up and about the next day. As promised, Wade took them back to the lab and performed some tests of the A-wave detector that he had constructed. The accompanying discussion revolved around the physics to begin with and was primarily between Wade and Shearer; but then Uberg widened it to encompass more of the botanical issues, which drew Elena in, and soon the four of them were engrossed in technicalities that Nick had heard before, and which were mostly lost on Jerri. The theorizing and debating continued through lunch, by which time it had become clear that this was only the beginning. Nick suggested to Jerri that they could leave the others to it, and he would show her around the place. At the same time they could take Nim out and give him a chance to start getting to know his way around. Jerri's head was spinning, and she gratefully agreed.

They omitted the upper part of the original house, which was reserved as private rooms for the residents. After a tour of the library, sitting rooms, and other parts of the ground-floor level, including a look around the kitchen, they exited into a herb and vegetable garden at the rear, behind the laboratory extension. The fission module that had been "borrowed" from Revo base was housed in a low, bunkerlike cellar adjoining it. As with the ones that she and Marc had seen previously, Jerri found nothing remarkable about it as far as appearances went—a dome-topped cylinder with electrical hardware connecting to a panel of switchgear and indicators. A short distance away, practically hidden by the surrounding trees, they came to a low-roofed log-built structure that was more interesting, if noisy. It was practically a small factory inside, with Cyreneans applying themselves to a variety of tasks, directed by a sprinkling of Terrans. In one corner, a home-built machine powered by a Terran electric motor was pulling copper bars through a series of progressively smaller dies and winding the resulting wire onto a spool. A dozen or so finished spools were stacked nearby.

"It's amazing how easy it is to take an infrastructure for granted," Nick commented as they watched. "It's all very well having the fission can next door putting out juice, but what do you do with it? Make motors to drive things? But to that you have to have wire, insulation, castings, bearings. You can't just call your local supplies merchant here. They're planning on putting another of whatsisname's steam engines into a mill and foundry down in Ulla. That should make a big difference. It's the reason why Evan wants some of his boys to get involved in the project at Doriden."

They watched a simple grinding head putting the finishing touch to the lead screw for what Nick said would be a more accurate lathe than anything the Cyreneans had at present. In another room, a Terran who looked Asiatic was talking chemistry at a demonstration bench and chalk board in front of a group of about a dozen.

"It's not a matter of trying to compete in terms of scale," Nick said as they came back out and began following a trail through the trees to see the preparations being made for a new building on the slope above. "Evan knows they could never match Earth in volume, even at this distance. It's more a question of spirit. If you can get the Cyreneans believing in themselves, their own nature will do the rest." He snorted. "Then maybe one day they'll be building their own starships and exporting their system to replace the ruins of what's left of ours."

"But do you really think their system can stay the same?" Jerri said. "Or will things have to change eventually?"

"You brought that up last night."

"I know. It still bothers me."

"You mean because of some inexorable law like all of the house-trained professors back home teach? Numbers growing, competition for resources increasing, and all that kind of thing."

"Yes, exactly."

"I just hope Evan's right," Nick replied. "He's pretty sure they'll steer clear of the pitfalls. They seem to have done all right so far. The way they go about things avoids the huge concentrations of wealth that cause all the trouble back home. Everything's distributed among small family businesses and local municipal bodies. If they want to take on something bigger, a bunch of them will get together and appoint a lead contractor to direct things. But they keep their independence. So the little guy doesn't end up with nothing. He owns a share in the product."

"I'm not sure how you mean," Jerri said.

Nick sought for an example and then waved at some felled trunks lying to one side, waiting to be hauled away. Ahead, where a site had been cut into the slope and leveled, Cyreneans with picks and shovels were digging trenches for foundations. "Suppose that you and I got those fellas that you met back in Doriden to make a machine for us that cuts timber faster."

"You mean a power saw, for a mill?"

"Yeah—something like that. And then we find a couple of guys up here, say Bill and Joe, to work it for us. Now the way it is back home, we'd pay them a flat wage and then own the lumber, which we'd then go out and try to sell. Right?"

"Okay."

"So now you've got a conflict. The less we can get away with paying Bill and Joe, the more we have to keep for ourselves. And once they've been paid, they don't give a toss about whether we sell the stuff or not . . . that is, until it turns out we can't, and they get laid off."

"So how is it different here?"

"All four of us own the timber. We provided the mill. Bill and Joe did the work. We split the proceeds between us, so everybody is on the same side with the same incentives. We all want to see it sell. No conflict."

Simple enough, Jerri thought to herself. But surely not something that could be universal. They had stopped to watch Cyreneans digging the foundation. She nodded, indicating them. "You're not saying it could work even for guys like that."

"Sure it can," Nick said. "Knowledge is a big commodity here. What comes out of Linzava will earn income from all kinds of sources. And every one of those guys down there can choose a small piece of it instead of a pay check—kind of like a stock certificate. You collect them through life—for all the enterprises that you've put something into. They might only be pennies in some cases, but they add up. You can trade them or sell them if you want. So even if you lose an arm and a leg, you've still got income. And that's what it's all about, isn't it?"

"So who takes care of all the record-keeping and paperwork?"

"Lawyers. Who else?"

They came back around to the side of the house where the stable was located, facing the paddock inside the gate. Nick suggested that they could use what was left of the afternoon to begin Jerri's riding lessons. "Great! Let's do it," she replied.

He led the way inside, and after exchanging a few words with one of the stable hands, went to a stall and led out a plain dun colored mount, smaller than the one he had ridden the day before and seemingly younger. "This is Sheila," he announced, patting the animal's neck. "Nice and friendly. Cyrenean horses are amazing. If you get lost just give them a free rein and they'll always bring you home." He selected a saddle and harness from several hanging on hooks on the wall, and carrying them under one arm, brought the horse out into the open. Jerri followed with Nim, who was accustomed enough now to Cyrenean animals not to pay much attention.

"You seem to be the animal expert," Jerri commented as Nick slung the saddle and began fastening straps and buckles. "I thought you said you were a physician."

"Aw, human animals, animal animals. Same thing, really. Didn't they say you're an anthropologist?"

"That's right."

"Well, there you are then. Same thing. You won't have a problem."

He let her handle and talk to the horse until each was comfortable with the other, and then went through the basics how to mount and dismount, and the elements of control. Then he held the reins while Jerri lodged a foot in the stirrup, lifted herself up, and swung her other leg over.

"Okay?" Nick called.

"Fine."

"I'll just walk her around the field for a bit first, to let you get the feel of it." They set off, heading out away from the house, Nick still holding the reins.

"So what part of Australia are you from?" Jerri asked.

"Adelaide, in the south—on the coast going toward the middle, west from Melbourne."

"Did you come to Cyrene from there, or had you moved?"

"I was still there when I applied for the slot—on the same mission as Evan. For some reason they weren't getting a lot of doctors."

"So what made you decide to go?"

"Oh . . . The payoffs from drug companies were corrupting everything. If anyone tried to speak out or blow a whistle, it was the end of their career. I suppose I'm too much of an idealist. I went through med school to learn how to make sick people better, not help stockholders get rich. So, all things considered, I figured there might be a better chance of making a go of it here."

The horse kept to a loose, steady rhythm, and Jerri was quickly at ease. "So you just came out on your own? No ties, or anything left behind?" she said.

"None that matter too much. But there's a neat Cyrenean lady down in Ulla that I've been kind of sweet about for a while now. Her name's Sakari. I guess you'd say we're serious." Nick looked up and winked.

"Does that mean little Nicks running around before too much longer, maybe?" Jerri asked; then she realized that she wasn't even sure if it was possible. She hadn't heard of any precedents on Cyrene, although it had happened on some worlds.

"I don't think anyone knows yet," Nick answered. "Some of the experts say yes, and others say no. But you already know what I think of experts. How about you? I guess you're just about set with that Marc, eh? He seems a pretty good guy. Sharp, anyhow. Reckon you'll make a go of it here?"

Jerri looked around at the forest, with higher peaks rising to the south above the pass over which they had come. It could have been the enchanted woods of an old European folktale set in Transylvania. The splendor of the raw, natural scenery reminded her of the approaches to Yosemite not far from Pinecrest, where she had lived, and places she had seen in her field trips back on Earth. "Oh yes," she said, and smiled.

"That's fine," Nick pronounced. "Want to take Sheila yourself for a bit now?"

"Sure."

He handed up the reins and stood back while Jerri guided the horse into a wide circuit toward the middle of the field. "Remember what I said. Loose on the grip, and gentle on the reins. Use your knees and your weight as a guide. She can read it. . . . You're doing great. Try opening it up a bit back here to me." Jerri urged the horse into a slow canter to complete the circuit. "Are you sure you've never ridden before?" Nick asked her as she drew up.

"I dabbled a bit here when I was a kid, but never anything serious."

"Then you're a natural."

"Although I did try a camel once." Jerri heeled Sheila into motion again and set off on another round. Nick stood and watched, his hands on his hips.

"You're joking! A camel? That puts you one ahead of me," he called.

"When I was in Algeria. It's like trying to stay on a roller coaster. They can be mean brutes too. Do they have anything like them here?"

"Oh, there are all kinds of strange creatures on Cyrene. The climate extremes produce some amazing adaptations. When the novennial cycle goes into the hard winter, this valley will be all ice. The Woohosey freezes solid."

Jerri reined to a halt beside him again. "It sounds as if there's going to be a lot to get used to," she said

Nick shrugged. "It's what life's all about, isn't it?" He looked around. Daylight was close to ending by that time. "I'll tell you what," he said. "It's a bit late for me to saddle up now. But first thing in the morning I'll take you on a ride down into the valley for a few miles.

Give you a chance to really get your hand in. What do you say?"

"Sounds good," Jerri agreed.

She dismounted. They were walking back toward the stable, when Nim looked toward the gate and barked a warning. The sounds of hoofs came through the trees, and then five mounted figures appeared on the road outside, coming from the same direction that the carriage had arrived from the day before. A horn sounded as they turned in through the gate and headed along the track toward the house. Nick stopped to peer through the fading light. "I recognize three of them. . . . But not the other two," he said. As the horsemen reached the door, other figures emerged from the house. "You go on," Nick said, nodding to Jerri. "I'll take care of Sheila. See you in a minute." Jerri gave him the reins and headed over toward the house as the group at the door began disappearing inside. Three who had been left to take horses around to the stable passed her coming the other way. Jerri attached Nim's leash and went in.

In the front hallway, wrapped in a dusty riding cloak, was none other than Jeff! With him was a Cyrenean in the process of handing his hat to one of the household staff. The Cyreneans who had accompanied them were talking rapidly with others, and somebody was hurrying out through a passageway at the rear.

"Jeff!"

He turned and saw her. His face was tired and grubby, but the smile was genuine. They hugged, and he clapped her on the back fondly. "Hi, Jerri. You guys didn't think you could get rid of me that easily, did you?"

"But what on earth . . . "

"It's not Earth."

"Whatever. . . ." Jerri found that she was too astonished to be able to frame a question.

"Strange things happen here, remember?"

"But how did you . . . I mean . . ." Then she realized that Marc had appeared from somewhere.

"What in hell? Jeff? . . ."

Before Jeff could respond, Wade appeared from the passageway at the rear, brought by one of the Cyreneans. Jeff and his companion disposed of the rest of their traveling clothes amid a babble of questions and fragmented introductions. The other was called Xorin, recruited by Jeff as a guide in Revo. But what was Jeff doing in Revo? . . . Then Wade ushered them through into a room opening off from the hallway, where they would be able to sit and talk more comfortably, and asked one of the Cyreneans to organize some kind of refreshment for the arrivals. As they moved on through, Nick joined them from the passage, having entered via another door.

Inside, Marc and Jerri immediately resumed pressing Jeff with questions. But he shushed them by shaking his head and making staying motions of his hands, conveying that he had something more important to say.

"Look, guys, before we get into all that, there's something I have to tell you. It's a confession. I was never what you thought. I was a plant ever since the briefing program in Redwood City—working for Milicorp. I was put there by Myles Callen."

Jerri forgot what she had been trying to say, and shook her head in protest, while the other Terrans stared disbelievingly. Even the Cyreneans who couldn't follow what was being said saw from their faces that this was something serious.

"Why?" Marc managed finally in a whisper.

"It was the whole reason why your application was rushed through, Marc." Jeff inclined his head briefly in Wade's direction. "To find Professor Wade. They knew that he'd set up a way to get you to where he was. I was supposed to go with you, and then let them know the location. But you caught them with their pants down when you pulled that stunt at Vattorix's." Jeff looked directly at Wade. "That was neat." Wade acknowledged with a gratuitous nod.

Jerri knew that Marc had had suspicions for a long time about his sudden release from Berkeley. What he hadn't been so sure of was why they were so anxious to catch up with Wade—although it seemed a lot clearer now."What was so important about finding Professor Wade?" she asked, curious to see if Jeff would bear it out.

"That wasn't something I was considered as having a need to know," Jeff replied.

"Oh, I think I do," Wade said in a voice bordering on a growl.

"So you lost us at Vattorix's," Marc resumed. "How did you manage to find us from there?"

"That's what I'm waiting to hear," Nick put in from one side. He sounded concerned.

Jeff shrugged. "Easy, really. I showed up in Revo with the story of having gotten separated and wanting to catch you up. If anybody checked, I already had the credentials of being one of the gang. And with people like these you can't go wrong. They can't help you enough."

"Very well," Wade conceded. His manner was grim. "But why are you telling us all this now?"

Jeff didn't smile. "Because . . . I don't really know how this happened. You hear about the things that come over people here. I turned into what I'd pretended to be." Jerri turned her face toward Marc. He shook his head and returned an equally strained expression. This was too much to take in all at once. "I'm with you guys now." Sincerity and anxiety were written across Jeff's face, a pleading to be believed. "Here for the duration—and whatever happens next."

Wade gestured shortly at Jeff's person. "But good God, man, aren't you hot?"

Jeff shook his head. "I got rid of that stuff. It's all a long way from here, at the bottom of the Geevar river."

Meanwhile, outside the stables, two of the Cyreneans who had taken care of the horses stopped to enjoy the night air before going back into the house for their supper.

"Look." One of them pointed to a light moving across the darkening sky. "The Terran ship that travels between the stars is passing over."

His companion scanned in the direction the other was indicating. "I see it." There was a pause, and his expression became a frown. "But there's something strange, Lun. Look again. I've never seen that before. Aren't there two of them now, close together?"

CHAPTER THIRTY-THREE

So it had been a setup as far back as the training week in Redwood City. When Jeff just happened to be behind Shearer in the checkout line in the cafeteria at lunch that day, it hadn't been accidental. All through the voyage he had been insinuating himself further. And they had just happened to end up as roommates in Revo base. It was clear now why, at times, Jeff had come across as just a little too inquisitive. But Shearer still had a lot of outstanding questions that Jeff would be in a position to throw some light on. And if Jeff wanted to make some amends for deceiving them, he would never be more disposed toward being cooperative than right now. Despite his journey and arrival late the previous evening, Jeff was up and about early the next morning. Jerri had left with Nick on a horse ride as they had agreed after yesterday's lesson. Shearer took the opportunity to steer Jeff aside and suggest an walk outside. It would be more private, he said, which in the circumstances hardly needed explaining.

They came out of a side door into the cobbled yard separating the stable from the house. Xorin still hadn't appeared, and Jeff wanted to check on their horses. "That must have been a long ride from Revo," Shearer remarked. "Was it something you did back home?"

"It was one of the things they put you through. CEP, it was called. Comprehensive Environmental Preparedness. "

"Uh-huh."

They moved clear of an angle of the building, and Jeff stopped to take in the vista of forested hills with peaks in the distance. "Mornings on Cyrene are a whole new experience," he said. "It's a feeling of being connected to everything alive in the universe—as if the universe itself is coming alive."

"I know." Shearer nodded. "The Cyreneans call it the cosmic consciousness. I'd read about it but never knew what it meant. It's something you have to feel. They take it as being self-evident." Jeff knew by now about the moon flower and certain other Cyrenean plants.

"It makes you feel as if the whole life you lived back on Earth was being only half awake," Jeff said.

"That seems to be how just about everyone who comes here ends up feeling. It just takes longer with some people than with others."

"So how was it with you—out of curiosity?"

Shearer had to think back. "I'm not really sure. . . . It kind of crept up on me during the journey from Revo. There wasn't anything like the sudden flash that you seem to have had. In fact, I'd guess that you're probably ahead of me."

"Are you serious?"

"Yes, I'd say so."

They reached the stable, and Jeff went on in. Shearer decided to wait outside and enjoy more of the morning sun. They still hadn't broached any of the issues that he wanted to discuss. He wanted to know more about the kind of information that was finding its way back to Callen, how many more Terrans he might send to work undercover in the city. How long could they realistically expect to remain undisturbed at Linzava? It had taken Jeff a matter of a day or two to find the trail that led here. Admittedly, he'd had Shearer to follow. But with the amount of stories and gossip that had to be circulating in and around the city, and with Callen in a position to employ multiple sets of eyes and ears, it could be only a matter of time. Maybe they needed to consider moving the whole operation elsewhere, much farther from Revo—possibly overseas, even.

Shearer had risen far earlier that morning than he had intended. He wasn't sure why. He had awakened to a feeling of restlessness, a vague foreboding of something about to happen that he was unable to relate to anything definite or that anyone else had said anything about. Nim seemed to have felt something too, and according to Jerri had woken her up in an agitated state. When Shearer walked out with her and Nick to get the horses ready for their ride, Nim had run round and around, circling toward the gate in a wide arc and then back again, barking, as if trying to draw them away from the house. To avoid waking up the whole place, Jerri and Nick had left right away, instead of coming back inside for a mug of *pikoe* first, as they had intended.

Now everything was still again. The hum and clatter from the workshops hadn't yet started. The trees above Linzava were a mixture of greens and gold, and the crags beyond, granite gray, catching the first rays of the primary sun as the first-dawn twilight turned to day. There were still moments when he wondered if they would really be doing the Cyreneans a favor by speeding them along the kind of path that Wade had mapped out—although the signs were all that they would have gotten there soon enough on their own in any case. Did technological advancement necessarily imply intellect at war with nature? Shearer didn't think so. A species that could produce Beethoven, Leonardo, Shakespeare, and Archimedes was not meant to exist in huts and spend a life of stoop labor in fields. The splendor of the Amazon forests and the Colorado Plateau could coexist with starships. But somewhere along the way on Earth, too many had lost sight of what it meant to be human, and it was they who dictated how the nuts game was played. Shearer believed with Wade that the Cyreneans would get it right. But sometimes he asked himself if it might be just wishful thinking. Or could it be some subtle emanation from a distant future being focused and infused into his mind? He smiled thinly to himself. If there was any way of telling, he had yet to find it.

The sound of barking came through the trees from the direction of the road. Evidently Nim still hadn't calmed down. If anything, he seemed more frenzied than when Jerri and Nick left. Shearer moved forward to where he could see the gate past the carriage they had arrived in, which was standing outside the stable. Then Jeff's voice came from the entrance as he emerged and began walking over.

"The nags are okay, Marc. So what was it you wanted to talk about?"

"Let's make it later. I think they're back."

The thudding of hoofs approaching at a trot became discernible, and then the two riders appeared. Moments later, Nim shot through the gate and past them into paddock, where he turned and started barking again, as if trying to drive them back out. The horses were shying and trying to pull away, clearly not used to this.

"What's gotten into him?" Jeff asked in a mystified voice.

"I don't know. I've never seen him like this." Shearer advanced a few steps farther and called out, extending his arms wide in a "come" signal. "Nim! Here! What's the big problem with you today, then, huh?"

Nim half turned, hesitated, looked back at Jerri and Nick, and then came running toward Shearer, barking loudly again. A groom came out from the stable behind Jeff to investigate the noise. Others were appearing around the corner from the front of the house.

"He's gone crazy," Jeff murmured, moving up to stand beside Shearer.

Then Nim veered to the side suddenly and raced to a pile of building oddments left outside a shed by a wall running behind where the carriage was standing. He rummaged underneath some boards leaning against a drum and dragged something out, juggling it into the air with his snout and a paw. It landed and tried to right itself, but before it could escape Nim was on it again, snarling and growling. Shearer ran over to investigate, expecting to find an animal of some kind. Instead, it was one of the strangest objects that he had ever seen. About the size of a human hand, it had a body of angular planes and protuberances that was clearly artificial, and multiply jointed, spiderlike legs that thrashed and flailed in the air as it tried to break free, while Nim used paws and jaws alternately to keep it pinned on its back. It looked like a modular robot assembly, but on a smaller scale than any that Shearer had seen before.

"What do you make of—" he started to ask as Jeff joined him, but cut off when he saw the look on Jeff's face. "What is it?"

Jeff glanced around, picked up a large stone from several stacked by the boards, and raised it with both arms . "Call him off, Marc!" Shearer seized Nim's collar and drew him back, barking and straining, and Jeff demolished the device as it righted itself and started to move away again.

"*Jeff, what is it?*" Shearer demanded again. But Jeff was looking upward apprehensively, turning his head one way and then the other to scan the skyline.

"Find Wade!" he snapped. "Get him out of here!"

"Jeff, would you mind just—"

"There isn't time. I'll grab some horses. We've all got to get away. Uberg too if you can find him. And Elena."

Jerri and Nick had drawn up, still mounted. Nim was pulling against Shearer's grip, barking frenziedly. "What's going?" NIck demanded.

"You've got to get out!" Jeff told them. "Now! Do it! Back along the road as far as you can get. We'll be right after you."

"Jeff, mate, what—"

"*Just go, Nick! Listen to the goddam dog!* . . . Jerri, drag him if you have to. There isn't time to argue."

Whatever was happening, Jeff knew a lot more about it than Shearer did just at that moment, which was nothing. "Do what he says," he shouted to them. "I'm going for the others."

For a moment or two they backed their horses away undecidedly; then Shearer released Nim, who flew at them, darting from side to side to herd the horses toward the gate as if they were sheep. Jeff ran behind waving his arms. "*Just go! Go!*" They turned and spurred the horses into a gallop back out onto the roadway with Nim following. Shearer was already on his way back toward the side door into the house. He heard the first whisperings of approaching aircraft just as he reached it.

By the time he had made his way through to the front entrance hall, consternation was breaking out. The sounds of engines were now distinct, seemingly coming from all directions outside. More people were following those who had gone out to investigate the barking and shouting. Wade appeared in shirtsleeves, coming down the main staircase. Elena was close behind. As Shearer hastened across to them, a military assault lander with Milicorp golden-lightning-flash insignias dropped into view in the front court outside the open doorway. Armed figures were leaping from the doors before it touched the ground. Seconds later, another came down farther back behind it in the paddock.

"What's happening?" Wade asked Shearer, seeming bewildered. Elena could only shake her head.

"We have to go. No time," Shearer told them curtly. Wade nodded numbly. "Where's Uberg?" Shearer asked.

"I haven't seen him this morning."

Jeff had arrived via the same door as Shearer. "There's nothing we can do," he told them, and beckoned frantically. "Come on! They'll be in here in seconds."

"Not that way," Wade said, recovering himself and waving toward a passage. "That yard's open to the front. Go through the kitchen." An amplified voice boomed from the front of the house:

"ATTENTION. YOU ARE SURROUNDED. KEEP CALM AND MOVE OUTSIDE PEACEFULLY. NOBODY NEED GET HURT." Then it began repeating in Yocalan.

With Wade leading, they came out of the house on the far side of the laboratory extension, where the trail led through the trees past the workshops and up the slopes at the rear where foundations for a new construction were being laid. As the path steepened over rocks, Shearer dropped back to give Elena a hand. Wade paused to catch his breath and waved Jeff to the front. "Keep following it on up," he gasped. "The path crosses a stream at some rocks. From there on the forest gets thicker. Bear to the right past the rocks." Jeff nodded and pressed on.

"What about Jerri and Nick?" Wade queried.

"They got away on the other side—down toward the valley."

Wade nodded, and they carried on.

As they came over a hump above the excavation site, they saw that Jeff had stopped to wait at the stream in front of a pool fed by cataracts running down a narrow fissure. Shelves of rock provided a way across. The forest beyond was dark and heavy with under-growth. Jeff motioned the others on past him. "I'll follow you guys," he told them. "We could get separated in yards in there."

Wade went ahead; Shearer and Elena followed. Tangles of vines snagged their feet, and springy branches swished at their hair and faces, but the denser covering brought feelings of security. Shearer glanced back to check that Jeff was still with them . . . but he wasn't. "Wait," he called ahead. Wade stopped. Shearer began cautiously retracing their path.

Jeff was still at the rocks. He was standing with his back to them and seemed to be looking back down the trail. Shearer worked his way closer. "Jeff," he called in a low voice. Still Jeff didn't move. Movements behind him told Shearer that Wade and Elena had come back to see what was happening. Without turning his head, Jeff moved an arm out behind him and part-lifted it away from his body, fingers open and extended, conveying in a way that couldn't be mistaken, *Easy! Move very, very slowly.*

Parting the leaves carefully, Shearer edged his way forward. A black shiny ovoid, about the size and roughly the shape of a football was hovering in the air five feet or so in front of Jeff's head. Sunlight glinted off its lenses and sensor housings. They were known as "roaches"—interdiction and reconnaissance drones. They could deliver anything from a high voltage jolt that would knock a man senseless to an explosive shell capable of blowing a head off. Or they could simply terrorize. Fugitives had been known to collapse and die from exhaustion when being relentlessly pursued by them .

"What is—" Shearer heard Wade say, moving up to crouch close behind him, and then a quick catching of breath. "Oh, God."

They saw Jeff move a step to the side, no doubt on command. A monotone voice issued from the drone. "*You people in the trees. Be informed that your companion is in target lock-on, termination mode. You move, he fries. Your call.*"

For several agonized seconds nobody moved. Shearer and Wade looked at each other with helpless expressions. "We can't," Elena's voice breathe from the rear.

"It's over," Wade said.

Raising his hands high, he straightened up slowly.

CHAPTER THIRTY-FOUR

Everybody from Linzava—Terran and Cyrenean—was brought back to Revo base. The majority of them, which included Elena and Uberg, went to join a numbers of other formerly departed Terrans who had been located and apprehended. Shearer, Wade, and Lang, however, were part of a group separated out for return to Earth aboard a fast military clipper called the *Ranger*, operated by Milicorp, which had arrived with a new Director and administrative staff within the last couple of days and would be returning immediately. Along with them were Emner, who had been Director at the time of the *Tacoma*'s arrival, and Colonel Yannis, his Milicorp security chief, both of whom had been relieved of command and were now included among the detainees.

A shuttle was already undergoing launch preparations when they arrived at the pad area, and they were aboard the *Ranger* in less than two hours. It seemed that the powers back home were very anxious to talk to Wade. Why Shearer and Lang's presence should be required so urgently was less obvious, but their guess was that it would involve corroborating parts of his account. And then it could have been for not greater reason than to fill available places in the *Ranger*—operators didn't like running interstellar ships at under capacity. Elena and Uberg were probably being kept back because of their knowledge of the local contact network around Revo, which would naturally be of interest to the new administration. The *Ranger* was under way before the day was out, speeding outward from the Ra system toward the H-point for its transfer out of normal space. Time

to Earth would be in the order of three weeks—a third that for a
Tacoma-class mission ship.

Vessels like the *Ranger* served the need for fast physical communications between Earth and its expanding web of colony worlds.
The *Ranger* itself was also fitted with an armament system, which Jeff
learned was a prototype long-range heavy-ion-beam weapon that it
was being used to test. Superficial observation of the layout and
structure of the vessel showed that it was designed to be capable of
carrying a lot more. Why a spacecraft should require weaponry at all
was a good question, since none of the worlds so far discovered could
boast a civilization anywhere close to being a potential spacegoing
adversary. Of course, there was always the possibility of that situation
ending tomorrow, and being prepared was only a sensible precaution.
But if the earlier age of colonialism on Earth was any guide, a more
likely explanation seemed to be insurance against future rivalries,
and a message to would-be interlopers that the new players of the
game were prepared to defend their turf. In short, the old, familiar
pattern was emerging to begin another cycle.

Around three dozen escapees and others who could be thought
of as malefactors were being brought back to Earth aboard the
Ranger. The latter included some crew members from earlier missions
who, while not having actually vanished from the base, had contrived
to go missing at the time their ship departed. There were also a few
from the *Tacoma* who had indicated a reluctance to return and were
therefore not considered reliable enough to continue with their
duties. Although they were not labeled prisoners as such, their movements were restricted to quarters in the *Ranger*'s midships section.
These comprised two rooms of double-tier bunks, evidently intended
to accommodate military contingents, with an adjoining mess space
and a small kitchen. Since the *Ranger* was designed for small-scale,
special-purpose tasks, not as a general transport for personnel or
cargo, they used the same dining and exercise facilities as everyone
else, but at their own set times in keeping with the general policy of
segregation.

Emotions aroused in a dream, or maybe new sentiments that are
opened up regarding a situation or a relationship, often persist after
the dream has faded, or even been forgotten. After the *Ranger*

entered Heim space and as the first days of the voyage home passed, Shearer noticed that the feelings he had developed of strong positive associations toward Cyrene and the prospect of a future there persisted more vividly than could be attributed to memory alone. It was as if the sense of being in touch with a "cosmic consciousness" that he had described to Jeff, once awakened, refused to be extinguished. And conversely, the thought of having to return to Earth and all that it implied loomed colder and larger like a dark, threatening specter. He talked to one or two of the others, and they felt it too. He began to wonder just how general this effect was among those who had been exposed to Cyrene's unique environment—apparently even for a period as short as a week or two.

One morning, shortly after the detainees had returned to their quarters from breakfast, two troopers from the *Ranger*'s Milicorp complement appeared, identified Shearer, and took him to an office cabin in the inner part of the ship, where he found Callen waiting, seated at the desk. He hadn't even known Callen was aboard. For about an hour Callen worked through a series of questions from a prepared list, not pressing Shearer strongly for answers it seemed, but more testing his attitudes and reactions. Shearer got the feeling that this was a preliminary to more interrogations that he could expect in the weeks ahead, and Callen was merely preparing his ground.

But Shearer noticed something else too. This was not the same coldly efficient, single-minded Myles Callen who had interviewed him in Redwood City in the week before the *Tacoma*'s departure. Somehow, he seemed less sure of himself, less focused. He went through the questions with the air of one enacting a routine that he was committed to, but with a verve that was diminished compared to what had once been. Shearer wasn't sure what to make of it.

Wade was taken for questioning by Callen later that same day, but he was unable to augment Shearer's impressions because, not having met Callen before, he had no previous experience to go by. Wade did say that Callen had expressed a lot of curiosity about the kind of world Wade envisioned Cyrene as becoming.

They asked themselves why Callen should have been recalled to Earth so quickly. It seemed a meager return after bringing him so far. With the kinds of problems that base had been experiencing there should have been a lot more for him to do beyond just tracing Wade and shipping him back. Since he had never been involved with Wade previously and hadn't had time to become expert on what Wade had been doing on Cyrene, it seemed unlikely that he would have much to contribute to whatever proceedings were to take place upon Wade's return. The other possibility was that it had to do with some sudden change in the political climate affecting Milicorp and Interworld. The changes that Shearer had seen in Callen would certainly be consistent with the stresses and strife that constantly plagued the predatory world that people like Callen lived in.

Or could it, Shearer wondered, be the result of something in Callen having changed at a more profound level? . . .

That evening, after they had returned from their hour in the cafeteria, Shearer made his way over to Emner, who was lying on one of the lower bunks by the wall, pen in hand, studying a page in a book of crossword puzzles. They knew each other from the chatter over meals, but so far had never had any particular reason to talk person-to-person.

"Do you do cryptics?" Emner greeted as Shearer pulled a chair from the narrow table in the aisle behind.

"What've you got?" Shearer asked, turning it around and sitting down.

"The clue says, 'Tuo down under.'"

"How many letters?"

"Seven."

Shearer thought for a few seconds. "Outback."

Emner raised his eyebrows and nodded. "Good one." He wrote it in and then set the book down. "We never even got to meet before you went over the hill. You and that lady you were with must hold the record for the shortest stay in the base. What was it—one night?"

"Yes," Shearer said.

"What happened to her? I didn't see her being brought in with the rest of you from that place up north of Revo."

"She got away just before the raid. I guess she's still with the Cyreneans."

"Were you close?"

Shearer nodded. "We had plans for starting over on Cyrene. A home . . . everything."

"Too bad."

"You must have seen it lots of times," Shearer said. "This change that comes over people. A lot of them disappeared during your watch."

Emner snorted. "Cyrenean siren song, we called it. The scientists thought it was something chemical in the air, but they never found anything."

Shearer and Wade had decided not to rush into divulging what they knew until they had a better feel for the situation. "Yet you never did anything to stop them," Shearer commented.

"Oh hell, Shearer, you're not going to start into all that, are you? I've been grilled enough on it already—ever since the *Tacoma* arrived."

"It seems to me as if you must have gotten bitten too," Shearer said.

Emner didn't deny it. "Uh-huh. Why else do you think Callen took over, and I'm on my way back?"

"So why didn't you go over the hill too while you had the chance?"

"Oh. . . . Hum. . . ." Emner made rocking motions in the air with a hand, and then ran it through his hair. "There were a lot of conflicting issues. I've got family back home. Maybe, if the truth were known, I just wanted to be sent back and have an end to it. I don't know. . . . Why are you asking all this?"

"I'm trying to get a better feel for how it works. To know the signs. What kinds of patterns you've seen." Shearer paused, but Emner said nothing, waiting to see where this was going. "What's the story with Myles Callen?" Shearer asked finally, lowering his voice. "He was sent out to do a job. Okay, he'd taken over command, but that was only temporary. The *Ranger* needs three weeks to make the transit, so the decision to bring in the new team must have been made before the *Tacoma* arrived. He was sent to Cyrene to do a job. When the *Ranger* arrived, it should have freed him up to get on with it. But it didn't happen. All of a sudden he's on his way back too."

Emner shrugged. "Somebody must have changed their policy."

Shearer shook his head. "His job was to find out what was screwing up on Cyrene. That didn't change. Something in the relationship between him and the corporation changed."

"Why do you care?" Emner asked.

"When I'm in a situation like this, I like to have as good a handle as I can get on what's going on?"

"What good do you think it'll do you?"

"I can't tell if I don't know, can I?"

"So what makes you think I can help?"

"Ah, come on. You were base Director since the *Boise*. You know your way around, and who sees the traffic from Earth. And you're in this same situation too, right?"

Emner studied Shearer's face at length, as if trying to discern a motive. Shearer met his gaze evenly. He was making no attempt to hide anything, for the simple reason that just at that moment, he didn't have anything to hide. The candor must have struck a sympathetic chord in Emner.

"It's something that blew up within the last week," he said. "Callen was recalled."

"By Milicorp, you mean?"

"It goes further than that. Callen is known as a shark, which makes him good material for the kind of business that Milicorp is in. But when it reaches the point of bonking the wife of one of the clan that owns half of Interworld, you're taking on a different league." Emner raised a hand as he saw the objection forming on Shearer's face. "Yes, I know it happens all the time, and it's just not something you hear about. But in this instance somebody had a reason to make sure word got back to the Corbels' head honcho, and guess who just happens to be his favorite niece. She might even have done it herself, for all I know. I don't have to tell you how insane these things can get. She sounds dumb enough and mean enough. . . ." Emner shrugged and left it at that.

Shearer was already shaking his head incredulously. "And it could become an issue between corporations . . . over something like that? It's too crazy."

"Not if it were left to the business managers," Emner agreed. "But when the tribal chiefs get dragged in it can get out of hand. Don't forget . . . Marc, is it?"

"Right."

"You're talking about egos that live in a different world from the rest of us. These are people who'll keep a war going for years rather than back down and admit they can't win. Right now, from what I can make of it, whether Milicorp gets to stay as Interworld's security contractor could be on the line. Callen is being hauled back as the sacrificial offering to straighten things out. So you see my point about who might have set him up. It would suit someone like her just fine, wouldn't it? And you can always bet there will be a line of people with holes in their backs who have been waiting for a chance to balance the books. What goes around, eh?"

Shearer didn't answer at once, but picked up the crossword book and ran his eye idly over the partly completed page. A train of thought of some kind had started somewhere in his mind, but at this point, where it might be heading, he wasn't sure. "So going back to Earth might not be exactly the most attractive of propositions for Callen right now," he commented distantly.

"What else is he going to do?" Emner asked with a snort.

Shearer had enough to chew over for now. It was time to change the subject. He put the book back and looked up. "How about you?" he asked. He got the feeling that Emner had been looking for someone with whom he could share confidences.

"Oh . . ." Emner leaned back against the pillows that he had stacked at the end of the bunk and clasped his hands behind his head. "As I said, I have family back home. . . . But, do you know, I'm not really sure I think of Earth as home anymore. Does that sound crazy to you? It's one of the things that happens with the big-C siren song." His voice fell almost to a whisper. "I'll tell you what I'm going to do, Marc. When I get back, I'll tell them all what it was like and how it feels out there. And then one day—I'm not sure when or exactly how . . . we'll come back to Cyrene. All of us together. I *know* that's where the future is. Hey, you were there, Marc. You know what I mean."

CHAPTER THIRTY-FIVE

It was a little late in life for such things, Callen admitted to himself, but he had decided that he was going soft. It was one of those eat-or-be-eaten situations where coming out on top depended on nerve, ruthlessness, and outthinking the shifting alliances and temporary truces among those who were out to bring you down. Normally it was something he excelled at and thrived on, with adrenaline rushes that his system was deliciously attuned to. As he had anticipated, his sources on Earth were reporting that the story there was being twisted to make it seem that the *Ranger* had been dispatched specifically to effect *his* replacement after a negative assessment of his ability from an unnamed authority aboard the *Tacoma*. To forestall such accusations, Callen was taking them Wade's head on a plate, tracked down and brought in along with his partner in a matter of days, and their whole subversive operation with the Cyreneans uncovered. And as a bonus he was delivering a renegade Milicorp undercover operative cleared by the people who assigned him to Callen, but whom Callen's experience had taught him to watch nevertheless. They'd have a hard time nailing him with that record to point at.

But of course it wouldn't stop there, because that wasn't really what it was all about. That was merely the pretense they would play out for the sake of external appearances. In reality it was a hatchet job ordered by Joseph Corbel personally after the brat-bitch fed them the story that *Callen* had suckered her by intimating that he was in a position to recommend her as Cyrene's ambassadress as an enticement for services rendered during the voyage out, when in fact an instruction to that effect had already come in.

Ordinarily it would have been a good fight, with Wade, Shearer, Dolphin, and the others who had been rounded up nothing more than unlucky victims to be written off if that was what the game called for. And over the years Callen had seen plenty of splattered limbs and entrails from collateral damage who had been a lot more unfortunate than these particular victims. Such had always been one of the things to be accepted about life. The world was a harsh place. But now he found it strangely troubling for reasons he couldn't put his finger on. That was why he told himself that he must be going soft.

His attitude toward academics and intellectuals had always been contemptuous. They waffled and talked, safe within protective borders that others defended. He had watched them projecting themselves into fantasized alpha roles with affected verbal aggressiveness, but never incurring any real physical risk. But there was something about the way the people on Cyrene had quit and vanished that stirred a grudging admiration in him. Instead of fawning, groveling, and falling over themselves to pander to the whims of the institutions that succored them, like all the ones he had known, they had turned their backs on all of it and struck out into the completely unknown. Even on an alien world light-years from home, where the security symbolized by the one link to Earth should have been the overriding consideration, they had opted for independence to follow what they believed in. That took guts and conviction. And Callen thought he had glimpsed why they did it. Once again he was unable to pin down the specifics, but there was something about Cyrene, something vibrant and fresh in the culture emerging there that made Earth feel diseased and degenerate by comparison. And others who had sensed it had gone out to help build what could have been, and to become a part of it. . . . Yet he was a part of the powers that would destroy all that—just as they were equally prepared to destroy him. Why? Because it was what he had always been.

He thought ahead to the confrontation that awaited when he arrived on Earth. Even if he recruited enough pull on his side, made the right moves, and came out of it with all the tokens to establish himself as having "won," the thought had little appeal. What would it all be for, really? To impress and gain the favor of worthless people who didn't interest him? The phoniness and cowardice behind it all

James P. Hogan

repelled him. He felt like a pit pony that had been allowed to see sunshine and know the freshness of open air, being taken back down to the gloom and stifle of the mine. It made no sense. He had hardly been out or seen anything beyond Revo base in the brief time he was there. But already, in some strange way that he didn't understand, he was beginning to miss Cyrene.

The whine of the cabin door sounded, and a moment later Krieg appeared. He had been up in the communications room behind the bridge, checking on the latest to come in. Krieg was being recalled to Earth too, officially for "reassignment," since he no longer had a role on Cyrene as Callen's associate. Callen had little doubt that the real reason was to be pumped for incriminating information that could be used in the forthcoming bloodletting.

"From Cyrene," Krieg announced. "The last of the natives who were being held at the base have been let go." Callen nodded. That was to be expected. There were no grounds for holding them. Preferred policy was to induce them into dependence, not start a war. "The Terran property at Linzava has been recovered. No information on the progress of inquiries concerning Uberg and the others."

"Anything new from Earth?" Callen asked.

"Just routine stuff."

Callen motioned him down into the fold-out seat between the hinged surface that served as a desk and table below the com screen, and the washbasin. This was definitely not E Section accommodation in the *Tacoma.* "We need to talk about the reception party when we arrive. Something we have to be prepared for is that Borland could bounce the wrong way." In a situation like this it was a legitimate consideration. The top management at Milicorp wouldn't hesitate to dump Borland if it meant placating a client like Interworld, which meant that Borland would try to disassociate himself. In fact, Callen had already learned from a sympathetic quarter on Earth that a story was circulating to the effect that Borland had opposed the choice of Callen for the Cyrene mission and been overruled. Who but Borland was likely to have originated it?

"Fishes swim. Bosses do whatever it takes to save their necks," Krieg agreed.

At times, Callen envied him. He personified the ultimate in reductionist materialism, viewing the world in its simplest mechanical terms, which he accepted pragmatically without moral scruple or value judgment. If he had been affected by Cyrene, he had neither mentioned it nor shown any indication.

"I want you to give me an account of the Amaranth operation," Callen said. "Names, places, everything that happened. It doesn't have to identify you as the originator. Just facts I can throw at people, that they'll be able to verify if they check."

For once Krieg managed to look surprised. "What does Amaranth have to do with it?" he asked. That had been the operation where they installed a controlled prophet in the king's court through the device of a manufactured plague, which Krieg had masterminded before being spirited away to Cyrene.

Callen had decided it was time to reveal a few things. "I met Borland in a room in the San Mateo Marriott when he gave me the orders for Amaranth. It was a room that a friend of mine in the state security police recommended. They arrange for foreign visitors that they're interested in to stay there." Which was another way of saying that it was bugged. "I've got it all, Jerry. Even a vid of Borland and the hooker who showed up after I left. It'll nail the line down all the way back to the treetop at Interworld. A veep at Milicorp didn't dream up something like Amaranth on his own."

Krieg whistled silently. What Callen was saying was more than a landmine under the other side's position. The Asian and South American interstellar outfits would run with it. The questions it would raise could have repercussions that would last for years. The simple answer was, it *couldn't* be allowed to get out.

"That's . . . interesting," Krieg said. He gnawed at the edge of a thumbnail and then smoothed it with a finger. His expression was thoughtful and distant. "Very interesting."

Callen's price would be a ticket to comfortable obscurity, effectively at whatever figure he chose to name. Even so, he found himself able to summon up little enthusiasm for the prospect. And he didn't have to be told that life in such circumstances, for people who knew things that made powerful interests decidedly uncomfortable, had a tendency to be inexplicably accident-prone.

There had been an incident once, when Lang was with a Marine unit attached to a force occupying a city in southern Asia. It was in one of the endless actions involving insurgents who were sabotaging oil pipelines that had been laid from somewhere inland to the coast. The unit was on a house-to-house search detail for weapons, explosives, and suspects—kick down the door, go in screaming, knock down anyone who gets in the way. They were trained to disorientate and intimidate any opposition by shock, speed, and violence. The trouble was it could go to your head, and you got carried away—especially if you drugged up before setting out, as a lot of guys did. A terrified boy came out of a doorway onto the street and ran straight at them. Kids had been known to be strapped with bombs—at least, so you were told—and the man working flank to Lang's right blew him apart with a six-round burst on automatic. The boy wasn't packing anything.

Later, Lang was standing guard over a teenage girl and her mother who had been brought outside while the squad trashed the house and everything they owned, and beat up the males who hadn't been hauled off in a truck. The girl had just stood there, staring at him, her eyes unwavering. She didn't show emotion or attempt to appeal to any sense of humanity in him—implying that there wasn't anything there to appeal to. In the end she said, "Why are you doing this to us?" Lang had no answer. He'd felt like a reptile.

The incident itself wasn't particularly exceptional. The reason Lang recalled it now was that the boy reminded him of Mutu, the ferryman's son. Similar in build and looks, about the same age, impatient to begin the great adventure of learning to become an adult and go out to meet whatever life had to offer. Young people on Cyrene didn't spend extended childhoods in artificially structured social environments or immersed in electronic make-believe realities that had little relation to the real world and seemed only to generate resentment at being alienated from it. Cyrenean children began learning the skills of the farm and workplace, and assimilating the rules for getting along with others at an early age. Adults were expert at the things they knew they would have to know, and so commanded a respect that came naturally. Lang had never been interested in marrying and starting a family back home. He'd seen too many of the walking wounded that came out of being trapped in years of wage and tax slavery, and then seeing the kids that it was all for taken away and turned into monsters by the state. But maybe, if the day ever came when somehow he could go back to Cyrene . . .

"Jeff. What are you looking so lost in thought about?"

Lang turned his head to find Wade standing by the bunk. "Hey, Evan. Aw, this and that. At least thinking is something there's plenty of time for here, for a change." He swung his legs off the side and sat up. "So what's up?"

"Some of us in the next room are setting up a poker table. Do you play? Five stud."

"You guys might not know what you're taking on here. You're talking to the man who cleaned out the Marine Corps."

"I'll risk it. So are you in?"

"Sure. What are we betting?"

"Anything you've got that's Cyrenean—coins, trinkets, buttons, beads. Lou says it all fetches good prices back home."

"I've still got the pouch I was wearing when they picked us up—full of coins and things. And I think I might have a few pins and a hat badge."

"Perfect. There's no rush. We won't be starting for about half an hour."

Lang slid down from the bunk without using the steps and moved to the end of the aisle, where the stand with the coffeepot was. "Coffee," he said over his shoulder as he filled a mug. "Now, that's something I did miss on Cyrene. Do you think it would grow there?" He saw that Wade had followed him to do likewise, and moved out of the way.

"I don't see why not," Wade said. "Life there seems remarkably compatible. You'd need to talk to somebody like Dominic Uberg about that." He poured himself a mug, stirring in some creamer, and eyed Lang as he took a sip. "What made you ask that, Jeff? Been having thoughts about going back one day?"

Lang grinned faintly and didn't try to deny it. "Hasn't everybody?"

"Has Marc talked to you yet?" Wade asked.

"Marc? What about?"

"He's sounding people out on how they feel about going back to Earth. He seems interested in the ones who don't have strong ties there and liked what they saw on Cyrene—like you, Jeff."

"What's going on?" Lang tried his coffee. It tasted good.

Wade shrugged. "I dunno. He hasn't said. Maybe he's thinking of writing a book."

Jerri sat out on the wooden deck at the rear of the house in Ulla, watching the boats on the broad sweep of the Woohosey river. Nim lay by her chair, sprawled alongside Sakari's *glok*, Roo—named by Nick. The two animals had become inseparable and were sleeping off the exertion of an afternoon romping around the town on expeditions to shops, and visits for Jerri to be introduced to friends. The first evening nip was in the air as Cyrene moved toward the cooler part of its orbit, and Jerri had put a cloak around her shoulders, over her sweater and skirt.

The laboratory and workshops at Linzava, higher in valley behind the town, had looked bare and dilapidated after being cleaned out of their Terran equipment and then subjected to the none-too-gentle attentions of the Milicorp soldiers, but since then the soldiers hadn't returned. All the same, everyone had agreed it would be a prudent for her and Nick to move down to stay with his Cyrenean girlfriend. Sakari framed pictures and dabbled in printing decorative patterns, pamphlets, and books. Jerri had experience in editing and desktop publishing, and it seemed that each of them would have something to learn from the other. Nick had his eye on some empty rooms in the building adjoining the house, with a view to maybe setting up a physician's practice.

The raid had concentrated on bringing back Terrans, whom the authorities at the base evidently considered to be still under their jurisdiction, and repossessing the equipment that had been taken from the base. Although some justification for the latter couldn't be denied, the Cyreneans were astounded by the means employed. Surely there were other ways in which the case might have been presented, they said. The significance of all the plants and the botanical experimental work in progress had apparently been missed completely. Since there had been no return visits to investigate further, it seemed safe to conclude that nobody had divulged the nature of Wade and Elena's discoveries.

Although the disruption of the work at Linzava represented a setback from the expansive visions that Wade had entertained, it was far from a disaster. It meant, simply, that instead of taking a fast track to an infrastructure to support oil and electricity, the Cyreneans would fall back to the more sedate course already being explored by people like those ones they had met at Doriden, in their own way, and in their own time.

In fact, there were many who were of the opinion that it would be better that way. After all, Wade's prime motivation had been to forestall Earth's economic imperialist schemes by setting the Cyreneans on a path to self-sufficiency before they could be lured into a condition of dependence. The reality of any real threat in that direction now seemed doubtful—certainly in the short term. As far as could be made out from the reports finding their way through from Revo, while the lock-in at the Terran base was still being enforced, the new administration that had replaced Callen seemed to have gone into some kind of a funk. Communications with Vattorix had been minimal, with little evidence of significant new activities. If Jerri's understanding of how these things worked was anything to go by, the *Tacoma* had be at the limit of the maximum time it could be permitted to stay, and there didn't seem to be enough going on to justify sending another ship to relieve it, let alone expand the traffic. It was as if they had no policy and didn't know what to do. Nick had heard rumors from Terran sources scattered around that Interworld was contemplating chucking the whole thing and pulling out— which would have been a first. Others said they were reconnoitering elsewhere on Cyrene to see if what they had encountered in Yocala was typical. But nobody really knew.

Nim lifted his head suddenly and looked toward the house. Moments later Sakari came out carrying a wine flask and cups, set them down on the table in front of Jerri, and pulled up a chair. She was tall, long-legged, and sturdily built, with olive skin and long honey-blond hair hanging forward over her shoulders and fastened by clasps. Jerri thought she would raise a fine family if events ever went that way.

"Nick is back," she said in Yocalan. "He will be out in a moment." The NIDA pair that Jerri had brought with her had run down and there was no way to recharge it, so they were back to basics. It was probably a good thing, Jerry had decided. She was going to have to learn the language anyway. Sakari surveyed the animals. "Look at that lump of mine, not even stirring. Nim shames us."

"Roo's at home," Jerri pointed out. She stood the cups and held them for Sakari to pour.

"Well, it's supposed to be Nim's home too now."

"I like that . . . what do you call it?" Jerri indicated the thick, garment, like a cardigan, that Sakari was wearing. "The reddy leafy brown suits you. I haven't seen it before."

"It's called a *kishelin*. Istany made it for me."

"The woman in the place where we got the bread and cakes?"

"Yes. It was for some designs I did for the walls. And see how the collar gathers for when it gets cold."

"Those designs with the fish and the shells and the water plants? Did you do those? I thought they were wonderful."

"Well, thank you."

A clumping of feet on boards sounded from behind. Nim's tail added a few thumps, and then Nick sat down looking jovial as always. "Hi Jerri," he greeted. They made it a rule to speak in Yocalan when Sakari was present. It was all good practice anyway. "I hear you've had a busy day."

"Just helping Sakari get some things. And learning to find my way around. Anyway, who told you?"

"Oh, I get around too, you know." Nick looked at Sakari. "I talked to the man who owns those rooms. I think it might work out."

"Very good."

"It sounds is if you're really getting settled in, Nick," Jerri commented.

"Well, not just me Jerri. You're one of the family too, now. Isn't that right?" His eyes took on the faintest touch of a more serious light. It was a hint to her to be realistic. But Jerri just smiled and sat back to taste her wine.

"Well, for the duration, anyway," she conceded.

Nick grinned and tilted his head in a way that said he wasn't going to argue. "You really think he'll come back, Jerri? But how could that happen?"

Jerri looked out at the river and up at the first stars of evening. The *Tacoma*'s orbit wouldn't bring it overhead tonight, but she had seen it that morning. "I couldn't tell you how, Nick," she replied. "But it shouldn't come as any surprise to you by now. On Cyrene, you just know these things."

CHAPTER THIRTY-SIX

The two troopers brought Shearer to the cabin that Callen used as his office during the day. One of them opened the door; the other motioned Shearer through. They withdrew, closing the door behind him.

Shearer sat down in the chair on the opposite side of the narrow metal desk. The routine was familiar by now. Callen made a play of scanning over the notes displayed on a flatpad lying in front of him. He looked weary. Shearer had formed the impression that he really didn't care whether he won or lost the fight he would be going back to. Superficially he seemed a shadow of the man that Shearer had met before the voyage out. And yet, in another way, Shearer sensed a deeper, more profound man.

"This job description that was posted for an assistant to go and join Wade on Cyrene," Callen opened. Shearer raised his eyebrows and waited. "Why did you apply for it?"

"To get away," Shearer answered. "What chances were there for working in real science back there? Nastier bombs? Better technology to boost profits a tenth of a point? The project I was on was being wrapped up. The only gain it stood to offer was in knowledge."

Callen looked dubious; but there was also a hint of genuine curiosity on his face. "And what do you consider to be real science?" he asked.

Shearer shrugged. "What I just said. Pursuing knowledge for its own sake. Wanting to know what it's all about—how the universe works. Where it came from and what it's there for. But nobody in your world wants to hear about things like that."

"Why do you call it my world?"

"Okay, then, your kind of people. They created it, and your job is to defend it for them. How do you like the results?"

"And what makes knowledge so important? Why should anyone want to know?"

"Humans are born wanting to know. It takes professional educators twenty years to kill it and turn them into what the system wants. Or if you won't fit, you're weeded out. Nobody's going to change it now." Shearer showed his hands briefly. "So you get away. That's what I did."

Callen stared for a second or two, but didn't seem inclined to pursue it. "So what makes you think the universe is there for any reason at all?" he asked, picking up Shearer's other point.

"Look around. Open your eyes. How could anyone think it's not?"

"I thought scientists didn't have time for ideas like that."

"You're talking about technicians that the system has bought. They peddle the kind of world that suits it, and tell everyone they'd better buy into it because that's all there is. Real science just follows whichever way the evidence seems to point. You don't decide in advance what kind of answers you'll accept and what you won't."

"So what's the reason?" Callen challenged.

"I don't know."

"Did you think you'd find it on Cyrene?"

"Maybe. . . . I don't think it was to produce Interworld Restructuring."

Callen's mouth twitched. He shifted his gaze back to the notes on the flatpad and flipped the image to a new sheet. "Wade disappeared from Revo base shortly after filing the application."

"If you say so."

"Things like that don't happen on the spur of the moment. Why would he file for an assistant if he was planning on disappearing?"

Callen was obviously cross-checking answers. Shearer could see himself getting tangled up in contradicting details for no good reason if he let himself be drawn in. "He's here. You can talk to him. I was in California. I can't second-guess his motives," he said.

"But you were in contact before he disappeared."

"His messages never went into it. We'd worked together before.

That seemed good enough for me." As Callen would no doubt be able to verify—and very probably already had.

"I put it to you that you had already agreed it between you," Callen said. "Even at the time Wade departed from Earth. You both have the same political views. You'd worked with him since arriving from Florida. The intention was for you to join him at the first opportunity."

Shearer spread his hands in feigned innocence. "He just filed for an assistant."

"Oh, come on. He was stuck with procedures. The spec had your measurements like a suit."

"Okay." Shearer held up a hand. "So we think alike, and we work well together. Where I was at, I was going nowhere. This could have been a whole new start. What's so strange?"

"What did you think you'd find there?"

"I had no idea. All I'd seen were the regular releases, same as everyone sees."

Callen checked his notes and moved to a different angle. "The work you were doing at Berkeley involved a new kind of quantum wave. Want to tell me about it?"

Shearer drew a long breath. He must have been asked this dozens of times, both before leaving and during the voyage out. It could get involved. He had learned to try and keep things as short as possible. "The formal quantum wave equations give two sets of solutions. One kind are called 'retarded,' which have been used in physics for over a century. The other kind—'advanced'—involve negative energy and travel backward in time. Traditionally they are treated as an artifact of the mathematics and not attributed any physical reality."

"But some years ago, Wade came up with a theory that they're real." Technically inclined or not, at least Callen had been doing his homework.

"Yes," Shearer said.

"And his work at Berkeley was aimed at trying to prove it. Which you continued."

"Yes."

"And was it getting anywhere?" Callen's expression said that he doubted it. Why else would the project be shut down?

Shearer made a face. "Obviously the people funding it didn't think so. We were getting results, but they were judged inconclusive. Right on the edge."

"What do you think?"

"I'm probably the last person you should ask. People who want to believe see things that aren't there. Trying to eliminate wishful thinking is what half of science is all about."

Callen sat back in his chair and steepled his fingers for a moment, as if contemplating an outlandish question. "Was Wade continuing with that same line on Cyrene?"

It took Shearer by surprise. His first reaction was to stall while he collected his thoughts. "There's nothing like Berkeley there. They're only starting to dabble with steam engines."

"You arranged for some specialized hardware to be shipped from his private lab. Then he managed to lift enough gear from Revo to outdo Edison—including a ten megawatt fission module, for heaven's sake!" Callen leaned forward and shook his head, as if none of this should need spelling out. "But he didn't wait for you to arrive, did he? Suddenly he vanishes from Revo to go and join Elena Hukishido, who had gone there on the same mission but disappeared a couple of months before he did. Her field was biophotonics. And the person who stayed back until you arrived, and who had a conduit already set up for you, was Dominic Uberg, a plant biologist." Callen sat back, inviting Shearer to consider his case. "So what were they on to out there, Mr. Shearer? The intelligence agency that backed the Berkeley project thought it might give them a means of seeing into the future—which a report written by you did nothing to dispel. It must have been something very exciting."

Now Shearer thought he saw what was behind all this. Callen was going back to a bloodbath involving high corporate politics and out-raged Brobdingnagian egos of a kind that Shearer was grateful not to have to deal with. Callen was scouting all the angles to prepare his position. In the bizarre way that events had turned out, he was sounding Shearer out, in effect, as a potential ally to his cause. But there was no way that Shearer could oblige. He and Wade had agreed adamantly—and could only hope that noting had transpired since on Cyrene to confute them—that there could be no revealing of what the work at Linzava had established. For after the bonanza that the Heim discoveries had unleashed, the news of yet another new realm of physics being opened up would trigger a rush of commercial speculators that would dwarf everything that had happened on all the other colony worlds put together. Callen was so close . . . This had to be killed in the bud.

"Sure—he was interested in continuing working on his theory if he could," Shearer said. "A man doesn't forget something like that. It was a passion with him—and still is. But it didn't go anywhere." He paused pointedly. "And if you want my frank opinion, I'm glad it didn't."

Callen's eyebrows arched in surprise. "How so?" he asked.

"Come on." Shearer got a kick out of throwing Callen's own phrase back. "That wasn't why you set me up, or something Interworld was interested in." They had been through the questions of Shearer's application being rushed through, and the role played by Jeff Lang, in an earlier session. "You've just told me you'd read the funding agency's assessment. Interworld was panicking because the buzz coming in from Revo was that Wade was organizing a network of relocated Terrans to help the Cyreneans stop their planet from being turned into another industrial plantation. But it's already a lost cause, Mr. Callen. You admitted that yourself when you ordered the gates on the base to be closed. That planet will entice away everyone they send there. Three missions are going to have to be written off. Interworld's first big bust. How are the company's damage control doctors going to spin that in the stockholder reports?" Shearer shook his head in a way that said he was glad it wasn't he who was going back to it. "They're going to want heads. It'll be blood all over the walls back there. I don't think I envy you in your position . . . on top of everything else."

"Meaning?"

"Ah . . . talk goes around. Let's just say that Milicorp might have their own reasons for needing a body for the wolves."

Callen stared at Shearer long and hard. A change had come about in the atmosphere. Although the protocols of the situation didn't permit it to be voiced, there was a mutual recognition of their positions as being more congruent in some ways than adversarial. The conversation was no doubt being recorded, but Shearer assumed that the interrogator would have editing capability. "My compliments on your reasoning," Callen said finally.

"That figures both ways," Shearer replied. And meant it. He

snorted and smiled faintly. "It's too bad you're going the wrong way—back to a meat grinder. Your kind of thinking would be priceless to the Cyreneans. They put great value on knowledge too. But they're more intuitive. Rational analysis is something they need to work on—especially given the direction they're heading. And they'll do it without all the bloodbaths and the slave camps. Knowledge to create a better life for everybody, not just the leeches."

"What is it about Cyrene?" Callen asked distantly.

Shearer shrugged. "That's another thing Wade was hoping to find out more about. He thought Elena Hukishido might have been on to something. That was what got him excited. Some kind of euphoric or mild hallucinogen produced by plants, that Terrans react to. . . . They were still working on it." Callen would know that the labs inside the base had been following that line with negative results.

Callen seemed to dream for a few seconds longer. Then he brushed it aside abruptly and said in a brisk voice, "But that's not the way it is, is it? Life is about playing the hand you're dealt. We're heading for Earth." In that moment Shearer had glimpsed what he had been looking for since he sat down. If there was to be any chance at all of pulling something off, he had no choice now but to go for it.

He studied a knuckle while he picked his words, and then asked in a curious voice, "But does it have to be that way?"

Callen frowned. "How else could it be?"

"Listen to what a lot of people's instincts have already told them: Go where they know the light is. Be a part of that."

"You mean Cyrene?"

"Why not? Why go back to a nightmare?"

Callen gave a sharp shake of his head, as if to be sure that Shearer wasn't taking leave of his senses. "Even if I thought you were serious . . . how do you intend getting there? You can't just show up at an airport after you get home."

Shearer gestured briefly to indicate their surroundings. "Why wait till you get home? The means is right here."

Callen looked incredulous, and then laughed derisively as if he were agreeing to share a sick joke. "And how do you propose persuading the captain to turn the *Ranger* around? None of the crew were down on Cyrene. In any case, I don't think he'd be interested in trading places for a brigantine out of Revo."

Shearer maintained a serious expression. "It will need at least two surface shuttles to take everyone from the *Ranger* down after it docks with the transfer satellite. You could lose the crew if they were assigned for relief on the first one—not unreasonable, since they've just done an interstellar round trip without a break. And people from Cyrene who have reasons for wanting to go back to Earth could be included on it too, such as Emner. That would leave a majority up at the satellite who want to return to Cyrene—enough to take over the *Ranger* if they were properly equipped and organized, had speed and surprise on their side. Any additional ones wanting to stay could be left on the satellite to be picked up."

"And who's going to take the *Ranger* back? You?" There was still mockery in Callen's tone but it had lessened. His eyes played over Shearer's face searchingly. He was listening.

"Colonel Yannis has done full military space piloting and commanded Heim ships. I guess you already know his record."

"It needs more than a captain," Callen pointed out.

"Getting us there would just need propulsion and navigation. We can forget communications, weapons control and targeting, and other specialized military functions. Berger and Polapulos were first and second drive officers on the *Tacoma*. They're being shipped back because they were in contact with runaway Terrans. Sengatrow was a master fields engineering specialist from the *Boise*, before the *Tacoma*. Wen Siyu supervised drive and generating controls instrumentation. They were picked up at Linzava. In addition there are four others who could be brought up to speed for regular duty shifts. After something the size of the *Tacoma*, they shouldn't have much trouble handling the basics of this kind of ship. Recharging the D-T primary f·el bank and restocking from the transfer satellite could be done in under an hour."

Shearer left it at that. Either Callen was with him now, or else there was no point in continuing anyway. His only choice had been to stake all or nothing. He raised his chin and waited.

Callen regarded him with what looked like open disbelief for along time; then he exhaled sharply, shaking his head. "You obviously have it all figured out. . . . And these people you mentioned would be favorably disposed?"

"Oh, I'd say so. Sure."

"How do you know you can trust them?"

"Obviously there are going to be risks. Evan Wade is pretty good when it comes to judging and recruiting people who won't talk too much. You should know that. "

Callen shook his head again, but it was from wonder more than anything else. His eyes came back to meet Shearer's. Shearer read in them a look of disbelief that Callen could think the things he was finding himself thinking.

But Shearer was getting used to that. He had seen that look many times now. Cyrene did crazy things to people.

CHAPTER THIRTY-SEVEN

For a smaller craft like the *Ranger*, the H-point could be closer in to Earth than had been the case with the *Tacoma*. It reemerged into normal space a less than a day's flight time from the transfer station designated DSX-14. As they made final approach, Shearer and his companions were able to verify its form on one of the cabin wall screens as a toroid surrounding a cylindrical central structure. Callen, who by this time was fully committed, had provided details of the internal structure and layout. A shuttle to take the first batch of arrivals down to the surface was already attached at one of the four docking ports. Of the remainder, one was occupied by a cargo shuttle, another out of use while undergoing overhaul, and the last, reserved for the *Ranger*. Also, standing off at a distance of a mile or so, waiting to move in, was a robot freighter that one of the company identified from its markings as having come from Cyrene. It was not the one that had been in orbit, loading, at the time of the *Tacoma*'s arrival—which couldn't have made it to Earth in the time since, anyway. Shearer guessed it to be the one that Uberg had said departed earlier, on which he had sent his consignment of botanical seeds and samples for study. It appeared have arrived shortly before the *Ranger*—possibly a matter of mere hours—and been put on hold to give servicing of the manned vessel priority.

The escape plan that started as an impossible brainchild of Shearer's had gradually come together and taken form under Wade's quiet but skilled direction. Three quarters of the detainees being brought back from Cyrene were involved, who knew the plan and were fluent in their roles. Wade had broken the group down into teams who talked to him and Shearer but not among each other. Individuals who, for whatever reason, had elected not to be included, such as Emner, were not conversant with the details, although under the conditions of their confinement it would have been impossible not to have some idea of what was going on. There was really little else that could be done to preserve secrecy. In the final measure they depended on trust in the goodwill of their fellows, which they knew was always a risky business in situations where there could be something to be gained by plea-bargaining. But what was the alternative? Shearer remarked to Wade that if they had thought to bring some moon flowers to brighten up the place, they might have been on surer ground. The strangest thing about it was the realization that he hadn't been joking.

Callen had turned out to be not just an asset, but essential. As appreciation deepened of just what would be entailed, it became apparent that the cooperation of somebody in a position of influence on the outside was indispensable. Not only had he been a source of vital information on the numbers and disposition of the ship's crew and the Milicorp contingent that it was carrying, but his position gave him a say in deciding the makeup of the shuttle passenger lists. In addition, his access to Milicorp's records enabled him to identify four troopers and a sergeant from earlier missions who were being recalled on grounds of suspected unreliability, having been replaced by new blood that arrived with the *Tacoma*. Guarding nonviolent miscreants aboard a spacecraft was looked on as a "soft" duty that would at least get some useful work out of them on the way back, and Callen had arranged for them to be retained in this capacity and among the contingent that would stay with the *Ranger* when the first descent shuttle left. After putting out guarded feelers, Callen had succeeded in recruiting the sergeant, whose name was Osterman. He had been contemplating making a break on Cyrene since learning that returning to Earth would mean having to face a former wife and a militant attorney waiting to put him through a blender. Having Osterman won over gave access to the ship's small-arms armory.

The final lists had the first shuttle down as carrying the *Ranger*'s captain and senior officers, the major part of the crew, the hard core of the Milicorp contingent, and some people from Cyrene who were returning on official business. Those left at DSX-14 to await collection by a second shuttle would be the detainees—including the ones who were not planning to return, since there was no logical grounds whereby they could be separated out—a guard detachment, which included as many judged to potentially "friendly" as Callen had been able to have picked, and a skeleton crew under the *Ranger*'s second officer, who would be responsible for post-flight system checks and shutdown prior to handover of the ship to a service crew.

Callen's rationale for remaining was that he had been specifically entrusted the task of bringing back Wade, and he would remain with his charge until delivery was completed. He had mulled for a long time over what to do about Krieg. He knew of no strong ties or affiliations that should bind Krieg to Earth, but then Krieg had never shown any emotional disposition or attachment toward anything. In the end, he had decided not to put Krieg in the compromising position of having to declare loyalty one way or the other. Callen would wait until the moment came for those returning to Cyrene to divide themselves from those who would remain on the satellite, and let Krieg choose for himself then.

The odds had thus been rendered as favorable as possible. The general feeling was that they could have been far worse. Callen was forced to agree with Shearer that betting high on the hand that gets dealt in life comes more easily when one has had a hand in stacking it.

Shearer sat with Wade and Lang at one of the tables in the detainees' mess area. Around them, and back at the two bunking rooms, everyone was waiting with topcoats on and personal belongings packed, ready to go. There was little talk. Even those who had opted for Earth were tense now that it was plain that the moment had arrived. Without the constant sensation of power pulsing through the structure, felt more than heard, and the rest of the background to being under way that had become so familiar as to cease registering consciously, the ship seemed dead and still. The only sounds now were the humming of the ventilators and the whines and clunks of unseen machinery securing the docking latches and service umbilicals. There was no reason for delay. Shearer estimated that the first batch to be departing should already be assembling in the core zone of the ship, where the main lock was situated.

The signal to move would be when Callen appeared, accompanied by Osterman, which would mean the bridge had received confirmation of the shuttle's departure. Earlier, Osterman had concealed caches of pistols and small arms at a number of strategic locations where the breakout groups would be able to retrieve them en route to their designated target areas. First priority was to seize the bridge and communications room before an alarm could be raised. Callen would head for it directly with a picked group, while Osterman led a second to subdue the remaining Milicorp detachment, some of whom he hoped could be induced into collaborating. Lang, meanwhile would lead a third group in a fast rush through to the satellite control center at the top end of the central cylinder, which it was vital to secure before word of trouble arrived. With those objectives attained, the way would be clear for Shearer, Wade, and a guard detail to escort everyone not wishing to return to Cyrene off the ship and onto the satellite to await later collection. At the same time, a technical squad commanded by the former mission ship officers would commence recharging the *Ranger*'s power banks and restocking with water and supplies for the return trip. They expected to have everybody reembarked and to be ready to detach in under an hour.

Never had Shearer known minutes to drag so slowly. He felt clammy, his stomach tight. Somebody farther along the table was drumming his fingers incessantly. Another somewhere behind clenched his teeth audibly every five seconds or so. Anticipating it got to be like listening to a dripping tap. Shearer wanted to scream at him to stop it. Wade caught his gaze and raised his eyebrows resignedly. Emner, who was nearby, leaned forward and murmured quietly.

"I take it, gentlemen, that this is where we part. Good luck to you all. Maybe, one day, I will see you again." Wade nodded almost imperceptibly.

"Thanks," Shearer whispered.

Footsteps sounded on the metal stairs a short distance along the corridor outside. Moments later, Osterman stepped in through the doorway, brandishing an automatic pistol, nodded curtly, and with a wave of his arm stood aside, holding the door. The lead squad, who had been waiting just inside, moved quickly and silently past him to follow Callen, also armed, who was visible beyond. Osterman's group were already moving up behind, while Jeff Lang and the fast team closed in from the sides to group for the run into the satellite as soon as the way through the ship was clear. Perhaps thirty seconds passed. Then Lang's voice came from the front in a low but commanding "*Go!*" and the waiting figures melted away into the corridor.

Everything seemed to be going quietly and smoothly. Surely if anything had gone wrong on the bridge they would have heard hints of it by now. Two of those who had gone ahead reappeared to station themselves inside the door, now carrying weapons. Shearer got up and moved forward to join them. One handed him a pocket two-way radio and a pistol. Shearer had no experience of using a gun. The whole idea was not to have to. It was intended primarily as a badge of authority.

Behind him, Wade addressed the eleven detainees who were left. "Okay, no surprise. This is it. There's no time for speeches. We're taking the *Ranger* back to Cyrene. Anyone can stay aboard who wishes to. Everybody else will be taken off the ship now. You'll be collected from the satellite later. Please cooperate. Nobody wants to see any unpleasantness."

They were prepared for something like this. A couple seemed to be in a mild state of shock. Nothing happened for several seconds. Then Emner, smiling faintly to himself, got up and moved calmly toward the door. One by one, others began following. A woman called Jaynie, who had been at Linzava, and Ted, a steel erector from Revo base, who had become friendly with her during the voyage hung back, looking uncertainly at each other. Then they exchanged silent nods. Ted looked at Wade. "We're staying," he said.

Wade nodded. "Just remain here for now," he told them.

Shearer and the man who had given him the pistol led the rest out into the corridor and up the stairway to the main inboard deck, where an armed trooper in Milicorp uniform ushered them on through to the core zone—one of Osterman's defectors. A wider corridor and another stairwell brought them to the access ramp and lock antechamber. It had been secured by a rearguard from Jeff Lang's squad, who had already gone through. Controlling the lock was one of the crucial parts. *God, we're going to pull it off!* Shearer told himself.

This was where they were supposed to meet Osterman, bringing the *Ranger*'s second officer, crew members, and disarmed Milicorp remnants to join the others being taken through to the satellite. One of Lang's rearguard confirmed that they hadn't shown up yet. Shearer tried to raise Osterman on the radio but without success.

"We'll wait here for them," Wade said to Shearer, indicating himself and two of the company. "You go ahead with the others."

The connecting ramp to the satellite was clear. A guide posted by Lang waved Shearer and his party on through a gallery crossing the main toroid into a second ramp leading to the central cylinder. They would deliver the stay-behinds to the control center, they had decided. The satellite crew there would know how best to accommodate them until a relief shuttle arrived. They came to the access shaft leading up to the end of the cylinder where the control center was located, and reached the entrance. Two more of Lang's squad were posted outside. Leaving his charges with the guards, Shearer went inside to check on the situation.

Lang was there with the remaining few of his own squad . . . and nobody else. The room was empty, its monitor stations and control desks unmanned. He was looking bemused, staring out through one of the large, angled viewing panes at a shuttle that was in the process of pulling away from the far side of the toroid on reverse thrusters, evidently having just detached. As Shearer watched, it slowed to a halt, and then began sliding forward again and turning to cross in front of the dumpy silhouette of the robot freighter hanging in the background.

Just detached?

But the shuttle was supposed to have detached before Callen came down to the detainees' quarters. His cue to leave the bridge was to have been a signal being received there from the satellite that the shuttle had departed. How could it be departing only now?

One of Lang's troops looked up from a screen that he and another were operating. "Callen is back on the line now, Jeff."

Lang turned from the window and moved over. Shearer came forward to join him. The expression on Callen's face was just as bewildered as Lang's. "It's the same here," he announced. "Nobody. The entire bridge area is deserted. Same for communications and the propulsion section. They're all gone. Everybody."

Something was very, very wrong.

CHAPTER THIRTY-EIGHT

Callen stood amid the empty crew stations on the *Ranger*'s bridge, facing the screen showing Lang and Shearer. Colonel Yannis had come with him to survey the bridge layout, and Wen Siyu was already bringing up screens of system information on the flight engineer's console. Berger, the former first drive officer from the *Tacoma*, had joined them moments before to report that no *Ranger* or Milicorp personnel were present in the power and propulsion sections of the ship. Clearly, they had all left on the shuttle that Lang had just seen detaching.

So what did it mean? Other officers were arriving in the control center to take charge of servicing procedures for the *Ranger* and direct transfers from the satellite's stocks of supplies. Callen waved Berger forward to liaise with them while his mind raced over the events of the past ten minutes.

He had arranged to be here, on the bridge, at the time the shuttle was supposed to have left carrying the allocation of passengers that he had helped draw up. And he had definitely heard the communications officer announce receipt of a signal from satellite control saying that the shuttle was detaching. At that point, Callen had left the bridge to collect Osterman and set the plan moving as arranged. The *Ranger*'s second officer and his skeleton staff who were supposed to have stayed had been here then. They must have left while Callen and Osterman were down at the detainees' rooms on the lower decks, which meant that the shuttle hadn't left at all at that time; it had waited for them. So there never had been any signal from satellite control. They had known the whole plan. It was a setup.

Who, then, had given them away? An informer planted among the detainees back at Revo? Could his own plant, Dolphin, in fact have been a double plant put there by the corporation? Betrayal by those one thought were closest was an accepted part of the way this insane game was played . . . But no, neither of those possibilities made sense. *Every one* of the group brought back from Revo—even those having no part in the escape plan—was still here now at DSX-14. An informer would have made sure to be separated out somehow by now, and have gone on the shuttle.

The only other answer was that the office in which he had conducted his interrogations, which was when he and Shearer had discussed and worked out the details, had been bugged. But one of the tasks that Krieg would have performed routinely, and which Callen had specifically made a point of checking with him, was to go over every inch. . . .

And then Callen groaned. He looked around reflexively from one side of the bridge to the other, but he already knew it didn't need verifying. Krieg wasn't around anywhere.

So Krieg had had his own line back to Milicorp corporate all along. And Krieg knew that Callen had evidence of the complicity between Milicorp and Interworld in engineering the plague on Amaranth and was prepared to use it. Even if the present fracas were to be resolved without a public scandal, the continuing existence of such a threat would never be tolerated. And now Callen, and everyone else he might have talked to among the renegade group from Cyrene, had been isolated on an abandoned satellite in high orbit above Earth. The implication was now glaringly obvious: None of them would be allowed to come down from it alive. But exactly how was something like that supposed to be effected? Callen asked himself.

And then he remembered Milicorp's orbiting bombardment platform, *Marduk*.

In the Opcon room on *Marduk*'s Control Deck, a communications officer turned from a console and nodded to Rath Borland, who was standing with the Commander and a retinue of Milicorp staff officers. Borland moved over, and the operator directed him to one of the screens. "Code word *Shellfish* received, signed X-Man," he read. Borland nodded. X-Man was the designation given to Krieg in his concealed role as Borland's agent on the *Tacoma* mission. The message meant that all had gone according to plan, and the shuttle had detached from DSX-14. Temperamentally Krieg was not suited to step into the place of someone like, Callen but his services to the corporation would stand him in good stead.

Borland turned to the group of figures in olive green uniforms lavish with medal ribbons and braid, and shiny Sam Browne belts, standing a short distance apart from the Milicorp officers. "The objective is cleared," he told them.

The delegation of senior military staff was from one of the newer states that had emerged from the turmoil in central Asia. Impressed by *Marduk*'s recent performance in helping subdue the insurrection in Tiwa Jaku, they had prevailed upon their government to consider contracting for similar support services and had come up on a preliminary assessment visit. They were already clients of a little-publicized department of Milicorp that nobody talked about very much, that dealt in techniques and training for countersubversion and "extreme" methods of interrogation.

A confidential directive delivered from the top level in Milicorp had called for elimination of the threat that X-Man had reported Callen as representing, along with everyone that Callen might have divulged his information to. It wasn't a time for half-measures or squeamishness; the stakes were too high. And the obvious time and place to do it was right now, while they were all together and in a situation that had been rendered free of complications.

Borland's arranging of the timing such that the military delegation would have the bonus of witnessing the operation had been deliberate. Although it was guaranteed to provoke bilious reactions when word reached the right quarters in the Milicorp-Interworld stratosphere, he expected to come through unscathed, and thereafter to be invulnerable. For once Callen was removed, Borland could well find himself the next in line to be set up as a sacrificial victim. So he was taking out insurance, just as Callen had sought to take out insurance. The difference, however, was that Borland would be able to threaten exposure if anything untoward were to happen to him. He felt reasonably secure against any risk of being compromised by the Asiatics in his turn. For one thing, they had no motivation to see him brought down; on the contrary, he had a solid record of dealing dependably with them, which it was in their interests to perpetuate. And for another, nobody would be likely to mess with a person commanding the kind of firepower he did, while he was still around.

"At which point will you send in the backup?" the leader of the delegation asked. He was a heavily built general with a smooth head and a cruel face. By backup, he meant the two military shuttles standing by in lower orbit, carrying assault troops with heavy equipment.

"We'll give them three passes," Borland replied. The general nodded, his expression conveying reluctant acceptance. Borland knew he would rather that he and his party got a chance to see *Marduk*'s long-range X-ray laser weapon in action.

Borland had prepared for two eventualities. According to the information from X-Man, the renegade group intended to make its break for Cyrene as soon as restocking of the *Ranger* was complete, which they hoped to accomplish in under an hour. If they adhered to that plan, they would be taken out as soon as *Marduk* was in a position to fire. This could vary from immediately the *Ranger* cleared the satellite to a maximum of twenty minutes later, depending on where *Marduk* was in its orbit, since for part of the time they would be in mutual eclipse with Earth between them. This gave the target no chance of getting out of range. Even if they were to forgo the normal practice of running on conventional drives to the H-point—involving relative gravitational field intensities and done to maximize economic operation—which for a vessel the size of the *Ranger* would be about a day out, technical considerations following from standard operating procedures precluded an early enough escape into Heim space. After engine shutdown and recharging, the *Ranger* would need over an hour of running on conventional drive to build up suitable field conditions again before a transfer could be initiated, and this was well within Marduk's window of opportunity.

The other possibility was that the renegades would realize their situation, refuse to expose themselves to fire from *Marduk*, and stay put. Borland would allow three passes of *Marduk* through its optimum targeting position. If the *Ranger* had still made no move by that time, the backup force would be sent in. Either way there would be no survivors.

The official story would be that the *Ranger*, an armed interstellar vessel, had been seized by mutineers thought to be intending to take up a piratical existence among the Terran colony worlds. However, prompt action by the ship's Milicorp contingent succeeded in evacuating the crew and the satellite staff before they could be made hostages. The ship posed a danger to everything in the vicinity of Earth, not to mention the havoc that could ensue elsewhere if it disappeared into Heim space. Mindful of its responsibility as possessor of the only means presently available to thwart such a the threat, Milicorp had issued several warnings. When they went unheeded, the corporation had taken it upon itself to initiate appropriate action. There was little likelihood of other accounts appearing later that would refute this version of the story. Communications from both the *Ranger* and DSX-14 had been disabled.

Whether as a result of those aboard the *Ranger* failing to appreciate their predicament, or if they realized the risk but decided to try a run for it anyway, given the choice, the Milicorp executives involved would also have preferred the first alternative. Not only would present an opportunity to test the effectiveness of *Marduk*'s long-range weaponry in the space environment, but it would also send an important message. As more contractors worldwide entered the lucrative defense and security business, analysts and political realists agreed it would only be a matter of time before mercenary organizations hired by rival interests found themselves directly in conflict with each other. This was felt to be as good a time as any for Milicorp to stage a show of strength affirming its readiness and ability to assert itself belligerently if challenged.

CHAPTER THIRTY-NINE

The business of bringing the *Ranger* up to flight readiness proceeded regardless, with the primary fuel connection established and recharging initiated. Polapulos, one of the former *Tacoma* officers, had arrived in the satellite's storage section with a labor detail to take care of the supply transfers. Shearer was still with Lang in the control center when Wade came back in after going out to explain things as best he could to the confused group of intended stay-behinds, who had thought they were to be be collected by a second shuttle. All Wade had been able to tell them was that the crew members and others who were supposed to have joined them had already gone, and nobody knew what it meant or could say for sure what would happen next.

"Where are we at?" Wade asked, looking around. The screen was still showing Callen on the *Ranger's* bridge.

"All long-range communications are out—from here and from the ship," Shearer told him. "Obviously nobody's interested in talking."

Wade took a few moments to digest the implication. "So whatever happens next, the world only gets to hear their side of it."

"Exactly."

Callen had described the potency of the weaponry carried by Milicorp's recently commissioned orbiting platform, *Marduk*, and confirmed that it could be deployed to engage long-range targets in space as well as for surface bombardment. It was painfully clear now that they had walked right into a stratagem whose sole purpose was to set them up as an easy mark. *Marduk* was equipped with a prototype

X-ray battle laser, which at this range would pick the *Ranger* off like a duck in a barrel the moment it detached from DSX-14.

Marduk had emerged from behind Earth in the last few minutes and was just starting to cross the planetary disk. Lang had been for trying to make a run for it as soon as *Marduk* entered eclipse again, but Callen had dissuaded him. Just estimating *Marduk*'s orbit by eye, Colonel Yannis had given them no chance. Even if *Marduk* had been orbiting in the same plane as the satellite, which would have given a maximum obscuration period of something like forty-five minutes, it wouldn't have made much difference. The energies involved in Heim electromagnetic-gravitational conversion were so tremendous that field buildup had to be done gradually. Once the Heim field had been allowed to collapse by a full system shutdown for recharge, at least an hour of running under conventional drive would be needed before it would be ready to effect a transfer.

Wade exhaled a long sigh and seemed to deflate visibly. Shearer knew from long experience how much it took to make Wade this disconsolate. The vision he had held for what Cyrene could become, and his dream of being a part of it, must have been more intense than even Shearer had realized. "So they've got us cold," Wade said in a dull voice. "We have to stay put until they're ready to round us up, and then we get marched off. I guess we get that paid vacation in a camp somewhere after all, Marc. I hope it's not one of the ones up north. I never did care too much for the cold."

Shearer shook his head violently. "Evan, that's not the way it works. You haven't figured it through yet."

"What are you taking about?"

"Callen's been spelling it out to Jeff. The next things coming to DSX-14 won't be bringing nice guys in gray tunics coming to take us away. They'll be in heavy-duty suits with EV gear and assault cannon, blowing their way in through the walls. If we fly or stay, it won't make any difference. Nobody's going to walk off of here."

Wade was shaking his head disbelievingly. "But what . . . Why?" He turned to the screen showing Callen. Yannis had moved into view behind. "Why would they take such extreme action? We're no threat. . . . Very well, okay, we had a plan to try and go back. . . . It's over." He threw up his hands uncomprehendingly. "Are they concerned about the *Ranger*'s armament? But nobody here knows how to operate it, even if we wanted to. So we set up a light signal that they can see. Doesn't the satellite have approach beacons or something? We only have to let them know."

On the screen, Callen was shaking his head. "You don't understand, Professor. They cut our communications precisely to avoid anything like that. Marc Shearer already said it. They don't *want* to talk."

"But why? . . ."

"Let's just say, big-time corporate politics. We represent a risk that's unacceptable. There's a lot about the way they run their business that they don't want the world to hear about. It's nothing new, Professor Wade. Just about all of history is a much dirtier affair than the sanitized version everybody gets taught. Nothing was ever truer said than that the winners and whoever they pay are the ones who write it."

Lang had been staring out through one of the control center windows at where the *Ranger*'s upper core section and part of the main structure were visible over the curving top of the toroid. As the satellite turned, optical shutters automatically blocked off the window panels on the sunward side to shield the inside.

"Doesn't the *Ranger* carry a couple of ship's boats?" he asked suddenly, turning back to the screen. He meant the two small daughter vessels normally berthed in housings on opposite sides of the peripheral ring. They could be used as surface landers or as lifeboats in an emergency, and were to have been the means of getting back down to Cyrene if it turned out that the *Tacoma* had departed by the time they returned.

"What about them?" Callen asked.

"Ramships!" Lang said. "What kind of speed could one of them get up to over the distance to *Marduk*? Enough to take it out, surely."

Callen turned his head inquiringly toward Yannis. But the colonel looked dubious. "I can't see it. You'd have to aim it by sight after *Marduk* appears over Earth's rim. They're not Heim drive. The run in would take too long."

"What other chance do we have?" Lang insisted.

"He's right," Callen said. "With the weapons and targeting that *Marduk*'s got, boats like that would never get close."

Wade turned away in frustration, clenching his fists. "There *must* be something we can do. We can't just sit here."

"What?" Lang asked him in a flat voice.

"*The freighter!*" Shearer exclaimed. He was looking out at the robot vessel from Cyrene, still standing off while it awaited its turn to unload, just coming into view again as the satellite turned. "It's a Heim ship. I don't know. . . . Would it have shut its field down already?"

"No. . . . It wouldn't." On the screen, Yannis stepped forward alongside Callen. "You do that after you dock, so the field energy can be tapped and stored. It's still hot out there." He licked his lips and looked at Callen. "He might be onto something."

"How would you fly it?" Callen asked.

Yannis was obviously thinking frantically. The others fell silent. "It would have been brought in under remote control from DSX-14 after reentering three-space. There should be a drive profile with parameters all set up still live on the system, somewhere over there where you are." An excited note crept into his voice. "If I can find it, all I'd need to do is switch it back to Active. That should give me full access to the Heim system too. I'm coming over there!"

Callen turned to ask something, but Yannis had already disappeared. "Wen Siyu," Callen called up past the screen to somewhere in the background. "Keep an eye on this channel. We're going over to the control center." And then he disappeared too.

"The laser is fired from a self-aiming ordnance pod ejected to a safe distance from the platform," Borland explained to his attentive listeners. "Energy from a fission device detonated in a precisely shaped cavity is focused via a set of heavy metal lasing rods in the instant before they are vaporized. At this range a target the size and hardness of the present one will be annihilated instantly. With progressively longer dwell times, we can guarantee total lethality for such a target up to a hundred thousand miles in less than five seconds. It would even be an effective weapon for, say, interdiction and harassment operations against the lunar surface, should such things ever become a consideration there."

"What about targets on Earth's surface?" the smooth-headed general asked.

"Absolutely," Borland replied.

"How would it compare in ground suppression capability with the strike at Tiwa Jaku? Could you achieve obliteration power levels over a greater area?"

"Not significantly. But within the kill zone you would be talking about neutralizing targets of considerably greater hardness."

"Do you have the resolution and tracking capability to target, say, individual vehicles—aircraft and ships?"

"That is the next intended development phase."

"I see. Very good." The general sent an inquiring look to his colleagues, who returned satisfied nods.

The officer who was monitoring *Marduk's* orbital progress turned from his console. "Five minutes, Mr. Borland." It meant that DSX-14 would be coming out from behind Earth for the third time. This was the decision point at which Borland had said he would send in the assault force. A preview of DSX-14 coming in from a surveillance satellite on the far side of Earth showed no change in the situation, or any indication that the *Ranger* was preparing to move.

"We were hoping very much to see the laser in action," the general said pointedly.

Borland bit his lip. There was no question that it would be straightforward to take out both the ship and the satellite together. It would certainly provide a more spectacular and convincing demonstration—and the complication of having to justify undesirable collateral damage in the form of extraneous personnel had been removed. They would probably be talking about a lawsuit involving the owners of the satellite or their insurers, but taking care of things like that was what legal departments were for.

"Nobody would deny Milicorp's obligation to put the safety of its visitors first," the general pointed out. "We would, of course, be willing to corroborate that use of offensive weapons against *Marduk* appeared imminent."

Borland thought for a few seconds longer. Then he looked across at the ordnance officer, manning another console. "Prime the laser for ejection. Target on computed rise of DSX-14. Set trigger arming to code three. Maintain safety override."

Colonel Yannis had located the control log from first contact with the freighter after its reentry into 3-space, and from there retrieved the file of course directives and settings used to bring it in to where it was now waiting. Although no longer active, its main drive was still idling in accordance with normal practice, the Heim field intact and uncollapsed. Everything depended now on Yannis being able to figure out the command protocol that had been used. His needs were a bare minimum. First would be to renergize the conventional nuclear drive in order to launch the freighter on an intercept course as *Marduk* came into view, for which he estimated a run of between ten and fifteen seconds would suffice; next, flip a transfer into Heim space before *Marduk* could respond; and finally—trickiest but most crucial of all—estimate the moment for flipping back to 3-space. The last would have to be by pure guesswork, since there was no time to set up an exact computation. Yannis would have one chance. Making a Heim transfer this close in to the gravitating mass of Earth would soak up just about all of the power reserves, but since there would be no drawn-out voyage to anywhere to make allowances for, it really didn't matter.

Recharging and restocking of the *Ranger* was complete, and everyone not involved in the last activities taking place in the satellite's control center were reimbarking, disconnecting the service couplings, and making ready for immediate departure. If this crazy gamble with the freighter worked, the sooner they were away from any reserve force possibly lurking in the vicinity, the better. If it didn't . . . well, it would have been a way of keeping them busy. The group who had intended going on to Earth had reconsidered and were throwing their lot in with those heading for Cyrene. If *Marduk* was taken out, they didn't want to be the only ones left around to face whoever showed up next in the kind of mood they were likely to be in. Their futures on Earth, they had decided, would be better negotiated more amicably and in a calmer atmosphere at some later time, via whatever administrative channels proved to be available.

Shearer had just about contributed all he could. His role now was reduced to watching some ancillary displays for any changes in radar signatures that might be significant, while an operator monitored a telescopic view of Earth's rim. Yannis had moved the freighter to a position in-line between the satellite and the point where *Marduk* would appear, its thrust axis trained like a rifle barrel. The image slid slowly across the screen as the satellite rotated. Every ten seconds, the view switched to a different camera around the satellite's toroid to keep the freighter and target area in view.

At the console that he had linked as a remote control station,

Yannis read off check functions to another operator, who responded with numbers from a status screen showing readings from the freighter's Heim system.

"C-field J vector?"

"Seven-seven-zero."

"Ramp at max?"

"Check."

"Injector phases?"

"Two-five; four-four; and, ah . . . zero-one-three."

As Shearer listened, the chilling awareness crystalized that the future before him had reduced to just two extremes. Either he would very likely die within the next few minutes if Yannis failed and *Marduk* fired its laser; or he would see again all the things he had remembered and dreamed of since leaving Cyrene.

Strange though it had to be at a moment like this, he thought of Jerri and all they had talked about and planned. He wondered where she was and what she was doing right now. Was she still at Linzava, and what was happening there? Or would she have moved somewhere that would be safer? He thought about the hills and forests of Yocala, Revo with its lake on one side and the sea on the other, the color and life of the town, and its people leading lives of kindness, trust, honesty, and integrity. Never had he been more mindful of how much it all contrasted to the things they had returned to. He found that he was easy in his mind that it had all come to this. It simplified all the heart-wrenching and soul-searching. If the alternative of returning to Cyrene was not to be, then he would be content to accept the other. Earth, he now realized, was not an option that he could live with. A number in one of the displays he was watching changed below a critical value.

"Thirty seconds," he said, alerting the operator.

The operator checked and called to Lang. "Rising imminent. Due in twenty-eight seconds."

"Roger. F-main and boost, ready to fire?" Yannis had the alignment view copied to his console.

"Ready."

"Fields loaded for immediate cut-in?"

"Check."

Yannis took a final glance over his screens. At the same time he managed to muster a faint grin. "I've never heard of anyone flying an H ship by the seat their pants before."

"Please concentrate on the objective, Colonel," Callen pleaded dryly from one side.

"Twelve seconds."

The view on the screen switched to another camera, resetting to one side the image of Earth's curve with the freighter hanging in the foreground, which then began the slow crawl back toward the center.

Five seconds. . . . Four . . ."

"*Marduk* sighted!"

Lang's voice came in. "Trim attitude left point six, up point three."

Yannis tensed over the console, his eyes judging the angle and distance, fingers rapidly entering last-moment corrections. "Let her come. . . . That's it. . . . Just a little more, baby. . . ."

The surveillance operator checked a screen again. "Mr. Borland. Something's changed here."

Borland moved to investigate. *Ranger* was still docked at the satellite, but a freighter that had been standing off to one side had changed its position and was now in front of it. Borland frowned. The control staff from the satellite had all been taken off. And why should they want to move the freighter anyway?

"Is something wrong?" the general asked from the visiting military group.

"I'm not sure."

"Radar alert. The intervening object is beginning to accelerate this way."

Borland stared in confusion for several seconds, and then it clicked. They were going to try and use it as a ram. A good try, he complimented inwardly.

"Intercept ETA?" he queried.

"Thirty-seven minutes," a voice responded after a short pause.

Desperation, the mother of invention, Borland thought to himself. He turned to address a different sector of the Opcon room. "Ordnance. Retarget intermediary object and lock on."

"Target accelerating rapidly," the surveillance operator interjected. "Revised ETA thirty-four minutes."

"Reset trigger arming code to five," Borland intoned. "Unlock safety override and stand by." This would be a better demonstration than they bargained for. And he could still send in the assault ships without having to take out DSX-14, with all the attendant inconveniences.

"Trigger arming reset. Safety unlocked."

"*Target has disappeared!*"

"What? . . ."

The surveillance operator turned a baffled face. "We've lost contact. There's no reading on anything."

Yannis stared fixedly at the screen, silently measuring the time like a musician listening to an internal beat. Since the satellite wasn't connected to the freighter by a Heim link, there was no way of communicating with it now. Reentry into 3-space would be after a pretimed delay, which to be on the safe side he had set to occur at a point some distance short of the target.

It reappeared suddenly out of nowhere, enlarging with frightening speed to blot out all else as it came hurtling at them with the momentum it had built up in Heim space. None of the petrified faces fixed on the screen had time to utter a sound. . . .

And the interior of the control center lit up with new light flooding though the windows on the unshuttered side, away from the sun. The spectacle flared for several seconds, and then died, leaving just a cloud of debris dispersing rapidly into space. It was said afterward that the explosion was seen from Burma to Pakistan.

"Let's go," Callen said to the awed company around the room.

Ten minutes later, the *Ranger* detached from DSX-14 and headed for deep space. After little over an hour later, it engaged Heim drive and blipped out of the normally perceived solar system. . . .

While behind it, high over the surface of Earth, pieces of debris, materials, and particulates from *Marduk* and the freighter from Cyrene that had vaporized with it drifted down in an expanding cloud that on its lower fringes was already beginning to mix with the upper atmosphere.

CHAPTER FORTY

Revo base had undergone a transformation in the two months that had gone by since their return. With the gates open again, and passage in and out unrestricted, the semblance to a prison camp or military installation had largely disappeared. Many of the once-departed Terrans had reappeared, some of them on a part-time basis while they continued to reside or involve themselves in other business elsewhere. The skies were turning grayer and Ra Alpha was receding, and the backlog of outstanding work on the buildings and structures was being cleared to prepare for the approaching cold season. All the same, a lot more flowers and plants were in evidence to brighten the place up.

The *Tacoma* had long since departed, taking Gloria Bufort and her briefly lived court back to what whatever bickering and infighting between Interworld and Milicorp awaited them, but truth was that nobody on Cyrene really cared all that much. The administration that arrived with the *Ranger* on its first visit had succumbed to the planet's pervasive influence and were keeping things going on a genial caretaker basis until some kind of a policy was decided on how future relationships were to be managed. Even if Interworld decided to pull out, with the diversity of interests on Earth and the dynamic expansion of interstellar activities generally, it was unthinkable that some kind of contact wouldn't continue, even if no more than as occasional visits to satisfy scientific and cultural curiosity. In fact, most of the Terrans who would be making their homes there were agreed that something like that would suit them just fine.

In the meantime, the new A-wave laboratory on the east side next to the flight operations zone, comprehensively equipped and with all the facilities of the base to draw on, surpassed anything that Wade could have dreamed of at Linzava. A new model of adtenna was already producing unequivocal results, and the staff included a coterie of Cyrenean students and technicians, who, although not fully up to the intricacies of quantum mechanics yet, were unequaled in eagerness and desire to learn. Shearer, Uberg, and Elena took care of most of the work there these days. Wade himself spent more time at places like Doriden and Linzava pursuing his prime interest of helping the Cyreneans achieve a smooth and trouble-free technological transition. At the base, around the city, and in all the other locations where they had established a presence, the Terrans were already highly revered by the population on account of the things they knew and what they could *do*. Many Cyreneans commented that the Terran authorities at the base seemed to have changed its ways lately from what had been seen in the early days. The Terrans told them it was because they were turning into Cyreneans. And in a kind of way, it was true.

Shearer thought that Jerri looked something like a lady from English Georgian times but without the skirt bustle, when she arrived at the edge of the flight landing area. She was dressed in formal Cyrenean style, with a long saronglike garment hanging elegantly almost to the ankles, a light purple cloak, and an ornate hat with a flower and feathers. One of the Cyrenean lab staff had fashioned a collar for Nim to match the clasp of the cloak. Shearer had outdone himself by taking to Cyrenean trousers and boots, though with the trousers less baggy than the native norm, a satiny yellow shirt with a floppy collar and maroon neckerchief, and a long brown coat with golden buttons and braid that he had bought when a traveling trader stopped by the base one day.

"Come on, you're the last," he said as she took his arm. "They say there's a woman behind every successful man. And it's true. We're always waiting."

"The obligatory last-minute loose button. It's a law of nature. There's always something."

Shearer took Nim's leash in his other hand, and they began walking out toward the waiting aircraft. It was the same VTOL personnel transporter that Gloria Bufort and her entourage had used on the evening of their reception by Vattorix the day after the *Tacoma*'s arrival. Very fitting, too, Shearer thought to himself. A clunky sambot flyer like the ones the peasantry had traveled in wouldn't have suited this occasion at all.

Nick had opened his physician's practice up at Ulla, and already he had a list of patients, a fine reputation that was spreading across northern Yocala, and a couple of trainee Cyrenean nurses. He and Sakari were getting married today. It was the first instance of a Terran-Cyrenean match to be formalized, as far as anybody knew, and had become the major social event to be talked about for miles around. Just about the whole of the town of Ulla seemed to have taken upon itself to organize the celebrations and invite itself, and two boatloads of well-wishers had arrived via the sea route from Revo. Vattorix felt that such a symbolic union of the two cultures warranted some official recognition too. At first he had intended sending a representative with regrets that the pressures of his duties prevented him from being able to attend personally. Then Chev had pointed out that the Terrans could have him there and back in a day, and used the phone that he had acquired and never grew tired of showing off to get their ready agreement. Vattorix had promptly assented, and the VTOL's first stop would be at his residence across the lake to collect him.

Shearer unclipped the leash as they approached the open door of the aircraft, letting Nim bound ahead and up into the cabin. Colonel Yannis stood waiting to close the door. "Glad you decided to come," he said to Jerri as Shearer lent her a hand up and then followed.

"When did a woman ever miss a wedding?"

Yannis grinned, secured the door, and made his way forward, while Shearer and Jerri buckled themselves into the last two empty seats, alongside Uberg and Elena. Wade was already at Ulla, having arrived the previous day from somewhere in his travels. Yannis seemed to be back in his element, piloting again. With places like Linzava effectively becoming outposts of the base, and the demands for regular traffic increasing, he and the other pilots were always busy. The Cyreneans were awed by Terran feats of navigation. Chev liked to astound his friends by showing them their location on his phone's map display, pinpointed live from the satellite grid.

Two others who would be making their own way were Callen and Jeff. With sulfurous altercations and demands still singeing the stuff of Heim space along the communications link back to Milicorp, they had decided it would be both considerate and discreet, at least for a while, to leave no one with any need to lie when saying they had disappeared from the base. They were up at Linzava, coordinating its development as an offshoot enterprise, and had only a few miles to travel down the valley. Jeff had been administering the refitting of the workshops and was negotiating for another of Wolaxal's steam engines to be built there. After further deliberation—and perhaps, for all anyone knew, with the help of a little stimulated intuition—it had been decided to let the Cyreneans set their own pace and not reinstate the fission module. Callen was said to cut a good figure on a horse, and to be enjoying the life.

The engines started and idled for a few seconds, and then the note rose rapidly and steadied. Moments later, the craft started to rise. Outside, the buildings of the base shrank and fell away.

Elena leaned across to lay a hand on Jerri's shoulder. "What did you decide to get them in the end?" she asked.

"A window planter in a wrought-metal frame. Jeff has a black-smith friend somewhere along the Geevar, who made it. He picked it up for us, but he sent us some pics. It's really beautiful."

"It sounds very nice," Elena agreed.

"Appropriate for a wedding," Uberg put in. "An old Yocalan tradition says that every home should have some moon flowers inside. They bring luck and good fortune, you know."

The craft rose and turned, and the familiar expanse of Revokanta lake and its hills came into view ahead. Unlike the blue of the first time they crossed it to Vattorix's residence, the water was gray with reflected overcast, and the hills already shedding leaves and taking on a stark look in anticipation of the coming winter. Jerri slid a hand onto Shearer's arm and leaned closer to look past him through the window.

"It all feels so different from the last time," she said. "We were fugitives then. Now I feel as if I'm going home." She fell quiet. A look of sadness seemed to come over her as she gazed out.

"What is it?" Shearer asked.

"Oh . . . I suppose it was me talking about Cyrene as if it were home," she replied.

"Well, it's going to be now," Shearer said. "And it will be a fine one. You'll see."

"Yes. I don't doubt it. But that's the point."

"What do you mean?"

Jerri sighed and then smiled faintly, as if feeling slightly silly. "Everything feels so right here. And then I think back to that nightmare of a world that we lived in once, and it seems . . . I'm not sure. As if we're walking out on all of those people back there, somehow. Abandoning them. They're our own kind, after all. We've always said it's just a corrupt few who cause all of the grief. Most of the ordinary people just want the same as we do—to live their lives the way they want, and to be left alone. They believe the ones they should be able to trust, but they're lied to. They work, they suffer, and they try, but everything is taken away from them. They don't have any chance, do they?"

Shearer shook his head somberly. "I hear what you're saying, Jerri. But what can you do? We both know the reason now. Maybe the way you have to look at it is that every planet is a biological experiment. That all of life was supposed to fit and work together the way it does on Cyrene. Becoming fully conscious needs the environment provided by the plants. But Earth turned out incomplete. And so the intelligence that evolved on Earth is functionally incomplete. And the rest is what you get." He was about to say more, but then shrugged and left it at that.

The center of the lake was choppier than the last time they saw it, the boats fewer. In the distance, the higher peaks were visible, their tops already showing touches of white.

Yes, he was saddened by the thought too, he had to admit to himself. Earth had had its chance in the cosmic roulette game and been unlucky. Earth would have to live with it. There was nothing that anyone could do.

EPILOGUE

In a village in southern China, far above the city of Canton in the valley of the Bie river, Tsien-cho, the schoolmistress, came out to call her charges in from their morning break. The games were reluctantly ended, subsiding into chattering and giggling. As the children converged to file past her inside the door, one of the girls stopped and showed her a flower. "Can you tell me what this is, Miss? I've never seen one like it before."

Tsien-cho took it, and as she turned it over in her hands, her puzzlement grew. She had studied flowers assiduously since she was as young as the girl asking the question, but she had never seen the likes of this one either. It was like a small orchid, delicately formed, with petals of pale lilac showing a blush of pink at the base and white at the tips. But strangest of all was the dark red collar encircling the stem immediately below. It looked almost like a second set of petals, but curled shut.

"No, this is new to me," she confessed. "Where did you find it?"

"Over there, by the fence. There's a little bunch of them."

Beside Tsien-Cho, one of the boys pointed at the hillside above that side of the village. "Look up there!" he exclaimed. "There are hundreds of them! Everywhere!"

END